Windigo Fire

Windigo Fire

a novel by M. H. Callway

Seraphim
EDITIONS

The publisher gratefully acknowledges the financial assistance of the Canada Council for the Arts and the Ontario Arts Council.

 Canada Council **Conseil des Arts**
for the Arts **du Canada**

 ONTARIO ARTS COUNCIL
CONSEIL DES ARTS DÉ L'ONTARIO

Library and Archives Canada Cataloguing in Publication

Callway, M. H., 1947-, author
    Windigo fire : a novel / by M.H. Callway.

ISBN 978-1-927079-30-0 (pbk.)

    I. Title.

PS8605.A475W55 2014   C813'.6   C2014-905292-8

Editor: George Down
Author Photo: Claire Callway
Design and Typography: Julie McNeill, McNeill Design Arts

Published in 2014 by
Seraphim Editions
4456 Park Street
Niagara Falls, ON
L2E 2P6

Printed and bound in Canada

For Ed
Two cats forever

1

Evil exists and he was no better than the others. He knew that now.

Danny Bluestone twisted the spliff in his nail-bitten fingers, feeling the weed roll under the thin white paper like twigs and pebbles in a stream. Couldn't bag any decent bud this morning, so he'd settled for homegrown. Go organic. Support local industry. Smoke only nature's own Red Dog Gold.

Midnight on Fire Lake, stuck on an island deep in the forests of Northern Ontario. Fifty miles from the nearest town – if you'd call Red Dog Lake a town. The raucous sounds of the hunters funnelled down from the lodge buried in the thick woods behind him. He breathed in deeply, letting the pungent pine sap purge his spirit of their meaty white presence. Clear the landing. Get ready for take-off. His *Zippo* lighter rested heavy and cool in his hand.

Under the rising moon, the black silhouettes of the pines fringing the shore were etched as sharply as crystal, and Fire Lake had morphed into a silvery flat expanse. He wet the end of the spliff, straining to hear the eerie banshee call of a loon.

Nothing.

When he was a little kid, and his dad was still alive, they'd flown in here to fish for trout. The birds' snaky black shapes had been common at twilight when they'd camped on the island, but today he hadn't seen even one. And no fish in the acid clear waters of the lake.

No animals. No nothing.

"Hey, Danny boy!"

He started, barely rescuing the *Zippo* from sliding into the dark water at his feet.

"Come out, come out, wherever you are."

Like all day he'd been the invisible man. Now when he needed to be alone, trust them to whine for entertainment with him as the target. He hesitated, thumb on the lighter. Noises travelled in the still night air.

"Where'd he go?"

"Maybe he sprung a leak."

Drunken titters. What if the smoke of his smouldering joint travelled, too? Would the hunters' campfire mask it? They were using that stone oven on the veranda, the one that looked like a ripe beer gut. Dangerous, but way out here who was around to see? Sparks poured up in a fountain from the stove's chimney and drifted over the tops of the trees.

Damn, Danny thought. All along Highway 11, from Temagami on up to Red Dog Lake and Cochrane and beyond, the white forest fire signs were cranked to red on the dial. Extreme hazard. No camping. Especially no fires. The sharp-needled powdery ground under his bare feet was so dry that it crackled.

"Hey, where *is* the little jerk?"

That was Ricky, the American with the shaved head, the one who claimed to be some old rock star. His voice had a dark edge, matched by a flicker of something Danny had spotted in his small blue eyes this morning when they'd hit the island. Like he knew the joke and you didn't, and the punch line wasn't going to be pretty.

"Maybe hunting guides in Canada don't like getting paid."

"Sure they do." That was the flustered, placating voice of the older guy, Morty Gross, who had some political job down south in Toronto. "Danny's off being a native, some spiritual thing. Like I promised you. Authenticity."

"Sure you did, and a load of other bull." Ricky sounded closer.

Danny scrambled up and jumped lightly onto the rock face behind him. The heat of the August afternoon lingered in the ice-smoothed stone. He crept up its clean bare surface, climbing till he reached the thicket of blueberry bushes he'd scouted out earlier. From here, he could spot them easily enough, and they'd never see him.

"*Oh, Danny boy, the pipes, the pipes are calling.*" Ricky emerged from the trail, a bulky dark outline against the shimmering water. "Maybe he's watching us. He conned you, Morty."

"You wanted a native guide, I got you one. He came highly recommended."

"By you, no less. Turn around, I got some business here."

Danny heard the rasp of Ricky's zipper. Oh man, he thought, I have to drink out of that lake. All day long Ricky had been watering the blueberry bushes like a dog making his mark. Like toilets were for weaklings.

"Tell me you enjoyed the show," Morty said.

"Uh-huh."

"Look, I got us something to celebrate. Two words. Single malt. The best, used to be flown in special to the lodge, OK?"

"So don't disappoint me."

Morty coughed out a laugh, like he still had control of the party, and vanished back down the trail. Ricky sat down on a boulder by the shoreline, merging into the night.

I hate this job, Danny thought. Forget the money. Working at the stupid children's camp wasn't so bad compared to this. I want my old job back. Even though I'll have to beg for it.

He glanced down at Ricky and tucked the joint and lighter into his shirt pocket. He loved the crisp crackle when a spliff first caught fire. He could almost feel the acrid burn of its pungent smoke, resin and tar coating his lungs, almost see its end blossoming, shedding sparks into the night.

He pulled a plastic baggie from his jeans. The mushrooms were shrivelled ugly things, like shreds of dark flesh, but they were quiet and didn't cast an odour. Doing 'shrooms wasn't smart since he ought to stay alert, but …

He ate his usual number.

Then one more.

An ice-age boulder had carved a natural hollow into the granite beneath him. He settled his back into it and waited. He'd be safe enough up here. Unlikely to roll down into the water or anything.

"See? Here we go." Morty was back.

"So give the nice bottle to daddy," Ricky said, reaching out a heavy arm.

This is what I get for studying English Literature, Danny thought. Government gave me free tuition for a useless degree, a one-way ticket to that crumby counsellor's job at the kids' camp. Take it or go back on pogey like every other Indian round here. Some choice. He breathed quietly, waiting for Huxley's doors of perception to open.

He could never tell when he'd crossed the threshold. Back in college, he'd be wide awake, thinking he'd been sold Campbell's mushroom soup, then he'd meet one of Hunter S. Thompson's lizards on the Toronto subway, sitting there in plain view, reading the paper or something.

Even this long after sunset, the day's heat seeped from the smooth stone into his back. That's what they used to heat their houses in Scotland, wasn't it? Rocks. Once upon a time, he'd wanted to study at the University of Edinburgh, to visit the Isle of Mull to see if he could spot ex-Beatle Paul McCartney. Stupid, right?

"This isn't single malt, you liar," Ricky said below him.

"It's rye to tide us over." Morty sounded desperate to turn the insult into a joke. "Our friend Anderson, the Norwegian, is looking through our supplies. It's here, I swear. Where could it go? There's no way off this island."

"Maybe it's taken a walk with your guide." The beach pebbles screeched under Ricky's feet as he stood up. "Where's your Aussie pal, Hendrix? I'm thinking it's time for me to get in some crossbow practice."

"Ricky, for heaven's sake ..."

Fear erupted through Danny's chest, but he was falling into the soft fist of rock, tumbling, plunging into the clear lake water. It parted in fronds like syrup, till he stared into the droopy grey face of Old Devil, the trout monster of Fire Lake. Oh God, I'm drowning, he thought. Breathing water without knowing it. Or was he? Huxley's one-way door had closed and he was lost in the funhouse of perception.

From afar, Morty's voice: "Here comes Anderson. He found it, so make nice."

"Yeah, right, after he helped himself."

"See for yourself. The seal ..."

The seal ... Danny gazed up at its vaporous grey form in the clouds. The hard ground left his back, and he was lifting off, soaring on an iridescent dragonfly that droned through the air. Fire Lake fell away like a sheet of dark metal and they shot past acres and acres of green forest, wilderness as far as the eye could see.

No light penetrated through the trees. Their branches arched over him, forming a dark cave. Something stirred, a matted black bearskin that rose from the ground and took form. No flesh, no bones. Only darkness behind its eye holes. He pressed his face close to the black snout – still moist – and asked it what it wanted.

Are you a spirit?

Black ooze crept from the eyes. The white teeth parted and the stench of decay rolled over him.

I'm sorry, Pasha. I'm so sorry.

He buried his face in his hands, but tears were useless. Nothing would make it better. Ever.

Shivering and wet with dew, he sat up. His back and muscles ached from the cold rock that had drained the warmth right out of him. A thick blanket of white mist lay over the water, obscuring the dawn, drawing colour out of the world. Was he still ripped? He rubbed his face, shook his long hair. Standing up shakily, he felt a surge of telltale nausea, the flu-like fatigue that would dog him for three days.

The 'shrooms must be done. Must be morning.

He stumbled down to the slate-grey shards of the beach where he'd been sitting last night. A flash of gold. Something was floating in the water, bobbing gently with the wavelets slapping the stones.

He blinked. What was it? A dead fish? Without thinking, he waded into the lake to get a closer look.

A white arm stretched out through the clear water, fine blond hairs waving like seaweed, fingers spread like a starfish above a gold-linked bracelet.

Oh, hell, Danny thought. His throat was parched but his feet were icy cold. He scrambled back out. It's a flashback, that's all. A mirage.

Heart thundering in his thin chest, he staggered down the trail to the lodge. Darkness slept under the trees, the way he'd dreamed it last night. Utter silence except for his panting breath. Too early, too early, he chanted silently. He'd find the hunters asleep. Remnants of the 'shrooms lurked in his system. He couldn't be sure about reality just yet.

He reached the clearing.

He smelled it then, the metallic slaughterhouse reek of blood.

Images, but no focus.

The hunters were lying all over, splattered in garish colours. Humans couldn't bend that way, could they?

Dead, all dead.

A screech of panic tore out of his throat. The screams kept bursting from deep within, and he couldn't stop them even when he clapped his hands over his ears to shut out his own noise.

No one knew where he was, except Rachel, a ten-year-old kid back at the children's camp. The bush plane wouldn't be back for two days.

And, like Morty said, there was no way off the island.

2

Danny huddled on the dank stones edging the lake. He'd lost track of time. Thoughts tumbled through his brain.

Breathe, try to breathe.

He sucked in air, rasped it out, feeling the scratch of the weed he'd been doing all summer. His limbs kept shaking and wouldn't stop. I'm too scared to be scared, he thought.

Need to calm down.

He fumbled in his shirt pocket for the spliff. It jumped up and down in front of his face as he tried to light it. The *Zippo* slipped through his fingers and bounced into the lake. He groped through the blackish water and gravel to retrieve it.

Now it wouldn't work.

Furious, he shoved everything into his jeans. His throat was on fire. He swallowed, desperate with thirst, but nothing would make him drink out of that lake.

Not now, not ever.

There was fancy mineral water back at the lodge. He'd helped load boxes of it onto the float plane. Corazon Sinclair, the bush pilot, had been really annoyed, but Anderson, the Norwegian, had insisted. Very health conscious, Anderson was. Grey eyes intense behind his steel-rimmed glasses, he'd lectured Danny about the dangers of chlorine in tap water and parasites in lake water. He'd even been strung out about radon gas seeping from the granite rock on the island.

Well, that sure worked for you, Danny thought.

They'd had trouble taking off and Corazon swore there was no way she'd be hauling back any empties. The bottles would stay on the island. Forget the environment. He thought of those bottles now: they were a beautiful cobalt blue bearing a weird Scandinavian label, and they'd be nice and cold in the propane fridge back at the lodge.

What was he, crazy? He'd have to walk past *them*.

See *them*.

A sharp pain in his gut. He clutched the pine sapling growing out of a crack in the rock beside him. Man, how could he be hungry now? He picked a clear bead of sap off the tree's rough bark and poked it into his mouth. Pine sap, nature's chewing gum, his grandmother had told him. But the resinous, solvent taste made him choke. Hot acid boiled up from his stomach and he spat it out on the ground.

Silence, all around. The sun was still hidden behind the dark trees on the far shore. He shivered in the chill of early dawn.

He rubbed his arms. He couldn't just sit around with *them* lying there. He'd go crazy without help. Morty had used his cellphone yesterday morning before they took off for the island. Some problem he had to fix.

Danny's guts twisted at the thought of searching Morty's pockets.

Then he remembered: cellphones didn't work this far out in the wilderness. The third hunter, Hendrix the Australian, the one with the temper, thought the cops could track them through Morty's phone. Morty had to keep reassuring him that Fire Lake had no reception.

Then again, Morty was a worrier. What if one of the hunters got hurt? They were important dudes, after all. Maybe he'd brought along a radio phone in his luggage just in case.

Only one way to find out.

He stood up slowly, hanging on to the pine tree for support. The shaking had stopped, but his legs felt light, like ghost legs. He left the beach and started down the narrow trail to the lodge.

I won't look at them, he thought. I won't look. They can't hurt me. They can't hurt me because they're not real. They're dead, they're all dead.

He couldn't shake the image of Anderson's severed arm reaching out into the clear water, his gold bracelet shining ...

Daylight hadn't reached the clearing. Everything was so still. The bodies rested where he'd seen them before, grey amorphous lumps at the edge of his vision.

Don't look. Don't look.

But he did. He stumbled over a tree root and retched.

A black coldness seemed to leak through the open door of the lodge.

I have to go in, no choice.

He stepped through the doorway like an explorer venturing into a cave.

"Oh man," he said aloud.

The interior lay in shadow. The generator had stopped. Starbursts of blood plastered the walls. It must have started in here in the great room, he realized. The killer got Morty and Hendrix on the patio. Chased Anderson down to the lake.

Broken glass and plates all over. Tipped beer and whisky bottles staining the big pine table. The hunters' bags had been ripped open and their guns scattered across the plank floor.

He crunched through the debris and found the propane fridge propped up against the back wall. The blue bottles stood inside unharmed. He grabbed one, unscrewed the cap and drank deeply.

Something's wrong, he thought, setting the bottle down. He stifled an absurd laugh. What else could go wrong? He sensed a scorched odour, an undercurrent in the air around him.

It's nothing, he told himself. It's the ashes from the campfire last night.

A fine mist hovered in the still air of the room. He thought of the dry woods behind the lodge and the sparks roaring up from the beer-gut furnace.

What if the hunters had started a forest fire?

He stumbled and banged his leg against the wooden arm of the rustic sofa. He had to call Corazon, the cops, anybody. Which bag was Morty's?

Was he imagining it or was the smoky mist getting thicker? Maybe Old Devil had tried to warn him in his dream last night. Maybe he hadn't been ripped on 'shrooms. His grandmother believed that message-in-a-dream stuff.

The sharp crack of a twig outside.

His heart took off like a wild bird. The 'shrooms had made him stupid. He'd made a mistake. A bad one. They'd been five altogether, the four hunters and him. Only three were dead.

He wasn't alone on the island.

Ricky, the killer, was still there.

3

Red Dog Lake, Nirvana Children's Camp,
August 9th, 9:00 AM

I'm ten. Danny doesn't treat me like a baby.

Rachel Forest glared at the weathered picnic bench that served as the craft table for Nirvana Children's Camp. Of all the lame activities in Nirvana's forced-jolly universe, crafts shared the trough with worms and cockroaches. It was Barry's favourite disciplinary alternative, so here she sat, forced to make garbage with garbage.

From her vantage point on the granite outcropping under the pines, she could scope out the whole place – from its smelly outhouses to the chilly lake. The cries of the other campers sounded like shrill far-off birds. She watched the old school bus from Santa's Fish Camp crawl like a yellow caterpillar down the dirt road to park outside the mess hall. Someone clanged the dinner bell. Kids streamed off the playing field and began lining up beside the bus.

Funny, their field trip to Santa's Fish Camp was supposed to be on Monday.

Rachel shrugged and pistoned her leg in a seemingly artless tic, jostling the splintery underside of the bench with her knee, sending ratty pine cones, faded sparkles, fossilized pasta bits and dried-out paint pots rattling into erratic orbits. And when she intensified the rhythm, they hurtled over the earth's flat edge into the far lost reaches of space – or at least down onto the soft pine needles beneath the bench.

She thumped her knee. *Stu-pid. Stu-pid.*

She curled her thin fingers around a crusty bottle of black paint. Flicking off its white plastic lid, she drove her thumb down through the watery grey fluid into the rich dark slime at the bottom. Warm and sweet, like the lair of Old Devil, the ghostly trout monster Danny had told her about at campfire. She dredged up a gob of pigment and, with hate-fired determination, slashed a black streak across each cheekbone.

I am a warrior. A ninja.

Funny how the other kids thought Camp Nirvana was so terrific – like getting onstage with a rock star or something. Couldn't they see how Barry, the camp director, was ripping them off? Even Dad, who was usually smart, had been taken in. And Dad didn't know what Barry did on his computer late at night.

Nin-ja. Nin-ja.

Dad's boss, Dr. Amdur, had visited her at school. Sitting her down like a patient, he'd explained how Dad was taking his first big step on a long healing journey. That showed great courage. From now on, they both had to help Dad.

What that really meant was that she'd be stuck here all summer. She hadn't seen Dad since the day he dropped her off at camp, not even once. And no phone calls either.

She squirted a dollop of slimy glue onto the cone of pink sparkles before her. With her index finger, she smeared a comet's tail across the limp piece of construction paper. The slippery feel and faint flashes of pink tingled up her arm.

I want to work on my real art. Mine and Danny's.

From what she'd overheard Barry say, Dr. Amdur was paying her camp fees to help Dad get back on his feet. Adult-speak for getting him off those little yellow pills.

"How are we doing, Rachel?"

She stifled an unpleasant twitch under her shoulder blades. Barry was always sneaking up like that, pressing too close. His pungent cologne pushed away the pure scent of the pines.

"I trust you used your quiet time to reflect," he said. Silence. "The trick you played on Adriana was, um, insensitive. We're all equal here at Nirvana."

To Adriana and her rich buddies who think I'm pond scum? I don't think so.

"It's time for our field trip."

"I'm not going."

"Of course you are."

Rachel's eyes lit on the craft table's one treasure, a fresh pot of indigo paint. Her hand hovered above the mucky paper, fingers aching for it. *Not while Barry's watching, you idiot.* She drew a deep breath and latched her arm under the bench. "I've been to Santa's Fish Camp three times already this summer. It's for babies." *And losers.* "I'm ten!"

She pounded her knee. *Los-ers! Ba-bies!*

"I don't make exceptions here at Nirvana."

"We're supposed to go on Monday when Danny gets back."

"We're going now."

She had a scary thought. Her finger tracked slick glue across the paper in an ever-expanding whirlpool. "Where's Danny?"

"That's anyone's guess."

"He told me he'd be back on Monday."

"That may be, but he won't be coming back here."

"Danny would never quit Nirvana."

"Who says he quit?"

She drove her knee so hard into the wood her teeth jarred. Macaroni scattered into the bushes. "Did you fire him?"

Barry uttered that weird clicking sound that meant he wasn't going to answer.

You can't fire Danny. I won't let you.

Twisting round, she threw him her scary stare. Being born with yellow eyes was an awesome weapon.

"Rachel, what have you done to your face?"

She turned back to her drawing. *I can play the silent game, too. And win.*

"That's an interesting creation," Barry said with sudden energy. He leaned closer. "What is it?"

Danny was right. She needed to watch out for Barry. She curled her fist under the table. *Any closer and I'll launch you into next year.*

"Politeness is the oil of civilization, Rachel. I asked you a question."

"It's dog do."

"We don't use hostile words at Nirvana."

"It's conceptual art."

"We're all aware that you took a children's art course. And I know when I'm being tweaked."

Like hell. "Dog do!" she laughed brightly. She'd get the cook's neurotically incontinent Boston terrier to wolf down those mangy pieces of macaroni. Ten seconds then up like a geyser over Nirvana's craft table – instant 'found art'. "Dog do!"

"What did you say?"

She pounded her leg. *Dog do. Dog do.* The cook's dog would eat anything.

"You'll have to speak up." He squeezed closer.

"Get away from me!" She rocketed her fist toward Barry's paunch. He jumped nimbly out of reach. "Touch me and I'll tell my dad."

"Fine, fine." He waved his hands as if warding off smoke. "Why don't you hand me your work?"

Grimly she tore her crumbling creation into bits. Too bad the bits were too wet and sticky to reach Barry. She watched him lace his fingers over his beige polo shirt. His soft belly and round rump made him look like a duck.

"Quack!"

"Excuse me?"

"Quack! Quack! Quack!"

"I'm not playing into your hands this time, my dear. I won't be calling your father."

Her leg froze. "Why not?"

"Because he's fed up with being hauled to the telephone every five minutes. In fact," Barry added gleefully, "we had a meaningful discussion this morning. Quite a meeting of the minds. He asked me to handle all future problems, my way."

It was like being underwater trying to breathe. "I don't believe you!" She leapt up. Anger roared through her body, a dark wind twisting through her arms, legs, and ribcage.

I'll use my karate.

"What are you doing?"

Her fists on the end of the picnic bench. Arms up and rigid, tilting the table. An avalanche of crafty garbage bounced into the forest for recycling.

"I am a Ninja!"

"Stop that!"

A savage cry erupted from her lungs. She jerked up her arms. Rusty nails sprang free of rotten wood. The middle board of the table vanished. For a heartbeat the two halves of the picnic bench hovered over the pine needles before collapsing into a pile of decayed lumber.

Awesome!

"You're – you're psychotic," Barry stammered.

Fun to watch him flush and stumble backwards. When she was certain that he was headed back to the mess hall, she dove into the wreckage of the craft table. And grinned.

She stood up, patting the back pocket of her jeans. *Now I've got my indigo paint.*

The dusty earth of the trail through the woods was soft velvet under her runners. She and Danny had taken it many times during the last six weeks.

Old Logan has a phone even if his zoo is wrecked. This time I'm calling Dr. Amdur. He'll phone Dad. And Logan is my friend. He'll help me find Danny.

4

Fire Island, August 9th

Danny froze, not daring to breathe. Something rustled down the outside wall of the lodge.

He hit the floor in front of the sofa. Sharp fragments of glass bit into his knees. He held his breath, listening …

He was wedged between a rough wooden coffee table and the seat of the rustic sofa. Its orange plaid back formed a barrier between him and the open door. Three feet in front of him stretched the long pine dining table. Under it, he spotted the Norwegian's prized gun.

Distinct footsteps now.

His pounding heart sent blood roaring through his ears. He stretched out his hand for the gun, his fingertips brushed the tip of its slim grey barrel. Couldn't reach it.

Peering over the back of the sofa, he saw Ricky's bulky shadow in the doorway outlined by the faint dawn light.

Have to get closer.

Slowly he shifted onto his hands and knees.

"I heard that."

The screech of an armchair pushed aside. "I know you're in here." Ricky crashed into the room, sweeping through the broken glass and debris on the floor.

Danny leapt and rolled.

"Stay back! I – I've got a gun, Ricky."

A dark laugh. The click of a bolt fitted into a crossbow. Danny imagined it tunnelling through the sofa upholstery, burying itself in his throat.

He fumbled frantically with the gun's complicated trigger mechanism. Where was the safety lock? *Was* there a safety lock? He should have listened to Anderson boasting about its advanced technology. Too late now.

"I know how to shoot." His bloodied finger kept slipping on the trigger.

"I'm going to skewer you like a hog."

Danny slammed the gun's barrel over the sofa's rigid back.

A hard vibrating missile burst into the upholstery.

Danny fired. His ears filled with the roar of sound. Pain crashed into his shoulder. Heavy white powder rained down around him. He was coughing, his eyes were stinging, he couldn't see. Anderson's gun had a kickback like a horse.

"Nice job redecorating the ceiling," he heard Ricky say.

Furious, he slammed the gun down over the sofa back. His hands were shaking.

No sign of Ricky.

"That was – that was a warning shot. Next time you're dead."

"You don't have the guts." Ricky had crept much closer.

"Come here and find out."

"*Gotcha!*" Ricky reared up like a grizzly behind the sofa. Danny froze, hands glued to the gun.

Shoot him, shoot Ricky.

Gun and crossbow pointed at each other, three feet apart.

Why doesn't Ricky shoot? What's he waiting for?

Silence.

The two stared at each other.

Slowly Danny creaked to his feet. His arms shook with the effort of keeping the gun pointed at Ricky's heart.

He's weighing the risk of firing. His bolt will jolt me into pulling the trigger. He can't dodge a bullet from three feet away. Even almighty Ricky knows that.

"So your buddies left you behind," Ricky said.

"What buddies?" Danny levelled the gun. If he lost focus, he'd die. Ricky was counting on that.

"Peeing yourself, aren't you?" Ricky went on. "Not so easy to kill a man when he looks you in the eye."

"Yeah, you should know, Psycho." Danny's arms throbbed from the weight of Anderson's gun. It was much heavier than the hunting rifles he was used to, loaded down with a lot of elaborate technology, scopes and stuff. Despite preaching about the purity of nature, Anderson certainly hadn't planned on giving it a fighting chance.

"Might as well make it easy on yourself."

"Back off! Get back or I'll blow your head off, I swear."

"No way, you murdering little freak. The minute I turn my back, you'll do me like you did the others. I'm a lot harder to kill than Morty, you'll find that out."

"I didn't kill anybody!"

"Bull crap."

"I got ripped. On 'shrooms. I passed out and woke up to – to all this."

"Like hell."

"I'm just a camp counsellor, for heaven's sake."

"What?"

A strange wheezing noise. Ricky was laughing. "Knew you were a fake," he said at last.

"I'm not a fake. I'm Cree, like Morty told you. He paid me to come along for the ride. To give you guys a real Canadian experience."

"You sure did that."

Danny jerked the gun back to level. "Stay where you are." He took one slow step to the side.

"Leaving?"

Where would he go? How was he going to get off the island? Swim? He'd never make it to the mainland. It was too far.

Ricky stuck a thick finger under the collar of his combat vest. "I never touched those guys," he said.

"What?"

"I said I never touched them."

"You killed them, nobody else."

"No." Ricky shook his head. "I went round the back of the island. To check on things."

"What's to check? The hunt's over."

"Had enough of Anderson's moaning and that Aussie jerk, Hendrix, dissing the US of A. Took the single malt Morty owed me and got tanked. Never heard a damn thing through those trees."

"You're lying! They had to be screaming."

"And you?" Ricky lunged forward. "What's your excuse?"

"I was ripped, man. I mean, I sort of heard something." The dragonfly carrying him over Fire Lake. "A plane, I think. I thought I dreamed it."

"That's convenient."

"What about you? You could have used that big bow of yours to help. Instead you hid in the trees."

"Shut up! You know what I think? I think you had it planned. You told your buddies a bunch of rich dudes were out here. They flew in when they figured we'd all be asleep. You let them do the wet work."

"You're crazy! I don't have any buddies. And even if I did, why would they smash up all the booze and leave your guns behind? Nobody knows we're out here."

"Except your pilot."

"Corazon won't tell." How much longer could he keep holding the heavy gun? One minute? Half a minute?

Ricky's eyes narrowed. "You think you're the only boy who grew up in a small town. Everyone in Red Dog Lake knows we're out here. And Hendrix had enough cash on him for an army."

"The money's still there. Lying where – where Hendrix is. Go see for yourself since you don't believe me."

Danny's arms were shuddering. The gun dipped.

Ricky lunged. The edge of the coffee table slammed into the back of Danny's knees. He hit the table hard. The gun flew out of his hands. Crashed onto the floor.

He stared up at Ricky. He felt the sharp point of the steel arrow scratch a bead of blood from his throat.

Why doesn't he shoot?

A trickle of sweat slid down from Ricky's cropped scalp and trailed past a dark mole on his cheek.

A loud report like a pistol shot.

Ricky twisted, faced the open door. "That's gunshots."

"No, no! It's a tree on fire."

"What?"

"The fire in the stove last night. It's started a forest fire. Let me up."

Another sharp report.

"Listen to me! When a tree burns, the sap boils. It explodes out of the wood. That's the noise it makes. I grew up here. I know what it sounds like."

Ricky hesitated. "OK, up. No tricks."

No time to think. Danny rolled off the coffee table. He scrambled away on all fours along the side of the sofa.

A loud bang. The steel bolt hit the floor inches from his hand.

A thick grey and white snake scuttled past him and disappeared under the pine table. The head of another snake shot through a hole in the floor. It wriggled out to follow its mate.

Ricky was sweating, feverish. "Hate snakes," he muttered. He took aim again, jaws working.

"Stop it. Stop! STOP!" Danny shouted. "They're milk snakes. They're harmless. Leave them alone."

Ricky's face contorted. "Why're they coming through the floor?"

"The ground's burning. It's cooler up here in the lodge. We've got to get out of here."

Slowly Ricky lowered his bow. "Fine, OK. Outside. And don't get smart."

Danny grabbed the arm of the sofa and pulled himself up. He moved down the pine table, steering clear of the broken glass, Ricky's laboured, moist breathing close behind him.

They reached the doorway. Danny blinked against the morning light. The air felt thick. A dark plume of smoke washed over the patio.

"One side." Ricky shoved Danny against the door frame and pushed past him onto the flagstones. More rockets of sound. "Where's that coming from?"

"From there!" Danny pointed over the roof of the lodge. "Holy crap!"

A tall pine reared up in a waterfall of flame. A branch blew off in a cascade of sparks.

Ricky stared, bow sagging at his side.

"Now do you believe me? The whole island is like dried-up dust. We have to get off now or we'll fry."

"How long have we got?"

"I don't know."

"Good, 'cause I'm not leaving without my prize."

"Are you crazy?"

"I paid thirty-five thousand bucks for that pelt. That's thirty-five thousand in real money, American dollars ..."

"Look ..." Danny rubbed sweat from his face, thinking desperately. "When this island goes, it'll blow up like a bomb. We can't outrun the fire, nothing can. We have to put water between us and the fire. It's our only chance. And we have to find Morty's radio phone and call Corazon. Get her to fly in and pick us up before the smoke gets too thick for her to land."

Ricky swore, rubbing his forehead with his free hand.

"Burning's the worst death there is," Danny said. "Is that how you want to go?"

"Fine, you win." Ricky shouldered his bow. "OK, so how do we get off the island, Genius? Swim?"

5

Logan's Zoo. Rachel had never seen a place so still. When she emerged from the trail, it felt like stepping into a chill mountain lake.

"Logan," she called out. "LO-OO-GAN."

No sign of him today. Maybe he was drunk again. Those times Danny would turn her round by the shoulders and march her back up the trail to Camp Nirvana. Let the guy keep his dignity, he'd say.

She picked up a dry tree branch and swished it over the earth as she made her way past a row of ratty old booths that had once held a shooting gallery, a fish pond and a maple sugar shack. The plywood Logan had nailed over their dark openings sagged from rusty nails.

The thought of stumbling across Logan's prone, drunken form made her shiver. Dad hated alcoholics. Before he went to work for the health department, Dad drove tow truck for a body shop. He'd cleaned up every kind of road accident there was, even one where a whole family got killed. According to Dad every death on the road was caused by alcohol and that's why he never took a drink. Ever. Except now he was in rehab because of those yellow pills, oxy-something they were called. Go figure.

In June when they were driving up to Camp Nirvana, they had to pass through Red Dog Lake. Dad got all excited and said they had to visit Logan's Zoo. He'd gone on and on about the animals they would see there: foxes and skunks, rabbits and goats, maybe even a cougar. Dad's mum had taken him there when he was a kid. Most of all Dad reminisced about Pasha, the Russian bear. She did neat tricks and for a reward Logan would give her a strawberry ice cream cone.

"How long do bears live?" she'd asked Dad, thinking that Pasha must be pretty old by now.

Dad didn't reply. He drove up and down Highway 11 looking for the entrance to the zoo, growing more and more silent when he couldn't find it. Finally he drove back to Red Dog Lake and pulled up at this big pink building called the Galaxy Motel. In the café, a fat lady called Corazon laughed when he asked for directions to Logan's Zoo. Dad got that empty look again, his dark eyes almost black. They took off again in the pickup, driving back and forth up the two-lane highway until he found a dirt road with a wire gate across it.

The gate wasn't locked. Dad let her jump out and squeak it open. They drove down the road, bushes and pine boughs scraping the sides of the cab. They ended up in a parking lot with green weeds poking through the cracked asphalt.

The main fairground sloped away from them. Dad pointed out the ramshackle booths, telling her about the cool prizes he'd won as a kid: a hockey puck, stick-on tattoos and chewing gum that turned your mouth black. They couldn't see Red Dog Lake but they could hear the waves. Dad said that the zoo didn't have a beach, only cliffs with a huge drop-off down to the lake. Folks worried that some kid was going to fall down and get killed because all the animal cages were strung out on trails that criss-crossed through the lake-side trees and Logan hadn't bothered to put in a guardrail. Dad led the way through the trees but the cages were only filled with leaves, sticks and dirt.

No animals.

They ended up at the main building which stood next to a small concrete amphitheatre and a large ornate cage. This was where Logan's bear, Pasha, performed, Dad explained. Up close the bars of the cage were pitted with rust. The door stood open. A soggy black sleeping bag lay dumped in the centre. Dad told her not to touch it.

Rachel kicked a stray pine cone up the slope. "Logan," she shouted.

Her voice echoed over the rocks and the pines. Maybe Logan had driven his bashed-up *Volkswagen* van over to the Galaxy Motel. Danny said that was why Logan stayed so skinny: he could only afford to eat at Corazon's diner twice a week.

The main building was a sun-faded wooden structure on two levels. On the ground floor, people used to buy their tickets and souvenirs and up top they'd sit out on the deck to eat their hot dogs from the cafeteria. That's where Logan kept his old black wall phone.

Rachel hesitated at the bottom of the rickety stairs to the deck. Would Logan be mad if she used his phone without asking?

I guess I can wait for him, she thought. She strolled back to the amphitheatre and climbed up the concrete benches to the top. She sat down, flicking dead leaves underfoot with her stick. Dad said Pasha was so smart she could do all kinds of complicated tricks. She could balance a red ball on her nose while rocking to *Smoke on the Water* by Deep Purple. She would fall over and play dead when Logan squirted her with a water pistol. At the end of the show she would give him a sloppy kiss to get her ice cream.

Bored now, Rachel sighed and made her way back down to the cage. The grotty sleeping bag was still there. She circled the cage, dragging her stick over the steel bars, making them clang. Maybe Logan got his cheque from the government today. Then for sure he'd disappear into the bar at the Galaxy Motel. Corazon held karaoke strip night the first week of every month to get everybody's welfare and pension money, Danny said.

Away from the theatre and the bear cage, under the leafy branches of a maple tree, she found the gravestones again: three small granite squares half covered with dry weeds and dusty soil. Nobody knew they were there, not even Danny. She traced the names with her finger: Brownie, Rusty and Golden. No dates though, so she still couldn't figure out how long bears lived.

She cracked her stick in half and tossed the pieces away, then headed back to the main building.

That first day, she and Dad had wandered all over the deck, peering through the darkened windows. Suddenly Dad said they had to go. Some tramp was living in the building. Those guys were desperate men, often in trouble with the cops. Bad people. He warned her never to go back to the zoo again, no matter what.

Later on she learned the tramp was Logan.

She pushed open the front door, wrinkling her nose at the sharp smell, a mix of mildew, stale coffee and cigarette smoke. The light switches never worked. The passageway to the old washrooms and office had sunk into purple shadow. She picked her way past the knocked-over cafeteria tables and chairs to the black rotary phone on the wall by the exit to the deck. She lifted the receiver and dialled zero to call the operator.

It took quite a while. The operator wouldn't call Dr. Amdur until Rachel gave her the number on the phone. She hesitated because Logan didn't have any money, but maybe she could get some money from Dad to pay Logan back.

"You are connected," the operator said.

Rachel listened to the rings. They seemed far away.

"Amdur here."

His voice sounded so near, it startled her. Now she didn't know what to say. "Hi, Dr. Amdur," she stammered.

"Rachel? Is that you? Is everything all right?"

"No." She wanted to tell him about Barry and the things stored on his computer, but then Dr. Amdur would know that she'd sneaked into Barry's office and hacked his password. "Barry wants me to go to Santa's Fish Camp again. It's for babies. Camp sucks. I want to come home."

"I see." Dr. Amdur sounded tired.

"I miss Dad. Danny, my counsellor, left on Thursday. Barry fired him for nothing."

"Now how do you know that?"

"Because Barry's a jerk and pervert! And Danny knows it." There, she'd said it. "I hate Camp Nirvana. I want to go home. I can live in Dad's and my apartment. I can look after myself."

"You know that's impossible, Rachel. Children aren't allowed to live on their own."

"Then I could stay with you till Dad gets better."

Dr. Amdur sighed. "That's not possible either. Remember what we talked about, about helping your father get better?"

"Yes, but I'm not *doing* anything. I can't help Dad when I'm at camp."

"My dear child, while you're at camp he doesn't have to worry about you."

He should. "That doesn't make sense."

"I know it's difficult to understand. I need you to promise me, Rachel, that you won't do anything silly. Try to be happy at camp."

"NO! I hate Camp Nirvana. I'm leaving and I'm never going back."

"Now see here …"

For the first time, Dr. Amdur sounded mad. That really hurt. Slowly and carefully she pulled down the metal hook for the receiver so he wouldn't notice her hanging up.

Adults always stick together, even nice people like Dr. Amdur. Everybody's mad at me, she thought. Barry's mad, and Dad is mad. Well, not mad exactly just quiet and not saying anything.

Loud footsteps on the wooden stairs outside. Rachel jumped. The receiver slipped out of her hand and crashed against the wall. The door to the deck flew open in a burst of light. Logan stood there, his long hair wild, a paper bag from the Liquor Control Board of Ontario in his fist.

And he looked *really* mad.

6

"OK, Genius, I'm waiting," Ricky said.

"There's a boat – a canoe," Danny stammered. "My dad and I used it. We went fishing here when I was a kid."

"There's no canoe. I've been all over the island and I've seen squat."

"Morty said you guys were going to bag Old Devil. The icing on the cake, right?" Danny felt sweat prickle under his arms. "Round here folks stash gear under the house. No basements. The canoe's got to be under the lodge."

A second pine tree roared into flame like a torch. Danny cried out, he couldn't help it.

"OK, OK, find the damn boat," Ricky said.

Danny searched his memory. He remembered his dad tugging on a padlocked gate that led to the underside of the lodge. In the early dawn, the sky had glowed pink over the tops of the pines pressing up against the building, so checking out the eastern side was the best bet.

But that meant he'd have to cross over the patio, passing the silent humps of Morty and Hendrix …

"Come on, wake up, we gotta go." Ricky shoved him.

If I stick to the edge of the patio, I can do it.

The flagstones stretched out in a long rectangle before them, about fifteen by thirty feet. Danny left the doorway and made for the bare strip of ground edging the stones. He headed down the short side of the terrace, dirt and weeds scratching his feet. When he reached the corner where the flagstones gave way to the trail down to the lake, he was forced to turn and face the dark forms of the bodies. He tried to look away from them as he headed east along the long side of the patio, but their icy presence reached out for him, pulling his eyes away from the trees to look at them.

A flicker of movement. He watched Ricky bend down over Hendrix's eviscerated corpse, scoop up a handful of hundred dollar bills and stuff them inside his combat vest.

"Robbing a dead guy, that's twisted. That's really sick, man," Danny said.

"Mind your own damn business."

Danny had reached the end of the flagstones by now. No choice but to cut through the pines, paralleling the lodge, for a distance of about fifty feet. At that point, he'd turn left, cut through the trees and end up at the eastern side of the building.

Throat dry, he plunged away from the flagstones into the thick woods. Sharp branches tore through his shirt. He pushed and shoved them away, his hands growing dark and sticky with sap. The crackling of the two burning trees was getting much louder.

The fire's going to jump to another tree. And another. And another. It'll storm through the treetops at sixty miles an hour ...

He turned left now, pressing on. Suddenly the trees ended and he was looking at the southeast corner of the lodge.

A lattice of treated wood lined the gap between the base of the building and the ground, a height of roughly three feet. He moved over to the lodge itself, crouched down next to the lattice and, shielding his eyes, stared into the damp darkness underneath.

A flash of silver like a fish at the bottom of a lake: an aluminum canoe.

Found it!

He gazed down the wall of logs that formed the eastern wall of the lodge, looking for the hatchway in.

There, halfway down, a pile of pine needles and a half moon of swept dirt. Someone had opened the gate, and not too long ago either. Its rusty latch was broken, hanging by one nail. He ran down to it, took hold of its flimsy handle and pulled.

The gate swung open easily. He bent down and crawled through the opening, his hands sinking into soft loam. The canoe shimmered in the dim light about twenty feet away.

He crept closer, passing a set of paddles – they'd need those. A piece of yellow nylon rope dangled from the bow of the canoe. He grabbed the rope and pulled.

The canoe barely shifted.

He wiped his face. *Keep it cool, man, or you're dead.* He breathed in, tried to focus. The ground sloped down toward the opening. The canoe would slide out no problem once he got it moving. It was probably stuck on something.

He tossed the rope aside and gripped the pointed bow with both hands. He tensed his muscles and pulled.

Nothing.

"What's the holdup?" Ricky's voice at the opening startled him.

"I found the canoe, but it's hung up on something," Danny said over his shoulder.

"You're pathetic! Go on, get out of there."

Danny scrambled back out, dragging the paddles with him. He dumped them on the ground and stood up, relieved to be back in the light. He watched Ricky barrel in through the gate, crawl under the lodge and seize the bow of the canoe, working to free it.

"OK, I need some muscle. Grab the rope," Ricky said. The yellow rope flicked through the opening. "And put some back into it."

Danny picked up the rope. At Ricky's signal, he dragged on it. His shoulder muscles burned from the strain.

"Pull, damn it!"

"This isn't right." Danny dropped the rope, hands on his thighs, breathing hard.

Ricky's round head emerged through the opening. "Some jerk shoved a load inside the canoe. Can't see what it is. Too dark under there."

A swath of burning pine needles rained down. Danny brushed frantically at his clothes and hair, searching for painful points of fire. Nothing, thank God.

"We've got to haul the canoe out no matter what," he insisted.

"Who's arguing?" Ricky vanished back under the lodge. Thuds and grunts of effort. "OK, I got it."

The metal end of the canoe nosed out into the light. Danny grabbed it and heaved. God, this was hard.

Half of the canoe flopped through the gate. Something yellow inside. A sturdy Kodiak hunting boot, camouflage pants.

Another heave. The rest of the canoe glided outside.

Anderson's bloodless face stared at the sky, eyes like boiled egg whites under his twisted spectacles. His mouth sagged open in grotesque mimicry of *The Scream*, his thin fair hair stirring in the hot breath of the fire.

Danny sprang back against the bushes. Hot acid boiled up his throat. He leaned over and coughed into the dirt until his stomach clenched in pain.

"Get a grip." Ricky had struggled back outside and sat crouched beside the canoe. "Yep, Old Devil, the monster trout, can snack on Anderson's arm all week. He won't be missing it."

"Oh man. He tried to get away, only he bled to death."

"Wake up, Sunshine, do you see buckets of blood? He got done someplace else and was stashed under here. Come on, grab the end. We gotta tip him out."

"No way, forget it." The shaking had started in Danny's limbs again. He blundered away from Ricky, heading along the southern wall.

"Get back here, you," Ricky shouted behind him. "Fine, say hello to Anderson in Valhalla for me."

There was no way he'd set foot in that canoe now that he knew Anderson had died in it. He had to get back inside the lodge, find Morty's radio phone and call for help. He stopped at the edge of the terrace.

He'd come back by the more direct route. Now he couldn't get to the entrance without stepping through the blood that had flowed from Hendrix and Morty.

Overhead a soft whispering like a campfire starting. He looked up. The cedar shingles on the roof of the lodge were smouldering. The logs of the walls were old, soaked in creosote to ward off insects and mice. Once the fire took hold, the century-old building would go up like a blast furnace and become ashes in minutes.

No time left.

He tried to keep to the narrow strip of earth rimming the flag-stones. That way he was able to avoid Morty, but Hendrix lay sprawled directly across his path. He swallowed. Hendrix's limp, liverspotted hand pointed into the trees from a black, insect-infested pool of blood.

I have to jump over him. No choice.

The buzzing of the flies and mosquitoes drowned out the noise of the fire. Danny closed his eyes.

I'm wasting time.

He leapt, blindly. Somehow he managed to clear the hump of Hendrix's leather-clad back. He charged over to the entrance, refusing to think of what had soiled his bare feet.

He hesitated in the doorway, eyes scanning the dim floor. A chaos of ravaged duffle bags and equipment sprawled under the table. The radio phone had to be there.

Most radio phones consisted of a black telephone receiver on top of a metal box about eight by ten inches in size. Should be easy to spot.

He ran over to the table, his eyes struggling to adjust to the dark, and crawled underneath it. The planking under his hands felt sticky. He prayed it was just dried-up liquor. He seized the torn remains of the bag lying on top of the pile and shook it.

Nothing inside, empty.

He tossed the ruined bag aside.

Next he found a black backpack, only slightly torn. He foraged through it. Again, nothing inside except for a white plastic medicine bottle. No label. Probably some weird medicine or a roll of film.

"That the Aussie's pack." Ricky said from the doorway. "Where's his gun?"

"Don't see it." Danny tossed the medicine bottle back into the pack.

A loud crackling sound. He squinted through the murk round the edge of the table. Smoke! Curling down through the joints in the ceiling.

The lodge was on fire.

There's no time left. No time.

The ropy strands of the last bag were stuck to the floor. He jerked it free. Beneath it, a sticky river of dried black fluid bore a detritus of shattered electronics, metal and glass. A shiny watch face glinted from the ooze: Morty's Rolex. He remembered Morty stripping it off and dumping it on the dining table while he, Danny, poured out the hunters' shots. Morty had raised his glass and declared that time didn't matter on the island.

Not any more.

"Do you see Anderson's gun?" Ricky again.

"No!" Danny flung the remains of the ragged bag across the floor.

A flash of copper metal nearly hidden under the rustic sofa. He groped through the dark and seized a black plastic receiver. Bright wires sprouted from one end.

"Found it," he shouted. He felt under the sofa and pulled out a dented metal box. An electronic circuit board poked through one shattered side. He grabbed Hendrix's pack and dumped the box and receiver inside. He'd fit everything back together, get the radio working.

A dull thump overhead.

Fire had broken in upstairs. *I have to get out of here.*

Danny went to stand up, and banged his head on the underside of the table. Man, that hurt. Even in the dim light he could see that dark matter had soiled his hands.

A chunk of plaster from the ceiling crashed down onto the table right over his head. Thank God, the table held. Smoke poured through the naked lathes like blood from a wound. He could feel the heat of the fire, radiating down from the ceiling.

"I need that gun," Ricky shouted. "What are you waiting for?"

He had to get out. Now. He grabbed the pack by the straps.

There, poking out from under the sofa, he spotted Anderson's gun. He reached to grab it.

A rushing sound. A sigh like snow shifting. An avalanche of plaster, wood and charred furniture broke through a tear in the ceiling.

And buried the table and sofa in a mountain of construction waste.

7

Logan moved through the room like a dark wind. He grabbed a stray chair, screeched it over to a stained plywood table and thudded down the bottle. He collapsed on the chair. The outside trees cast shadows through the speckled windows of the ruined cafeteria like silhouettes on waxed paper.

His mouth moved, no words came out.

Who is he talking to? Rachel dared not breathe.

Logan rubbed his eyes, banged his forehead with the heel of one hand, rocking rhythmically. Cold crept into Rachel's chest: she shouldn't be seeing this.

Down the phone line trickled a recorded voice nagging at her to hang up. *Shut up, shut up, Phone Lady.* She hauled on the slippery phone cord to catch the dangling receiver.

Logan's body grew rigid. He leapt up, a scarecrow come to life. Rushed at her, so fast. He wrenched the receiver out of her hand and slammed it back into place.

Rachel gasped. "Mr. Logan …"

He seized her shoulders, watery blue eyes unseeing, and banged her spine hard against the crumbling plaster next to the phone.

"Mr. Logan, you're scaring me. Stop!"

He blinked, confused.

"Mr. Logan?"

He shuddered and released her. "Bloody hell, Kid, don't sneak up on people like that." He stumbled back to his chair, sat down and tossed his crumpled stetson on the table. "Shouldn't you be at camp?"

"I'm looking for Danny."

"Naturally." He freed a shiny brown bottle from the paper bag and unscrewed the top. "Sorry, Kid, haven't seen him since the last time you two misfits went AWOL from Barry's plantation."

"I ... I didn't mean to scare you."

"Scare me? Not a chance."

"I'm sorry I used your phone without asking. I'll pay you back when I get some money."

"Forget it. Ma Bell doesn't know I rewired the sucker." He smiled, showing surprisingly white teeth. "Hell, she can afford it." He gestured at the kitchen cupboards behind them. "Don't stand there, gaping. Go on, get me a glass."

Relieved that he was back to normal, Rachel ran over to the counter, climbed up and swung open the cupboard door. One tumbler, milky with grease, rested on the middle shelf. She grabbed it, jumped down, and set it down on the table in front of him.

He grunted his thanks and poured out a dollop of tawny liquid. She wrinkled her nose at the sharp smell of alcohol. Canadian whisky, the label said.

"Dangerous to disturb a man's drinking, Kiddo," he said. "Your daddy should have taught you that."

"My dad doesn't drink."

"Is that so? You're making me nervous, Rachel Forest, hovering there all judgmental. Sit down for God's sake. I'm OK now."

Cautiously she righted a tipped-over chair and sat down, but not too close to him. She watched him take a deep gulp of the whisky. He had a wind-hollowed face beneath a stringy mass of yellowish grey hair. His jeans were frayed and slick with dirt and his worn black leather jacket had a large rip under the armpit. The edging at the neck of his faded T-shirt looked like it had been chewed by mice. So did the brim of his punched-down cowboy hat.

Probably the mice *had* chomped on them. She'd seen enough mice running around the place.

"What's the matter? Cat got your tongue?" he asked.

"I … I'm worried about Danny."

"Oh?"

"He said he'd be back at camp on Monday, but Barry fired him."

"Surprise, surprise. Well, you could see that coming ten miles away."

"That's not fair. Danny's my best counsellor. He didn't do anything wrong."

"Danny's a grown man, with a grown man's problems. Let it go. How old are you, Kid? Ten? Eleven? Go on back to camp, there's nothing for you here but a wrecked-up old vet and his addiction." He poured himself another glassful.

"I'm never going back to camp. Barry made everyone go to Santa's Fish Camp. I hate that place. It stinks!"

Logan's glass couldn't hide his smile. "You got that right."

She felt in the pocket of her jeans for her precious bottle of indigo paint. Danny was coming back, he had to. He cared about their art even more than she did.

She looked at the far side of the room where Logan's battered red tool chest rested on rusting wheels: the hiding place for their art. Its drawers were wide and empty, perfect for storing her large blue-checked sheets that resembled old-fashioned graph paper. Danny maintained that Logan would never look inside it because he'd sold off his tools for drinking money ages ago.

She watched Logan down more alcohol. Maybe it wasn't smart to show him where they'd stashed their art. Dad told her drunks tore their houses to pieces looking for booze when they ran out. What if Logan opened the drawers and the mice got in? Mice ate through anything and everything: wood, soap, paper … especially paper.

Still, she wanted to make sure their art was safe. She slid off her chair and crept over to the tool box, careful not to distract Logan. Taking hold of the rusty steel handle, she pulled open the top drawer.

Empty!

Fear ripped through her body. She pulled out the drawer underneath. And the next one. All empty, everything gone.

Rachel cried out, her pain a rushing tide. "Our book: it's gone! All of it."

"What the hell!" Logan banged down his glass. "Keep it down, Kiddo."

"My paintings, they're gone!"

"What paintings? Stop hyperventilating. Let me think for a minute. Oh, yeah, right. The comic book."

"It's not a comic book, it's a *graphic novel*." She didn't want to make him mad again, but … "Did *you* take it?"

"No, I don't read. I'm not the cultured type."

"You did read it. You said you liked our story."

"Hey there, get a grip." Logan held up a hand. "On my life, I swear I never touched your art."

"Well, somebody did. Somebody stole it."

"Use your head, Kid. Nobody comes here but you and Danny. Only one answer to your mystery, sorry to say."

Rachel frowned so hard her forehead hurt. "Danny wouldn't take our art without telling me."

"Maybe he wants all the credit for your comic book."

"Danny wouldn't do that to me. We're partners."

Logan sighed and refreshed his drink. "I've known Danny since he was your age living with his grandmother. The boy means well, but he finds staying on the righteous path a slippery proposition. Lack of moral fibre, I suppose, not that I'm a shining example of virtue. Your Danny drifts through life and when things blow up in his face, as they usually do, he might, on a good day, take a second to think about it, and his insight won't last much longer."

"I don't know what you mean."

"OK, fine, my guess is Danny said 'see ya Monday' so he wouldn't have to deal with you getting all emotional. And he took your art with him because Barry fired his ass." He drained his glass. "Better get used to getting dumped if you want boyfriends."

"I never want a boyfriend. Why are you being so mean? Danny visits you all the time. You act like you like him, but now you just sit there and drink and say bad things about him."

"Rachel Forest, you are the essence of tact." He reached again for the bottle.

Rachel clenched her fists. "I bet Barry fired Danny because he found out he was moonlighting ..." The words stuck in Rachel's throat like hard pebbles. She'd promised Danny she wouldn't tell about his special job.

"Moonlighting where?" Logan asked.

"Nothing."

"Cat got your tongue again, I see."

She watched him drink another shot. How many drinks was that? Three? Four? He really was a useless drunk, just like Dad said.

Logan sighed and set down his glass. "Where did Danny say he was moonlighting? Don't just stand there staring at me with those big yellow wolf's eyes of yours. You want me to help find him, don't you? Where was the job?"

"He ... he said he couldn't tell me. It was safer that way."

"Why?"

"He didn't want his grandmother to worry. Or me. He was acting weird."

"Oh?"

"He was *scared.*" There – she'd said it.

"And you know what being scared looks like." The mistiness in Logan's eyes had vanished: he looked like a blue-eyed eagle.

"Sure. I've been scared lots of times." *Playing Ninja, looking in through Barry's office window late at night.*

Logan shook his head. "No, you don't, Kid." He screwed the top back on the whisky bottle and grabbed his hat. "OK, guess it's time to fire up the VW. You coming?"

"I'm not going back to Camp Nirvana. Ever."

"I heard you the first ten thousand times. I'm heading down to the Galaxy. Thought you'd be hungry."

She did feel hungry. "I can't go. I don't have any money," she said.

"Who says you're paying?"

"You don't have any money either. Danny said so."

"Then Danny knows as much about me as the rest of the fools in Red Dog Lake." He shoved his hat over his tangled hair. "We're eating at the Galaxy because the only person who might know where Danny put your art works there."

"I don't want to talk to that fat lady Corazon. She's mean."

"Yes, the only thing stonier than the farmland around here is Corazon Sinclair's heart." He started toward the outside door. "Hurry up now. We need to catch Odile before she goes off her shift."

"Who's Odile?"

"She's the closest thing to a saint in Red Dog Lake." He held the screen door open to let Rachel out. "Thought Danny might have told you. Odile St. Pierre is his grandmother."

8

Grit packed Danny's mouth and nostrils. He coughed and spat, desperate to breathe, rubbed his eyes to clear them. Smoke and dust shrouded the great room.

He was still under the table. Somehow he'd survived. The pine dining table had held up to the collapse of the ceiling. Ugly stuff built to last, just like Morty said.

Hard metal poked his thigh. Instinctively he reached down. Felt the barrel of Anderson's gun beside him. He curled his fingers round it and jerked the weapon free from a mound of plaster and broken wood.

I have to get out.

The end of the dining room table pointed toward the outside door. Though he couldn't see anything through the smoke, if he crawled forward in that direction, he told himself he couldn't miss it. He pulled up onto his hands and knees and fumbled for Hendrix's pack with the radio phone. He managed to loop one arm through its straps. Dragging it and the gun, he started for the door.

Breathing the thick smoke was like inhaling a garbage bag full of Santa's high-octane weed. Intense heat pressed down on him in a searing impenetrable wall, blistering his skin. He crawled forward through heaps of glass, ashes and rubble.

From sweat lodge ceremony he remembered that the air at ground level had less smoke and stayed cooler. He bellied down onto the planks, coughing violently. The air might be cooler next to the floor, but it still felt like it was melting his bones.

Twenty feet ahead, slightly to the left, a hazy glow: the door. He wormed his way toward it, squinting through the smoke.

Give it up, man. So easy. What have you got to live for? Crap job, no future.

The air felt cooler. Maybe he was kidding himself, but the light seemed brighter.

He reached out. Struck a raised piece of wood.

The threshold … the door!

He groped for the cool, smooth flagstones beyond the doorstep. Bracing his hands on them, he pushed himself up and heaved his body out the door.

He flopped onto his back, gasping like a spent fish, staring up through the burning treetops.

Thuds and groans as more logs collapsed into the flaming lodge. He had to get clear, get down to the lake.

He staggered to his feet, picked up Anderson's gun and slung Hendrix's pack over one shoulder. Through the shifting bands of smoke, the trail down to the lake beckoned like a beam of light.

Ricky had vanished. Left him to die.

Where the hell was he? Had he hauled the canoe down to the lake? Or had he decided to swim for it? He was a big guy with layers of fat like a marine mammal, probably a natural-born swimmer. He'd make it across to the mainland, no problem.

Danny limped dizzily down the trail. Smoke streamed through the trees like black mist. He was marooned on the island: what could he do to save himself? Get in the water and stay under, obviously. But would the fire boil up the water in the shallows and cook him like a chicken? When he surfaced to breathe, would the incandescent air char his lungs and skin? Would the flames eat up all the oxygen and suffocate him?

Water, he needed water. He thought of Anderson's blue bottles of mineral water exploding back in the burning lodge. He could see them, taste the frothy metallic water inside.

A blue mirage shimmered in the air before him like a jewel. He was hallucinating, losing it for sure. He rubbed his eyes with his free hand.

The blue of the lake – that's what he was seeing. Beyond the burning island, the sun streamed down on the sparkling waves of Fire Lake in a perfect August day.

Ricky was standing on the beach, bent over the canoe, his hunting boots tied by the laces and slung round his neck. The shale screeched against the aluminum bottom as he shoved it into the water.

Danny stumbled, willing his legs to move faster. By the time he emerged from the trail, Ricky had waded knee-deep into the water. He slung one bare foot into the canoe and leaned on it. The metal boat wobbled frantically, tipping on its side. Water sloshed in. Swearing, Ricky leaned over, grabbing both sides. He pushed down and tried to jump into the middle with both feet. The canoe flailed wildly and flung him into the water.

Ricky surfaced like a mad walrus. He seized the canoe, dragged it out of the water and banged it down on the rocks of the beach. Furious, he picked it up and bashed it again.

"Stop!" Danny screamed.

He rushed at Ricky, swinging the pack.

Hitting the American's massive shoulder was like running headlong into a side of beef. Danny crashed down on the black gravel of the beach, one arm tangled in the straps of the pack. Anderson's gun flew out of his hand.

"You little jerk!" Ricky seized him by the shirt. He banged him painfully against the stones. "Don't – you – ever – sneak – up – on – me."

Danny swung at him, striking nothing but air.

"Ease up!"

"No, you left me to die!"

"Stop it or I'll crack your skull open."

Ricky had him by the throat, jamming the back of his head so hard against the stones that his ears hummed. He wanted to tear Ricky's face off. It took all he had to force himself to lie still.

"Are you going to behave?" Ricky's small eyes bored down on him.

"Yes, *yes*! Let me up."

Ricky relaxed his grip. Danny rolled over on one elbow, coughing for air. Ricky snatched Anderson's gun from where it had fallen onto the stones and tossed it into the canoe with a metallic clang. He'd already secured his precious bow to the underside of the middle seat.

"That gun's mine," Danny lurched to his feet.

"You snooze, you lose."

"You left me to burn. Why didn't you help me?"

"You never served your country, did you, you pathetic excuse for a man? A weak soldier guts the troop. In combat, he goes down to save the warriors. That's survival."

"You were never in the army. You're a washed up rock star who gets off on playing Rambo. A mark who pays thirty-five thousand dollars to shoot a tame old bear who never hurt anybody. Really big man you are, Loser."

Ricky came at him. Danny swung Hendrix's pack like a shield, but Ricky tore it away.

Behind them a dozen more trees whooshed into flame.

"Time to go," Ricky said. "Stay back or you're dead." He tossed Hendrix's pack into the canoe.

Danny rubbed his face. He moved away from the water, keeping Ricky in sight until he reached the edge of the rock cliff where he'd hidden out the night before. He retreated up the sloping granite and slumped down next to the blueberry bushes. Now he had nothing, not even the ruined radio phone. He spotted his runners in the crevice where he'd stashed them yesterday. He tied their laces together and slung them round his neck like Ricky.

From his perch he watched the beefy American slog back into the water. This time Ricky slammed against the canoe with his gut across the midsection. Once again it spun and threw him in the water. It rocked dangerously – the crossbow, Anderson's gun and the pack rattling around inside.

Ricky surfaced, soaked through.

Bad comedy, Danny thought. *We who are about to die can't laugh any more.* "You don't know the first thing about canoes, do you?" he called down.

Ricky ignored him, shaking water out of his ears. He seized the boat again.

"I can show you how," Danny offered, coming down from the rock.

"Like hell."

"Guess we'll both fry then." Danny hunkered down on the beach, waiting. He picked up a broken pine twig and poked at the dark pebbles. Time for him to get in the water no matter what. The charred odour of burning wood overwhelmed his senses. It wasn't the comforting scent of a warm campfire, but the penetrating acrid smell of a thousand furnaces. Smoke burned his eyes, blotting out the sun.

He had scraped away the shale and was boring his twig into the grey mud beneath when Ricky appeared, brandishing a paddle. Danny held still, staring at the black curling hairs on Ricky's pale elongated toes.

"Give up?" He tossed aside the stick.

"Don't try anything."

By now they were both wheezing, eyes and noses streaming. They stumbled over to the spot where Ricky had beached the canoe.

"OK, I'll steer," Danny said. "You go in front." He pushed the canoe out till it was floating in one foot of water. "Wade out to the middle."

Ricky grunted and moved into the water still holding the paddle.

"OK, now lean over and grab both sides. *Both* sides, I said."

Ricky glared at him over his shoulder. He dropped the paddle in the canoe and took hold of the gunwales.

"Now step right in the middle. One foot, then the other."

"It won't stay still, damn it."

"I'm holding it still. Just do it."

The canoe reared and wobbled wildly. Danny could barely hold it level. Ricky's two hundred pounds crashed down on the central thwart. When Danny tried to dislodge the canoe, it stayed stuck on the rocks.

"Move forward. Forward, damn it!"

Ricky swore and hauled his bulk down onto the gear then back up onto the forward seat. Coughing through another intense surge of smoke, Danny forced the canoe off the stones. The lake bottom dropped off sharply. In seconds, he was waist deep in icy water. He seized the stern in a frantic embrace, hooking one foot over the side. He pushed down hard with his heel, tipping the canoe to get his arm in.

"Hey!" Ricky shouted.

"Balance me!"

Danny's muscles burned with effort. It was easy playing warrior when you were ten years old, skinny-dipping at Catholic camp, but he was twenty-four now and his sodden jeans dragged him down like cement. The bottom vanished. Beneath him he sensed only still black water, the haunt of water demons.

He wrenched his upper body out of the water. The canoe bucked violently. Ignoring Ricky's shouts, he rammed his knee against the oncoming boat bottom.

"Get over!" he cried.

The boat rocked and tumbled. He wrenched and pulled, feeling the hard side and edges of the canoe bang against his ribs.

And then he was up, free of the water, cold air beating on his wet clothes.

He shook the wet hair out of his eyes. He was straddling the stern, his back to Ricky, staring at the island. They had already drifted several yards from shore. Black smoke towered over the trees in a thunderhead, crimson flashes of fire like lightning underneath.

He twisted round to face Ricky and sat down carefully in the stern. Water streamed from their clothes, puddling in the bottom round their gear.

"Quick, hand me the other paddle," Danny said.

"I only got one." Ricky held it up.

Of course, one person, one paddle. Idiot!

"You can't steer from the front end, Ricky. You'll have to give it to me."

Ricky thought this over, sucking his cheeks in and out.

"OK, the farther out we go into the lake, the higher the waves will be. We'll tip over. Hope you can swim."

"Take it!" Ricky pitched the paddle at him. It rattled on the metal bottom.

Danny snatched it up. He dipped it into the water on his left, making the familiar J-stroke, correcting, balancing. Hard work with Ricky's weight sinking them close to the waterline.

He counted silently to keep up the rhythm. Ricky folded his arms, scowling like a disgruntled tourist. Every few minutes, Danny leaned over panting, resting the paddle across his knees, to give his arms and shoulders a break.

He glanced back. By now they were far enough off shore that distances proved deceptive. The beach and white granite rocks of the island had merged into a flat featureless line.

Fire was spreading relentlessly through the island trees, consuming the crime scene and turning evidence into ashes. The cops would never find out who had killed Morty and the others. They'd nail him for it: they'd say he was a weirdo local native with a hate-on for white tourists. This stupid Indian guide gig was a mistake that would rub out his life.

Still he felt sorry for Morty, a lot sorrier than he did for the other two. Morty was full of nervous self-importance, trying hard to be politically correct around Danny, but at least he was human. "I'm sorry about the bear, Kid," he'd confided to Danny at the end of the hunt. "The boss upstairs says make these guys happy, I jump up and do the tango. It's economics, Kid, it always is. These weapons guys can give us jobs and, God knows, Ontario needs 'em."

Right, nice jobs making arms and bombs to kill people.

"Hey, wake up, Sunshine." Ricky sounded unsettled. The wind had picked up. The waves were two-foot swells with clear rippling wavelets on the surface. The canoe slid down the back of a large wave, floundering in the trough.

Danny plunged the paddle back into the water, pushing down hard, cursing Ricky for being a self-centred moron who thought television was life. They needed that second paddle and Ricky's muscle to fight through this mess. He spun the bow around to meet the next wave head-on. His arms and shoulders burned with the strain. How long could he keep this up?

"Hear that?" Ricky shifted suddenly.

"Sit still, damn it!" The canoe bobbed like a cork, sending stabs of fear through Danny's chest.

"Something's coming."

Through the slapping bursts of wind, a faint insect-like drone.

"It's a plane!" Danny's heart raced. "It's Corazon! She's flying in to check on us!"

"Where's she coming in? She's gonna land right on top of us."

It was a fair observation, given that they'd reached the middle of the lake. Exactly where Corazon would set down her float plane to stay clear of the trees and rocks along the shoreline.

"She'll see the fire. She'll do a flyover before she lands. She's super-careful." Danny shaded his eyes, trying to spot the plane. "We've got to make sure she sees us. Grab something, anything. Wave, shout." He started undoing the buttons of his shirt. "Have you got a mirror?"

"For what?"

"To shave your pointed head. To signal her, for heaven's sake!"

"Shut up." Ricky jerked a small pair of black binoculars from his combat vest and focused them on the horizon.

The plane appeared to the east, a tiny mosquito hard against the sky. Danny waved his free arm and shouted Corazon's name.

Waves bucked the canoe. Danny scooped up the paddle, his strength returning. They had to get out of the flight path, they had to move. He pushed hard, aiming for the mainland.

The rhythmic throb of the plane's rotor grew louder. *Two engines ... Corazon's plane is a Piper Cherokee, single engine ...*

The plane crossed over the island well above the fire, heading west toward the far end of the lake. Suddenly, it banked steeply, its aluminum skin flashing silver in the sun.

Corazon's plane is red and white.

"That's Santa's plane," Danny said.

"It's turning around." Ricky stared through the sights of the binoculars, following the plane's trajectory. "They're coming in. Stay down!" He sounded nervous.

"What for?"

The silver float plane swooped down in a roar of sound. Wind battered them as it flew over them frighteningly low. It stayed low over the water before climbing east to clear the trees.

Ricky stuffed the binoculars back into his vest. "What are you waiting for? Get going."

"It's OK, they saw us. There's no way they missed us."

"Didn't you hear me? We're a sitting target out here."

"OK, OK." Danny resumed paddling, heading toward the mainland, which seemed to dance through the waves without getting any closer. "Look, it doesn't matter if it's Santa's boys or Corazon come to get us. That plane is our way out."

The plane cut a long graceful arc over the trees and returned, flying so slowly its motors sounded on the verge of sputtering out. Ricky reached for Anderson's gun.

"What are you doing? Are you crazy?" Danny cried.

"Shut up!"

The plane's shadow chased them over the waves. It passed overhead so low Danny could see scratches on the bottom of the floats.

The canoe crested a wave, nosing deeply into the trough.

Ricky aimed the gun at the retreating plane.

"Don't!" Danny shouted. "They're trying to save us, you moron!"

"They're coming back to kill us."

"What?"

Ricky pulled the trigger. Nothing. "Hell! It's jammed." He dropped the gun and pounced on the centre seat to untie his crossbow. He jerked and pulled at the lashings, struggling to free it.

The plane returned, flying even lower. The props thundered down. Coming for them.

Ricky stood up. Danny screamed a warning. Felt the canoe lurch madly.

He fell. Water smothered him in a cold translucent blanket. It poured into his mouth and ears. He couldn't see.

Couldn't breathe …

The water devils had caught him at last.

9

Every day Corazon Amorsolo Sinclair stepped onto the porch of her fine log home and breathed in the vista of pines and lake water, the band of highway drilling north to Cochrane, and the brilliant pink complex housing the diner, rooms and bar of the Galaxy Motel.

This is my world, she thought. Mine, all mine.

"Mine!" That first word had emanated from her sturdy thirteen-month-old frame with such ringing clarity that Mama Filomina cried out, convinced that a burglar had invaded the nursery. Filomina never felt safe in Manila with its fifteen million people, despite the high metal security fence around the Colonel's estate. She rushed to her priest, but he did not address her worries with nearly enough gravity. He patted her hand, invoked the Holy Mother and reminded her to keep the Catholic faith. All would be well by the time of the children's first communion.

Filomina obeyed faithfully, watching her twin son and daughter with an eagle eye, disconcerted by each aberration she discovered. Corazon wanted to play with cars and electric trains; Franco only wanted to play with dolls. Corazon began to read at the age of four and begged Mama to teach her numbers; Franco cared nothing for his letters and foraged passionately through Mama's cosmetics and jewels. Filomina dared not breathe a word of her discoveries to her husband, the Colonel, who had great plans for his son.

On the eve of the children's first communion, she realized beyond all doubt that the Colonel's mistress, that witch, that *bruja*, had cursed her, the Colonel's rightful wife. She had unwrapped Corazon's white lace dress with its pretty pink ribbons, ordered specially from Madrid. With a great deal of effort, she tugged it over her daughter's husky body, praying for a miraculous transformation. No matter how much she fluffed the flounces of the skirt, or fussed with little Corazon's limp hair, nothing could disguise the fact that her daughter was homely, a fat sausage in fancy trim. A strange compulsion seized hold of her. She slipped the dress over thoughtful little Franco, telling herself it was only a joke. If the Colonel knew nothing of it, what harm could it do? She stepped back to view her handiwork and nearly expired. Franco had disappeared. In front of her stood an angel, his face and dark curls heartbreakingly beautiful.

Terrified, Filomina crossed herself. The priest would be helpless against this evil. She must visit the *albularyo*, the shaman. She dared not breathe a word of her intentions to the Colonel, who harboured a strong distaste for superstition and a profound faith in engineering mechanics and the scientific process. The *albularyo*, a leathery toothless man who smelled of sweat and tobacco, forced her down into the dirt of his garden and extracted a lump of dark matter from between her thighs. Here was the evil, he said, holding it under her nose, here was proof of the curse that the Colonel's mistress had brought down on the children. She had forced the migration of the children's souls: her son's spirit lay trapped in Corazon's body and her true daughter in Franco. To remove the curse would require ten thousand American dollars. Cash up front.

Filomina paid him immediately. The Colonel, when he found out, was predictably furious. "Barbarism, pathetic ignorance," he ranted, though he had just squandered an equal sum on diamond earrings for his mistress. Puberty would sort out the children. Franco would study mechanical engineering and Corazon would study fashion and marry, end of discussion.

None of this came about, Corazon reflected. She had, of course, overheard every word, since her parents' passionate disagreements provided much entertainment for her and Franco. Later that night, alone with her dire reflection in the bathroom, the tropical humidity seeping from the sticky white tiles, she made a vow. She would grow beautiful and marry well. She would make Papa proud of her.

Puberty, however, was only kind to her brother. Corazon's body and chin remained round and her eyebrows grew thick and angled sharply upwards, giving her a perpetually startled, almost cartoonish expression. Mama, bitterly disappointed, sighed and took refuge in her romantic novels whenever she could wrestle them away from Franco. Rich men only marry thin, beautiful women, she reminded her daughter. Corazon must lower her expectations.

This Corazon had no intention of doing. She set about beating her baby fat into submission through a brutal regime of team sports and vigorous exercise. She excelled at softball and running but, alas, she had inherited her father's stocky build, and no amount of training could reshape her bones or alter her God-given physiology. She flattered Franco who had developed an encyclopaedic knowledge of cosmetics and their function, real or imaginary. He taught her the nuances and artistry of makeup. She ruthlessly uprooted and reshaped her brows, enduring an exquisitely painful cosmetic procedure known as threading. But the Colonel only shook his head and sighed when she dressed in her Sunday best to accompany him to Mass.

On their seventeenth birthday, Franco vanished. The house was in an uproar. The police were summoned and Filomina suffered yet another breakdown. Franco surfaced three months later, the winner of a spectacular beauty contest for drag queens, contests he continued to win handily despite his fondness for drugs and debauchery. The Colonel no longer dared to intervene, since Franco's lover was a four-star general. Grudgingly he allowed Corazon to study mechanical engineering, if only to distract his fellow officers from the antics of his diva son. Corazon excelled, but first-class student or not, prominent father or not, men refused to hire a female engineer.

Or marry one.

By the time of Corazon's graduation, Filomina had fallen deeply into the clutches of the *albularyo*. The Colonel, disgusted, moved in with his mistress. Corazon stood at the crossroads. If she remained in the decaying family home with her mother, she would dwindle into a hopeless spinster. She packed her suitcases, boarded the city bus and moved in with Franco and his lover, the general, working as their unpaid maid.

The lack of money weighed on her. She began to crave the comforting weight of change in her palm. She dreamed of the slippery, sensuous feel of paper money, but Franco, like the Colonel, wanted her poor and dependent.

Her former classmate, Teresa, worked in Toronto as a nanny. Corazon knew little about Canada other than it was full of snow, but its southern boundaries hugged the far more desirable USA and its precious hordes of American dollars. How hard could it be to slip over the border? The day the Canadian authorities approved her visitor's visa, she pawned Franco's jewels for the airfare.

The plane to Toronto landed in the middle of a January blizzard. Her plastic raincoat cracked and her gloveless hands turned purple from the cold. Her throat closed, her bones turned to crystal. She had to spend nearly all of Franco's money she had left on winter clothes just to survive.

Teresa had taken a lover, a grey-haired schoolteacher who viewed Corazon's intrusion into their lives with a jaundiced eye. Despite the fact that Corazon slept on a cot in their dank windowless basement, the teacher extracted Corazon's share of the rent to the penny. The remainder of Franco's money lasted barely a heartbeat. To feed herself, Corazon cooked and cleaned for them, even servicing the teacher's most prized possession, his Harley Davidson V-Rod Muscle motorcycle.

Desperate, Corazon went to confession in a stone church near the core of the city. She poured out her heart, dizzy with hunger. Franco's money was tainted, the priest told her. Tainted from the sin of homosexuality and the sin of theft. She must work to expiate these transgressions. She must work for the church. For him.

And so she exchanged one basement prison for another, slaving for food. When she complained, the priest threatened her with the immigration department. Her flesh melted from her body, her skin hung in folds. In time, as she had feared, the priest began to demand sexual favours. As his moist and corpulent body thrust into hers, she felt annihilated, less than nothing, less than the prostitutes who lined the streets outside.

The priest had another weakness. He loved to gamble. Thursdays were his poker nights. She would set out the whisky bottles and glasses on a dark green tablecloth that hung over the round table in his office. She would serve him and his cronies roast beef sandwiches and potato salad, clearing their plates and emptying their ashtrays while they, intent on their cards, paid her not the slightest attention. She watched the piles of winnings, noting the exact number of bills and, more importantly, who they went to.

The priest was a mediocre player but one night he won big.

She stood at the sink in the vestry kitchen after the gamblers had left, her hands deep in soapy water. She fingered the submerged edge of the knife she had used to slice up the meat for their dinner. It was at this unfortunate moment that the priest pulled up her skirt.

He had greatly underestimated the depth of her hatred. And her physical strength, hardened by months of strenuous labour. She stabbed him until he crumpled to his knees. He shrieked for mercy.

Corazon straddled him, the knife high in her bloodied fist. "Why should I show you mercy, you puffed-up toad, you devil? I was destitute and starving and you took advantage."

"Yes, yes, forgive me. I took advantage."

"Give me the key to the safe."

"Never, you little whore." He tried to buck her off.

Corazon gripped him more tightly in this macabre parody of sex, momentarily amused. She pressed the tip of the knife into the flesh under his chin. "I am not a whore," she said. "I am a university graduate from a fine family. And," she leaned forward, "whores get paid. For that I am going to cut off your balls."

He screamed, but no one heard, any more than the times she had screamed for help trying to fend him off. The moment he yielded up the key was a moment like no other. She stood up, reborn.

"For the love of God, call an ambulance," he whimpered, clutching himself, blood streaming through his fingers.

"We'll see," she said and showed him the knife again. "Pray you told me the truth."

She stepped over his prone body and climbed the stairs to the vestry office. The key slid easily into the lock of the safe. Her heart leapt when the door swung open. Ten thousand dollars at least, far more than his winnings. She grabbed the wastepaper basket from under his desk, found a plastic bag inside and stuffed every last bill into it.

Back downstairs, she stripped, showered and changed into jeans and a shirt. She shoved her few belongings into a black garbage bag – and her ruined bloody clothes and the knife into another.

He was breathing strangely when she returned to the kitchen. He no longer replied to her questions.

"I'm not a monster like you," she told him. She picked up the telephone and punched 911 for help.

She slipped outside and waited in the shadows until the ambulance pulled up to the vestry door. The thought that he might be dying set her limbs trembling.

She walked into the night, heading for the house Teresa shared with the teacher. They would turn her over to the police in an instant, but in their garage rested the key to her freedom.

Within the hour the teacher's prized Harley Davidson was purring between her thighs.

For someone with Corazon's mechanical skills, it had been trivially easy to break into their garage, disable the bike's alarm system and start the engine. She headed north up Yonge Street leaving the city.

The cold night wind blew through her clothes, clearing her mind. Her odds of escape were not bad provided she could disappear. The government put no energy into chasing up foreign visitors who failed to leave. People at the church paid her so little attention they hadn't bothered to learn her name. Her unremarkable face would blend into one of thousands of illegal immigrants. Teresa and her lover were happy to be rid of her. The Riverdale neighbourhood, where they lived, was a mixed area: thefts of cars and motorcycles were a regular occurrence.

Yonge Street transformed into Highway 11. She rode through Barrie, Orillia and North Bay, stopping only for coffee, gas or to relieve herself. Dawn found her in Temagami. She pulled off the highway and sank the garbage bag with her bloody clothes in a nameless lake. The knife she buried in a pine forest.

A few hours later, the bike's temperamental engine sputtered to a halt in a dump of a town called Red Dog Lake. She wheeled the bike over to a dilapidated pink building with a rusting gas pump and defunct coffee shop. Inside she found its equally decrepit owner, a man named Lester Sinclair.

That had been twenty-five years ago.

No *albularyo* could have predicted her life from that moment, the life she had forged with her will – and her fists when necessary.

A life that could disintegrate in a heartbeat if the cops ever tracked her down. Lately she'd seen far too many TV documentaries about police officers doggedly pursuing and solving cold cases.

She chewed her lip, staring down at the Galaxy. She hadn't been able to sleep for weeks. The economic recession had hammered her like it had every other business, and the collection department at Canada Revenue Agency was pressuring her about her back taxes. The five thousand dollars to fly Morty Gross and his buddies in and out of Fire Lake had seemed like a godsend.

At first, she hadn't been too worried despite Mayor Fortin's nagging about the need for secrecy. She could be discreet: after all, she and Fortin had always done friendly business and neither of them followed the law exactly to the letter. What could be so special and mysterious about this particular fishing trip to Fire Lake? Morty Gross had been a good customer of hers for years. He seemed a decent enough sort though he drank and sweated too much. In her opinion, he fooled his VIP guests into believing that they were getting an exclusive, forbidden and naughty experience all paid for by the Ontario Government. In reality, the trout, pickerel and bass could swim unharmed, because Morty and his guys spent their time getting drunk while littering the environment with their empties.

Last night's group, though, had been different. Morty had barely greeted her: he was unusually jumpy, on his cellphone every two minutes. No fishing rods in the cargo, but plenty of other heavy gear. She knew a gun case when she saw one. And that big American, Ricky, had brought along an evil-looking crossbow. To spear trout? Hardly.

Anderson, the Norwegian, had been cold and standoffish, treating her like a servant, forcing her to take on those heavy crates of useless mineral water. Worst of all was the Australian, Hendrix, who didn't speak at all. He stared at her in a dark, knowing way that made her feel instantly vulnerable, and he was wearing an expensive leather jacket and black dress shoes, not outdoor gear like the others.

Then Danny showed up. And he let slip that Santa had set up the whole show.

And she'd sworn she'd never do business with Santa.

Too late to back out. The plane was loaded and Morty's five thousand dollars were in her pocket. She and Mayor Fortin were going to have a long talk this morning.

She hated leaving Danny alone with those guys. Whatever those guys had planned, he was so out of their league.

She shivered and zipped up her pink cardigan. It was well past her time to check in with the staff at the diner.

She climbed down the stairs to her deck and took the path through the trees that led to her kingdom. All the way down to the Galaxy, an acid disquiet chewed through her, a foreboding so dark, she could have sworn Filomina's spirits were shrieking out their indecipherable warnings to her.

10

Bumping along the highway in Logan's VW, Rachel felt so hungry she nearly threw up. The fumes in the van and the ruts in the road didn't help either.

"Hydraulic lifters are sticking again," Logan muttered. "Need Corazon to work her magic."

"The fat lady can fix engines?"

"You bet. She maintains her own plane, too."

Rachel thought this over. "I didn't think she was that cool," she said.

"The Cobra Queen's allowed one good quality."

Logan swung the van into the parking lot of the Galaxy Motel. To Rachel, the building looked like a pink three-legged octopus: its head was the garish neon sign that crunched down on the hub where the three wings of the motel joined together. The tavern, bristling with antennas and satellite dishes, looked like a bulbous purple growth at the end of the monster's northern leg. The café was a narrow aluminum fish swimming in the shelter of the leg to the south.

Dad had gone on and on about the café being a neat retro diner. Rachel liked the shiny metal siding and the green and white trim on the outside, but the inside looked boring: a row of plywood booths lined up against the outside windows and six aluminum-edged stools set along the counter that faced the kitchen. Glittering amoeboid shapes danced in the Formica tabletops. A faint twang of country music filtered in from the loudspeakers, but that was okay because Dad liked it.

She climbed out of the van and followed Logan up the concrete steps leading to the diner's entrance. He looked down at her. "What's with the war paint on the face, Kiddo?"

I am a ninja. "Nothing; do I have to wash it off?"

"Nah, leave it."

He ushered her in ahead of him and pointed her to the counter. They sat together, facing the kitchen. No other people in the café except an old bald guy eating by himself in a booth at the far end. He wore a blue plaid shirt and emerald green suspenders.

"That's the mayor, Maurice Fortin," Logan told her.

Rachel twirled gently back and forth on her seat listening to Logan trade funny insults with a man in the kitchen who was wearing a purple bandana tied over his head. Logan said he was Joseph, the chef.

A young blond woman in a pink waitress uniform slapped down cutlery and glasses of ice water in front of them. She didn't look pleased about it.

"That's not Danny's grandmother," Rachel whispered to Logan.

"Odile's on break. She'll be here," Logan replied. "Joseph's fixing us the Trucker's Special, but Charmaine here doesn't think I can pay for it."

Charmaine ignored him. She strolled down the length of the bar, pausing at the cash register to look outside.

The roar of a powerful engine. Rachel leapt off her seat and climbed into the booth opposite them to look through the window. A red-and-green-striped Hummer had pulled into the parking lot. Its seats were red leather trimmed with fake white fur and the hood ornament was a tacky plastic reindeer with a glowing red nose. Two men got out. One wore a green elf hat and a pair of denim overalls with nothing underneath except a thick coat of body hair. The other was Santa himself.

She charged back to the counter. "Mr. Logan, it's Santa." Logan's fingers curled tightly round his water glass. "What if he

sees my T-shirt? What if he asks why I'm not with the other campers at Santa's Fish Camp?"

"Sit tight. We'll say you're my granddaughter."

Rachel grabbed her water and sucked out a piece of ice. Her
stomach hurt, but she wasn't hungry any more.

The door whooshed open.

"Merry Christmas," Santa announced, waving like the Queen
from a motorcade. "Merry Christmas, all you mothers."

Charmaine loved it. Maurice Fortin creaked his stiff back,
turned around and beckoned Santa to join him.

"Bring us some coffee, will you, Darling," Santa said to
Charmaine. "I've only got half an hour before dear sweet Barry
Tucker buses in the next batch of ankle-biters to the Fish Camp."

Logan stared straight ahead. Peering past him, Rachel watched
Santa and his elf join the mayor in the far booth and settle in.

Santa doesn't look like a real Santa, she thought. He isn't old
and fat enough and his white beard is too short. And his red suit has
oily black dirt all over it.

"Two Trucker's Specials," Joseph called out through the order
window.

Charmaine bustled over and grabbed them. Swooping past
Rachel and Logan, she headed for Santa's table.

"She's taking our food," Rachel whispered. "She's giving it to
Santa."

At that moment Corazon sailed into the diner from the kitchen.

"Eyes front, Soldier," Logan said. "The Cobra Queen is back
on her throne."

Corazon eased one plump buttock onto the high stool behind the
cash register. Santa looked very comfortable indeed in the far booth
opposite that snake, Mayor Fortin. Crushed up against Fortin, she
recognized the portly form of Edgar, Santa's head elf, half-naked in
spite of her prominent sign: No shirt, no shoes, no service.

Santa, that Aussie slime. From the first time he'd eaten at the
diner, he'd made it clear he planned to take over the Galaxy. Now

he was sitting there making nice with Mayor Fortin right under her nose.

And making sure everyone in town knew it.

Three years ago Santa had appeared in Red Dog Lake as suddenly and cleanly as if Scotty had beamed him down. He'd bought up fifty acres of bush that Mayor Fortin had been trying to unload for years, and over the next six months he'd built Santa's Fish Camp using mostly outside contractors. Mad that he hadn't hired enough locally, and that he was trying to put Logan's Zoo out of business, Corazon and the rest of Red Dog Lake had settled back to watch him flame out.

Yet Santa had thrived. Logan was the one who went broke, even if Pasha, the dancing bear, was a legend. Local word was that Logan was feeding Pasha roadkill at the end. Maybe even eating it himself.

These days Santa's elf, Edgar, drove him around in that tacky Christmas-themed Hummer. And his pilot, Tear Drop, flew him all over the wilderness in his Twin Beech: a rare and expensive float plane. Both toys were funded by the ticket sales to a bunch of tawdry statues of fairy-tale characters, no doubt.

Any idiot could add two and two and get five, to use Mayor Fortin's favourite shopworn expression, Corazon thought. Before Santa, the locals grew their own weed to get high. These days modern hydroponics and dark advances in genetic engineering produced plants that dripped THC. A few crusty leaves packed the same wallop as flowers did twenty years ago.

Thanks to Santa, Red Dog Lake had finally struck green gold.

She'd love to know who he really was. Santa relished tweaking people who asked him pointed questions. His one-word reply was invariably: "Santa." Who are you? "Santa." Where are you from? "Santa." Who funded the Fish Camp? "Santa."

Last week in the Galaxy Tavern she'd overheard Edgar, Santa's beer-soaked elf, call him 'Mr. Easter'. *In vino veritas*. And their creepy companion, a pale dude who showed up from time to time on a Harley Night Rod Special motorcycle, had called him 'Meredith', and later 'Merry'. 'Merry Easter' indeed. That night she'd fed everything into her computer's search engine, but as usual had turned up nothing. Astonishing that Santa never shed a scrap of personal information in cyberspace. And that wretched satellite Internet was costing her a fortune, too.

She glanced down the length of the diner.

Logan was sitting at the counter, far removed from Santa. A scruffy-looking kid wearing a white and blue T-shirt from Camp Nirvana sat huddled next to him. She had the weirdest yellow eyes ... Corazon had seen that kid before – but with a young, good-looking guy, not Logan.

Charmaine squeezed past. Corazon glanced over Santa and Edgar's meals. They were tucking into the $8.99 Trucker's Special: basted eggs shiny with grease, their edges crisped to a delicate lace; heaps of home fries; a sizeable fruit salad heavy on the melon (woody and tasteless but durable and cheap); and – wait a minute – bacon, *six* pork sausages *and* fried ham cut twice as thick, no make that three times as thick, as the usual serving. She watched Charmaine wiggle her curvaceous butt over to Santa's booth where all four of them shared a laugh while she wrote up their bills.

That little jerk!

As Charmaine sashayed her way back, Corazon snatched the order book from the girl's pocket. Ignoring her protests, she thumbed through the pages. Just as she thought: Charmaine had billed Santa and his buddies for the $2.99 Early Bird Special. Cheated Corazon out of nearly twenty bucks, more if you counted the extra food.

She used a black marker to fix the problem, ripped out the pages and tossed the order book on the counter. "Next time you're out," she said.

Charmaine blinked, mouth wide.

Santa was waving at them with his coffee cup.

"I'll do it." Corazon picked up the glass carafe from the coffee machine and balanced her way over to Santa's booth.

"Ah, Her Majesty herself," Santa said. "Oh-ho, you look mad as a cut snake, my girl. Am I in trouble?" He pushed his thick white and green mug over for a refill, black eyes glittering.

"All your life, Santa." Corazon poured their coffees.

"What did you say to Charmaine just now?"

Corazon arched a plucked eyebrow, set down the carafe and slapped their bills on the table beside it. Santa set down his knife and turned over his bill, glanced at it and cleared his throat.

"You got a problem with the bills, boys?" Corazon asked.

"No, no problem," Fortin stammered, leaving his bill face down. "And the food is great like always, eh, Santa?"

Santa permitted himself a thin smile.

"You there, Mr. Elf," Corazon said to Edgar. "You obviously can't read so I'll explain for you." She tapped the dress-code sign on the wall next to them. "Tonight is Karaoke Strip Night. You want a beer, first you gotta strip. English style, 'The Full Monty'. Show us what little you got."

Edgar swallowed, looked vainly to the others for support.

"That's hard, Corazon," Santa said. "I thought you didn't like men."

"That's right. Only sheep, like you, Santa."

Logan and the kid had left the counter and were making for the door. Good, Corazon thought. She had enough problems. At six-four, Logan could be a handful.

"Bloody hell, look who's emerged from his cave," Santa muttered, then yelled: "You're too early for the pub, Mate." Logan stared at him. "Who's the little Lolita?"

"My granddaughter," Logan said.

"Really. Where's your other wife? The nice one with the black fur coat."

Logan's stillness stifled all sounds in the place. Joseph and the kitchen staff stared through the order window.

"Ah, John Logan, the man who loved animals," Santa went on. "Too hard and too often."

A rush of movement. Corazon felt herself roughly shoved aside. She crashed into the wall next to her dress-code sign.

Logan was leaning over Santa's table. The kid stood behind him, tugging on his leather jacket.

"Please, John, go sit down," Mayor Fortin said. "He's just jerking your chain."

"Shut up, Maurice," Logan said. He seized Santa by his short white beard.

Edgar and Mayor Fortin shouted in protest. Logan twisted his grip, dragging Santa up from the bench despite his struggles. And judging by Santa's shrieks of pain, the beard was real, not part of the costume.

"Please, John, don't go crazy now. Santa was making a joke," Fortin pleaded. "A bad joke, but he meant nothing."

"Sure." Logan's eyes were remote, his face stony.

Edgar the elf stared as though his eggs had stuck halfway down.

Joseph had stepped out of the kitchen. "Take it easy, *Maskwa*," he called out. Corazon signalled to him frantically.

"Let me go, you wet maggot." Santa's hands flailed uselessly against Logan's arm.

"Please, Mr. Logan, stop," the kid said.

Logan snatched up the steaming coffee pot with his free hand. Calmly, he dropped a gout of boiling coffee onto Santa's round cheek.

Santa screamed in outrage. "Help me, you bastards!"

"*Sancta Maria*," Corazon said. "Constable Michael comes in for his coffee in two seconds. Logan, put him down. You got enough problems."

Logan raised his arm again and poured. Everyone cried out.

"He's trying to kill me," Santa screamed, twisting madly to shield his face. "Stop him for Christ's sake."

"John Logan," said a quiet voice. "Listen to me. Let him go."

"Look, Odile, I've got him." Logan squeezed Santa's whiskers more tightly. "I've caught him by the beard."

"Yes, I see. We all see." A smooth dark hand reached over and touched Logan's bare wrist. "Put down that coffee, Bear Man. Listen to me now. Someone will get hurt."

Logan released Santa so abruptly he bounced down on the bench as though he'd fallen through a trap door.

Santa clutched his cheek, face crimson. "You bloody psychotic. Who let you out of Penetang loony bin?"

"Shut up," Corazon barked and pried the coffee pot out of Logan's grip. She turned her blazing eyes on him. "Behave yourself, Bear Man. You're scaring the kid. Go sit down."

Logan stared at her. He tore off his hat, slapped it against his thigh, but did as she said, the kid trailing after him.

Corazon nodded to the small silent woman in the black waitress uniform. "Odile, get Santa some ice. Then take Logan's order."

"Yes, Madame." Odile moved back to the counter as quietly as she had appeared.

"Take his order? What the hell's wrong with you?" Santa said. "Throw him out on his arse!"

"This is my place and don't you forget it," Corazon said. "John's a local. He gets served."

"Obviously, *I'm* not a local. You hear that, Maurice?" Santa said to the mayor. "According to that Filo illegal, I'm not a local, but she is."

"She married a local guy." Fortin shrugged and smiled sheepishly at Corazon. Edgar the elf tried hard to stare at nothing.

"Tell you what, Santa," Corazon said. "When Constable Michael drops by for his coffee and blueberry muffin, I'll tell him you got a complaint and send him over."

Santa muttered and picked up his fork.

Didn't think so. You don't like cops any better than I do.

She headed for the cash, shouting at Joseph and the others to get back to work. A black and white Ontario Provincial Police cruiser had appeared in the parking lot. Constable Michael was early. Good thing those two had settled down.

A figure in a dark navy uniform stepped in.

Corazon took in the glossy black wing of hair, the gravely perfect features and flawless olive skin.

Not Constable Michael. A new cop. A woman.

They've found me.

The glass carafe slipped from her fingers. Crashed and shattered on the linoleum tiles.

11

Danny sank. Down in the dark to the detritus on the lake bottom: rusting beer cans, twists of fish line, mud-encrusted bottles. His flesh dissolving, translucent ...

A giant force seized him by the scruff of the neck. Yanked him up into a burst of light and wind. A brutal blow to the cheekbone punched him back into the world.

The side of the canoe.

He grabbed at it and swore, but all that came out was an anguished wheeze. Something kicked him in the face – his runners, bobbing around his neck. The laces were caught in his hair.

"For God's sake, hang on," Ricky said beside him. He flopped Danny's arms over the side of the boat.

Danny coughed and retched as reason slowly returned. The canoe was full of water. The waves must have swamped it when it tossed them out.

"I thought you knew how to paddle one of these things," Ricky said.

"You stood up in the canoe, you jerk," Danny panted. "You're certifiable, trying to bring down a plane with a hunting rifle."

"That is a Dragunov SV-137 Russian sniper rifle, Baby. Semi-automatic and gas-operated." Ricky worked his way round to the front of the canoe, hanging onto the gunwale. His combat vest was sodden.

The canoe breached another glassy wave. Danny's arms were shuddering. His soaked jeans were pulling him under. Had to get them off. He clutched the side with one hand and fumbled with his zipper with the other, struggling to free his legs. With a great heave, he chucked the sopping mess of cloth into the drowned canoe.

"Ricky, get your clothes off," he shouted through the wind, but the American had already figured that out for himself. His black combat vest flew into the canoe followed by his saturated pants and the crash of his heavy combat boots. Ricky's shaved head and heavy white shoulders surfaced near the bow.

"Which way is land?" he yelled back at Danny.

Truly Danny had no idea. All he could see was water, rising up in one mountain after another. *The sun, find the sun.* There, burning a hole through the gathering smoke, right at mid-sky.

Danny took a guess. "Keep going, this direction."

Ricky grunted in reply. He slung the yellow painter over one beefy shoulder and swam, using the breaststroke. Danny kicked his legs, to propel them forward. His teeth were chattering. Had to stay warm, had to keep moving. Ricky looked like a powerful swimmer, but how long before the cold water leached away his strength?

Got to help us move, got to. He kicked, counting to thirty, then drifted for a brief rest, counted and drifted, counted and drifted …

"Wake up!" Ricky had surfaced beside him, shuddering with cold.

"Sorry," Danny mumbled.

"Did you hear what I said? Did you see where that damn plane went?"

Focused on survival, Danny had heard nothing. He shook his head.

"Speak up," Ricky shouted.

"No, I didn't see where it went," Danny yelled back. "Maybe they gave up. The waves are too high. Landing's too risky." A distant throbbing motor above the tumbling slap and hiss of water. "They're coming back."

"No kidding."

"If they buzz us again, they'll fly too low. They'll catch a pontoon and flip over. Crash and die. They can't be that stupid."

"Heads up."

The plane was roaring down to land on top of them.

"Get under!" Ricky dived down, a white whale flashing in the murky water. Danny clung to the canoe, not daring to let go.

The plane droned over them, skimming across the waves like a skipping stone. He heard its engine pitch higher as it climbed to clear the trees on the far shore.

Ricky broke through the surface. Hurled his arms over the side of the canoe, breathing heavily. "Is it gone?"

Danny nodded.

"Only way to make them stop … is to … play dead. Next time go under and stay under."

"No. I'll lose the boat."

"Do it or we're finished."

"I don't hear the plane any more. Maybe they won't come back."

"Hendrix never gives up."

"Hendrix died on the island."

"You think?" Ricky swam back to the front end of the canoe and started pulling again.

Danny was too tired to argue. A large wave heaved over him and the canoe. His nostrils filled with the smell of dead weeds, drifting sediment and mud.

Kick, drift, kick, drift … Above the slosh of water, a faint throb.

"The plane … it's back."

Ricky kept swimming, an elephant fording a river. Couldn't hear. Danny's ears were sharper, younger. "He's coming back again," Danny cried.

"Dive down," Ricky yelled as the roar of the engine approached. "Do what I tell you." He vanished.

Thwack! A stone, burrowing through the water. Hail pelted the lake surface.

Bullets – they're shooting at us!

Danny let the water take him. He sank down, ears throbbing, lungs burning. He forced his eyes open. A blurry grey everywhere. The water closed round him in a thick suffocating jelly ...

Thrashing and screaming, he broke through into the air. Alone in a desert of water. No canoe and no Ricky. Nothing but waves and the sky.

The plane had vanished. He couldn't hear the engine.

Didn't matter, he was going to drown.

He shouted Ricky's name, frantically treading water. He bobbed up the surface of an oncoming wave. There in the trough, Ricky hauling the canoe. He paddled madly after them but when the next wave flung him up, they'd disappeared.

Every instant he was losing strength. His arms and legs churned uselessly.

The gym teacher claimed he lacked willpower. Didn't matter what he screamed at his limbs. They wouldn't obey him, couldn't move, couldn't ...

He was drifting again, sinking ...

He coughed back up, in one last pathetic struggle ...

Sank ... and felt a rock.

He fought back up to the surface. The waves had eased. About one hundred yards in front of him, trees and thick bush pushed down to the water's edge.

The mainland.

He'd been lucky, damn lucky.

Slowly, a few strokes at a time, he paddled toward the trees. At last his bare feet were sliding on the slippery rocks. He sloshed toward the bushes, biting back the pain in his feet as he trudged over the black shale.

No sight of Ricky or the canoe anywhere.

He stopped, gasping for air, and called out Ricky's name.

"I'm right behind you." Ricky stumbled past him, hauling the canoe. Water tracked rivulets through the sea growth of his body hair. He dragged the canoe onto the rocks of the beach and collapsed beside it.

Danny followed, the wind blowing his skin into goose bumps. He fell down next to Ricky, thanking all his grandmother's saints and spirits that he was free of the water.

He stared back at the island. Even this far away, he could see the flames eating through the trees, breaking through to the shoreline. "The wind," he panted. "It's blowing this way. It'll carry the fire over here."

"Great," Ricky said. "Any more good news?"

"They tried to kill us. Why?"

"Hendrix is a whack job." Ricky poked a thick finger through a round bullet hole in the side of the canoe. "Hates witnesses. Scorched earth, clean the house, that's his creed."

"Hendrix died on the island."

"No, uh-uh." Ricky shifted on the stones. "The guy on the island wasn't Hendrix. That was Curtis, Hendrix's bodyguard. Curtis bought it on the island."

"I don't get it. Why would Curtis pretend to be Hendrix?"

"Hendrix switches ID's with Curtis when he gets antsy." Ricky stood up. "Come on. We gotta get our stuff out of the canoe."

Danny lurched over with him to the boat. Anderson's Russian sniper rifle had vanished. The paddle, too.

He gathered up his wet clothes and the Aussie's black pack, heavy and streaming with water.

Ricky untied his crossbow from the thwart and shovelled his clothes and gear together. He dumped everything into the weeds and splashed back into the water. "Give me a hand. We've gotta push this sucker back out into the lake."

"No way. I nearly drowned. I'm not going back in."

"Drowning's gonna look like nirvana after Hendrix gets finished with you."

"The wind will blow the canoe back here. Stash it in the bushes."

"It's metal. He'll see it."

"I don't hear the plane any more. Maybe he gave up."

"You don't get it, do you? Hendrix is a pit bull."

Ricky waded out into the water, dragging the canoe. A moment later he was swimming, towing it back out into the lake.

"Ricky, this is crazy. Come back."

Danny waited, straining to hear the sound of the airplane engine over the wind and the water. Nothing. He grabbed his clothes, wrung out his jeans and shirt and spread them over a bush. Last night he'd felt the first bite of autumn in the night air and caught the first glint of gold in the birch trees. He kept telling himself you couldn't die of hypothermia in August.

He rubbed his numb arms, trying to keep sight of Ricky. He saw the silver canoe flip over like a breaching dolphin and the small pale dot that was Ricky start swimming back to shore. What a stupid waste of energy, he thought.

Fighting through the water had made him desperately hungry, but there was nothing to eat except pine sap and birch bark. That might ease his stomach pains but would provide no energy. He needed fat, protein.

A loud roar. Ricky stood up in the water and sloshed back to shore, swearing at the rocks underfoot. He staggered over to weeds where he'd thrown his gear and seized his precious crossbow, fingers probing the wires and mechanism. Grunting, he set it down and foraged through the pockets of his combat vest, pulling out a crumpled foil ball. He tore it open with his teeth, ripped off a chunk and tossed it at Danny.

"Protein bar. Better eat up," Ricky said.

Danny stared at the gooey yellow mess, the soggy remains of a dried-out cereal bar, the kind southern hikers and cross-country skiers liked to eat. He chewed it down, trying not to gag.

The shiny metal bottom of the canoe bobbed in the lake about one hundred yards off shore. He listened again for the plane. Nothing. Smoke was drifting out over the water from the island. How long did they have before the wind blew the fire over here?

"I'm not going to sit around waiting to get burned up and shot," he said.

"You got no choice, Sunshine," Ricky said. "Better pray I can fix my bow."

"Remember when we flew out here, Corazon took us over an old mine."

"So what?"

"It's the old Archangel uranium mine. People say the tailings poisoned Fire Lake and the groundwater round here."

"So now I'm gonna glow in the dark. What's your point?"

"The mine isn't that far away. We could walk to it."

"You mean tromp through the bush in the middle of nowhere trying to find a mine that's been closed down for years? Just so some hunter can stumble across my bones. Forget it."

"I can find it."

"And if we did get to this stupid mine, is there any food? A phone?"

"Probably not."

"Great idea. Real bright."

"Listen to me. That mine's got something better than food."

"What?"

"A road out to the highway."

That got Ricky's attention.

12

Barry called that lady cop, Rachel thought. She shrank down next to Logan who sat still as a rock.

The lady cop had impressive gear: a stick, a bulletproof vest and a gun. Her uniform was dark navy blue with a gold badge pinned to her chest. She stood in the middle of the diner, scanning the booths and the counter. Corazon, the Cobra Queen, looked like she was going to throw up.

"I'll get that mess cleared away for you, Madame," Joseph said to Corazon through the order window. And it was a real mess, too – shining glass and mud brown liquid everywhere. He came out of the kitchen carrying a brush, dustpan and mop.

Corazon muttered her thanks, moved back to the cash register and sat down behind it.

Dead quiet. Down at the far end Mayor Fortin crumpled his paper napkin and tossed it over his unfinished eggs, fidgeting to squeeze past Edgar the elf. Santa attacked his meal with diligence.

"Hi there, Raven," Joseph said to the cop. "Been a long time. Thought you worked out of OPP headquarters in Orillia."

"Yes," the lady cop said, but she didn't sound friendly. "I see you're still here in Red Dog Lake. Heard you quit law school."

"It's not a waste," Joseph said without heat. "I like it up here. Got a family now."

"Heard that, too." She stepped aside to get out of the way of his cleanup. "I need to speak to Mrs. Corazon Sinclair. That's you, isn't it?" she said to Corazon. She went over to the cash, flipped open a small black leather folder and showed it to her. Rachel caught the glint of a gold shield.

"Sergeant Raven McKenna of the Ontario Provincial Police," Corazon read out loud. She made a face as though the ID was a dirty bandage. "Impressive. Up to now in Red Dog Lake we've only had one junior constable for fifty thousand square miles. How come the government's spending money on a big sergeant? Where's Constable Michael?"

"I'll ask the questions, if you don't mind." McKenna put away her ID.

"OK." Corazon folded her arms.

McKenna pulled a photograph from her tunic and slapped it down on the counter next to the cash register. "Four men chartered a bush plane and flew out of Red Dog Lake yesterday. I need to speak to their pilot. Have they been through here?"

"I can't say."

"You're not looking at the picture."

Corazon glanced at it. "It's upside down."

"Take a closer look." McKenna spun the picture round with one finger.

Corazon shrugged. "I never saw those guys before. Did you, Maurice?" The mayor, who stood by the cash register foraging through his wallet, shook his head vigorously. "Tell you what, why don't you ask Santa? He's sitting right over there."

Santa's coffee mug froze halfway to his mouth.

"I'm asking *you*," McKenna said.

"Look, Sergeant, August is high season. Loads of tourists come through my place. I can't tell one bunch of fishing guys from another."

"Really? I'm sure you recognize the little guy, Morty Gross. The Protocol Office always books him and his guests into the Galaxy. And the SUV he rented is parked right outside."

"Well, it could be him," Corazon said, not looking at it. "What do you say, Maurice?"

"No, sorry, I did not bring my glasses." Fortin shoved his glass-es case deeper into the pocket of his blue plaid shirt.

McKenna frowned, moved over to where Logan was sitting and plunked the photo in front of him. "Maybe your memory's better."

Logan stared straight ahead.

Rachel peered over Logan's arm at the digital print of four men boarding a small Air Canada jet. A little bald guy was first, followed by a tall man wearing a leather jacket and jeans. The third man had round, steel-rimmed glasses like a Nazi. He was dressed in camou-flage gear and carrying a rifle case. The last guy looked scary: he had a shaved head and was dressed in black like a member of a police SWAT team. He was the only one smiling into the camera.

"Well?" McKenna asked. Logan shrugged.

"It's illegal to have guns on planes," Rachel said.

"Why hello there," McKenna stared down at her over Logan's head, making Rachel wish she'd kept quiet. "You're right, Kid, it's illegal. But our government paid for their private charter, so they can do what they want."

Odile, Danny's grandmother, was standing by the swinging door to the kitchen. At a signal from Corazon, she nodded, got busy and set down a mug of coffee, cream and sugar in front of Sergeant McKenna.

"It is good to see you back in Red Dog Lake, Raven," Odile said. "*Tan-si*? Are you well?"

"I'm OK, Grandmother," McKenna replied, sitting down on the stool next to Logan. She went on to say something long and complicated in Cree.

"Can you understand what she's saying?" Rachel whispered to Logan.

"Uh-huh," Logan said. "Raven is showing Odile respect. Odile's got a big reputation in their community."

McKenna dropped a toonie coin down on the counter and picked up her coffee.

"Oh, there's no charge," Corazon said from her spot behind the cash.

"Can't do that," McKenna said. She shoved the coin to the opposite side of the counter and waited until Odile picked it up. "I don't do business the way Constable Michael was doing business."

Corazon cleared her throat, giving McKenna the evil eye. "Odile, get John's order," she said.

Odile appeared in front of Logan, order book at the ready. Her face had the stillness of a plaster saint in a church.

She's so tiny, Rachel thought, not much taller than me even if I'm nearly eleven. And she doesn't look old even if the long braid down her back is silver.

"What can I get you, *Maskwa*?" Odile asked Logan.

"What does *maskwa* mean?" Rachel said.

"*Maskwa* means 'bear'." Odile smiled at her. "We call John 'Bear'."

"Because of Pasha."

"Of course, and your name is *Nisimis*, 'Little Sister'."

"That's what Danny calls me!"

Sergeant McKenna threw Rachel a sharp look. "Would that be Danny Bluestone at Camp Nirvana?" she asked.

Logan laid a warning hand on Rachel's arm and ordered two toasted western sandwiches. Joseph had finished cleaning up. Odile followed him back into the kitchen.

McKenna sipped her coffee. "I seem to make you nervous, Mrs. Sinclair."

"OK, you got me." Corazon slid off her stool. "You see, when you came in just now, I thought to myself, *Sancta Maria*, that lady cop, why she looks just like my twin brother, Franco."

"What?"

"Hey, I'm a little older than you, but Franco still looks good." Corazon smiled like a shark. "He's a top drag queen. He does a cop routine, a real showstopper. Lots of black leather, bondage gear, you know, nice kinky stuff."

Stifled titters from the kitchen staff. McKenna's expression would have frozen a tractor trailer in its tracks.

"Hey, Franco can pass for real, no problem," Corazon added.

"I've heard about your karaoke strip nights," McKenna said. "I'm putting your liquor licence under review."

"What? Don't you dare leave, Maurice." The mayor shivered, skewered in the middle of escape. "You gonna stand there like a fat *putain* and let her pull my licence?" Corazon jabbed him so hard he winced. "Santa put you up to this, eh?"

"*Tabernacle!* No, Corazon, for heaven's sake," the mayor stammered. "Nobody did nothing. Look you," he said to McKenna, "you see anyone drinking here? You got no cause to pull Madame's licence."

"Then answer my questions. Who flew Morty Gross and his party into the bush? And where did they set down?"

"Why do you want to know so much?" Corazon asked.

"Morty Gross calls in to the Protocol Office twice a day. Only he hasn't, not for twenty-four hours."

"So what?" Corazon said. "Maybe last night those guys killed a forty-pounder. They're sleeping it off."

"That may be," McKenna said. "But the Ministry of Natural Resources just got a satellite report of a forest fire breaking out near Red Dog Lake."

Rachel gripped Logan's arm. "Where are the forest fires?" The words came out of her mouth by themselves.

"You look scared, Kid," McKenna said. "Do you know something you want to tell me?"

Rachel shook her head so violently her teeth scraped together.

"I see you're wearing a shirt from Camp Nirvana. What's your name?"

"Amy … Amy Logan." The lie slipped out but McKenna kept staring at her.

"You wouldn't happen to be the girl Barry Tucker reported missing, would you?"

"Of course she's the girl, Sergeant." Santa and his elf joined Mayor Fortin at the cash. "Arrest that man." Santa pointed at Logan. "Ask him why he spirited her out of Camp Nirvana. A girl he's passing off as his granddaughter. Ask him what he's doing with her."

McKenna's laser eyes moved to Logan. "I'll need to see your ID, Sir. And the kid's."

Rachel's heart was pounding like a drum. Through the order window Joseph, the chef, pointed over his shoulder and mouthed the words "out back".

She scrambled over the counter. Knocked over the drinking glasses in a flood of water and ice. Heard shouts behind her. She plunged into the kitchen through the swinging door. Landed painfully next to the black metal grill. The hiss of steam and smell of burning grease choked her.

Joseph pulled her up. Pushed her toward the open back door. She dashed out into the cool air.

Behind her people were yelling and knocking stuff over. She ran, panting, down the concrete path that edged the motel. She spotted the black rectangle of an open door right where the wings of the motel joined up, under the Galaxy's neon sign.

She ran so hard her feet burned from banging against the pavement. She charged through the opening into darkness.

And let Corazon's big pink octopus swallow her up.

13

Santa clutched the makeshift ice pack to his cheek, watching Edgar struggle to get behind the wheel of the Hummer. Fat git, he'd have to suck his gut back to Toronto to squeeze in, Santa thought. Now what was he doing? Staring at the reindeer hood ornament for an answer to the meaning of his pathetic life?

"That cop, Santa, that cop ... we should have looked at the photo she had," Edgar said.

"No point. Come on, start the bloody motor before she realizes we're gone."

"But, Santa," Edgar fidgeted with the steering wheel as though it had been sitting in the burning sun all day. "What if those guys are Morty and the others?"

"Of course it's them. And because it *is* them, it's not them."

"Yeah, OK, but what about those forest fires?"

"For God's sake, rub those two brain cells of yours together and generate a few sparks. Morty What's-his-name would have radioed Maurice Fortin if there was a problem. Or Charlie Hendrix would have called us. That copper's bluffing."

"Why would she do that?"

"Just bloody take me back to work."

"OK, OK, no problem." Edgar reversed out of the parking lot and turned south onto Highway 11.

Santa settled back, comforted by the roar of the Hummer's Detroit Diesel Turbo V8 engine, though ice water was trickling down his neck. He gazed out the passenger side. Trees, trees and more trees gliding past. Nothing but bloody trees. If the greenies got the finger out and travelled up to Red Dog Lake for a look-see at Canada's arboreal splendour that might put a cork in their whinging.

"Your cheek, um, looks real painful," Edgar said. "That's gonna blister up real bad."

"Shut up." Santa lifted the towel with its load of ice cubes, winced and pressed it back down. "Logan just moved to the top of my shit list."

"Um, that's a real bad word, Santa."

"What a little girl you are."

Edgar sniffed. He seemed to have a perpetual allergy these days. "I thought Corazon was top of your, um, list," he said.

"That dingo's leg-over. What did she say to Charmaine anyway? The poor girl looked scared to death."

"I think … I think maybe Charmaine shouldn't have fixed our bills."

"Bloody hell." That's all he needed. Charmaine lying in wait for him back at Santa's Fish Camp ready to soak his suit with tears. Not that she wasn't a splendid girl … "If she's there when we get in," he said, "you tell her again there's no jobs at Fish Camp. I can't have her hanging about. Even you should understand that. Women muck things up. Only one use for them really."

"Sure, Santa." Edgar fixed his round green eyes on the two-lane highway, hands rigid on the steering wheel in the prescribed ten and two position.

Some poor misguided souls imagined a bovine sweetness in Edgar. Bollocks, Santa thought. Edgar was far short of a full quid, but not so dim he couldn't focus on the necessary, without straying into questions of legality or morality. A man of few talents, our boy Edgar, but he did have one overarching useful quality: he liked to be told what to do. He positively craved it.

They passed the green and white mileage sign at the edge of town. Two hundred kilometres to North Bay. Up here it took a bloody lifetime to get from Point A to Point B. Like being back in the outback except for the wretched climate.

"Do we have go to karaoke tonight?" Edgar asked.

"Too right we do."

"Don't let Corazon make me strip."

Santa smiled. "What, and miss my chance to see you wave your old fella at your banjo-playing aunties? *I'll* make you strip."

"That's not funny."

"For God's sake, if you bothered to wash the wax out of your ears, you'd know you were off the hook. That she-wolf copper pulled the Cobra Queen's liquor licence. Absolutely brilliant, that was."

"Oh, the liquor licence won't make any difference. I mean, it's karaoke strip night. One cop can't come between two hundred people and their beer." Edgar sniffed again, thinking. "What if she follows us back to Santa's Fish Camp?"

"Do us a favour, just shut up and drive."

How could anyone be so bloody thick? Santa yanked on his baggy red velour pants. They never failed to twist his undershorts and squeeze him like a vice. He flung the remaining scraps of ice out the open window and pressed the lukewarm, sodden towel to his face.

"Mr. Easter, I really don't want to go to karaoke tonight," Edgar persisted.

"For the love of Mike, stop whinging. And don't call me 'Mr. Easter'."

"Sorry, Merry – I mean, Santa."

Meredith Easter: Santa enjoyed that name. In fact, he'd enjoyed several names throughout his career, but he especially liked that one. It bore a slight resemblance to the one he'd been born with. 'Merry Easter' was gloriously over the top, but even that low wit was lost on the gormless inhabitants of Red Dog Lake.

God how he missed the tropics, even the pig-stinking heat and thunderous rains. No colour up here; everything was a sort of monochromatic greenish-brown. All the fish had grey skins and bland white flesh that tasted the same, one species to another, unless you were a fantasist. Not like Asia at all. The plants, the fish, the animals, the girls: all sporting such vivid colours they burned your eyes. Oh, to be strolling through the close streets of Bangkok, breathing in those rich odours: fry-ups in rancid cooking oil, ripe garbage, sewer gas, all overlaid with the musk of incense and phallic flowers.

He'd run into Hendrix in Bangkok, in a nostalgia bar for Aussie expats. At the time, he'd been dabbling in the skin trade and funnelling along Afghani hash whenever he could nab some. Hendrix was tapped into a higher league, shifting arms through Pakistan. Dead easy money, he maintained, since AK-47's were piled up like bananas in the open-air markets. They'd sunk a dozen *Coopers*, moved on to a bottle of *Talisker* single malt whisky and opened up to each other like brothers. A creative, entrepreneurial spirit, that's what they had in common. Over the years, Hendrix had steered him to a few winners and he'd done his bit, done Hendrix proud, and more besides.

Flesh and guns. Demand wasn't a problem, the world had a limitless appetite for both, but supply could prove tricky. It was the bloody Thai police getting stroppy that had done for him in the end. All that UN claptrap about human trafficking. He'd had to hop it to England, ostensibly to visit his sister, but when the London police started pressuring him about Hendrix, he'd done a runner, slipping off his Chicago-bound flight in Toronto. Like Hendrix said, it never hurt to be generous with baggage handlers at major airports.

He hadn't thought much about Canada before then except that it struck him as the most boring place on earth. But surfing the Internet at his sister's in Putney had opened his eyes to its potential. While Canadians might seem so pathetically wet they'd say please and thank you to an automated banking machine, scratch the surface and underneath it you found a nation of petty thieves, drug dealers and swindlers. Canadians ran top boiler rooms that drained money from marks around the world, and they grew enough marijuana to rival Mexico.

Hydroponic gardening had been the answer to his cash flow problem, and the vast bland suburbs of Toronto the location for his enterprise. The inhabitants of the burbs remained sealed in their SUV's and IKEA-furnished four-bedroom homes. They didn't know their neighbours, and they didn't want to. Absolutely ideal for setting up shop. Plenty of floor space in a monster house to turn a quick, tidy profit, although the mould and the humidity ate through the flimsy wall board like crikey, and the sulphurous smell was a problem.

Hendrix had kicked him the funding and he'd set up shop straight away.

How was he to know that two Iranians had a grow-op on the same bloody street? The stupid whackers decided to tap into the electrical main to cut hydro costs. Instead they drilled into a gas pipe and turned themselves into crispy bacon. And flattened their bloody house. Three-tier response all round – every fire truck, ambulance, and police car in the area, a bang-up catastrophe. Say what you want about Canadian coppers, lazing about in the nearest Tim Hortons doughnut shop, but once they got a hard eye on your business, they never gave it a rest.

He'd had to leg it before his first harvest, thanks to that prize idiot driving the Hummer.

Edgar had been the two dead Iranians' plant expert. He'd escaped the explosion only because he'd been off at the local Tim Hortons getting sustenance for the crew. He ended up on Santa's front lawn, open-mouthed and drooling, holding a raft of coffees in a pressed cardboard tray. The only thing missing was a flashing neon sign saying "Arrest me". Santa had hustled Edgar inside as much for the fresh coffee and Timbits as the cops lurking about.

Edgar had been inordinately shocked and grief-stricken over the demise of his departed masters. Nevertheless beer and sympathy had opened him up like a tin of sardines. The offer of a replacement job at an admittedly downscale operation had wiped away his tears, and he proved himself useful, coaxing bushier, healthier plants out of the cut-rate seedlings Santa had been saddled with. At least until the day one of the late Iranians' widows spotted Edgar unlocking their front door and called the cops.

He'd told Edgar and told him. Go in the back way. Never go out during the day. But the lure of Tim Hortons had proved too much.

He'd had to torch the place the day before harvest – that really hurt.

Not to mention the pain of Hendrix's displeasure. Hendrix didn't handle hits to the bottom line well and tended to remedy red ink on the balance sheet with red bodily fluids. He'd had to do another runner quick fast until he could repay Hendrix his seed money.

Ironically, Edgar had furnished their salvation. Every time Edgar landed in trouble – a frequent occurrence – he'd dash up Highway 11 to hide out with his mother in Red Dog Lake. This time he brought along his dear friend, Mr. Easter. They'd spent the summer in a derelict trailer buried in the bush, living on blueberries, lake trout and pickerel, and the occasional handout from Edgar's mum.

"Here we are, Santa." Edgar turned in to Santa's Fish Camp.

The main gateway was a knock-off of a flash iron gate that he, Santa, had admired at a cattle station in the outback. A short dirt road led to the parking lot and ticket booth. Only a few cars remained in the lot this late in the afternoon, including a battered blue Honda Civic.

"Hey, that's Charmaine's car," Edgar said.

"I can see for myself. Pull up over there." Santa pointed to the spot where Mother Goose's Woodland Trail exited into the lot. He flung the wet towel onto the ground and adjusted his hat. Wouldn't do to be seen out of costume, though one of his local employees was playing Santa at the Christmas Fish Pond while he was out on break. "Let's take a walk." He pointed Edgar up the trail and they set off, going in the reverse direction.

He'd lifted the idea of nursery rhyme characters along a forest trail from the layout of Logan's Zoo. All the woodland trails led straight to the Christmas Fish Pond, gift store and photo-op with

Santa. His backstage operations, under the guise of generators and storage sheds, remained deep in the woods, locked and off limits, guarded by Santa's not-so-friendly pilot, Tear Drop.

Pines, pines and more pines, Santa thought as they puffed up the incline. The leaves on the birches already showed hints of yellow. Winter came on so fast here. In two months they would be arse-deep in snow.

That oncoming cold weather had spurred his entrepreneurial instincts three years before. That, and Hendrix's temper when he'd run them down.

His first impulse was to set up a knocking-shop, but the inhabitants of Red Dog Lake were already at it like rabbits. You couldn't sell what everyone gave away for free. Alcohol had been his fallback option. Hereabouts liquor control meant that the LCBO closed down on Saturday because they were sold out by Wednesday. But when he'd stuck his nose into the moonshine racket, he'd run afoul of Mayor Fortin and his clan: they'd been bootlegging over the Quebec-Ontario border for the last century.

Bloody Canadians! Not so much bent as bendy, and cliquish, too. At this point spending the winter in a nice warm jail cell had looked preferable to frostbite in the unheated trailer and Hendrix's thirst for revenge.

Then he'd gotten cosier with Edgar's mum.

A bit of coddling and the old ratbag was fairly panting to sign over her pension and life savings, catapulting him back into the horticultural business, mining green gold. Three years later, flush with cash and toys, back in Hendrix's favour, his life should have been top dollar.

But it wasn't. Not by a long chalk.

"Santa." Edgar's plaintive voice again. "Do we have to walk the trail?"

"Procedure, Boy. We don't want tourists winding up where we don't want 'em."

"What about Charmaine? She'll be waiting."

"Let her wait. We'll sink a few cold ones with her later. And a few hot ones after."

"That's rude. Charmaine's a nice girl."

"Just a joke, Mate."

Edgar stopped, panting, next to the statue of Little Miss Muffet and her hairy black spider. He wrenched off his green elf hat and wiped his armpits, casting off an eye-watering pong.

"Santa, that cop, what do you think she knows about the bear hunt?" he asked.

"Not a damn thing. She's on a fishing expedition."

"What if she finds out about the bear?"

Santa looked up and down the trail to make sure no straggling visitors were about. "She looks like a career-monger, that one. She won't want to cross her political masters in Toronto. In a day or two, she'll forget all about Morty's VIP guests shooting a bear out of season."

"Not just any bear."

"Shut up." Santa pulled a half-finished Cuban cigar from his jacket pocket, lit it and tossed the match away. He made for the statue of Little Jack Horner and his plum pie, leaving Edgar behind.

"Oh man, Santa, there's a red fire hazard." Edgar pounced on the match, tucked the charred stick into his overalls and struggled to catch up. "I was thinking, um, maybe Corazon, should, you know, fly in to Fire Lake. Check that your friends are OK and all."

"No, not her."

"Well, maybe Tear Drop and I could fly out in the Twin Beech."

"Bloody not! You stay away from Fire Island, do you hear me?"

"OK, OK, but what if there really is a fire?"

He grabbed Edgar by the overall straps, the glowing end of his cigar frizzling the elf's thick chest hair. "Now you listen to me for once in your blighted life. Hendrix and the hunt are off limits. Out of bounds. Do you understand?"

"Why?"

"Because Hendrix is a fella who likes to cut out your kidneys, fry 'em for breakfast and make you watch while he swallows them."

"Jeez, Santa, I didn't mean nothing by it. I don't want to upset anybody." Edgar followed along silently, but Santa's bliss was short-lived. "Look, it's not just the hunters," he started up again. "Danny's with them. He's a local dude."

A local.

Santa hit Edgar then. He couldn't help himself. And hitting Edgar felt bloody marvellous, his flesh ringing wetly against that ham of a cheek. Edgar's wounded kitten reaction was better than sex.

"You hit me!" he cried. "Why?"

"Because you never bloody listen." Santa flexed his hand and puffed on his cigar, feeling the bitter carcinogenic smoke curl round his tongue. Three years in Bear Shag, Ontario, and he was still stuck with Edgar, his sole gateway to the north. Forget getting cozy with Maurice Fortin's clan. Those froggies stuck together like soiled undersilks. And as for the Crees – The Community, in politically correct parlance – if he was lucky, they ignored him.

Bloody locals.

One day soon, Edgar ...

He'd do the necessary himself. After three years in Red Dog Lake, he'd earned himself that pleasure.

14

Danny had no choice but to get back into his wet clothes. His shirt stuck to his skin and his soaked jeans cut into his legs. Squishing into his runners made him think of foot rot in WWI trenches.

The overturned canoe rocked in the waves of the lake, a silver log framed against the burning island.

And drifting back to the mainland beach exactly as he had predicted.

"I can get us out of the bush," he said to Ricky, who was pulling on his gear.

"Sure you can."

"Look, Fire Lake is shaped like a wolf's head." Danny sketched the boundaries of the lake in the air. "Fire Island is the wolf's eye. We need to head northeast, where the spine enters the skull, between the wolf's ears. Have you got a compass?"

"I thought you Indian guides knew how to get around without tools and crap."

"A GPS would be even better."

Ricky sighed and pulled an enormous skinning knife from his combat vest. A tiny water-logged compass was lodged in the blunt end of the handle.

No point asking him to hand it over. Danny leaned over the American's burly forearm and tapped the compass to dislodge the trembling needle from a bubble of cloudy water.

"That's north," Ricky said, pointing.

"Well, magnetic north. It doesn't line up with true north. And there are magnetic anomalies round here that throw things off." Danny searched through the sky. The sun's disk through the gathering smoke looked like a fading searchlight.

"And big duh, that's west." Ricky gestured at the sun.

"No, southwest. The sun lies fifteen degrees south this time of year. We should head that way," Danny stretched out his arm, "and stick to the shoreline for as long as we can."

He didn't want to tell Ricky that it might take them a full day to struggle through a couple of miles of bush. His best guess was that the Archangel Mine lay six miles away to the northeast. If they were lucky, they'd run across a rock outcropping and get high enough to actually see the wretched thing. If they didn't, and his reckoning was off, they would wander aimlessly until they died.

He strapped on the Australian's drowned pack. "OK, let's go," he said.

He set off, leading the way along the fringe of gravel that skirted the shore. He sensed Ricky behind him, grumbling, following at a distance.

His legs felt rubbery from the water. Ricky's protein bar had coalesced to a lump in his stomach. Better than nothing, but no use if he couldn't keep it down. Normally they'd have run across some blueberries, but this summer had been too dry for them. Made for lots of bears in the garbage dumps.

Hungry bears.

How had he gotten himself into this mess?

His night off. He'd hitched a ride with one of his Fortin cousins down to the Galaxy's diner to visit his grandmother, Odile, hoping that Joseph, the chef, would slip him a freebie, a grilled cheese sandwich or a leftover lunch special if Corazon wasn't looking. The Cobra Queen was mad at him these days: he hadn't stayed over enough.

So what if she made him breakfast the morning after? He'd been thinking he'd rather go home to Odile at the Blue Sky Bookstore. He'd sleep in the book stacks the way he used to when he was a kid, when the aisles between the shelves became game trails or secret passages in castles. Maybe Odile would fry pickerel in butter for supper and make bannock bread for breakfast. Or cattail biscuits.

But Mayor Fortin had driven Grandmother over the Quebec border to Rouyn for evening Mass and Joseph had left work early to take his kids fishing.

He'd ended up in the Galaxy Tavern. He was drinking watery draft beer on an empty stomach when Edgar had literally bellied up to the bar and steered him over to Santa's table. Santa's flushed face matched his red lumberjack shirt. His bushy silver hair was wet with heat and sticking up all over, but he was buying. Talk turned to an easy job. Play the Indian. Fly out into the bush with some rich white hunters and tell native stories, preferably sexual in nature.

"Discretion though, my boy," Santa had said. "These fellas are on a tight schedule. They can't wait until bear season opens. They need us to stage the event, if you follow me."

"So it's a set-up," Danny mumbled through his beer fuzz. "Where are you getting the bear?"

"Don't you worry about that. So what's your answer, Danny Bluestone?"

He'd hesitated. Canned bear hunts were illegal and really sick when he thought about it.

"Still dithering?" Santa had said. "Well, now that Edgar and I have let you in on our little secret, we'll have to kill you." And then he'd laughed with the tiniest hesitation that gave Danny a dark nudge.

So I sold my soul for fifteen hundred bucks and a bag of weed.

The throb of the single engine in Corazon's Piper Cherokee. His stomach dropping as she dipped lower, the blue strip of Fire Lake looking impossibly small, not at all like the wide waterway he remembered landing on with his dad. The lurch of the pontoons catching the water and the excruciating slow taxi toward the looming black shape of the island.

Blowing up the Zodiac. Loading the gear into it, stripping off his jeans and runners and walking the loads over to the island, trudging through the chilly water. Humping the hunters' gear, food and liquor to the lodge. Getting the propane fridge going. Offering to help the Australian carry his guns and being smashed up against the nearest birch tree for asking. Morty intervening, placating.

Foraging through the cupboards, shaking out the brown mouse droppings from four shot glasses. Pouring out the chilled vodka shots with Anderson insisting on his own aquavit with caraway seeds floating in it.

He'd fully expected to be asked to cook their meals, but Morty uncased a load of roast beef and salads, French cheese, smoked salmon, even Beluga caviar. Ricky had stuck to his beef jerky, chopping off pieces with a wicked-looking skinning knife with a handle like a bat's wing.

Forget the native guide act. They wanted a servant boy. Morty told him to stay back, clean up after dinner and set up the bar. They only called him out back because there were problems.

Stumbling over the roots in the dim trail, the sunlight fading already. The smell of green wood. The crudely built platform, the makeshift arena. A length of steel chain.

A bear slumped on the ground, her massive head resting on her crossed front paws. A black bear with silver on her muzzle. An old bear. A bear too sick and tired to stand.

"She needs water. When was the last time you fed her?" he asks.

Two dark eyes, wells of sorrow. She turns her head. Recognizes the boy who gives her ice cream. Strawberry ice cream.

Tears flooded his eyes. Wind battered him. Ashes drifted through the air. A bitter smell of charred wood and burning vegetation.

He stopped to look west over the lake. On Fire Island, black skeleton trees stood bathed in flame. Chunks of burning twigs floated through the air, sputtering out on the lake's surface.

Behind him, Ricky swore. "How long before the fire gets here?"

"I don't know. If the wind shifts west, we're in trouble. I need to see your compass again."

"Fine." Ricky groped through his vest and held out the knife.

Danny tried to snag a decent compass reading while eyeballing the shoreline. "OK, I'd say it's time we head into the bush. After we round the next point."

"Forget it," Ricky slouched down on a nearby log. "I'm not gonna fight through a bunch of weeds so some wolf can munch on my bones."

"No problem, the wolves will scatter your bones. No one will find you."

"Oh, funny guy. You said the lake got poisoned. So there's gotta be a river, right? A river from the mine to the lake. So follow the damn river."

"There is no river. Fire Lake is fed by groundwater. That's how it got poisoned. The tailings got into the groundwater."

"What about the bear? How'd you guys bring her in?"

He remembered Santa saying the elves had done it. "They tranked her and flew her in, I guess. She was groggy, remember?"

"Don't give me that. You had to truck that big bear in. There's gotta be a road."

"There is no road. You'll just have to trust me."

"Well, that just warms my heart." Ricky stashed the knife back in his combat vest.

Danny moved on, picking his way over fallen logs and scattered shale. The exercise had dulled the chill from his wet clothes, but they still were a long way from dry. Behind him, Ricky stumbled along, cursing all the while.

They reached the point. Danny gazed into a dark tangle of bushes and trees. "This is where we go in." He turned to look at Ricky. "I need to ask you something."

"What?"

"Why did you pull me out of the water?"

"That's a good question."

"You left me to burn in the lodge."

"Get over it. The ceiling caved in. I thought you bought it."

"What were you guys really doing up here?"

"Paying thirty-five thou for a lousy bear hunt."

"Yeah, and what else? Morty was government. Why was he kissing your butts?"

"Business."

"It's the arms business, isn't it? Anderson had that pricey gun. And Hendrix or Curtis or whoever kept making cracks about selling AK-47's to Pakistani schoolchildren."

"You done now?"

"Is it nukes? Are you planning to open up the Archangel Mine again? What are you, Ricky? CIA?"

Ricky gave him the finger and walked past him down the beach. Danny picked up a handful of beach gravel and lobbed it at Ricky's back.

"Ow! The hell's your problem?"

"I want an answer! I nearly died twice because of you."

Ricky turned, sliding the bow off his shoulder. "Shut up. We've got bigger problems." He pointed to the lake.

The wind had died. Danny sensed a great stillness, the hush before a cold front rushes through. Towering over the burning trees and the smoke of the forest fire, a black thunderhead as big as a castle. Lightning crackled from its ramparts.

Danny swore. "We need to find shelter. We've got maybe two minutes."

15

A cluster of vending machines marked the hub where the motel's three corridors met up in the belly of the octopus. Their plastic compartments housed soft drinks, condoms and DVDs with lots of cars, guns and naked women on the covers.

Rachel ran down the long corridor, turning one stainless steel doorknob after another.

All locked.

Halfway down there was a door with no room number on it. This time the handle turned. Wall racks holding white towels and folded bed sheets stretched up over her head. She slipped inside the linen closet, closed the door and crouched down next to a laundry basket on wheels.

Total silence and darkness. Nothing but the clink and wheeze of the nearby ice machine.

I am a ninja. I can hide here forever.

Last Thursday, Danny had told her a big secret: he was going to pretend to be sick that weekend. Some rich tourists wanted a native guide. He'd make more money in two days than he would at Camp Nirvana for a whole month. A few more gigs like that and they could publish their graphic novel, he'd said. He'd have enough money to move back to Toronto and find a decent job.

The luminous green numbers on her digital sports wristwatch flickered by. Ten minutes had passed. Now it felt creepy sitting next to the dirty sheets and towels in the laundry hamper. The linen cup-board smelled like an old basement. She crawled back to the door, opened it and looked out.

The empty corridor stretched away from her like a tunnel.

The sharp click of a lock. Somebody walked out of a room at the end of the hall. She leapt back, but kept the door open just a crack. Heavy boots whistled over the rust-coloured carpeting.

Silence. She peered through the narrow opening. A tall thin man was standing in front of the pop machine. His skin was as white as thin milk. The buckles on his dark jacket and heavy boots creaked and rustled. He looked like a pale insect wearing a black leather skin.

She dared not breathe. Coins dropped into the vending machine. The roll and thump of a soft drink can.

He picked up the can and turned around. His pale eyes looked right into hers.

"I see you," he said.

Rachel flung open the door and burst into the hall. She ran down the corridor, away from the pale man and the vending machines. She crashed through the steel-handled doors at the end.

She landed in a huge, faintly lit room where all the walls were painted black. Round wooden tables and steel-rimmed chairs hemmed in a raised stage. A mirrored disco ball hung high over her head.

The man … she searched frantically for a hiding place.

A chrome and wood bar stretched along the wall to her right. She ran behind it and squeezed down next to a shiny metal barrel of draft beer. She held her breath, listening.

Nothing.

Right next to her, a glass-fronted fridge held bottles of vodka coolers in blue, pink and green. Looking up, she could see the bottoms of the brown liquor bottles lining the glass shelves that stretched across the bar mirror. And way up, a lofty ceiling pep-pered with fluorescent stars.

The door to the tavern opened and closed. She gasped, she couldn't help it. Her heart beat so loudly she could hardly breathe.

"*Nisimis,* are you in here?"

Rachel stuck her head up over the edge of the bar. Odile, wearing a white cardigan over her black waitress uniform, was standing in the light cast by the mirror ball.

"It is not good for a child to be running around the motel with many strangers. You must come out now." Odile held up a brown paper bag. "I have your western sandwich here."

Rachel stood up and found her voice. "Where is Mr. Logan?"

"He has left."

"I got him in trouble."

"Yes, perhaps."

"Did you see a man at the pop machine?" she asked.

"I did not see anyone, Rachel Forest. We must leave now. Mr. Fortin will drive us."

I don't want to go back to Camp Nirvana. But that pale man ...

She came out from behind the bar and crossed the floor to join Odile.

Danny's grandmother was so tiny her feet didn't reach the floor of Maurice Fortin's pickup. Rachel squeezed in beside her on the passenger seat. Odile dragged the safety belt around Rachel, clicking it into place.

No sign of Logan's van or McKenna's police cruiser in the Galaxy's parking lot.

Mayor Fortin balanced his white stetson on his knees. He was really old and ugly, Rachel thought. He had brown age spots all over, even on his bald scalp. She pulled the western sandwich out of the paper bag and wolfed it down while Fortin started up the engine and pulled onto the highway.

"I am thinking we should skip Sunday Mass tomorrow," Fortin said, as they headed north. "Big storm warning tonight. The road into Quebec, it will be flooded out."

Rachel saw no dark thunderclouds through the passenger window, only the rose and blue of the late afternoon sky.

"Maurice, I must ask you something," Odile said. The mayor obediently turned down the country music station. "You were sitting with Santa and Edgar today."

"Well, you know, I got to keep everybody in Red Dog Lake happy. Santa's not a local guy, but many people are getting off pogey because of him. And Santa's Fish Camp brings in plenty of tourist dollars."

"Yes, I know that," Odile said. "But Santa did not look at Raven McKenna's photograph. He made trouble for John Logan so he would not have to."

"Logan tried to cook Santa like a lobster. So Santa gets back at him a little bit. You cannot blame him for that."

"Did you see those businessmen in Raven's photograph?"

The mayor stared through the windshield, blowing air in and out through his nose, a big nose, too, with red veins on it like rivers on a map, Rachel thought.

"I want you to tell me the truth, Maurice."

The mayor's thin purple lips were working. "OK, sure, I seen them on Friday. They were waiting at the float plane dock to fly out into the bush. They were trout fishing."

"With guns? Hunting season has not started yet." Odile fingered the small silver cross on her necklace.

Mayor Fortin laughed the way Barry did when Rachel asked him where Dad was.

Odile frowned. "Who flew them out? Was it that Tear Drop person, Santa's pilot?"

"*Non, non.* Not Tear Drop, not him, *mon dieu.* Look, Morty's not a bad guy, but these guys with him, well, they were stuck-up guys, full of themselves. We locals fly the bush all the time, but this time our local pilots are not in their class. Morty brought in his own pilot."

"I see. You should have said so to Raven."

"Odile, what can I tell McKenna that she don't know already? Nothing."

"Did Danny fly out with those men?"

The pickup lurched as a tractor trailer barrelled past them in the opposite lane. "Stupid trucker," the mayor said. "Doing one-forty clicks 'cause he knows we only got one cop round here."

"Answer me, Maurice."

The mayor shrugged and turned up the radio. "Shania Twain," he said, smiling at Rachel. "Our beautiful girl from Timmins."

"Stop the truck." Odile's chest heaved in and out. "You will let us out here."

"*Tabernacle*, Odile."

"Do as I say."

The mayor sighed and pulled over onto the gravel shoulder. Rachel barely had time to undo her safety belt before Odile threw open the passenger door and pushed her along so they could both get out.

"Odile, this is crazy," Fortin said, looking down from the driver's seat. "You cannot walk along the highway all the way to Blue Sky Bookstore."

"Maurice, we are family and old friends. When you tell me the truth, then you may drive me home and take me to Mass." With that Odile slammed the passenger door shut. She took Rachel's hand in a strong grip for someone so small. "Come along, Rachel Forest. You will have supper at my place. John Logan is waiting for us."

The Blue Sky Bookstore didn't look like much from the outside, Rachel thought. It was a long, low building with sections linked together like a train. Parts of it were covered with silver-grey shingles, other sections built of concrete blocks. In the gravel parking lot, a metal post held up a clock with a white face and black lines instead of numbers. Long ago, Odile told her, Danny's grandfather, Albin, ran a gas station at Blue Sky. Nowadays everyone drove over to The Community because low taxes on the reserve made the gas there a lot cheaper.

Blue Sky had more books than a library. At the front door where customers first came in, Odile had set up a long oak table stacked with bestsellers and modern books. The rest of the building was a rabbit warren of metal shelves holding, to Rachel's mind, every book ever written. Lots were old books with leather covers and titles in gold writing.

"Where is your house?" Rachel asked.

"In the back," Odile replied. She went behind the cash register and unlocked a door framed by two metal shelves. "Albin's grandfather built it. It was his first home, but his children felt ashamed to live in a log house. They did not want to look like poor people so they built Blue Sky all around it. To hide it."

A short passageway led them into a comfortable room with red armchairs clustered around a stone fireplace. A steep wooden staircase that looked like a ladder led to a sleeping loft above.

Rachel followed Odile out of the main room into a simple kitchen at the back. Logan sat slumped on a chair beside a kitchen table that had aluminum all around the edge. Retro, Dad would say. Like Corazon's diner. A large Styrofoam cooler stood on the floor.

"Joseph dropped this off," Logan said without saying hello. "It's a smallmouth bass."

Odile knelt down and lifted the lid. A large fish with red eyes and black stripes down its side was lying on a heap of ice. "Yes, it is a beauty," she said. "It will make good eating. Rachel, why do you not help John clean it?"

But Logan's hands were shaking so badly, he couldn't hold the sharp filleting knife Odile took from the kitchen drawer. In the end, she brought Rachel outside through the kitchen's back door and showed her how to do it. She stuck the knife in the fish's bumhole and sliced through the belly. The guts slid out cleanly and they threw them into the bushes for the animals. Odile cut off the head and tail and scraped the scales off the skin. They looked like little bits of clear plastic.

"Rachel, you will set the table while I get the food ready," Odile said.

For once Rachel did not mind being told what to do. Odile acted like a strict schoolteacher, but she wasn't afraid of anybody, not even fat old Mayor Fortin.

Rachel found the plates, glasses, and cutlery in the drawers and cupboards and set the table the way she did for her and Dad. The plates were the same dark blue and white pattern Mum had liked: 'Blue Willow' she called it.

Dinner was bass fried in butter with rice and salad leaves with a peppery taste. Dessert was tea and homemade blueberry pie. Odile said grace and crossed herself before they ate. Logan hardly touched his food though it really tasted good.

"I'm sorry, Odile," Logan said, pushing his food around with his fork. "I can't, I'm sorry."

She nodded. "I will wrap it up for you. For later."

After dinner Odile washed the dishes while Rachel dried them. Rachel glanced out the back window. Logan had wandered out behind the house to the spot where he'd parked his *Volkswagen*. She watched him search under the passenger seat and pull out his bottle of whisky. She dumped the clean cutlery back in the drawer with a loud crash so Odile wouldn't notice what he was doing.

Odile wiped her hands and hung the kitchen towel to dry over the stove handle. "John will drive you back to Camp Nirvana when he is feeling better," she said.

"I don't want to go back there," Rachel said.

"I know you do not want to, but your father will be worried if you are not safe at camp. Now before you go, I must show you something."

She led the way back into the bookstore. Rachel followed her past the meandering bookshelves to a space that looked like a clearing in a forest of old books. There stood a large oak table with a drawer underneath. Odile pulled it open.

"My art!" Rachel cried. "You have my art!" She rushed over and ran her hands over her precious drawings. Electricity flowed into her from their vivid colours.

"Danny brought your drawings here last Thursday. For safekeeping," Odile said. "I told him not to risk his job at Camp Nirvana. That it is a steady income at least, but he did not want to listen. We had words."

"Mrs. St. Pierre … I'm worried about Danny. I-I think he's with those men in the photograph."

"Yes, of course he is. Tell me everything he told you, *Nisimis*."

So Rachel did. Even the part about Santa giving Danny the job.

16

Danny crashed through the woods to a thick clump of chokecherry bushes. He trampled the lower leafy branches, crushing out a hollow big enough to hold him and Ricky.

The wind was picking up. The tops of the red pines waved like black banners. Drops of water splashed his skin.

"Give me your knife," he said to Ricky.

"No way," the American replied.

"Then cut us some branches unless you aren't wet enough already."

Grimacing, Ricky pulled out his knife. Danny tossed down the Australian's pack and foraged through the groundcover, pulling up a dead pine branch, then another.

"Heads up." Ricky threw a live branch at him.

Crack! A bolt of lightning seared Danny's vision. He counted: one thousand, two thousand, three thousand ...

Thunder ruptured the sky. The full rain hit, bursting against the leaves and branches. He dove for the hollow under the bushes, shouting to Ricky to follow. The American squeezed in beside him.

Danny laced together the branches they'd collected, layering them over the pack to form a rudimentary roof. Rain pelted down in a waterfall.

Another flash of lightning. *One thousand, two thousand ...*

"This rain should kill the fire," Ricky shouted above the noise of the storm.

"No, it won't be enough," Danny said. "The fire's burning underground. That's why the snakes came up through the lodge floor. Once the storm's over, it'll start up again."

Another bolt of lightning. And another. It felt like they were crouching in a forest of knives.

One thousand ...

"The trees," Ricky shouted, leaning over to make himself heard. "We're sitting in the middle of a bunch of trees. Trees, lightning, get it? You're going to get us killed."

"OK, go stand on the beach," Danny shouted back. "Go make like an antenna and see what happens."

Another flash. Thunder in an ear-splitting roar directly overhead. Too many lightning bolts to count. Sky as dark as night.

Wet, cold, he'd never get dry, Danny thought. Couldn't remember how it felt to be dry. The smells of wet leaves, mud and damp cloth overwhelmed him.

If the storm ever stopped, they'd have to plunge back into the bush. Press through till last light. Temperatures might dip down close to freezing tonight. With their wet clothes, would hypothermia get them?

"Hey, the rain's slowing down," Ricky said.

The darkness seemed to be lifting. Danny shifted his feet in the mud under the bushes, trying to get his blood flowing.

"We're done here." Ricky pushed out of their bush cave and staggered to his feet.

"Wait!" Danny tried to hold him back. "There's still lightning. There's still ..."

A thunderbolt like the wrath of ancient gods. A tall pine exploded in a shower of sparks.

Ricky swore.

The crown of the pine toppled to the earth, landing twenty feet away.

"Now will you listen? Stay down, damn it," Danny said. "You have to wait ten minutes after the storm passes. Most people get killed by lightning because they head out right after the storm is over."

"That tree's burning. Hell, it's gonna start another fire."

Lightning or not, they had no choice. Danny crawled out and joined Ricky. Together they ran over to the fallen pine. Ricky began stamping on the flames. Danny dug up handfuls of mud and earth wherever he could reach and caked it over the charred wood to smother the embers.

Daylight had returned. The thunder sounded distant.

Exhausted and filthy, Danny staggered back to the lake, kneeling on the shale gravel to rinse off his hands and arms. On Fire Island, smoke mingled with the scraps of dark cloud trailing the storm. The flames had subsided to a fiery pool lapping the charred tree trunks.

"So you were right," Ricky said behind him. "The fire's still going."

"No kidding." Danny held up a hand, gauging the wind. "The wind isn't blowing south anymore. It's shifting. It's shifting west."

"And right in front of me I see this big damn lake."

"We need to get going."

Danny returned to the bushes where they'd sheltered and picked up the sodden pack. Through the trees he studied the sun, retracing the direction they must take.

"OK, follow me," he said.

Ricky grunted, shouldered his bow and fell in behind him.

They pushed through alder and chokecherry bushes and thick clumps of nameless weeds. Trees and rocks and pine needles, all looking the same.

Deep in the woods, daylight was already fading.

"We've gotta move faster, come on," Ricky said. "My grandmother and her walker go faster than you."

"Shut up!"

"What did you say to me?"

"Look, do you want out of here or not? We have no food, we need to save our energy. And if one of us falls and breaks a leg or whatever, we're done for."

"Hendrix will be coming after us."

Hendrix, Curtis, whoever, Danny thought. "Well, he'll have to find us first."

"Oh, he will. He's ex-military, an expert tracker. And he never gives up."

Danny stepped over a small ditch. Normally a spring would have been running through it but with this hot, dry summer ... Water, his clothes were so wet he hadn't thought of thirst. They should have found a container, filled it with lake water.

Too late now.

A hazy purple twilight seeped through the trees. Not dark enough to kick in his night vision, but so faint that his day vision was failing. A stone rolled under his foot. He clutched a nearby birch branch to save his balance.

They'd reached a long downhill slope, covered by a rockfall. Lichen spread across the granite boulders.

Danny set down the pack. They might as well stop here overnight. The rocks could provide minimal shelter against another storm.

"We need that big knife of yours again," he told Ricky.

"What for?"

"To cut some branches. Unless you like sleeping on rocks."

Ricky sighed with drama, but got busy cutting. Danny picked his way down over the rocks to the bottom of the hill and scanned the woods for anything to eat. This deep in the forest, the shade choked out much of the groundcover.

"OK, Mr. Native Guide," Ricky tossed down an armful of saplings halfway up the slope. "What's for dinner?"

"Not much. I see some chokecherry bushes over there. Don't eat the seeds, they'll make you sick. And there's pine sap. We can chew on that."

"Mr. Comedian, I ain't laughing."

"I'm serious. You can scrape lichen off the rock and munch on that but it tastes like gravel. My grandmother uses it to make a curing tea."

"One way to lose weight." Ricky settled down on a boulder, unhooked his bow and set it down well out of Danny's reach. "Forget the weeds. I need protein."

"Well, even if you bagged a chipmunk with that big bow of yours, we'd have to cook it. And that means lighting a fire, which we can't."

"Oh, come on. A little ground squirrel sushi; be a man."

"You obviously never heard of tularemia."

"Sure I did." Ricky looked up, suddenly alert. "Tularemia's a bioweapon. Washington, DC, The Mall, September 24, 2005, let off by a mob demonstrating against our fighting men."

"Suit yourself." Danny made his way over to the chokecherry bushes he'd spotted. The berries weren't ripe, but he chewed down the bitter, dark red fruit anyway, taking care to spit out the seeds. He picked a few clusters for Ricky, leaving the rest on the bush for the morning. From Odile he'd learned that the berries spoiled quickly.

Ricky, naturally, refused to eat them.

Danny finished off Ricky's share then divided the pile of branches and saplings Ricky had cut. He dropped his half in a hollow between the stones a short distance away from Ricky. He hunkered down on the branches, drawing his knees to his chest, shivering. Ricky pulled a small package from his combat vest and unfolded a thin sheet of metal foil.

"Thermal blanket," Ricky said. "We take turns. First me, then you."

They sat in silence while the dark deepened around them.

"You know," Ricky said into the night, "the best food is what those South American football players ate. Got all the proteins, enzymes, minerals."

"You Americans, one day without meat and you make like you're on the Franklin Expedition. In the old days, most of what

my people ate was plants." He thought a minute. "We had canni-
bals, too."

"Do tell."

"There are legends about the windigo. It preys on you in lonely
places. Pure white, twenty feet tall, with blood-red fangs."

"Sounds like Bigfoot crossed with a vampire."

"The windigo can take any shape. It lures you into its tent so it
can devour you. The worst thing is ..."

"What?"

"Just by closing in on you, the windigo's evil can infect you.
You become a windigo yourself."

"Nice campfire story, Mr. Camp Counsellor." The thermal
blanket rustled as Ricky shifted his weight.

"It's more than that. My grandmother ..." Danny's teeth were
chattering. He hoped Ricky was serious about sharing that blanket.

"What about your grandmother?" Ricky asked.

"She's a shaman. People in The Community call her in for help
all the time."

"Like The Exorcist."

"Well, a lot of folks take it seriously. They say my grandmother
is the only shaman round here powerful enough to get rid of a
windigo."

"You're full of it."

Two days ago Danny would have agreed with him. From childhood, he'd written off Odile's secret life as superstitious nonsense.

But now, staring into the dark, her beliefs didn't seem so ridicu-
lous. Odile would say that a windigo had torn Morty, Anderson
and Curtis, the Australian, to pieces.

Was the windigo lurking in the trees, watching him and Ricky,
waiting to finish the job?

He didn't believe in Odile's two faiths, but he did believe in evil.

For evil had invaded his life the moment he sat down with Santa
and Edgar in the Galaxy and let them buy him a beer.

17

The staff had lit up the Galaxy's blinking neon stars and wheeled out the illuminated notice board, which read:

"KARAOKE Strip Nite. U buff? U hot? Get lucky 2-nite."

The brilliant signs couldn't dispel the encroaching darkness, Corazon thought. On starless nights like this one, spirits seemed to seep out of the trees and the ground, eroding her shield of science and reason. The realm of the spirits more properly belonged in the steamy tropics, she felt, where they could work their mischief on Mama Filomina and her *albularyo*. She'd banished that nonsense when she fled the Philippines. Nothing was as incompatible with silly spirits as the cold clinical steel of North America.

Well, in the cities, perhaps. Not up here.

She'd learned about the hidden spiritual world of the Cree soon after she moved in with Sinclair, but, unlike Sinclair, she had no wish to dip into The Community's secret faith. She made it clear to everyone that she had no use for religion, especially priests of any description. As long as no one bothered her about that stuff, she wouldn't bother them either. These days, if staff didn't show up for work for ceremonial or ritualistic reasons, she worked around it and kept quiet. After all, Joseph was the best short-order chef within a hundred miles. Her bouncers, bartenders, musicians, waiters, cleaners, well, in truth, the whole Galaxy was run by The

Community. She wouldn't be in business without them – and they knew it.

Two worlds: the theatre of the real world and the mirror world, the shadowy one ... No better example than Odile, that grey little waitress. According to Joseph, Odile was a powerful shaman yet she drove over the border into Quebec with that self-serving hypocrite Mayor Fortin to attend Mass twice a week. Covering both bases, no doubt, Corazon thought sourly. Odile was quiet, neat, methodical and self-effacing, and she scared Corazon to death.

What if she knows about Danny and me?

For years Corazon had had as little use for sex as she did for religion. She'd made that clear to Sinclair from the beginning: separate bedrooms, no touching, no wheedling or begging for more. Not that it mattered, diabetes had rendered him incapable. In public, though, she played the comedy of their hot sex life, which suited both of them, and even gained Sinclair a modicum of status.

Later on though, after Sinclair's final and fatal illness, her treacherous hormones had led her to venture slowly and carefully back into the world of carnality. She had a recipe for lovers: young was better, looks a bonus, and discretion essential. She'd stuck to tourists and truck drivers until Danny. His being local made him a risky exception, but he was young, quite cute, and oh so grateful. The gulf in their ages ensured he'd keep quiet: he'd be too embarrassed to admit he'd slept with a woman old enough to be his mother. Besides, if he ever got difficult, she'd tell everyone in town that he'd been a virgin their first time. Nineteen and still a virgin? That was positively geriatric by Red Dog Lake standards.

Showtime, Corazon reminded her reflection in the bathroom mirror. She dabbed more glitter on her cheekbones and stretched and tugged her red-sequined tunic over her thick midriff. Forty-five isn't old, not by today's standards, she told herself. Gotta get sexy, gotta earn big tonight. Be like Franco, your dear brother. He worked his drag act through hangovers, detox, the general's infidelities and rejections from the young ones. Always a hit and always gorgeous.

She rubbed her bare arms. She just couldn't get warm.

That damn cop, McKenna, had stayed put in her cruiser outside the diner for hours. Waiting for me to make my move, Corazon thought. Waiting for me to fly out to check on Danny. Itching to throw my butt in jail, and probably Danny's, too, while Santa and his grow-op get away with murder.

You better be lying about those forest fires, McKenna, she thought. Just try and mess with my karaoke strip night. Just try it and I'll give you a night you'll never forget.

Logan was back inside Blue Sky Bookstore. Rachel listened to his footsteps wandering aimlessly through the book stacks. She turned back to her art and spread it over the wide oak table to show Odile.

"Danny thinks it's important that kids read books," Rachel said. "Kids like movies so we decided to write a graphic novel."

"Comic book," Logan returned, at a distance.

"Danny liked to read many graphic novels. *Bone* when he was little, and *The Watchmen* when he was a teenager," Odile said. "Both are excellent stories."

"Danny wants kids to learn about Cree legends. Our first story is *Wesakechak and the Bears*," Rachel said.

"Ah, *Wesakechak*, the trickster." Odile pulled out a chair and sat down next to Rachel. "He spots the bears fishing in a river and tries to outdo them."

"Yes, and he's crappy at fishing, so all the bears laugh at him." Rachel pointed to her paintings, one by one. "See, here he is falling into the water."

"*Wesakechak* looks like John Logan."

"Yes, and I made the head bear look like Pasha. Mr. Logan showed me an album full of pictures of her." Rachel hesitated. "Do you know how long bears live?"

Odile sat back. "Black bears live a long time. In the woods, thirty years or more. A tame bear like Pasha could live to be thirty-five, maybe even forty."

"Awesome! My dad saw Pasha when he was a kid, so I could still see her. Where does Pasha live now?"

Odile laid a warning hand on her wrist as Logan stumbled over to the table. "Show me your next story, *Nisimis*."

Why does no one answer me? Rachel thought. She pulled out her next story. "This one is sad," she said. "It's called *The Traveler*, about the man who was mean to animals."

"My grandmother used to tell me that story," Odile said. "The Traveler was a powerful warrior, but greedy. He was cruel to his wives and children and everyone around him. The only thing he cared about was his fine horses."

Rachel turned over the page. "Here are his beautiful horses. One day the Traveler finds an old white horse grazing in the field with them. He's never seen that horse before. He gets a stick, hits the horse and hurts her just because she is old." She looked up. "I had to draw that bad part, because it's in the story."

"Show me what happens next," Odile said with a glance at Logan.

"That night The Traveler has a dream. The old white horse turns into the most beautiful horse he has ever seen. See how I used the blue and silver colours in her coat? That's where I'm going to add my indigo paint."

"Yes, beautiful," Odile said.

"The horse says, 'You are a bad man'," Rachel continued. "'Because you are cruel to animals, I have taken all your horses away.' He wakes up really scared, runs out to the field, and all his horses are gone, even the old, sick one he hurt."

"He deserved to die for what he did to that horse," Logan said.

Rachel said: "The next night the white horse comes back and tells him: 'Your horses are by a lake, two days north.' So he runs to find them but they aren't there. And that keeps happening. The spirit horse keeps telling him where his horses are hiding and every time he travels to find them, they are gone. The spirit horse makes sure he wanders forever."

"My grandmother would say that if I listened, I would hear the hooves of the horses in the wind, and the voice of The Traveler calling for them," Odile said.

"And did you?" Rachel asked.

Odile smiled.

Logan moved restlessly. "A windigo, that's what The Traveler became. A demon, cursed forever for what he did to that horse. Put that in your comic book, why don't you?"

"We do not speak of the windigo. To speak of him is to summon up evil," Odile said.

The loud roar of a motorcycle startled all three of them. The bike didn't pass by Blue Sky: it stopped.

"Are you expecting anybody?" Logan asked. Odile shook her head. "Did you lock up?"

"My door stays open to The Community."

Logan held up a hand. "Let me check it out. Where's Albin's gun?"

"No guns, there is a child here." Odile turned to Rachel. "Put away your art. Make sure it is safe."

Rachel felt glad to do something normal. Her hands kept fumbling the pages. She slid them down all messy into the open table drawer. Finished, she looked up. Logan had vanished.

"Stay with me," Odile said and reached for Rachel's hand. "We must lock the front door."

Inside the Galaxy Tavern, the bartenders were wiping glasses, cutting limes and lemons, filling the ice machine, and loading beer and coolers into the fridges. Members of the local rock band, *Black Thunder*, were onstage testing the sound system with loud squawks of noise.

A few early drinkers were there, the loners and hard core mostly. Corazon spotted Maurice Fortin nursing a *Brador* beer at the bar, his white stetson shading his eyes. She signalled to the nearest bartender, who handed her a bottle of *Sauza* tequila. She grabbed two shot glasses and walked down the length of the bar to join him.

"Mass in Rouyn versus strippers, eh?" She jabbed him with her elbow. "See that table over by the stage? The Galaxy's buying."

Fortin sighed, slid off his bar stool and lumbered along beside her, clutching his beer.

The table was well out of earshot of the other drinkers. She slammed down the bottle and glasses on its bare surface and poured out two shots.

"You're a bad girl, Corazon," Fortin said. "And I'm a bad man. But you knew that already."

"So go to confession tomorrow." She sat down and kicked out the chair opposite her. "Sit down and drink up."

He took his seat, sighed and stared at his beer bottle, watching moisture trickle down its sides. "Odile is mad with me," he said at last. "She knows Danny flew out with those guys. The spirits tell her things ..." He massaged his wrinkled forehead. "My cousin, Albin, her late husband, he was strange like her. Seeing ghosts ever since he was a kid ..."

Here we go, Corazon thought and downed her shot. "We gotta talk, Maurice."

"I know."

She leaned over the table. "What the hell did you get me into? I don't do business with Santa."

"Look, Morty he likes you. Trusts you. About Santa, maybe I should have explained, but he was only a little bit part of Morty's show. I am sorry. Truly sorry."

Like hell you are. "Morty's guys weren't fishing. It was a canned hunt, a set-up. And don't you go shaking your head at me, you fat *putain*, pretending you didn't know nothing. What were they gonna shoot, those rich bastards? Wolf? Fox?"

"No, nothing like that."

"Those stuck-up guys were talking round me like I'm some robot flying my plane. The big American, the one dressed all in black like Rambo, he said they were gunning for bear. So don't lie to me."

Fortin shrugged and downed his beer.

"I got a damn good idea where they got that bear, too," Corazon said.

"*Tabernacle*, keep your voice down."

"How could you, Maurice? How could you do that? And I helped." She rubbed her stinging eyes and when she dropped her hands on the table, she saw they were smeared with mascara. "How much did Danny know about it?"

"You're not gonna like this." Maurice swayed in his seat like he was casting for trout. "Santa gave Danny the job."

"What!" This time Fortin grabbed the tequila bottle and poured. Corazon downed her shot, held out her glass for another and downed that, too. "Fine, Danny can stay out there on the island. Burn up with the others."

"Don' be hard on the boy," Fortin said. "He needed the money. Like you, like me. Look, for sure McKenna is bluffing about the forest fires. There's no problem. No radio message from Morty means no problem, right?"

"You think so, huh? Joseph told me about that cop, McKenna. They grew up together. She's a real straight arrow, Joseph says, a real pit bull. Her dad was a cop and her two brothers are cops. The word in The Community is that she's making detective in September."

"That's nice for her, no?"

"You idiot! McKenna works narcotics out of Toronto. She's in town on a case."

"Yes, well, maybe ..." Fortin lowered his voice. "Now look, tomorrow afternoon like Morty planned, you fly out and pick them up. Only you don' take them back here to Red Dog Lake, where McKenna's waiting. You fly them down to Temagami. My nephew will drive Morty's SUV to meet you. Then Morty takes his guys back to Toronto and we are out of it."

"You think that will fool McKenna, huh? When Morty radios in, tell him to hire another damn pilot." She looked up at the stage where the night's first performer, Robert, was testing the pole. "You do that 'cause I'm out of it. Now I got a show to run."

Rachel stared into the night, pressing her face against the narrow side window bordering the front door to the bookstore. A large black and chrome motorcycle stood parked under the old illuminated clock.

"I don't see anybody," she said.

"He is here," Odile said beside her. She moved to lock the front door, but it swung open, startling both of them.

A great stillness flowed into the room with the chill night air. A man in black motorcycle leathers stood in the doorway, his skin pale as milk …

The man from the motel.

Rachel bit her hand. *I don't want to scream, I don't want to.*

Odile stepped in front of her, shielding her with her body. "We are closed for the night," she said to the man. "That should be obvious even to you, *Machi Manito.*"

"What did you call me?" The man's voice was deep, with an Australian accent like Santa's.

"I called you by your name, Demon."

"Demon? That's hardly friendly." He smiled. "No drama. I'd like a book. Loud goings-on back at the Galaxy. You Canadians make far too much noise when you sink a few."

"Do not waste my time, Demon. What do you really want?"

"Right then. Your boy, Danny, flew out into the bush with a mate of mine. Their camp on the island is gone."

"What do you mean?"

"The island's been swallowed up by a bloody great bushfire."

"Danny!" Rachel cried out.

"How do you know this?" Odile asked.

"Don't you worry your head about that, Darling. You just tell me where to find a road in to Fire Island and I'll go fetch your boy for ya."

Odile grabbed the silver cross on her necklace. "There is no road in to Fire Island. And even if it existed, I would not tell you."

"I see." The man reached inside his jacket. "Is that your final answer?"

Rachel caught a flash of silver. *He has a knife – a knife!* She wanted to run, but she couldn't move. Her bare knees knocked together.

"I wouldn't do that if I were you," Logan's voice said behind them.

He was pointing a long black rifle at the man. Rachel watched Logan step forward and shove the end of the gun into the loose white flesh under the man's chin.

"This here's a Winchester M-70 rifle and it's loaded," Logan said. "Hands on top of your head."

"You're overreacting, Old Son," the man said. "I only came by to buy a book."

"Do it."

The man sighed and placed his hands on top of his thin fair hair.

"Rachel, Odile, get in the van," Logan said looking down at them over his shoulder. "Go on, run!"

Odile seized Rachel's hand. Together they dashed past the man through the open doorway. They ran round the building to the back parking lot where Logan's rusty van rested beside a clump of pines.

The passenger door was open. They tumbled inside. Rachel watched their breath fog the inside of the cracked windshield.

The boom of a shot. The roar of a motorbike.

A figure came loping through the darkness, holding the rifle. The driver's door flew open. Rachel stared, too scared to scream.

For a moment she only saw white skin. Then she recognized the beard and wild grey hair.

Logan tossed down the gun under the driver's seat and climbed in behind the wheel. "It's OK, he's gone. Good thing you never cleared out Albin's things, Odile. I found his gun in the tool cupboard like always."

Odile stared straight ahead. "Did you shoot him?"

"I fired into the air to get him moving."

"What does he want with Danny?"

"Nothing good." Logan fumbled with his car keys. "I'm taking you over to Joseph's place."

"Joseph is working as bouncer for Madame tonight," Odile said. "Take us to the Galaxy."

"No!" Rachel cried. "The man is staying at the motel. He'll find us."

"Do not worry," Odile said. "He cannot hurt us at the Galaxy. Too many people. Besides, we must tell Raven McKenna what happened."

"Then we should drive to the police station," Rachel said.

"No, Raven will come to the Galaxy tonight. To close Madame down," Odile said.

"Yeah, I guess you don't need the spirits to tell you that," Logan grunted, and started the engine.

18

Branches poked into Danny's back. Intense cold from his damp clothes made sleep impossible. "It's my turn for the thermal blanket," he said into the dark.

A rustling beside him. "I'll trade you," Ricky said. "One hour blanket time for some of that nice weed you've got."

"I don't have any weed," Danny said automatically.

"Come on. I was in the music business, remember?"

Danny felt in his shirt pocket and found his stash.

He opened up the wet plastic baggie, fingering his last remaining spliff: mangled but miraculously dry even after his dump in the lake. "I've only got one joint, that's it," he said.

"So bring it over."

Danny crawled through the dark toward Ricky's voice. A football-sized stone rolled away under his foot. He listened to it rattle down over the rockfall and thud to the forest floor below them.

"You sure make a lot of noise," Ricky said.

Light flared out, blinding Danny. Ricky was holding a small LED flashlight between two thick fingers about three feet away.

"Come on, stop wasting my batteries," Ricky said.

"What else have you got in that big vest of yours?"

The LED went out. There was a boulder next to the one Ricky was sitting on. Danny reached through the dark and ran his hands over its rough contours. Slowly he crawled over to it and sat down.

"Fire up that mother and give it to daddy," Ricky said.

"My lighter's dead."

Light burst through the trees as Ricky fired up a tiny match. Danny poked one end of the spliff into the flame, puffing frantically to get it going. The match sputtered out, but the glowing ruby of the joint's burning end remained in the night.

Ricky reached over and nabbed the spliff. Danny listened to the big American's lungs fill and empty.

"All right! We have liftoff, Captain," Ricky said.

"Fine, give me the blanket."

A rustling and crinkling. Hard to imagine that foil as thin as newspaper could provide any warmth, Danny thought as he took it from Ricky. He wrapped it tightly around his shoulders and waited. Slowly his shuddering eased.

By now the air was thick with the pungent aroma of smouldering weed.

"Your toke," Ricky said.

The red dot moved in his direction. Danny took back the spliff and inhaled. Smoke flooded his lungs and Santa's high-grade THC whistled through his nerve endings.

"Hey, gimme." Ricky snapped his fingers. "I said a toke, not burn me down to the roach motel." Danny passed it back. "This isn't bad weed."

"It works." Danny stared into the night. What was he doing getting stoned? Weed gave him the munchies and those chokecherries had done nothing to stay his hunger. "I didn't think a hard-core Republican like you would touch weed."

"You'd be surprised."

"Morty said you were a rock star. How come I never heard of you?"

"'Cause you're ignorant." Ricky laughed and wheezed. "Your turn."

"Sure." The ruby moved his way. Danny took another hit, thinking of carcinogenic tars four times worse than cigarettes. A familiar dizziness was seeping into his brain, and with it the eerily heightened perception that surfaced to haunt him whenever he was stoned. "You didn't answer my question."

"OK, you never heard of me because you've been wasting your time listening to pathetic crap like *Radiohead*."

"*Radiohead* is genius. I'm not into bad 1980s electro-pop."

"Are you kidding? I'm a Kentucky boy, I'm proud to say, and I play rock and blues, tried and true. Next time you're stealing downloads off the web, look up *The White River Rats*. Our music will crush that emo junk of yours." He snapped his fingers again. "Don't bogart that joint, my friend."

Danny passed it back. "Do you guys still play?"

"Naw, got divorced. Every gig we play, my ex gets a chunk." Ricky puffed in silence. "Do you want the end?"

Badge of honour to bag the roach, but Danny had lost his taste for it. "No, it's OK. You have it."

"Suit yourself." The ruby sputtered out. Ricky stretched, cracking his shoulder joints. "That was dynamite. Homegrown you said."

"I didn't say."

"Come on, where'd you get this?"

"From Santa."

"Santa." Ricky had the weed-giggles now. "So I'll have to line up with the rug rats and sit on Santa's knee to buy more Canadian sweet grass. Or do you locals have another way?"

"How about you answer my questions instead? How long have you and Curtis and Anderson been in business together?"

"Never saw them before."

"Come on, you were acting like old buddies. Why is my government throwing a party for a bunch of arms dealers?"

"Money. To give you Canadians jobs during the recession. Where is Santa's weed garden?"

"Santa."

"How many elves work the harvest?"

"Santa."

"Cut it out." A hard edge in Ricky's voice. "OK, an easy one. How much does Santa charge for a baggie?"

"Fifty to a hundred. More if he figures you're good for it. Less if he needs a favour."

"What kind of favours?"

"Well, let me put it this way: Charmaine, the waitress at the Galaxy, gets hers for free."

"And you?"

"My turn now. You're a rock star, or you say you are. How come you're knocking around with arms dealers like Anderson and that Australian guy, Curtis?"

"I'm helping out some people back home."

"People? A senator? The FBI? The CIA? Who are you, Ricky?"

"Uh-uh, my turn. How long have you been working for Santa?"

"I don't work for Santa. I mean, except for this gig. He'd like the whole town to be working for him, but it's not going to happen."

"Wake up, Sonny boy. It's already happened."

Danny shivered. All around him the woods stirred and whispered. "Are we done here? 'Cause I need to get some sleep."

"No, we ain't done. If you don't want to answer any more questions, gimme back that blanket," Ricky said.

Danny handed it over. The chill night air sent him into a fit of shivering. He slipped his way back down, feet first, over the rocks to his pile of branches.

Odile had told him that vision ran strong in their family, but even as a child he'd known that that gift, like so many others, had passed him by. Only the women in our family get vision, he'd remind her.

He'd never mentioned the weird insights and revelations that happened when he smoked up.

Like now.

He knew what Ricky was. And why Ricky had been hunting a tame bear on Fire Island with gunrunners and criminals.

19

"*WELCOME, ALL YOU MOTHERS! IT'S KARAOKE STRIP NIGHT!*"

Lights, music, thunderous cheers and rhythmic clapping. The bottle of *Macallan* whisky gleamed like a lighthouse among the drained beer glasses crowding Santa's table. Tobacco smoke swirled in a lilac fog round the mirrored disco ball. Life doesn't get much better than this, Santa thought.

Charmaine hugged him, her mouth wet and sloppy with alcohol. Too many Brown Eyes, the house specialty: a shot of *Jägermeister* topped with *Crème de Cacao*. Santa shuddered at the defilement of decent drink. At least Edgar, mournful as ever in his pointed green hat and stained overalls, was sticking to plain draft beer.

Santa, too, had stayed in costume for the evening. Maybe later he'd jump up onstage and give them all a Christmas treat, wave the hefty fire hose he was right proud of. Charmaine looked especially appetizing in that tight red leather jacket and matching stilettos. He'd booked them a motel room in anticipation.

Right now Corazon was introducing the first act, Robert, the French Canadian Stallion. Smart of the Cobra Queen to start off with a crowd-pleaser. Robert sported a red and black checked lumberjack shirt, knitted toque and red satin hockey shorts. He bounced up and down the stage to the Willie Dixon tune, *Built for Comfort*. Plenty of earthy innuendo in old Willie, and the young fella certainly knew how to milk it.

"Oh, he is so gorgeous," Charmaine breathed as Robert doffed his shirt to reveal a trim muscular torso.

"Steroids, my dear," Santa said. "Shrinks yer old fella to nothing."

"Oh, he's got plenty." Charmaine made another Brown Eye disappear.

"More, more, more," the crowd chanted.

Robert dived into the Hank Williams classic: *Hey, Good Lookin'*. And, Santa observed sourly, Robert did have plenty of meat to slap on the table. He kicked the table, spilling Edgar's pint.

"Your turn next, Mate," he said.

"No, no way." Edgar shook his head. Alcohol was making him mulish. "I miss my mum. I miss her so much."

"Oh, for God's sake," Santa said. "Can't you have one beer without getting maudlin?"

"Where is your mum?" Charmaine asked.

"With my Aunt Vera up in Buggy Lake." Edgar sniffed and wiped his nose. "No phone, no nothing. And it takes two days to drive up there. Can't afford the time off work. I haven't seen her in six months."

"Get Tear Drop to fly you up," Charmaine said.

"Give it a rest," Santa said. "Why don't you strip, Darling?" He nuzzled her smooth silky neck, thinking that once they were alone, he'd pour *Macallan* all over those melon breasts and lick them off. "Go on, get up there."

"N-no." Charmaine shook her head. "Corazon will kill me. She's so mad at me – she'll fire me for sure."

"The old cow won't be able to once I own the Galaxy, will she?"

"She'll never sell the Galaxy. She'd die first."

"Exactly. Look at her in that sparkly shirt – she looks like a pork sausage wrapped up in red tinsel."

Corazon, as host, was marching along the stage in a skin-tight, red-sequined tunic while the band thumped out the Donna Summer disco classic, *Hot Stuff*.

"*I need some hot stuff baby tonight*," Corazon yelled into the mike.

"Strip, strip, strip!" the crowd chanted.

"Oh, you want hot stuff." Corazon arched a plucked eyebrow. "OK, you're gonna get it." She blew them a kiss and dropped the tunic to bare one shoulder.

The audience loved it, banging the tables, shattering beer glasses.

"OK, next act: Edgar the elf." Corazon held out a plump arm.

The floodlight moved to Santa's table, blinding them. Edgar buried his face in his hands. Feet kicked his chair, beer showered down on his hunched shoulders. Eventually, the bouncers left the front door and hauled him up onstage.

Edgar slouched next to Corazon, wringing his green elf hat.

"So what's your song, Big Guy?" Corazon shoved the mike in his face.

Edgar sniffed. "My mum's favourite, *Having My Baby*, by Paul Anka."

Boos and jeers. Santa laughed so hard, he choked on his Scotch.

"Now you be nice," Corazon said to the audience. "This is Edgar's first time."

More catcalls. Shouts of "Aw, he's a virgin", "I don't do charity work" and "Hey, did your hand get a headache?" surfaced over the general brouhaha.

The band started up.

"*Having my baby*," Edgar crooned into the mike. "*What a lovely way of saying how much you love me ...*"

Dreadful, excruciatingly awful singing, if you could even call it that, Santa thought. High-pitched and nasal, not one note on the mark.

Beer mats, empty chip bags, half-eaten food sailed through the air. Edgar, oblivious, eyes closed, began a strange undulation, starting with a slow roll of the buttocks. He reached for his right shoulder and undid one metal clasp.

"What happened to the karaoke machine?" Santa shouted in Charmaine's ear. "I mean you do have *karaoke* on karaoke strip night, don't you?"

"Oh, the band smashed the karaoke machine last month." Charmaine stared at the road accident that was Edgar's burlesque.

"They needed more paying gigs so they ran over it in the parking lot."

"Enterprising bastards." Santa grabbed the *Macallan* again and poured.

"*Having my baby.*" Edgar had undone the second clasp. The top of his overalls flapped around his waist, revealing his exceedingly hairy torso and prodigious gut.

"Hey, Edgar," yelled some wiseass. "It's not one baby. It's triplets, man."

But Edgar was on a roll, entranced by song. He dropped his pants. He wasn't wearing boxer shorts.

A collective gasp.

"Well, that ain't rubber," the wiseass shouted.

A rhythmic thumping of tables began at the back and circled round the tavern. "Edgar, Edgar, Edgar."

"Well, he's got no reason to feel ashamed," Charmaine said and demolished her eighth Brown Eye of the evening.

Corazon gyrated to the audience's rhythm. "Hey, we got us *some hot stuff baby tonight.* A star is born!" She scooped up Edgar's overalls from the stage. "Here, cover up that cobra, Baby, you gonna scare the kids. I'm gonna name you … what you say, you mothers? It don't matter he can't sing with a talent like that. We're gonna give you a new name, Edgar. We gonna call you The Red Dog Grizzly." She winked broadly at the crowd. "And I don't think you'll be a virgin after tonight." She ushered him off stage.

"Hey, who'da thought?" Charmaine giggled, draining Edgar's half-finished beer. "Edgar, the stripping bear."

"Bloody shut up about bears," Santa said. His wonderful mood had evaporated. Even a long nourishing slug of *Macallan* didn't help. He felt a nasty chill between his shoulder blades. He turned to see people coming in from outside.

That tall fellow, Joseph, the cook at the diner, was talking to Logan in the doorway and ushering in the old waitress. And that scrawny kid Logan claimed was his granddaughter. He watched Joseph seat the waitress and the kid at a table at the back. Logan, thankfully, stayed outside.

He wiped his face with his Santa hat. Weed sales had tapered off tonight. He'd stationed his pilot, Tear Drop, outside in the parking lot with a supply of baggies, but the Red Dog whackers were sticking to sex and beer.

Another act started up; Monique LaRoux, a statuesque redhead, took the stage. Charmaine whispered that LaRoux used to be a man down in Montreal. Regardless, her pole-dancing was impressive.

"There's an underage child in here," Santa pointed at Rachel, itching to make trouble.

"Sure, lotsa kids here tonight," Charmaine said. "Everybody comes out for karaoke. No way you can get a babysitter."

Over by the bar, Edgar was back in his overalls, surrounded by patrons who were buying him beer.

"I'm going to water the roses," Santa said.

He hitched up his red velour pants, slammed his way past the crowded tables and chairs and staggered out the exit, squinting at the bright lights in the motel hallway. The washrooms were located near the humming vending machines. He wandered over, his black boots catching on the scratchy carpeting, and swung open the door to the men's room.

Empty except for a grungy metal bucket. The mop was missing.

Hardly his problem. He stepped over to the gurgling urinals, yanked down the elasticized waist of his red pants, pulled out his old fella. And waited. He'd had a spot of trouble lately, dribbling rather than passing his usual Niagara. Maybe he should see a doctor.

The door to one of the cubicles opened. He kept his eyes forward, staring at the cracked white tiles, breathing in the sickly sweet smell of bathroom 'mints'.

Finally things were happening. He let fly. God, that felt good.

A rush of movement. A brutal force seized his neck, smashing his raw cheek into the mirror so hard his blisters popped. He staggered, coughed, tried to not to wet himself.

Impossible.

Another jarring smash. The mirror gave way and cracked under his flesh.

"For God's sake," he croaked. He slid face first down the tiles, streaking them red.

Black Doc Marten boots. A blow to the stomach sent him sprawling, his sodden pants around his ankles. He couldn't breathe, the pain was killing.

He huddled in a fetal position, hands over his naked self. "Please, for God's sake. If it's money, just take it."

The attacker grabbed his tunic. Hauled him up, squashing his bare buttocks into the cold wet urinal. Desperate, he tried to shield his face with shaking hands.

"Wake up, Merry," a deep voice said.

"Hen-Hendrix?" He blinked uncomprehendingly. "Charlie?"

A knife flashed close to his eye. "You know what a Colombian necktie is, don't you, my son? The drug lords slit your throat and pull your tongue out the hole. Me, I like to go one better. I carve off your old fella while you're still breathing and poke it through."

"Charlie, for God's sake." Santa coughed and wheezed through his alcoholic haze. "Why-why are you back from the island?"

"That's a damn good question."

A brief flash of a white skin and black leather. A hard ringing blow to the face choked him with saliva, pain and tears. Blood poured into his mouth.

"Please, Charlie," he spluttered. "What's wrong?"

"God, you're pathetic." Hendrix released him.

Santa tottered to his feet, hauling up his pants to cover himself. He staggered over to the sink and coughed up a mess of blood and bile. With trembling hands, he turned on the tap and tried to rinse away the damage.

"You broke my nose." He felt the cartilage move under his fingers. A face like battered beef stared back at him in the mirror.

"Look at you, playing the clown in that naff red suit," Hendrix said. "You draw far too much attention to yourself."

"People expect it. They want a showman. What's the harm in giving the whackers a bit of fun?"

"You never could let it alone. A smart lad stays invisible. Hires the locals to play Santa and run the fish camp. Minds the product himself. Strictly export, no sales to the buggers in town. Never foul the nest."

"What's the harm if I spread a little green gold locally? It's profit. We're businessmen, Charlie." His eyes drifted to the washroom door.

He had to make a break for it. The bugger of it was that he had no knife or gun. The shards of the mirror hadn't broken free, so no joy there.

He leapt back, startling Hendrix. Hurtled to the door.

Too late he saw the mop shoved through the metal handle, barring the door.

Hendrix was on him like a tiger, nearly wrenching his arm out of its socket. A blow to his old fella crumpled him to his knees in agony. Hendrix dragged him over the filthy floor tiles and heaved him into a cubicle. When he clawed the metal wall to get his footing, Hendrix tumbled him onto his knees facing the toilet.

"Not smart, Merry."

"I don't understand what I've done, Charlie."

"You've landed us in a pile of crap, my son, that's what you've done."

"Why aren't you on the island?"

"Never went. Curtis took my place. He played me."

"But it was a business opportunity. For you, Charlie. Morty connects with the politicos, all strictly top drawer." He sniffed back blood. "And it was a spot of fun."

"Shooting a tame bear, that's cruel. Not a lark."

And you in the arms business, Santa thought, but wisely kept quiet. He sniffed up more blood. "I'll clear us a hundred grand on that bloody bear."

Hendrix slammed his head so hard into the side of the cubicle, his ears hummed. "That bear is going to cost you all you've got."

"Please stop hitting me. I don't know what you want. I don't know what you want, damn it!"

"Tear Drop got a wee whisper from that bent copper in Red Dog Lake," Hendrix went on. "Now what do you suppose he heard from dear Constable Michael?"

"I-I don't know. Tear Drop keeps his own counsel."

"A couple of buggers in your hunting party are turners. We've got ourselves rats in the nest. You want to live, you tell me who they are. Let's start with your mate, Morty, the government toady. Maybe the coppers had a word with him."

"Morty can't be the rat. He's been flying VIPs up here for years. Fortin said so." Santa fingered his swelling nose. "I say it's Anderson, he's a cold one."

"Bad guess," Hendrix said. "Known him for years. Bloody obsessed with technology, Anderson is. Not interested in money, not really. What stirs him up is a gun that goes bang with Nazi-precision."

"The big American, the rock star, it can't be him. He's just a limp whacker with too many millions."

"He's a nark!" He forced Santa's head against the rim of the toilet. "And he's got help."

"Danny?" Santa coughed. "You're saying Danny's a rat? He's just an idiot kid who works at the children's camp. Lived here all his life."

"The bent copper told Tear Drop that McKenna creature works narcotics. And she's native, like your friend Danny. Get the picture?"

"Oh God …" Santa rubbed his sore face. Everything he touched turned to crap. "I can't believe it."

Hendrix flexed his hand. "Curtis radioed me last night. Never heard a damn thing after. Had Tear Drop fly me out in the Twin Beech this morning. And do you know what I bloody found?" He thumped the wall of the cubicle. "Do you?"

Santa shook his head.

"The whole place has gone up in a bushfire."

"What!" Santa stared into the stained toilet bowl. "Oh, my God, what's happened to them? Are they dead?"

"Now that's the question of the day, Mate. Couldn't see through the smoke. Couldn't raise Curtis on the radio. But I did see two daft buggers paddling a canoe. And one of them looked a hell of a lot like that native kid. Now you tell me: where would they be headed?"

"Don't know, I swear."

Hendrix's hand seized the back of his neck. The stained porcelain of the toilet bowl flew up at him. He went under the water, gargling, swallowing.

He struggled madly, arms flailing.

Suddenly air, he could breathe. He clutched the rim of the black toilet seat, beard and hair dripping.

"I want answers," Hendrix said. "If Curtis is dead, you're dead."

A loud bang on the washroom door. Santa's heart leapt. Intermission, he was saved. The crowd would be storming in here to empty their beer-inflated bladders.

"Hey, who locked the door?" a man cried. "Open up."

Hendrix flicked open his knife. "Answer my question."

Santa's buttocks trembled. "I've no idea. Please, Charlie, the product's safe. Take it tonight, if you want."

"I don't care for that answer." The knife tip hovered over Santa's eye.

"Please, I don't know, I swear to God. There is no road. Flying's the only way in."

Several bangs and thumps on the washroom door.

"Hey, man," someone shouted. "Better finish what you're doing. The cops just showed up."

He felt Hendrix grab his tunic and haul him up. He leaned against the cubicle, legs shaking.

"Up and out. We'll finish this in my room." Hendrix heaved him out of the cubicle to crash against the urinals. He seized him again and shoved him at the washroom door. "Now pull out that broomstick so I can shove it up your backside."

The mop was tightly wedged in. Hendrix's impatience was electric. Santa hunched over the door. Whimpering, pretending.

Hendrix kicked him. Bastard!

Santa got a strong grip on the handle. The mop surged free of the door. He spun round.

Cracked Hendrix full in the face. Heard his nose give way. Bloody good!

Hit again, quick fast. Hendrix staggered back and tripped over the metal bucket. Dark madness rushing in now. Smash, smash.

Hendrix moves fast, the slippery bugger. Rolling away, arms and legs kicking. Can't get at his vitals. Can't reach that crispy skull, smash, smash.

Behind him, a walloping crash as the door burst open.

"Hey, man! What's going on?" Three husky men stared into the washroom.

Santa dropped the mop. Heard it clatter on the tiles.

"Hey, man. Are you crazy?"

Had to get out, had to. Santa ran at the men, barged his way through, leaving their shouts and protests behind.

The cool air in the hallway doused him back to sanity. He fled down the south leg of the Cobra Queen's octopus, heading for the parking lot.

Run, had to keep running.

Because he hadn't had time to kill Hendrix.

20

Walking into the Galaxy Tavern was like walking into a tunnel full of light and noise, Rachel thought. The band's thumping bass guitar made her ribs vibrate. Joseph had put her and Odile at a small round table near the back corner of the room.

None of the other people in the bar paid them the slightest attention, because up onstage a tall woman with fiery red hair was twirling round a metal pole. Why was everyone hooting and getting so excited? The lady's legs were white and bony and her shiny silver bikini made her freckles stand out. Now she tore off her bra. Her round boobs looked like they'd been frozen solid. Gross!

Lots of people were smoking cigarettes, too. Dad would nail them with tickets, if he was doing a health inspection here. Smoking indoors was illegal in Ontario even in bars. Rachel fidgeted on her hard plywood chair, searching the crowd for the pale man. Where was Sergeant McKenna?

"Do not worry about that man," Odile said close to her ear. "Joseph and his friends are big, strong men. And Logan is staying in the parking lot until Raven arrives."

With that gun next to the driver's seat, Rachel thought and shivered. Dad hated guns. He said the government should make stronger laws so that no one could own one.

"Why are you so sure that Sergeant McKenna will come here?" Rachel asked. "Is it because you're a shaman?"

"No," Odile smiled. "Madame Corazon gave Raven a hard time today and she will not forget it."

The lady with the frozen boobs left the stage. Now Charmaine, the mean young waitress, climbed onto the stage. Actually two men rolled her onto it. She had a hard time standing up. She wobbled around in her high-heeled red shoes, shouting at the band to play Shania Twain's *Man! I Feel Like a Woman!* Corazon was leaning on the bar, her plump arms folded over her sparkly tunic. She didn't look mad that Charmaine was acting drunk. Instead she was laughing.

I'll never understand adults, Rachel thought.

The band started up again. The audience screamed at Charmaine to take it off. Swaying to a rhythm that had nothing to do with the song, she fumbled with the zipper on her red leather jacket. After several tries, she managed to drop it down onto the stage. Now the blouse. She frowned in concentration, her fingers slipping on the buttons.

Why are people cheering? Rachel thought. Charmaine isn't singing.

The outside door whooshed open. Sergeant McKenna stood in the doorway, gazing around the room, one hand on her nightstick. Light sparked off the police badge on her chest.

The band stopped in mid-note. Charmaine staggered, her blouse gaping open to reveal a lacy black bra. The room that had sounded as loud as cars in a drag race now fell quiet as a deserted church. Rachel noticed several people slipping out the exit at the far side of the room.

Joseph whispered to McKenna, pointing to Rachel and Odile. McKenna frowned and turned her dark stare their way.

"Hey, she's hot," someone in the audience shouted. "Is that uniform for real, Baby?"

"Make her strip and find out," another man yelled back.

"Yeah, make the cop strip. Take it off."

"Strip, strip, strip." The room erupted in a crescendo of sound. McKenna's hand moved from the baton to rest on her holster, her face stony.

Joseph rested one large hand on her shoulder. Together they pushed past the crowded tables over to the spot where Rachel and Odile were seated.

"You wanted to see me, Grandmother," McKenna shouted over the noise.

"Strip, strip. Come on, take it off," the audience chanted.

"Sure, come on up, Sergeant McKenna." Corazon jumped back onstage and wrestled the mike from Charmaine's fist. "We love a woman in a uniform. How about a little girl-on-girl action with Charmaine here?"

"Strip, strip, strip."

"It's time to leave, Sergeant," Joseph said. "You're just here to see Odile, right?"

"I would say yes," Odile said. "And quickly."

McKenna glared at the room, nodded her head briskly and helped Odile up from her chair. "You too, Kid," she said to Rachel over her shoulder.

Walking out of the tavern was like walking through a wildly moving cornfield. People hooted and hollered all around them. Rushed up and veered away, slopping beer. They were saying, "Aw, too bad." "What are you, stuck-up?" "Can't wait to see what you got under that badge, Baby."

Joseph threw open the outside door and hustled them out. Rachel looked all over the parking lot for Logan, but both he and his van had disappeared.

As they moved into the pool of light shed by the single lamp in the parking lot, she could see that McKenna was sweating.

"You OK, Raven?" Joseph asked.

"They're animals. Pumped up by that Corazon creature. I saw at least twelve citations." She pulled off her hat and ran a hand through her thick dark hair. "I'd love to nail their collective butts."

"Let it go. You can't lock up the whole town." He glanced back at the closed tavern door. "Next time, bring backup."

"There is no backup. It'd take an army to round up that zoo in there."

"Where's your buddy, Constable Michael?"

"He's not my buddy." McKenna shoved her hat back on. "And he's not coming back. Red Dog Lake has a brand new junior constable to corrupt, if and when the brass sends him down from Kirkland Lake. For now, you better get used to me."

"What's going on, Raven?"

"I'm on a case. You know better than to ask me about it, Joe." She sighed. "The dispatcher called me at six o'clock. There's a forest fire up north near Malartic. A bad one. Ten campers are trapped and cut off from the road to the highway. The chief decided I should stay here. Only now ..."

"He's ordered you back to Kirkland Lake after all."

"Yeah, the firefighters need every resource we've got." She looked down at Odile. "You wanted to see me, Grandmother?"

Odile clasped her hands. "A man came to Blue Sky tonight, asking for Danny. Danny flew out with those men in the photograph."

"The guy pulled a knife on her," Joseph broke in.

"What!" McKenna straightened up.

"The man's staying here at the motel." Rachel found her voice. "I saw him at the pop machine this afternoon."

McKenna felt in her tunic and pulled out the photo she'd shown in the diner earlier that day. "Was it one of these men?" Rachel shook her head. "Can you tell me what he looked like?"

"He was pale like a vampire. And he was riding a big black motorcycle, a Harley, when he came to Blue Sky."

"I see," McKenna bit her lip.

"You know who Rachel's talking about," Joseph said.

"Oh, yeah. Where is he now? In the tavern?"

Joseph pulled a face. "I heard his bike pull out. Right after we went inside to get Grandmother."

McKenna swore.

Joseph glanced back at the tavern door. Patrons were leaking out the entrance and drifting into the shadows by the walls to light up cigarettes, legal and otherwise. "Look, I gotta get back inside. I'll give you a shout when he shows up."

"OK, but stay away from this dude. He's bad news. Nobody goes near him. That means you, too, Joe, got it?"

"Like I said, shout if you need me." He started heading for the tavern door.

"You better be listening to me, Joseph Wren." She watched him until he vanished back inside. "Come with me, Grandmother. You, too, Kid."

She led Odile and Rachel over to the police cruiser. After she'd settled Odile in the passenger seat, she climbed in behind the steering wheel and pulled out her notebook. She made Rachel sit in the back.

"Tell me everything, Grandmother."

Odile told her all, including what Rachel knew.

"Did Danny tell you the name of the pilot who flew them out?" McKenna asked.

Odile hesitated. "We had an argument." She gripped her hands together. "This man who came to Blue Sky … he is a windigo. I am afraid for Danny."

"Me, too, but Hendrix can't get at Danny without a plane. You and I know there's no road in to Fire Island." McKenna frowned. "Maybe he was looking for the old mine road, you know, the road to the Archangel Mine. Danny and the others might try to walk through the bush to the mine if they're in trouble."

Rachel could feel her heart beating so fast she could hardly speak. "Danny is going to get burned up. You have to go and rescue them."

McKenna glanced at Odile and started the engine. "I'll try to get a rescue copter to fly out and check on them. I'll call in every favour I've got."

"Try?" Rachel cried. "Why can you only try to rescue Danny?"

"Priorities and not enough resources. We don't know for sure that Danny's in trouble. I'm sorry, Grandmother," McKenna said. "I'll do everything I can, but my hands are tied."

Odile stayed silent, twisting the silver cross at her throat.

Rachel had always wanted to ride in a real police car with flashing red and blue lights, computer on the dashboard and radio going off in bursts. Sergeant McKenna looked like a warrior: she had a gun and stick like a Ninja and probably a bulletproof vest under her blue uniform. But now all Rachel could think about was Danny dying in the fire. She stared out the passenger window, watching the chalky edges of the highway streak by like white foam trailing a boat in dark water.

"I want to call my dad when we get to the police station," she told McKenna.

"Sorry, but I have orders to take you back to Camp Nirvana." McKenna glanced in the rear-view mirror. "Don't worry. Barry Tucker assured me he won't let you out of his sight."

"I won't go back to Nirvana. I won't!" Rachel exploded. "Barry is a creep and a pervert."

"Those are pretty strong words, Rachel Forest. This afternoon you told me your name was Amy Logan and that you were John Logan's granddaughter. That wasn't true, was it?"

Rachel looked out the passenger window.

"Barry Tucker says you tell lies. I'm inclined to believe him."

"That's not fair. I only said I was Amy Logan because I didn't want to go back to camp. And Barry *is* a pervert."

McKenna turned off the highway onto the dirt driveway that led to Camp Nirvana. They passed through the familiar arched gateway with the old hippy peace symbol overhead. Rachel clutched the handle of the passenger door, staring at the silver undersides of the leaves brushing past the window, but the cruiser was going too fast for her to jump out.

McKenna finished radioing in her location to the dispatcher. Light streamed out of Barry Tucker's office window and glinted off Odile's silver cross. The older woman's silence was like a deep pool of water.

"Rachel will be fine, Grandmother," she said. "Hendrix won't come crawling around here after her. Too many people. It's you I'm worried about."

"Hendrix," Odile repeated. "So that is the windigo's name. I do not want to tell you your business, Raven, but now we are here, I feel that Camp Nirvana is not safe for Rachel. Her father must take her home."

"He can't. He's in rehab. She's better off without her dad for now."

"At least her father is trying to get better."

"I wasn't criticizing, just saying."

McKenna started the engine, turned the cruiser around and headed back down the dirt road. She stifled a yawn when they turned onto the highway. Her contact lenses burned her eyes like hot sand. How long had she been up? Eighteen hours? Twenty?

At least an hour's drive to the OPP detachment. Nothing along the empty highway. No cars, no service stations. Beyond the windows of the cruiser, only blackness: the overcast had blotted out the moon.

"You must take me home to Blue Sky," Odile said.

"Can't do that," McKenna said. "It's not safe for you to be on your own with Hendrix around."

"I have lived on my own since Albin died and Danny went to college. I can take care of myself."

A flash of light in the rear-view mirror. McKenna reached up to adjust it.

"Raven, are you listening to me? You must turn around and take me to Blue Sky."

Old people, McKenna thought. A vehicle was roaring up behind them, coming on fast. Probably a drunk from the Galaxy Tavern.

"*Cist!* Listen to me," Odile said. "We must turn around. Now – for both our sakes."

The car pursuing them drew closer. One of its headlights was out.

"Writing you up is going to make my night, Buddy," McKenna muttered, staring into the mirror.

Scorching light flooded the cruiser. The vehicle wasn't a car, but a motorcycle rapidly closing in on them. It surged around the cruiser's back fender, veered into the oncoming lane, and drifted up to the driver's window, the biker a hunched dark shape, the crest on his helmet flashing silver. He kept pace with the cruiser for a heartbeat then rocketed past, the bike's tail light fading to a tiny red dot.

"That's him. That's Hendrix." McKenna flicked on her lights and pressed down on the accelerator. "Hang on, Grandmother."

Odile stared unblinkingly through the windshield.

McKenna felt her pulse surge, all thoughts and vision narrowing down to focus on the black ribbon of oncoming highway. The motorcycle's lights had vanished. Where was Hendrix? How far ahead?

She scanned the road, blinking back the grating pain of her contact lenses. The road surface was uneven, rutted by the snow and ice of past winters. Hard rock cuts lined the highway on both sides. She pressed on, searching …

"There!"

Odile's wild gesture broke her concentration. Too late she saw the motorcycle straddling the centre line, the driver immobile beside it.

She hit the brakes, her thigh muscles screaming from the strain of pressing down. She felt the grind of the ABS kick in, pulsing through the sole of her boot. In a long dilated instant, the car transformed into a wild thing out of control. And in that instant, she became a mere spectator, suspended in time, watching her fate.

The car rotated as slowly and methodically as a carousel. There was a horrid grinding of metal as the right side of the cruiser scraped along a rock face. A crunching force flipped the cruiser back onto the highway facing the motorcycle. The passenger door burst open.

For a moment McKenna saw only the trail of metal and glass on the road in front of her. Her chest ached intolerably. Her hands, slick with blood or sweat, slipped along her seat belt and jerked the catch open. Odile lolled in the passenger seat beside her, stunned by the crash.

McKenna leaned over and unclipped Odile's belt, easing her sideways onto the seat.

"Grandmother, are you all right?"

Odile moaned softly.

"Stay down."

Through the windshield, McKenna watched the driver of the motorcycle take shape. Tall, hunched shoulders. Black leathers, a starkly pale face. Holding what appeared to be a slim grey rod across his chest: a Dragunov SV-137 Russian sniper rifle.

She undid her holster and punched the radio. "McKenna here. I need backup."

The windshield ruptured in a starburst of crystals, glass tearing through the upholstery of the seat. McKenna pulled out her gun and kicked open the driver's door.

Hendrix took aim again.

She rolled out the driver's side onto the hard roadbed. Ignoring the shriek of her injuries, she crouched behind the open driver's door, her .40-calibre Sig Sauer semi-automatic pointed and ready.

"Charles Hendrix, you're under arrest," she shouted through the open driver's window. "Hands on your head. Put down your weapon."

He kept coming.

"Odile, Grandmother, nod if you hear me." Odile stirred. "Get out of here. Run!"

A strange, hollow noise. Hendrix was laughing.

McKenna's ears filled with the roar of sound as she pulled the trigger of her semi-automatic. Pain from the kickback slammed through her wrist.

A huge force punched through the cruiser door, opening up the metal like a monstrous flower. A blow to her chest like no other. She felt herself drifting; the night sky above her was spinning.

She heard Hendrix's footsteps crunch through the debris on the road. Something heavy rested in her right hand.

My gun. Her numb fingers bent around it.

She rolled onto her side. Got on her knees.

The passenger seat, thank God, was empty.

"Run, Grandmother," she whispered. She forced up her gun and steadied herself in the regulation shooting position.

The night air shattered with the burst of two guns firing at once.

21

Grandmother!

Danny sat up in the dark, awake all at once, instantly alert.

He'd seen a train pulled by a large black locomotive, the one in the famous Alex Colville painting, *Horse and Train*. Odile stood on the silver rail tracks, illuminated in the headlight as the engine bore down on her. Relentless, unstoppable ...

He squeezed his knees to his chest, shaking with cold. So stupid to end up in a fight with her last Thursday. He should've known better. He'd stomped out of Blue Sky like a dumb teenager. That's how she'd remember him: surly, stoned half the time, turning into a bum like everyone else in Red Dog Lake ...

And Rachel, *Nisimis*, Little Sister. Everybody pushing her onto a shelf, telling her to shut up and not bother them: her dad, Barry Tucker, even that older guy, Dr. Amdur, who supposedly was looking out for her. She'd be asleep now back at Camp Nirvana. Had she snuck off to visit Logan today? Danny tried to rub life back into his frozen limbs. He'd forgotten to tell her that he'd moved their graphic novel to safety at Blue Sky. Logan had been drinking way too much lately. Only a matter of time before the old guy set himself and the ruined cafeteria building on fire.

He stared into the dark. Had Santa set up the bear hunt on the island to kill everybody? And if so, how had he, Danny, not picked up on that? Sure Santa was a sleazebag, like any doper, but a murderer? And how could Santa even dream that he'd get away with offing important people like Morty and the hunters? It just didn't make sense. What Santa really cared about, more than anything in the world, was saving his own butt. So why lend his prized Twin Beech to Hendrix, knowing that Hendrix had murder on his mind.

Unless Santa didn't have a choice.

Hendrix hadn't been alone up there in the Twin Beech. It took one person to pilot the damn thing, another one to shoot.

Santa didn't know how to fly, but Edgar did – sort of. And Edgar had been in and out of jail, though only for small stuff like growing weed. That left Tear Drop, Santa's mysterious pilot and a real piece of work. Everyone in town knew that the blue tattoo under Tear Drop's eye meant the Aryan Brotherhood and hard time in the pen. So, no duh, it had to be him.

Which of the three hunters had been their real target?

Didn't matter. Once the sun came up, Tear Drop and Hendrix would be back.

Don't think about them. Keep moving. Find that mine.

He could make out the rockfall now: the stones seemed to cast off a faint luminescence, like the useless light shed by solar-powered garden lanterns. Slowly the tree trunks of the forest around him began to take form.

Dawn, at last.

He looked up. Beyond the treetops, the sky was still too dark to tell the weather. He creaked to his feet, wobbling on his bed of branches. Slowly, painfully, he swung his arms to get the blood moving. He felt his shirt and jeans. Not too damp considering, but his runners still oozed water. Without a fire they'd never dry out.

He held his breath, listening for sounds.

Nothing.

He turned, started to climb up the rockfall toward Ricky and smelled smoke.

Quickly he checked his shirt sleeves. The charred smell of the forest fire lingered there, but this new odour was fresher and stronger.

"Ricky, get up. We've got to go." He looked up the slope, searching for the American.

Gone, vanished.

Danny charged up the rest of the slope. By the time he reached the boulders where they'd shared the spliff, he was panting.

"Ricky, damn it! Where are you?"

He stared at the bare rocks, trying to get his breathing under control. Typical nark: share a spliff, gain the sucker's trust.

During the night Ricky must have decided that he could make it out of the woods on his own. Probably had a GPS stuffed in that big black combat vest. Didn't need Danny anymore, so forget him. Let him burn and die.

Danny brushed the hair out of his eyes. So what if Ricky had taken off? What did he need him for anyway? No more arguing, no more listening to his bluster and whining. He'd move faster. He'd …

A stone rolled down the slope toward him. He spun to avoid it and stumbled back over the boulders. Ricky stepped out of the trees at the top of the rockfall, fully dressed and ready to go.

"Where the hell were you?" Danny said.

"Taking a leak. What's your problem?"

"I smell smoke. The forest fire must've hit the mainland. We've got to move."

"OK by me."

Danny slid back down to his sleeping spot, retrieved the pack and searched out the chokecherry bushes. He was losing time, but they needed food. He stripped off the last few berries and dropped them into the pack. By the time he finished, Ricky had joined him.

"This thing's done." Ricky stared at the compass in the handle of his skinning knife.

"Let me see." Danny held out his hand.

"No way."

"I'll try to fix it, but you'll have to give it to me."

Grudgingly Ricky let Danny pull the knife out of his fist. The tip of the needle was glued to the glass.

Holding the compass level, Danny tapped the handle to dislodge the needle. For a moment, it swung free, then settled to point northwest, not northeast, its tip still stuck to the glass. He tapped it again. This time it landed vaguely north. He kept trying, but each time, it stopped in a different direction, with no order or pattern.

"You're right, the magnetic anomalies are messing it up. Too many ore bodies around here." He looked up. Still no sun. He'd have to trust that he'd stayed true to their northeast course so far.

No time to waste.

"OK, this way," he said, hitching up the pack.

"Aren't you forgetting something?" Ricky snapped his fingers.

"Here, catch." Danny tossed him the knife and plunged into the woods away from the rockfall with Ricky behind him.

Five in the morning. Colourless light from the parking lot leaked into the Galaxy Tavern through the open exit door. The cleanup crew, toiling between the tables, looked like bent dark shadows.

Corazon sat by the bar, trying to decide if that last shot of tequila made her an all-night party girl or an early-morning alcoholic. A purple *Crown Royal* bag with last night's take rested on the counter in front of her. She could really have used the two thousand bucks it contained – net of the usual payoffs – but the trashed men's room was going to eat it all up, and more besides.

Her feet ached and her shoulders felt like they'd been bound with wire. Three locals had walked in on a vicious fight between Santa and that tall pale buddy of his. By the time she, Joseph and the bouncers arrived, both had vanished. The men's room was a real disaster: blood, broken mirror glass, even a tooth on the tiles.

Santa again, ruining her life.

Time to stash the money in her safe. She slid off the barstool, picked up the bag and headed for the exit, threading her way past the beer-soaked tables, pasting on a smile for the cleaners' benefit. The sharp smell of disinfectant couldn't drown out the sour odours of stale cigarette smoke and spilled beer.

Why should she be surprised about Santa getting into a fight? He and Logan had mixed it up at the diner, and he'd been pretty drunk at karaoke last night. Probably he needled the wrong guy this time. His pale ex-buddy didn't look like he had a sense of humour.

Serves Santa right and about time too, she thought, but I'm the one stuck with the bill.

Joseph wanted her to report the fight to Sergeant McKenna. No way, she'd told him. That cop still has my liquor licence. And, in case you hadn't noticed, she's not exactly my best friend right now. But Santa, that bugger, he's banned from my place. Unless he gives me three thousand for the washroom. In cash, not dope.

No cops, not now, not ever. I solve my own problems.

She stepped out the exit door into the empty parking lot. No sign of McKenna, thank heavens. Every minute that cold-eyed cop didn't show up felt like a reprieve. Fun to give McKenna a scare last night so she'd learn who was really boss in Red Dog Lake, but now in the cold light of morning, Corazon realized she'd been stupid. Really stupid. Those extra shots of tequila were going to cost her big time.

She rubbed her bare arms. Already she could sense the frost of autumn in the air, the Arctic ice reaching down to steal summer away. Mist from Red Dog Lake floated like tufts of wool around the light standards. The lights in the windows of the Galaxy Diner made her think of a submarine diving into a cold sea.

What did McKenna want with Odile? McKenna didn't look like the type who believed in spirits or the old Cree religion. What if she wasn't bluffing about the forest fire? What if she'd picked up Odile because something had happened to Danny …

Danny … She bit down on her forefinger, a habit she'd had since babyhood. Should she risk flying out after all?

Mayor Fortin was sleeping it off in his usual room at the motel. The whole night he'd avoided Santa as assiduously as she had. He'd conveniently forgotten to tell Santa that she wouldn't be picking up Morty and the others. Typical of Fortin, that slimy snake.

Either way I lose.

Sleep, she needed sleep. At least four hours if she was going to take up the Piper Cherokee. Crash now or crash and burn later.

She stared at the concrete stairs to the diner. Normally she'd step inside and join the early fishermen and lingering survivors of karaoke night for the Early Bird Special.

Forget it, too tired.

She trudged round to the back of the diner, pausing for a moment by the open kitchen door to breathe in the smell of hot coffee, frying bacon and sweet maple syrup over pancakes. She sighed, skirted the battered metal garbage bins and started up the soft forest trail that led to her log house. She walked slowly, inhaling the earthy smells of the dripping trees.

Dead quiet in the woods this morning. Not even a bird. She hesitated, clutching the velvet bag of cash to her chest. At this point in the trail, she could no longer see the Galaxy or her house.

A haunted sense of being watched crept over her. Was it an animal? She strained, listening for the slightest sound, heart pounding.

Nothing.

Fifteen years ago, she and Sinclair had run into a starving bear at the town dump. They'd stood frozen, garbage bags in hand, praying it would ignore them, but instead it had charged at them like a train. Corazon wet herself running back to the car. She made it, but Sinclair was much older and heavier. The bear caught him, sinking its teeth into his work boot. For some forgotten reason, they'd stashed a shovel in the back seat. She hauled it out, ran back to where the bear was mauling Sinclair and smacked it on the nose. The bear barely blinked. Sinclair screamed something about his shotgun in the trunk. In the end, she managed to find the gun and load it, but her hands were shaking so violently, she'd missed the bear even at point-blank range.

The noise was enough though to make the bear think of alternatives for dinner. It took off into the forest. Miraculously, the only thing Sinclair lost was his boot.

She'd never told Logan her famous bear story, him being so crazy about Pasha and the superior spirituality of animals. He'd never understand the primordial terror she and Sinclair had felt: the fear of being eaten alive.

After that episode, she always carried a gun in the wilderness and she'd made damn sure to learn how to fire Sinclair's shotgun. Only now the gun was locked up in her house, one hundred yards away.

The garbage bins behind the Galaxy were always locked down, she assured herself. But this summer had been so dry, wild bears had no food. They might still try for the garbage out of desperation.

Quickly, she undid the straps of her high-heeled sandals and pulled them off. She shoved the bag with the money down the front of her tight satin pants. Shoes in one hand, house keys in the other, she sprinted up the trail, her chilled feet sinking into the damp forest dirt. By the time she caught sight of the round golden logs of her cabin, she was gasping for breath.

She bounded up onto the deck. Her key slid and scratched over the front door lock as she tried to shove it in.

Come on, come on.

Finally! She kicked open the door, clutching the frame to catch her breath. She reached in for the light switch.

A body blow knocked her inside. She staggered, lost her balance. A brutal hand twisted her short hair, wrenching back her head. Her body slammed against the log wall of the entranceway. A penetrating sewer smell of body sweat and urine overwhelmed her.

It was an old mugger's trick, rushing someone when they opened their front door. He must have been waiting under her deck since his fight in the men's room.

"You Filo bitch," Santa panted, his sour breath hot in her ear, his moist sticky body pressed against hers. "Now I've got you."

22

The spare room in Camp Nirvana's office cabin was a tiny space, no more than a cupboard really, backing off the main office where Barry Tucker kept his computer. It held a cot, a night table and a cheap bookcase, empty except for grit in the inside corners. A rough, grey Boy Scout blanket covered the cot's bare mattress.

Barry had shoved Rachel into the spare room the minute Sergeant McKenna headed back to her cruiser. Its door had a shiny brass lock that he bolted shut from the outside. For hours she'd sat huddled on the floor, back to the bare plywood wall, struggling to stay awake in case Barry came back.

Thankfully, he never did.

Sometime in the night she had crawled onto the cot and fallen asleep. She woke up, curled on top of the blanket, light trickling in through the single dirt-streaked window. She felt cold and stiff, and she needed to pee.

She sat up, chewing her thumb. Barry can't keep me locked up here forever, she thought. For one thing, I'll pee and poop all over the floor. But from the way Barry was acting, he'd never let her back into camp, even if she swore to act like a team player.

Fear gnawed through her stomach. Barry would never call Dad; he'd call the social workers. They'd grab her and give her to foster parents and she'd never see Dad again. Barry would keep her locked up until the social workers arrived. If she peed her pants, he'd say she did it on purpose. If she complained that he didn't give her any food, he'd say she was lying. Sergeant McKenna had called her a liar, too. That's what adults always said, especially when she was telling the truth.

I want my dad.

She tasted blood on her thumb. *Stop being a baby.* She jerked it out of her mouth and wiped it on her shorts.

By now Odile and Sergeant McKenna would have been at the police station for hours. She wanted to believe that rescue helicopters were flying out to Fire Island to pull Danny out of the forest fire. But she couldn't. It felt too much like having faith.

After Mum died, the priest kept telling her and Dad to have faith. That meant sitting around, going to Mass and praying all the time. Faith never stopped her wishing that Mum would come home from the hospital. Faith never stopped Dad from getting sad and taking those yellow pills.

Faith was useless.

She could see Danny's smooth olive skin, blistering and charring in the flames. Getting burnt up would hurt so much …

I have to get out of here.

She leapt off the cot and ran to the window. It was made up of a large single pane of glass set above two narrow overlapping panes, which slid sideways to let in the air.

The window catch on the sliding panes was stiff and rusty. She bruised her fingers trying to work it loose.

She kept at it but it wouldn't budge.

Santa was groping at the waistband of Corazon's satin pants. Even if she screamed at the top of her lungs, no one in the diner would hear her. Too far away.

She forced herself to go limp. "I know it's you, Santa."

"Merry Christmas, now give it to me," he breathed.

"I'm a lesbian, you know."

He stopped for a moment. "So bloody what?"

"I bet that excites you."

"Don't flatter yourself, you dingo's legover. I want that money you've got shoved down your drawers."

"Go to hell!"

He swore and banged her head brutally against the hard wall. The blow stunned her. She managed to grab and hang onto an empty coat hook above her head. She mustn't fall down. If he got on top of her, his crushing weight would trap her without a shred of hope. He'd been beaten and humiliated, he was lashing out for revenge. She could feel the fire of his hatred burning through her clothes.

"OK, OK, I'll give it to you," she gasped.

He eased off her so that she could turn around and face him. The *Crown Royal* bag was already hanging over her waistband. He jerked it out the rest of the way, hauled off and hit her in the face.

She collapsed onto the floor, her mouth full of blood. He kicked her viciously in the buttocks and once more in the ribs. With a grunt of satisfaction, he began foraging through the bag.

The main floor of her cabin combined the sitting and dining rooms with the kitchen stretching across the far wall. Weapons lay there ...

She had only one try. She had to outrun him or she would die. Adrenaline had muted her pain. She lay still, waiting until he pulled out the wad of bills and started counting.

She sprang up and charged madly across the plank flooring into the kitchen. He was after her like the wind. Her Henkel carving knife rested on the draining board, the same type Joseph used in the diner kitchen.

She seized it, wheeled and lashed out at him, the way her twin brother, Franco, had taught her.

"Bloody hell!" Santa stared down at the gash in his scarlet tunic. "You cut me!"

"You bet I did." She swung the knife again. "Stay away from me, Easter or whatever the hell your name is. Stay back or I'll kill you."

"You don't have the bottle."

"I've done it before."

"Oh, me, too."

He leapt at her like a wild man. She gripped the knife desperately, but a deadly force wrenched it out of her fist.

Santa thudded down onto the planks, shrieking in shock and fury. The knife was sticking out of his thigh.

He had more to him than she thought. He seized the knife and wrenched it free. Blood instantly soaked the leg of his velour pants. Dark red, venous blood.

She'd missed the femoral artery. Too bad.

"My leg. Help me stop the bleeding," he gasped.

"Go ahead and die, you rapist."

"Rape? What bollocks! Don't flatter yourself, I was after the money. Come on, Corazon, be a sport. Get me a towel, a rope, anything."

"Die, just die!"

She pulled out her cellphone to call for help. To her dismay and disbelief, he grabbed the knife, sprang up, and came for her.

She tossed the phone in his face. Dashed past him back into the sitting room. He plunged after her, hobbling as though he was in a bizarre stiff-legged race.

A Chinese chest served as her coffee table. She flung it open. The look on his face when she pulled out Sinclair's Mossberg 570 shotgun was priceless.

"Bloody hell." He paused, licked his lips.

"Want to jump me again? Go ahead and try. I'd love to blow you apart. Now drop the knife and the money and step back."

He opened his blood-stained fist and let the knife clatter to the floor. She gestured with the gun. He took one grudging step back.

"Give me back my money."

"You're overreacting. Thought you liked a bit of rough."

She shifted the handle to load, watched his eyes widen. "Even you aren't stupid enough to think you can dodge a bullet. Give me back my money, you sack of lard."

She knew instinctively he'd charge her. He seemed to move in slow motion.

She pulled the trigger.

The noise was deafening. The air seemed to rupture. The glass in her front window vanished.

Santa's face went pale as snow. He turned and ran like a rabbit, clutching his wounded thigh.

She followed him onto the deck, gun at the ready. He struggled down the steps, holding his right leg stiff as a log, dove into the woods and disappeared into the brush.

Everyone at the Galaxy Diner would have heard the shot. Santa knew that, too.

Corazon rushed back inside her cabin. With shaking hands, she set the shotgun down on the floor, slammed and bolted her front door. She collapsed back against it, pressing her hands over her hot flushed face.

To her horror, tears poured down her cheeks, her sobs shaking loose from an uncharted depth within.

It wasn't until the kitchen staff was banging down her door, demanding to know if she was all right, that she was able to pull herself back together.

And as luck would have it, Edgar the elf was with them.

23

Rough ground now, rocks and tree roots slowing them down. Danny tried not to think about their paltry progress or the dragon behind them.

Move, just move.

Time evaporated as they trudged through the endless bush. An hour whipped by in five minutes.

He could feel the stealth of dehydration creeping into his body, the nausea and dizziness, the scratch in the throat. He stopped briefly, praying for a faint sound of water.

"Man, there's got to be something to eat," Ricky said. "I'm dying here."

"OK, we stop. Two minutes, that's it."

Danny slid to the ground, bracing his back against a pine tree. He pulled the crushed chokecherries from the pack and offered them to Ricky.

"Forget it. Don't you have blueberries round here?" Ricky said. "There was a stand in Red Dog Lake. I saw it on the way to the float plane dock."

"They're farm berries. The weather's too dry for bush berries. Look, the chokecherries are better than nothing."

"You eat them. I'm gonna hunt something." Ricky fingered his bow.

"What are you going to hunt? Mosquitoes? Blackflies? What we really need is water." Overhead the sky was opaque with overcast.

Maybe if they were lucky, another storm might blow up. Rain could save their lives. He asked Ricky if he had a water bottle.

"Yeah, back on the island," the American said. "Quit asking me for stuff. Look in Curtis's pack."

Danny pulled it over, knowing his search would be futile. He searched through the outside pockets. Nothing. Inside it held only the shattered radio phone. Why was he still carrying that stupid phone around? Did he think it would magically repair itself en route?

He tried to fit the broken pieces back together. Water poured from the casing.

"You got any ideas?" He handed the shattered phone to Ricky.

"Yeah." With one powerful swing Ricky heaved the pieces far into the trees.

Danny sprang to his feet. "What the hell did you do that for?"

"Dead weight. It'll only slow you down. What else is in there?"

"Nothing!" Furious, Danny turned the pack upside down and shook it. The white medicine bottle he'd found on the floor of the lodge flew out and landed on the ground. He grabbed it and held it up for a closer look. It wouldn't hold enough water for a mouse.

He pried off the cap. Miraculously the inside was dry despite their dump in the lake. A few flat white crystals flecked with black rested on the bottom of the bottle. They cast off an odour reminiscent of new plastic.

Curious, Danny touched a finger to the crystals, then to his tongue. A bitter, corrosive taste. He spat it out violently.

"What is that?" Ricky asked. "One of Anderson's weirdo natural medicines?"

"Not unless he wanted to rot his teeth, fry his brain and turn into a mouth-breathing junkie. This is crystal meth!"

"And you would know that, how?"

"I read. You know, books, newspapers, the stuff you and your hunting buddies walk past in airports." He tried to toss the meth out, but Ricky seized his wrist and snatched the bottle away.

"That's evidence." He snapped his fingers. "Now the lid."

"I figured you for a nark." Danny threw the lid at him.

Ricky caught it and thumbed it back down over the white bottle, his face expressionless. Cops must practise that look, Danny
thought. He watched Ricky shove the bottle into his combat vest.

"Who was the crystal dealer?" Danny asked. "Anderson or
Hendrix?"

"You're dreaming."

"Maybe it's you. Maybe you're playing both sides, Ricky. If
that's really your name."

"You done?" Ricky stood up, shouldering his bow.

Danny grabbed the empty pack, turned away, and forced his
legs back into motion.

It took Rachel an eternity to work open the latch on the bottom
pane of the window in Barry's spare room. She slid it open with a
crash.

The morning air that flowed in felt cool. The aroma of cooking
bacon drifted up from the galley tent.

I'm so hungry.

The window opening was covered by a mesh screen. Nailed in.
She had no tools to pry it loose.

I am a ninja.

She took a deep breath, twirled and hit the middle of the screen
with a roundhouse kick. With a twang, it popped out of the window
frame and winged onto the grass.

Footsteps in the office. Barry!

Heavy boots tromped past the door to the spare room and wandered behind the desk that held Barry's computers. The office chair
squeaked as he sat down. Boy, he's fat, Rachel thought.

Now he was alternately humming and whistling, rolling the
chair back and forth over the plywood floor, making a dull grinding
noise.

Any second he'd be opening the door to check on her.

The window opening was so small. She tried to squeeze her
head through it, but the hard plastic edges of the liner around the
frame bit into her face. Now her head was stuck. She braced her
hands on the window sill, struggling to free herself.

Let me go, let me go.

She saw herself trapped forever, her head hanging out the side of the cabin like a gargoyle's.

A final painful wrench. She popped free of the window, tumbled back and tripped over the cot.

"Who's in there?" said a loud deep voice.

Santa! What was he doing here?

The chair banged against the desk. "Oy, Barry, is that you? Stop pushing up the zeds, you lazy bugger. Come on out. We need to talk, Mate."

A loud whack on the door sent her heart racing. He rattled the door handle. "Come on, open up. No point in hiding, you wanker."

Rachel searched the room for a weapon: nothing.

"I don't care who's in there with you. Bloody open up."

A heavy crash against the door made her jump. Santa heaved his weight against it again. Dust flew out of the hinges.

"What the hell are you doing? The whole camp can hear you." That was Barry's petulant voice. "Oh, my God, what happened? You look terrible."

"Well, aren't we sweet as cat's pee this morning?" Santa said.

"Your suit's all filthy. What if the children see you like this?"

"Then I'll wish them Merry Christmas and charge them double. Who have you got in the back room?"

"Nobody, nothing, I don't know what you're talking about." A sharp intake of breath. "Your leg. You're bleeding. You're dripping all over the floor."

Santa collapsed back into the desk chair. "Shut it. Grab me that first aid kit on the wall behind your head."

A lot of heavy breathing and shuffling. Suddenly Santa bellowed in pain.

"I'm only trying to help," Barry said. "First aid isn't going to work. You need stitches. Get Edgar to drive you to the hospital in Kirkland Lake."

"Can't. Had to hoof it over here. Edgar buggered off with my Hummer and my girlfriend last night. He's got stars in his eyes after singing karaoke, thanks to that Corazon monster. Which reminds me, I need a drink. I'm as dry as a dead dingo's dongler."

Barry sniffed. "You know I don't drink alcohol."

"And you fancy that questionable virtue cancels out the filth you mess about in. Don't make me laugh. Get over here and help me bandage this up."

More grunts and shuffles.

"That dressing isn't going to hold," Barry said at last. "And for heaven's sake, clean yourself up. You smell like a distillery."

Rachel heard a thud like meat being slapped on a countertop.

"You hit me!" Barry cried.

"You betcha, you stingy little lizard. I know you've got a bottle hidden in here." A banging and thumping of desk drawers. "Bingo!"

"Put that down. That's for guests."

The chair rolled and slammed into the wooden wall between the office and spare room, making Rachel jump. "Set your bum down, we've got business to discuss," Santa said.

"What-what business?"

"Don't play me about. The money you borrowed from me to set up your special websites. The ones you host and sneak a long peek at when you kid yourself nobody's looking, you pathetic pervert."

"Oh, those websites."

"I need my money back and I need it now. Plus a little sweetener, say five thousand or so, to stop me from telling dear, sweet Sergeant McKenna all about your nasty little hobby."

"I don't have to pay you a thing."

Another wet slap. "Keep messing me about and I'll turn really ugly."

Rachel pressed closer to the door, listening intently.

"It's all over. She was already here." Barry was sobbing now. "I sat up all night erasing my drives."

"You cretin," Santa said at last. "I watched that copper drive off from the Galaxy last night. She had that old native waitress from the caff with her. And that kid Logan was passing off as his grand-daughter. The kid wore a shirt from your precious camp. I say she belongs here and the copper was bringing her back. I say, the copper knew damn all about your computers."

"She knew everything. I saw it in her eyes."

"It's her job to make you feel guilty. Besides, a smart copper can read your drives even after you erased them."

"I'm not paying you a thing. I couldn't even if I wanted to. I don't have the money."

"You lying little worm."

"I need therapy."

"I'll give you therapy."

More slaps. Rachel clapped her hands over her ears; she didn't want to hear any more.

"For starters, I'll take that poufy hybrid car of yours," Santa said. "Give me the keys."

"I don't have them."

Barry let out a shriek of pure pain. Rachel rolled the nightstand onto the cot and shoved the bed over to the window.

"What's that noise?" Santa said.

She jumped onto the mattress, took a big breath and heaved up the nightstand. She crashed it against the large upper pane of the window.

The boom of shattering glass. Pain stung her bare arms and legs like a cloud of bees.

"Bloody hell!" Santa shouted behind the door. "What's going on? Give me the key!"

"Here, take it!" Barry said.

Rachel threw the grey blanket over the jagged glass sticking up from the bottom of the window frame. She stepped onto the window sill.

The grind of the key in the lock.

She clutched the top of the window frame. Balancing on the sill, she kicked over the bookcase. It crashed face down onto the floor in front of the door.

The door opened, banging uselessly against the fallen bookcase. Santa swore, ramming the door against it again and again. She heard Barry run out of his office.

No choice: she had to jump.

I'm cannonballing into the lake.

She swung her legs through the opening and dropped down into space.

24

The ground had grown treacherous, sharp rocks breaking through the thin soil under a cover of slippery pine needles. Danny picked his way in silence, swatting at the deer flies and mosquitoes that landed on his bare skin whenever he slowed his pace.

"You ever buy white crystal?" Ricky asked behind him.

Not in a million years.

"Well, did you?" he repeated.

"No, only morons get into that stuff."

"Oh, yeah? I bet you jerks in Red Dog Lake eat hemorrhoid cream just to get high."

"Right, sure, every day of the week. Why don't you admit it? You and Anderson and Curtis, all of you were stoking up on white candy. Giving yourselves a fake rush for a fake bear hunt, you bunch of pathetic losers!"

"Look who's talking."

"Some narks cross over the line. When did you?"

"I don't need drugs. The kill is enough."

"Yeah, right."

"You're a local dude buying weed from Santa," Ricky said, shifting his bow to his other shoulder. "So when did that fat Aussie SOB switch from green to white gold? I know he's cooking meth at Santa's Fish Camp. Come on, who's gonna hear you way out here? You can tell me."

"Ask Santa yourself. You're the cop."

They had reached a spot where the forest floor sloped up steeply to their right. Danny stopped to get his bearings, feeling the pull of gravity in his calves. Should he climb the hill? If they were lucky, its summit would reach above the trees and he'd have a clear view of their surroundings. Maybe he'd spot the mine.

Or see how fast the forest fire was eating through the bush behind them.

He wiped his face. What if he climbed up and found that the hilltop lay below the treetops after all? He'd have worn himself out for nothing. And lost critical time …

"Hey, heads up," Ricky handed him the knife with the compass.

He'd offered it willingly, at least that was something. But Danny still couldn't get the compass to work. "I'm going up," he said, handing it back.

Ricky grimaced. "After you."

They hiked up the hill slowly. To Danny's hopeful eyes, the light filtering through the trees seemed to be getting stronger the higher they got.

He climbed faster, breaking their pace, he couldn't help it. After twenty minutes, he ran into a sharply rising stretch of broken granite.

He looked up. Hovering high over the trees, he could make out a round patch of silver sky. Too hard to tell, even at this height, if the outcropping reached over the treetops or not.

"I'm going up the rest of the way," he said. "You coming?"

"Wait," Ricky tilted his head, listening. "I hear water."

On the edge of hearing, a slight gurgle. Danny closed his eyes, focusing on the sound, gauging its direction. "There!"

He scrambled over the stones at the base of the fractured granite rise and pushed through a patch of alder bushes. Water was seeping through a crack in the rock, oozing over a muddy fan of pebbles and weeds. No time to worry about dirt or parasites. He knelt down and drank. The water tasted like a slurry of grit.

"You've got to be kidding," Ricky said above him. "That's sewer water."

Danny kept drinking, absorbing the precious moisture. "We could really use a water bottle," he said, wiping his mouth.

"I told you. I left it on the island."

Drink what you can. As much as you can.

Danny tried to keep drinking, but his stomach rebelled. He staggered up, dropped the pack to free his hands and shoulders, and started up the rock face before he could change his mind. He heard Ricky follow him.

Once on the rock his feet kept slipping, he could barely find a grip. Gravity dragged on him, forcing his heart to beat wildly. Far above his head, the treetops waved against the silver sky: clouds or a haze of smoke blotting out the sun?

Halfway up, he became aware of a strange clacking noise. He paused, hands scraped and burning.

"Stop for a minute," he shouted down to Ricky. "I hear something."

Below him, Ricky paused and looked up. Danny strained to hear past the American's gasps for air.

There! The clacking wasn't random, but rhythmical. What the hell was it? It couldn't be human. No people out here.

He took a deep breath to ease the thumping of his heart. Odd things happened out in the woods. Once he and his dad had followed a weird noise for miles only to find that it was a broken branch rubbing against a half-fallen tree.

As Danny and Ricky climbed higher the strange sound stayed with them, growing then waning, sometimes vanishing altogether.

A flat smooth area dead ahead. Danny flopped face down onto it, breathing hard. He rested on his belly for a few moments, rolled over and sat up.

He'd reached the top. All around him the forest stretched out in a swelling green sea.

"We did it," he yelled down to Ricky. "We're above the treetops." Only the top of a single, tall pine tree broke his view. It rose twenty feet away from him, directly in front of the outcropping.

Breathing easier now, he saw that he was balanced on a flat, narrow ridge of stone. The side he had climbed was sharp but negotiable. The opposite side, the one he was staring down now, had a much steeper smooth stretch of rock that broke off into a sheer cliff, tumbling down to the forest floor thirty feet below.

He stood up, keeping well back from the dangerous edge, shielding his eyes against the brightness. Far to the west, black smoke shrouded the trees. So the forest fire *had* hit the mainland. Damn it, why did he have to be right all the time?

He scanned the northeastern woods. Where was the mine? It had to be there.

A flash of light at the point where the trees met the horizon. Could that be sunlight reflecting off a glass window in the abandoned mine building?

"I think I found it!" he shouted to Ricky who was labouring up the last piece of the climb. "Hurry up, I need your binoculars."

The clacking noise started up again. Now he heard a second sound, a strange cawing, like a deep-throated baby crying, coming from the cliff side of the ridge.

The single pine tree in front of the ridge lurched and swayed. He got back down on his hands and knees and cautiously peered over the edge.

In the tree, about mid-height, he spotted a brown shape. Hard to make out what it was through the thick tree branches.

The shape moved: it was a baby bear.

"Heads up." Ricky heaved his bulk onto the ridge, face slick with sweat, his vest muddy. He crawled over to the spot next to Danny.

The tree thrashed violently. It sounded close to breaking.

"What the hell is that?" Ricky pointed down at the tree.

"It's an animal. Ignore it." The cries burst out again, frantic, fear-stricken. "Give me your binoculars."

"We don't need 'em. I know what that is. Fresh meat." In a fluid motion, Ricky stood up and pulled the crossbow off his back.

"Are you crazy? It's a bear cub. Leave it alone."

Ricky slid a steel bolt into the bow.

"I said stop it."

Ricky lifted the bow and took aim. Danny lunged at him.

The bolt exploded out of the bow and winged over the treetops, wildly off course.

"You little jerk!" Ricky shoved him hard. "That's a stainless steel bolt you owe me."

"Stop it! Mama Bear just showed up."

Down on the forest floor, a dark shape melted out of the trees. At first glance, it looked like a matted black rug slung loosely over a wooden frame that had mysteriously come to life. The mother bear looked nothing like the round, well-fed animals scooping up spawning salmon in wildlife documentaries. Starvation had melted the stores of fat from her body.

The bear swung her head back and forth, sniffing the air, uttering the strange clacking sound Danny had heard on the way up.

"Keep quiet. For God's sake, don't move," he whispered.

"What's Mama Bear gonna do?" Ricky said at full volume. "Climb up and eat us for dinner?"

"Yes! Bears can climb anything. And she's hungry for two."

"Bull crap."

"She's trying to rescue her cub out of the tree. If she sees us, she'll go for us. Get back! Keep out of sight."

The mother bear rubbed her snout against the trunk of the pine tree, crying to her cub. A branch gave way. The cub let out a shriek and tumbled. A nest of branches broke its fall a few feet down the trunk.

The mother reared up into the tree. More caws and cries. The cub began an ungainly backwards struggle down the tree like a trapped house cat.

"Hey, Ugly Face," Ricky screamed down at the bear.

"Shut up, you idiot."

The cub let out a screech, bounced out of the tree and rolled onto the ground. The mother nuzzled it, coaxing it up onto its feet.

Ricky slid a fresh bolt into his bow. "Heads up, Mama Bear. Yeah, you too, Monster Baby. The nice hunter's brought you a big surprise."

The mother bear huffed at the air, instantly alert. She gazed up at the ridge.

Oh, hell, Danny thought.

His first instinct was to scramble back down the side they'd just climbed up and run for it, but that wouldn't help. Black bears could cover ground at thirty miles an hour. If he and Ricky managed to escape into the woods, the thickly growing trees had bare, thin trunks with no low branches they could use for climbing. And even if by some miracle they were able to get up a tree, black bears had powerful claws. And they were expert climbers.

The mother bear padded over to the cliff, rolling effortlessly over the rocks, the cub behind her. She reared up onto her hind legs, looking for a way up.

Ricky raised the bow. "I call this a two-fer. Two for one."

"Put that bow down."

"Pray I get her first strike or she'll be chewing your skinny butt for dinner." Ricky narrowed his small blue eyes, aiming. "Oh, sweet baby, Daddy's gonna bring you down."

Danny smashed his fist into Ricky's meaty cheek with everything he had.

Ricky staggered back. Spun with startling swiftness. And crashed the bow down on Danny's shoulder.

Pain shot through his arm. He fell and hit the stone platform. Momentum hurtled him out and over the ridge.

He threw out his arms, clutching madly at the rock face to break his slide. Gravity sucked him down, scraping him over weeds, gravel and stone. He dug in his heels, twisted and rolled.

Miraculously he stopped moving.

Pain screamed from his torn and bloody hands. He had landed sideways across the rise, wedged between a boulder and the granite face. Looking up, he could make out the outline of the ridge about fifteen feet above him.

He flexed his arms and legs; nothing seemed to be broken.

An unearthly roar rattled through the woods. The mother bear.

Gotta get back up there.

He dragged himself out of the niche behind the boulder and started crawling back up, ignoring the pain from a dozen scratches.

The bear roared again, a bellow of rage.

Pasha was dead. Two more animals were about to die because of Ricky's grotesque sense of entitlement, his aggressive, egotistical greed.

White-hot fury spurred him up the last few feet.

But when he reached the ridge, the stone platform was empty. No Ricky, no crossbow. He dropped down on all fours and bellied across the ridge to look down the opposite side.

Ricky was clinging spread-eagled to the steeply pitched stretch of rock that broke off into the cliff.

And below him the mother bear was closing in, showing her cub how to hunt.

25

"Ricky!" Danny shouted. "Are you OK?"

"No." Ricky winced, let out a cough. A thin worm of blood tracked down from his nose. "Guess you're gonna let me slide over."

"Hang on, I'll pull you back up."

"Forget it."

Danny crouched down. "Heads up, where are you hurt? Can you move?"

"Yeah, but ..." Ricky licked his lips. "Gotta a thing ... gotta a thing about heights."

Danny lay flat and leaned down over the steep rock face, bracing his weight on his hands, trying to get a closer look at where Ricky had landed.

From what he could see, nothing but friction was holding Ricky up. Ricky had travelled down the smoothly sloping rock to a spot where his boots rested six inches from the sharp cliff edge. If he slipped any further, he'd tumble thirty feet straight down into the bear's waiting jaws. As if on cue, she let out a cry that rattled through the trees.

The noise shattered Ricky out of his daze. His hands twitched on the rock. "Where is she? Is she coming up?"

The bear stood on the forest floor directly beneath him. She stretched her neck, sniffing and huffing at the air, working out the best way to reach the protein hanging so tantalizing overhead. The cub mimicked her motions, barking like an oversized dog.

"She's just wandering around and crap," Danny said. No point in panicking Ricky further.

"Guess you'll laugh when she spreads my guts out over the forest," Ricky said.

"Shut up. What's holding you up? I can't see from here."

"A big piece of rock jammed up my butt."

"You'll have to do better than that. Help me out here."

Sweat soaked Ricky's cropped hair. He squinted as though he were seeking a ship on the horizon. "OK, my right knee is wedged in a crack or something," he said.

Danny levered his body back to the safety of the ridge. He rubbed his face, trying to think. "Have you got a rope in that big vest of yours?"

"No, uh-uh. Nothing."

"OK, give me a minute." He'd have to climb back down to the forest floor and cut a thick branch long enough to reach Ricky. The bat-winged skinning knife would work perfectly, but it was out on the cliff with him.

"I'm sliding, man," Ricky called up. "If you're gonna help, now would be a good time."

Near the far end of the ridge, Danny spotted a crest of stone rising up from the edge. Ricky had at least fifty pounds on him, but if he could wrap his arm around that piece of rock and brace himself, he might be able to counterbalance the excess weight.

Quickly he tore off his runners and stripped down to his skivvies. He knotted one leg of his jeans firmly around his right forearm, got down on his stomach and curled his left arm around the rise of stone. He flung the free leg of his jeans down over the steeply sloping stone to reach Ricky. The frayed cuff brushed the top of the American's left hand.

"Grab onto my jeans. Use them like a rope," Danny shouted down. "I'll try to pull you up."

"Are you kidding me? A light beer has more strength than you."

"Quit arguing. Grab my jeans and press down on your right knee. Roll onto your right side, bend your left leg and get your left foot under you. Lean forward and climb back up."

"Forget it."

"You're right, forget it. You're so fat even Godzilla on steroids couldn't haul you up."

Ricky mumbled something inaudible.

"Come on, man, this is your only chance. What are you waiting for?" Danny said.

"Can't ..."

The bear let out a dark growl. Instinctively Ricky glanced over his shoulder. He swore and leaned his forehead against the stone.

"Don't look down. Pretend you're on the beach climbing a boulder."

A blur of motion. The bear reared up, clawing the air. "She's going for my legs," Ricky shouted. "She's gonna tear off my legs."

"Then move!"

"What part of 'forget it' don't you understand?"

"OK, fine, stay there. Let her eat you alive, piece by piece."

"Yeah, and when I fall, she's gonna tear me apart, so what's the difference?"

"What happened to your manhood? Guess it shrank in the wash. That's why you shot a tame bear. To fool everyone into thinking you're a man, you stupid nark."

Ricky let out a roar. He threw out his beefy left arm and seized the jeans.

The fabric clamped down on Danny's forearm in a brutal tourniquet.

Ricky leaned back, balancing precariously on his right knee. His two-hundred-plus pounds started dragging them down ruthlessly.

"Roll onto your side," Danny bit out. Ricky made to roll left. "The other way, damn it."

Ricky crashed down on his right side, legs dangling over the cliff. His free right hand scrabbled for a hold on the rock. His left foot slid and kicked to get purchase on the slippery granite.

"Get your feet under you. God ..." Danny wheezed in agony. The pain in his arm was beyond bearing, as though blood were bursting through the ends of his fingers.

Ricky let out a bellow to match the bear's. Suddenly he rose up on both feet in a sprinter's crouch. And made a wild leap for the ledge.

The force of Ricky's jump wrenched Danny's arm across his chest. Momentum tossed him off the ridge onto the sloping rock face. He slid down on his back, hanging by the arm tied to his jeans. He dug in his heels, groping madly for a hold with his free hand.

An agonizing wrench in his shoulder: he'd stopped sliding.

He rolled onto his front. Ricky lay prone on the ridge on top of the jeans. His bulk had saved Danny from sliding the rest of the way.

Danny managed to crawl back up to the safety of the ledge. He collapsed next to Ricky.

For several minutes, he lay on his back, staring up at the grey sky, listening to the wind groaning through the treetops. Blood from a cut inside his cheek leaked down his throat. His scratches burned like fire.

The odour of Ricky's pungent sweat flooded over him. He sat up and spat blood. "Get off my jeans. You're killing my arm," he said.

Ricky flopped onto his back, belly heaving with each breath. Danny tugged his jeans free, fighting to unsnarl the fabric knotted round his arm.

Finally loose, he flexed his fingers, but that only ramped up the pain. He untangled his pants and slipped them back on.

"What's the bear doing?" Ricky asked from where he was lying.

Danny had to force himself to lean over the cliff edge once more. He looked straight down into the mother bear's face. She eyed him curiously, grunted, reared up on her hind legs and swatted at him, black claws flashing.

"She's still there." He looked around for his shoes. "We're safe until she figures out how to climb up here."

"My bow," Ricky's hands groped the stone around him.

"Don't see it."

Ricky hauled himself to his feet, vest and pants torn, bare arms blotched with bruises. "You know what that bow cost me? Seven thousand dollars. You owe me. Don't think I won't collect."

"You shouldn't have pushed me," Danny shrugged. He found his runners and shoved them on. "And you shouldn't have tried to shoot those bears for nothing."

"Look down there and tell me bears are cuddly, you stupid tree hugger," Ricky said.

"If you want to stay out of her stomach, shut up. Bears are unpredictable." *And dangerous.* "If we're lucky, she'll opt for easier food and leave."

"How long will that take?"

"No idea." Bears are intelligent, skillful problem solvers, Danny knew. The mother might not give up at all. Odds were she'd dive back into the woods, find their scent and follow their tracks up the easier side of the rise.

A trivial climb for her and the cub.

Rachel landed on her hands and knees in the grass outside the back of Barry's office. Pointed pieces of broken glass like daggers lay everywhere.

"It's that bloody kid," Santa shouted after her through the broken window. "Stop her. Go get her."

She could hear him scrambling and tripping over the mess of furniture in the spare room. She daren't look back. She bolted away from Barry's cabin, heading straight down to the lake and the centre of camp.

"Rachel, Rachel Forest," she heard Barry call behind her. "Come back here! People, stop her."

She raced past a cluster of shed-like cabins where the youngest campers slept. She could hear Barry and Santa's shouts above the chatter of the white-shirted kids streaming out of the cook tent. They turned to stare as she tore past them.

She was running so fast, her breath was giving out by the time she reached the wooden dock fronting the lake. The battered canoes and piles of soiled life jackets offered no place to hide.

Footsteps were slapping the hard ground behind her. She turned left, leaving the dock behind her and headed out of camp, taking the long sloping footpath that led up into the woods. Running was agony. Her legs were tiring, slowing her down. Lungs bursting, her breath raw in her throat, she struggled to the top of the hill and limped past the remains of the rotten picnic bench that had served as Barry's craft table.

She found the familiar trail to Logan's zoo.

Luckily the path was flat. She half-ran, half-walked along it, her breath coming in wheezes. It took forever before she spotted the decaying, black-stained arcade booths at the end of the path.

Logan, where was Logan?

She dared not shout for him: Barry and Santa would hear her calling. They'd know exactly where she was.

Adult voices behind her. If she ran down to the booths and the old cafeteria building, they'd see her and catch her. She looked around frantically. And spotted a faded sign marked 'Woodland Trail' that pointed into the trees.

She stumbled over to the sign and recognized a narrow dirt trail that led away from the booths. She remembered how it plunged through the trees and ran along the cliffs edging Red Dog Lake. It was the same path she and Dad had followed past the empty animal cages, the path with no guardrails.

Breathing a little easier now, she fled down the Woodland Trail. She left the abandoned cages behind; they were traps for her, not hiding places. She reached a curve in the trail. She stopped and listened. The sigh of the waves of Red Dog Lake sounded very loud now.

"Where is she? Where'd she go? God, my bloody leg ..." she heard Santa say. He and Barry sounded very close behind her. They hadn't searched for her in the arcade booths: they'd followed her down the Woodland Trail.

They'll catch me for sure!

She left the track and dived into the brush beside it. She shoved and clawed her way through a thick clump of alders. Falling onto her hands and knees, she kept going, struggling blindly through tangles of twigs and leaves.

Suddenly, the knife edge of the cliff appeared in front of her: a startling schism six inches away from her hands. She gasped and stared down at the dark shale beach one hundred feet below.

"We've ended up in Logan's bloody zoo," Santa said. He must be standing on the trail about ten feet directly behind her. Only the alder bushes stood between them. "This is as far as I go," he panted. "That Logan's a bloody maniac."

She dared not move. She crouched in the leaves, waiting, listening. She heard Santa and Barry continue a little way further down the path.

"She always runs over to visit Logan," Barry coughed out. "I'll call the police again. They'll bring her back."

"Oh, *very* intelligent, my son. Print out the directions to your special websites while you're at it, why don't you? No, Mate, you waddle over to Logan's and bring her back."

"What if she won't come?"

"You squealing mouse, you're bigger than she is."

"What if Logan's there?"

"Pull your poncey officious act, the one you're so good at. Go on, bring her back here and I'll deal with her."

"What do you mean 'deal with her'?" Silence, except for a wheeze from Barry. "That-that's a bad joke, Merry."

"I'm not joking."

Where were the other campers? Where were the camp counsellors? Rachel prayed for the sound of more footsteps above the noise of the waves and wind.

But nobody else was coming down the trail.

26

The wooden float plane dock was a grey tongue stretching out into the waters of Red Dog Lake. High overcast, bit of haze, Corazon noted. Waves low, fine for takeoff. But she wasn't: she felt dry and hollow. Her legs were trembling as though she'd galloped five miles uphill.

It had taken her one or two seconds to make up her mind what to do. Her kitchen staff wanted her to call the cops, but McKenna was the last person she wanted to see right now. She'd fed them a lame lie about misfiring her shotgun. They didn't believe her, of course, but out of respect, they let it go. Everyone in Red Dog Lake knew Corazon Sinclair solved her own problems.

Finally alone, she'd stripped off her tunic and satin pants and pulled on jeans, a plaid shirt and her leather aviator jacket. On her way out, she'd stopped by the diner, grabbed some sandwiches out of the cooler and made up a thermos of coffee. Edgar was eagerly stuffing down the Trucker's Special – free of charge courtesy of the Galaxy Tavern. That should keep him busy, she thought. In a moment of foolish weakness, she'd promised to fly him up to see his mum. Maybe those fat-laden calories would make him forget the idea.

She had to move fast. She'd slipped out through the kitchen, wheeled her old Harley Davidson out of her private garage behind the motel and taken off.

Half an hour later, she was stowing her tool box back in her Piper Cherokee when she recognized the roar of the Christmas Hummer. She leapt for her shotgun resting on the pilot's seat, but when the Hummer pulled up at the end of the dock, it was only Edgar, not Santa, who climbed out.

Damn, Corazon thought. Doing what she had to do had taken far too long.

She released her grip on the gun and shoved it into its usual spot beside the pilot's chair. She watched Edgar jog down the dock to join her beside her Piper Cherokee PA-32S-300 seaplane.

"This is real nice of you, Corazon," Edgar panted. "Flying me out to see my mum before you go pick up those hunters. There's still time, right?"

"Sure, Baby." She rubbed her face, praying the trucker's caffeine tablets she'd downed would do their job.

She began her flight checklist. Edgar was immediately bored, twirling his elf hat and chewing on his thumbnail. Well, tough, she thought. She worked methodically through her list: wings, struts, floats, propellers, tail boom, all go.

She wiped the sweat off her face. "OK, let's get up in the air."

Edgar leapt nimbly onto the nearest float and shovelled himself into the cockpit through the open pilot's door. She watched him climb into the passenger seat, strap himself in, and slip on his mike and earphones with practised ease.

"You've flown a lot," she remarked. Edgar smiled in crafty complicity.

Her turn now. She untied the moorings and jumped, nearly sliding off the float. Getting inside was an ungainly struggle. She was too slow starting the engine and had to steer frantically to avoid the dock and pull the plane back onto a straight course to head out into the lake.

Edgar found the whole process amusing, the little jerk. She reminded herself to stay patient, for a while anyway.

She settled back into the pilot's chair, pleased that her cockpit looked perfectly neat, the way it always did. She taxied out into unobstructed water, running down her interior checklist: windshield wipers – check; radio – check; altimeter – check. Strange, she could taste smoke on the air blowing in through the open pilot's window.

She knew that smell. She'd lived through several forest fires.

Danny! She lunged for the radio. She'd call Morty now, make sure the hunters weren't just sleeping off their pricey liquor.

"You OK, Corazon?" Edgar was staring at her.

"Of course, I'm OK." She slammed the radio back into position.

"I mean, are you OK landing on Buggy Lake? It's real remote, you know."

"Yeah, I know that. And I know for a fact that its real name is Bouge Lake."

"Well, we all call it Buggy Lake. Look, maybe you could just fly me in to Kirkland Lake and I'll hitch a ride or something."

"Takes a day to drive from Kirkland Lake to Small Trout Falls. And another day to walk in to your so-called Buggy Lake." Corazon squinted at the dials on the controls. Compass – check; flaps – check. "This way I'll have us back by suppertime." Edgar looked thoughtful. "Don't get scared, Big Guy. I've landed on hundreds of lakes." She'd even landed on Buggy Lake once, but why tell him?

"Oh, I'm not saying you're not a good pilot. It's just that, well, now that I'm really going, I feel nervous." He rubbed his nose. "I miss my mum so bad. I haven't talked to her for six months."

"Long time." Battery – check; flight controls – check; clock – check … "Doesn't she have a phone?"

"No, uh-uh, no phone at my Aunt Vera's place. I would've wrote Mum, but Vera really hates me. She'd tear up my letters before Mum could read 'em."

Great, Corazon thought, growing more and more convinced this flight was a bad idea.

"Thanks for the shirt," Edgar said, stroking the Galaxy T-shirt he had on under his greasy overalls. "I should've had a bath, too, I guess. I really want to look nice for my mum."

"Quiet!" Corazon said, more sharply than she'd intended. She stared at the gas gauge, grabbed her logbook and flipped to her last entry. She'd filled up after flying out the hunters on Friday: 386 litres. Now the gauge indicated 200.

"Nobody touches my plane," she said. "Who touched my plane? Did Santa touch my goddamn plane?"

"No, no," Edgar shook his head wildly. "He doesn't know how to fly."

"What about your pilot, Tear Drop? What about Santa's creepy buddy, that Hendrix guy?"

"Mr. Hendrix and Tear Drop just use the Twin Beech, I swear."

"And what about you, Edgar? You seem to know your way around my plane pretty good."

"No, Corazon, I never touched your plane. I swear to God I didn't."

Edgar could swear all he liked but, in reality, anybody could have taken her plane. Like the other float planes, it rested at the dock unguarded. And nobody locked their planes in Red Dog Lake.

"Never mind, relax, Baby." Important to keep him happy. "But I need to turn around and gas up. How much cash you got?"

"Oh, um, I'm kind of cleaned out," he said. "Charmaine needed grocery money."

"Well, that's real helpful."

"I know you two don't see eye to eye, but Charmaine's a nice girl. Santa doesn't treat her right." He looked away. "He's a real jerk."

"You got that right." Corazon frowned. Time was getting short. "Forget it. We gotta get moving."

She revved the engine and headed into the wind. Takeoff in a float plane was always tricky. The ends of the floats dragged and tended to throw the nose forward. Worst case scenario, they could porpoise and capsize you.

She felt the familiar abrupt lurch as the floats lifted free of the sticky water. The nose of the Piper Cherokee swung up alarmingly; she moved swiftly to correct it.

"Scary," Edgar said through his mike as they levelled out. "I could take over on the way home if you want."

"You don't have your pilot's licence," she shot back, eyes on the dials while the plane chugged up to cruising altitude.

He shrugged. "It's just a piece of paper."

"I see, so piloting a bush plane is just a little skill you picked up, like playing elf at Santa's Fish Camp. But then you've packed in plenty of practice flying those great big loads for Santa."

"I don't know what you're talking about."

"Sure you do. Hey, I admire you for flying Santa's Twin Beech fifty miles out to Fire Island with a four-hundred-pound bear in the hold. Risk-taker, aren't you, Big Guy? You tranked her, sure, but what if you got the dose wrong and she woke up while you were still in the air? She'd have torn you to pieces before you hit the ground."

"What do you mean 'she'?"

"Come off it. We both know the bear was Pasha. Santa was just being practical, I can accept that. Besides he doesn't have the *cojones* to track down and capture a real wild bear."

"I figured there was a catch, you flying me up to Buggy Lake to see my mum. You just want to pick my brain." He stared out the window, sucking the inside of his cheek.

Buggy Lake, bug brain. Corazon thought. You'll be begging to spill your fat, greasy guts by the time I've finished with you.

Danny stood on the ridge of the granite outcropping, staring at the black tornado of smoke to the west. He tried to tell himself that the forest fire wasn't closing in on them. Below them, he could hear the growls of the mother bear and the chirps of her cub as they paced back and forth at the base of the cliff.

"How long are Mama and Baby Bear gonna keep it up?" Ricky asked. He had rolled up his pant leg and was daubing antiseptic cream on his many scratches.

"Till one of us jumps down and gives her dinner," Danny said. He could have used some of that medicine cream himself.

The sun burned down on them through the overcast. All he could think about was the muddy stream at the base of the rise. How much longer could he stand it up here without water?

"You know Raven McKenna?" Ricky asked, pitching the empty tube of cream over the side.

"Sure, I know Raven. She's with the OPP in Toronto. She grew up in Red Dog Lake."

"Yeah, I overlook that ugly fact on account of she's one hell of a cop."

"Raven's your contact, isn't she?"

Ricky reached into his combat vest, pulled out a slim leather folder and handed it to Danny.

Danny flipped open the ID and stared at Ricky's badge. "Special Agent Thomas Rudd, Federal Bureau of Investigation. There is no Ricky Fountain, is there?"

"Sure, there is. Ricky and I are buds, we hunt together. He loaned me his ID, trained me up. His son got into meth."

Danny closed the folder and handed it back. "You're American. You don't have jurisdiction up here in Canada."

Ricky grinned. "Cross-border project. You Canadians needed our help like always."

"Hendrix set up a meth lab with Santa, didn't he?" Danny said.

"No kidding. Hendrix and Santa are old buddies. Done a lot of stuff together."

"Then why haven't you taken out those two ratholes? We don't need outsiders like Hendrix and Santa spreading their crap around Red Dog Lake."

"We want to take Hendrix down for a lot more than one baby meth lab. That's how come I went gunning for bear."

"You bastard!" Danny leapt up. "I should push you over the edge. I should have let you fall. Watched the bears eat you alive. You got everybody killed!"

"Hey, cool your jets, Danny boy."

"Hendrix knew you were a nark. That's why he killed everyone on Fire Island. That's why he's after us now. Scorched earth, kill all the witnesses just like you said."

"Shut up!" Ricky bounded up, massive as a mountain. "You hear that?"

"Hear what?"

A faint whine below the wind. A dark mosquito-like smudge appeared on the north horizon. *Oh God, let it be Corazon, not Hendrix again.*

Ricky jerked the binoculars out of his vest pocket and stared through the sights, tracking the plane's trajectory. "I see your stupid mine by the way," he said. "Right where you said it was."

"What colour is the plane?" Danny asked. *Make it be red and white. Please God, make it be red and white.*

The aircraft floated over the faraway trees between them and the horizon, tracking lazy arcs back and forth. "It's heading our way," Ricky said, the binoculars fixed to his face.

"What colour is it?"

"Silver." Ricky lowered the binoculars.

Danny recognized the sound of the engine now. Not the spin of Corazon's Piper Cherokee, but the vibrating throb of the silver-skinned Twin Beech that had hunted them out on the lake.

And they were completely exposed up here on the ridge.

"Get down!" Ricky flung himself flat onto the stone.

Danny threw himself down next to Ricky. The plane appeared, skimming over the trees. It sailed over them in a deadly boom that echoed through the rocks of the outcropping. The downdraft blew down on them, twirling the treetops.

It roared away, banking over the pines to the south behind them.

"They saw us. They're turning around," Danny shouted.

But Ricky was laughing like a crazy man and pointing down the cliff.

Terrified by the noise, the mother bear was galloping into the woods, her cub struggling to keep up with her.

"And keep running, you ugly mothers," Ricky screamed.

Danny grabbed Ricky's arm. "We've got to get out of here."

Ricky stowed away the binoculars. "You first, Boy Scout."

Danny didn't hesitate. He plunged down the rock face, biting back the pain in his hands, jumping, sliding, anything to move faster. Ricky followed, in a clattering of loose pebbles and dirt.

The whine of the engine was getting louder and louder. And then the plane came screaming down on them.

A sharp sliver of rock pinged away a foot above Danny's head. "They're shooting!" he yelled.

Rocks and earth rose in a narrow fountain. Snaked up the slope. Ricky cried out.

He crumpled, lost his grip on the stone.

And then he was rolling and sliding. Crashing past Danny, rolling and sliding and falling.

All the way down to the bottom of the rise, where he didn't move at all.

27

"RICKY!" Danny shouted.

Ricky lay on his side, as still as a stone dropped from a balcony. Danny pushed off the rock. He slid down, oblivious to the pain that screamed from his hands.

Ricky had fallen near the muddy spot where water oozed out from the outcropping. Danny stumbled over to him.

"Hell of a way to get a drink of water," Ricky coughed out.

The silver plane had disappeared out over the trees. From the rev of its engine, Danny could tell that the pilot was banking again.

Turning back for another go at them.

"We've got to get into the trees," Danny said.

"Can't ..." Ricky gasped in pain and rolled onto his back. Blood soaked through his combat vest.

The roar of propellers. Bearing down on them quickly.

"GET UP!" Danny seized Ricky's shoulder. "Help me!"

Ricky threw out one hefty arm. Danny hauled it over his shoulder. Using the downward slope of the rise to help him, he tried to rock the beefy American onto his feet.

Ricky grunted in pain. "Can't do it ..."

Danny summoned his last shreds of strength, joints and muscles burning. "Help me or we're both dead!"

Ricky got one foot on the ground, dragged the other over, and leaned on Danny like a drunk hard off a bender.

A flash of silver: the plane.

Now they were caught.

The plane hovered over them at near-stall speed. "Under the trees!" Danny shouted, but the noise of the engine drowned him out.

Bullets thwacked into the mud inches from where they were struggling, chewed into the rock face and winged into the trees lining the rise.

It was over in seconds.

The plane passed over them and disappeared over the trees. Danny heard the by-now familiar banking and turning.

"Close one," Ricky wheezed. "You OK?"

"Don't talk, move!" *Must get into the trees.*

Ricky streamed with sweat, labouring as though they were trudging through deep mud. "Need to ... need to sit down." He flailed at the low-hanging branches with his free arm as they passed into the darkness under the pines.

The plane stormed back over the rise. Impossible to spot it through the canopy of trees.

Ricky's beefy arm slipped off Danny's shoulders. Danny fought to hold him up, but Ricky's weight dragged him off balance. Together they thudded heavily onto the ground.

"Come on, man. We have to go in deeper," Danny urged him.

"Sorry, Kid, no can do."

A heartbeat later, bullets thumped and pinged down through the branches of the pines and maples around them.

Danny dug his fingers into the dirt, desperate for the bullets to stop.

Rachel crouched behind the alder bushes, listening to Barry and Santa argue.

"Even if ... even if for one moment I thought you were serious," Barry was saying, "the whole camp saw us chase after her. People will follow us down the trail."

"She heard every bloody word we said. She'll tell everyone about your special hobby. You'll be out of a job, Dear Heart," Santa said.

"She's a liar. No one will believe her."

"All I'm saying is that accidents happen. Everyone says Logan should've put up a fence here twenty years ago. He'll be blamed. Bit of a blot on your camp's copybook, but you'll weather it."

"That's insane. You'd push a kid over the cliff just to get back at Logan. You're as crazy as he is."

"Fine then, take your chances. Give me the keys to your *Prius*." Santa snapped his fingers. "Stop dawdling. Hand them over."

"No, never. You can't have my car. You can't have it."

"Give me those bloody keys!"

Barry screamed. Grunts of effort. Slaps and blows. A huge thrashing of foliage as the two men grappled and crashed violently through the bushes. Rolling toward the spot where Rachel was hiding.

They'll knock me over the cliff.

She clawed away from their struggle, groping through snarls of weeds and branches. The cold wind blowing up from the lake seemed like it was dragging on her bare arms and legs, pulling her over the cliff edge.

She fought through the brush, pushing away from the deadly fall. Twigs stuck in her clothes like thorns. She felt like she was drowning in leaves.

At last she broke free and landed on the dirt path. In the bushes a short distance away, the two men fought and screamed like animals.

She shot down the Woodland Trail, not knowing where it led. All around her nothing but trees. Even the derelict animal cages had vanished.

Light faded this deep in the forest. Where did the trail go? Did it stop at a dead end somewhere? She'd have to turn around. They'd see her. She'd be trapped.

The path was curving to the right now, sloping down away from the lake. Something glimmered in the distance just beyond the trees: the rusty bars of Pasha's cage.

Her breath was coming in great heaves. She ran up to the cage. A familiar figure was sitting inside it.

She grabbed the cold, scratchy bars and screamed: "LOGAN!"

He stirred and looked at her with unseeing eyes.

Danny sat up. He could hear the plane droning above the forest, the noise of the engine growing louder, then fainter.

"He's circling us," he said to Ricky's prone form. "He's crazy obsessed. Maybe he'll run out of gas."

"Let's hope," Ricky muttered. He rolled onto his back, squinting at the dim light filtering down through the pine branches. "Did they stop shooting?"

"For now. How bad are you hurt?"

"Bad, Kid. I'm gut-shot."

So a bullet had found Ricky. Danny swallowed, feeling the prickling of sweat down his back. Here he'd been hoping, praying, that Ricky had been hit by a rock fragment, something that would give him a bad cut, not a mortal injury ...

Ricky tried to sit up.

"Take it easy," Danny said. "I'll help you."

Ricky protested but let Danny drag him over and prop him up against the nearest pine tree. He braced his back against the trunk, his legs stretched in front of him, and fumbled with the zipper of his combat vest. " Gotta ... gotta take a look," he said.

"Let me do it."

Ricky dropped his hands. Danny unzipped the vest. To his relief, he couldn't see anything. He was about to call Ricky a whiner when he spotted a small black hole leaking fluid three inches from Ricky's navel.

"Hey, it doesn't look too bad," he managed. "Looks like your vest took most of the impact. The bleeding's stopped. Well, mostly anyway."

"Like hell." Ricky winced, clutched his naked belly. "Come here. Run your hand down my back."

"What for?" Danny asked, though he knew Ricky wanted him to feel for an exit wound.

"Just do it." Ricky leaned forward.

Danny knelt down beside him. He slipped his hand under the vest. The skin on Ricky's back felt cold and rubbery, his body hair tickled Danny's palm. "This feels weird," he said.

"Don't worry, you're not my type."

Danny ran his hand up and down over the right half of Ricky's back. "You're solid there," he said. He stretched farther to reach Ricky's left side.

Now he felt fluid: a lot of it, close to where he guessed Ricky's left kidney would be. And he felt something else, a hard metal lump.

"What you got?" Ricky asked.

Danny pulled his arm free and sat back. His hand was bathed in dark blood to the wrist. "It's the bullet, I think."

"Let me see."

Danny spread his palm. Ricky bent over to examine it.

"Looks like it passed through you. That's better, right?" Danny said.

Ricky choked out a laugh, rolling his cropped head against the rough bark of the pine tree. "Stick it in your pocket. Do it!" He waited until Danny slipped it into his jeans. He wiped his face with his hand. "So thirsty."

Bad sign, Danny knew. Means he's hemorrhaging. "Stop whining," he said. "That bullet just sailed through your fat. That's your natural body armour."

"Funny guy."

"Hey, one of my Fortin cousins is a three hundred pounder. His ex shot him six times, but the bullets got stuck in his fat. He lived and she got off with a suspended sentence."

"I'd tell you to go to hell only I'm too tired." Ricky slumped against the tree.

"Come on, I'll fix you up. Give me your first aid kit." Danny held out his hand. "Come on, all you white tourists carry one."

"No point."

"Listen, we *saw* the mine. It's maybe two, three miles at most. We can do it, man."

"Nice try." Ricky reached into his vest and pulled out a small metal tin. "Here, take it." Even in the dimming afternoon light, he looked much paler.

Danny took the first aid kit from him and pried open the lid. The fixings inside were meant for casual scratches and insect bites, no help for a serious injury. He took out the roll of white medical tape. "OK, now I need your knife," he said to Ricky's stare.

A minute passed.

Ricky pulled out the skinning knife and dropped it on the ground next to his thigh.

Danny hesitated, listening. "I don't hear that plane any more. You?"

"No, nothing. Maybe he's on break."

"Good. I'll be right back," Danny said. He grabbed the knife and ran back toward the outcropping.

At the edge of the forest he paused, straining to hear the slightest sound. Still no sign of the plane.

Where had it gone? Why had it left?

A thin, acrid mist was drifting down the slope of the rise. Smoke!

That's why Hendrix had left. From the air he would have seen how fast the forest fire was moving and where it was headed. Why risk sticking around? Why not let the fire do his job for him and wipe Ricky and Danny out?

The flames must be nearly on top of them.

28

Rusty stains streamed down the greening concrete of Pasha's cage to the centre drain where Logan squatted in silence, Odile's Winchester rifle resting across his knees. Time had become elliptical and malleable. His past drew closer and closer, chasing him along a parallel track like a ghostly train, one that he stepped on and off freely, though the crossings now fell less and less under his control.

At times, such as now, the corroded bars of the bear cage would melt into the tall grass of the jungle. The Winchester became his M16, and the darkness within him bled out into an inky night that submerged the cage entirely even in midday. The quiet northern forest slowly filled with the rustlings of vividly coloured birds and sleek snakes, the creeping of thick vines, and the muffled footsteps of insurgents.

He'd fought being drafted. Not just because he opposed the Vietnam War, but because he bore a deep-seated, inborn mistrust of all governments and their endeavours, especially their haphazard choices of enemies and battles. He despised them all, from the White House down to the social workers who had taken him away after his father, The Preacher, died.

He had only faint memories of his mother, a pale shadow of a woman who was silently and unquestioningly obedient to her husband, The Preacher. She'd eloped with him to Montana when she was only thirteen years old to his forty-seven. Giving birth to Logan had nearly killed her; hard times had finished her off, leaving Logan and the Preacher alone. Logan figured his father kept him around for one reason only. As a sweet-faced youngster, he pulled in plenty of dollars and sympathy on the revival circuit and, more importantly, the women eager to comfort a poor lonely widower.

In their early years together, the Preacher did well expounding the Word of God. Usually he'd make more than enough to sustain the two of them through the brutal Montana winters, which they spent holed up in a log cabin deep in the woods. The Preacher held strong, idiosyncratic beliefs about the ungodliness of the public school system and a true, Christian education. He made Logan memorize long passages from the Bible and trained him how to speak in tongues, while refusing to teach him how to read and write. Logan learned how to hunt and fish, and how to brew moonshine in the radiator of The Preacher's derelict pickup. The lead that leached from the solder etched blue-black lines through the old man's gums, but that didn't stop the women wanting him. Logan would huddle outside the cabin, summer or winter, while his father had his way with them.

As Logan approached puberty, the lonely forest no longer calmed The Preacher. Instead it incubated his hatred of outsiders and the government. He became convinced that the aluminum fibres running through the dollar bills were wire taps inserted by the CIA, and burned their savings in the wood stove. He abandoned the revival circuit. To survive, they were forced to live off the land and the locals' garbage. Alarmed reports about a wild-haired man foraging behind houses and stores, and the gaunt, starving boy he kept with him, brought down the social workers.

For a time The Preacher managed to elude them, dragging Logan deep into the woods whenever he spotted their cars on the dirt road to the cabin. He used their subpoenas and court orders to light his wood stove, and took potshots at their retreating vehicles. But even as a child, Logan understood that that bizarre existence had to come to an end.

Logan raised his head, listening to the whistle of the ghost train in the distance. He stared through the bars of Pasha's cage into the dark alley behind a small-town diner. His father's blood mingled with the moonlight on the broken pavement. The police were everywhere, wielding their flashlights and guns, kicking over the restaurant's overflowing garbage cans, rampaging through the diner proper, their bodies blurred shapes behind the green window glass. The authorities never bothered to sort out who shot first, the owner of the diner or The Preacher. No one listened to his young son. Logan was just a kid, after all.

The social workers placed him in a foster home in Billings, the largest city in the state. He couldn't abide the lights, the people and their cars after the stillness of the woods. He only thought of escape.

The Ericsons were a middle-aged, childless couple who longed for a son. They were kind and unworldly, incapable of recognizing or dealing with evil, which made them perfect marks for the unscrupulous children's aid workers, Logan thought. He'd caused the Ericsons nothing but agony, first as an illiterate twelve-year-old, already familiar with alcohol, who equated learning with punishment. Then later as an adolescent who lied and stole, and abandoned them without warning or goodbye.

The ghost train drew alongside. He stepped into the car containing the Ericsons' living room. He smiled at the rose-patterned carpet, breathed in the scent of fresh floor wax and traces of Mrs. Ericson's perfume. It came in an exotic, dark blue bottle: *Evening in Paris* it was called. The year was 1956, so they had no television as yet, only a large brown Bakelite-encased radio on a walnut stand. A deep red, velvet armchair stood next to it. Old Man Ericson liked to sit there and read to him, classics that he thought boys would enjoy, though when he tried the Bible, Logan would clap his hands over his ears and scream. He'd had enough of religion for a lifetime even by then.

Old Ericson doggedly kept trying. Eventually it became clear that only animal stories appealed to the boy. Logan could recall the titles of his best-loved books even now, fifty-five years later: *The Black Stallion, Lassie Come Home* and *White Fang*. He hated *The*

Yearling though, hated the boy in the story for what he did to Flag, the deer he raised, hated him as much as he had hated and feared his father, The Preacher. After Mr. Ericson finished *The Yearling* Logan refused to listen to any more books. For weeks after, he would cry silently thinking of the deer's fate.

Sweet times though, Logan thought as he wandered through the ghost house. True happiness, but he'd been too ignorant and damaged to recognize it. He could hear the whistle of the pressure cooker boiling the vegetables for their Sunday dinner, smell the roast beef cooking in the gas oven. Mrs. Ericson would set the table with her best plates, white china with gold around the rim. She wouldn't let him eat until he said grace, but throughout dinner she would smile at him. For dessert they would have ice cream that came in a cardboard carton shaped like a brick. His favourite was strawberry.

Pasha's, too.

Distant shouts. Coming up the trail from the kids' camp. The Ericsons' home vanished, leaving Logan squinting into the afternoon light of the present.

More shouts. He gripped the rifle. He'd had enough lately. If strangers came running in here, bothering him, maybe he wouldn't be held responsible. The thought of firing the gun felt good, like the slow burn of rye whisky from a fresh bottle.

The voices faded in and out. Damn it, Logan thought. His hearing was going, his eyes too. Bolstered by the twin illusions of immunity and immortality, he'd been profoundly disturbed when overnight his familiar reflection in the mirror had transformed into that of a decaying old man. He'd punished and abused his body for years, and avoided doctors even more than the cops. No surprise he'd end up looking like a pile of rat dirt. Did he think he wasn't human?

He slumped back down on the floor of the cage and tried to summon up the Ericsons' house, but the train had continued relentlessly down the track and was gone. His foster parents had died young, she of cancer, he of a heart attack, both passing away while he was stuck in Vietnam. He'd brought them nothing but grief,

Logan thought. He had learned to read and write eventually, but he'd remained a mediocre student. Though he was fit and tough-bodied from roughing it in the woods, his years of solitude made team sports impossible. He'd failed high school, staggeringly and with flourish, and finally quit learning for good on his sixteenth birthday.

The army draft pounced on him when he turned eighteen. If he'd signed up voluntarily, like other dropouts, he might have had his choice of safe postings in Europe, but because he tried to escape over the border into Canada, they shipped him to Vietnam.

Ironically he proved to be a born soldier. Perhaps the Afghani hash he smoked out of the barrel of his M16 deadened his brain and gave him the detachment he needed. Perhaps it was simply his nature. He was assigned to a platoon that cleansed villages of the Viet Cong. He pitied the people huddling in fear, pleading for their lives, but he filled them full of bullets anyway. On leave he would get mindlessly, viciously drunk to obliterate the memories of what he had done.

And it was on one of these benders that he had his epiphany.

He'd staggered out of a seedy Saigon bar, groping his way into the alley behind it to be alone. He pulled out his hash for a toke and stopped.

He'd stepped into the very alley where The Preacher had met his fate. The same gleaming, obsidian walls, the same watery moon-light. He smelled the familiar sour tang of garbage and, under his feet, felt trickling moisture, perhaps water, perhaps blood.

A rattling noise from a trash can made him seize his gun. He turned and stared into the luminous eyes of a cat.

She was a scrawny creature, with tattered yellow-orange fur and tabby-like markings. She spotted him and froze, terrified. She had reason to fear him. People there ate cats. The city was overrun with rats and mice, but they ate the cats anyway. Logic never dissuaded humans from murdering each other, let alone animals, Logan knew.

The cat crouched low to the ground. She was starving, her sharp shoulder blades tenting her thin fur. He spoke to her, said something meaningless like "Hey, kitty". She turned and looked at him, her irises huge in the dim light, dark holes of sorrow. She felt the same terror and hopelessness that he felt. She had a soul as much as he.

More so.

A man came into the alley. He was waving a large knife and going for the cat. Probably he was simply hungry, trying to feed his family. No matter. Logan slit his throat with his own knife.

Under orders, he'd killed many innocents to beef up the body count for Washington's war statistics. This time he'd hadn't killed for the army. He'd killed for himself. For the first time, killing felt good: he'd saved an animal. He'd saved a soul.

The cat was still there in the alley, huddled against the wall. He reached out his hand. She rubbed her head against his open palm. He wanted to save her by bringing her back to the barracks, but he couldn't protect her. In the end, he'd be forced to abandon and betray her, the way Jody had betrayed Flag, the yearling.

The cat turned and vanished into the night. He'd prolonged her life, perhaps only by a few days; he'd have to be content with that. He knew now what he was meant to do.

Humans were obsessed with saving their souls. They had none; only animals had souls.

Soon after, he received word that Mrs. Ericson had died. Because of his distinguished war record, the army flew him home to Montana for her funeral. They never suspected a damn thing about his plans.

After the funeral in Billings, instead of heading back to base, he hitched a ride to the town of Morgan. Slipping over the Canadian border was trivial for a trained commando. He stepped into Saskatchewan, headed to Ontario and never looked back.

The voices again. A child was screaming. He recognized the voice immediately.

Rachel!

Logan seized the rifle and stood up in the cage. Rachel was standing outside, hanging onto the bars. Her black hair was full of leaves, her face a white triangle of fear.

In two steps he went over to the cage door and swung it open.

"Logan!" She rushed inside. Her arms clamped round him. She wouldn't let go.

He rested his free hand on her head. "What is it, Kid?"

"Santa … Barry." Her breathing cut through her words.

"They're after you."

"Yes. They're fighting."

He lifted her up with his free arm. She weighed practically nothing. Too skinny this kid, he thought. Living on nerves and little else. He carried her out of the cage back to the main cafeteria building and set her down at the bottom of the stairs.

"Go up into the cafeteria and hide," he told her. "Don't come out till I tell you."

"I want my dad."

"We'll find him. Now do as I tell you."

The kid to her credit knew when to take orders, and fast, too. She looked pretty banged up. She deserved better.

He loped down past the booths, staying alert, hearing nothing but the wind gusting through the pines and the far-off crash of waves along the rocky beach. He flicked off the safety on the rifle.

The trail that the kid and Danny normally took from Camp Nirvana tracked up from the south. Couldn't see anyone along it.

The kid had been standing on the west side of the cage, the side facing the lake. Maybe she'd taken the Woodland Trail. He followed it himself now, passing by the empty animal cages.

Halfway down the path, he spotted freshly torn leaves and twigs scattered over the ground. The vegetation beside the trail had been trampled and crushed, a riot of broken foliage. In their struggles, Santa and Barry had carved a green tunnel through the bush, leading west in the direction of the lake.

He walked over the trampled plants, following their trail, heading toward the top of the cliff.

A splotch of scarlet on the ground. More red splashed on the white bark of a birch tree. He aimed the rifle at the bushes surrounding him, heart pounding.

No cries, no shouts. No heavy breathing or groans of pain. Just the sigh of lake waves on shale far below.

He stepped over more broken branches, until he reached the cliff that dropped down to Red Dog Lake.

He peered down over the edge. Grey waves scraped back and forth over a band of sharp shale, tossing about a limp, beige shape. Water flooded over the dark blob of a head again and again.

Barry Tucker.

He mouthed the name even as a clamour of voices bounded down the south trail in the direction of Camp Nirvana.

They'd blame him. Recluse, bankrupt, alcoholic.

Convenient.

He lowered the rifle and struggled back to the Woodland Trail, following it down to Pasha's cage and the bear arena. He made his way to the cafeteria building. At the bottom of the stairs, he shouted Rachel's name.

She emerged cautiously onto the deck where tourists had once eaten their lunches in the sun. Smart kid, she wasn't taking any chances.

"Come on, Kid," he said. "Head for the VW. It's time to leave."

29

Edgar grudgingly spread out the chart of the area around Bouge Lake so Corazon could check it against her GPS.

"Hold that still," she snapped. "I gotta get this right. I only got enough gas for one flyover."

From the air, Bouge Lake looked much the way she remembered it, a typical ice-age lake: a long ribbon of water heavily wooded on all sides. She and Sinclair had landed on it fifteen years before to find a backwoods family cranking out legendarily cheap moonshine. Sinclair, naturally, thought he could cut a sweet deal and pass off the rotgut as Russian vodka back at the Galaxy.

"OK, I'm touching down," she said, dumping the chart on Edgar's lap.

She eased down the Piper Cherokee and skimmed over the dull grey waves. No rocks, logs or watercraft, thank God. The biggest problem would be finding Aunt Vera's damn cabin. All she could see around the shores of the lake were trees, trees and more trees. Edgar was no help at all, staring out the passenger window, determined to sulk.

She pulled up hard at the northern tip of the lake, banking over the woods to prepare for landing. They passed over a bald patch of ground like a white scar in the dark green forest. No house though.

"Is that your Aunt Vera's camp?" she asked him.

"I dunno. Everything looks different from the air. Never landed on Buggy Lake before," he sniffed.

Triple idiot, she thought, and concentrated on landing.

Once they were safely down, bobbing in the low waves, she set the water rudder and began a slow taxi down the centre of the thin lake. Couldn't see any cabins or shacks anywhere. Where had she and Sinclair met the moonshiners? She had no memory of the spot.

She opened the pilot's window to let in some air. "There's nothing here but mosquitoes. Are you sure your Aunt Vera lives on your so-called Buggy Lake?" she asked.

"Lots of people live back in the woods." Edgar opened the window on his side and stuck his head out. "Smell that? That's woodsmoke."

Great, Corazon thought as they continued taxiing north. Surrounded by inbred weirdos hiding in the woods like a bunch of wolves. What if Aunt Vera belonged to the moonshine gang? Sinclair's deal had gone sour almost immediately and those backwoods types tended to have long memories.

"There, see that cliff?" Edgar pointed excitedly. "When I step out Vera's front door, I look right out at Sparkle Cliff."

On the shore opposite Sparkle Cliff lay the clearing Corazon had spotted from the air. She idled the plane a safe distance from shore, while Edgar threw open the passenger door and climbed out, balancing on the float.

"I don't get it," he said through the open passenger window. "Where's Vera's cabin? I should be looking right at it."

"Look, we're really low on gas. I can't taxi all over the damn lake looking for nothing."

"Here comes somebody."

A man was paddling toward the plane in a tiny flat-bottomed boat that barely cleared the waterline. One of the banjo players obviously.

Edgar shouted and waved. The man waved back. He splashed up to the plane, tied up his preposterous boat and scrambled onto the float to join Edgar. The plane tilted precariously under their collective weight.

The man stuck his head in through the open passenger window, leering at Corazon with a mouthful of brown teeth. His skin had the dark patina of someone who had a bath once a year whether he needed it or not.

"'*jour. Bienvenu.*" The guy launched into a flood of backwoods *joual*, a harsh version of Québécois French. Corazon couldn't understand a word he said. To her surprise, Edgar replied in a fluent flow of the same *joual*.

"This here's Ratty," he explained, pausing for breath. "Jean-Pierre Rateau. We grew up together."

"That's nice," she said, resting her hand on her shotgun.

"Hi there, Edgar's friend," Ratty said in heavily accented English. "I was saying to Edgar that to see him is a big surprise. His *Tattie Vera*, she gone."

"What do you mean gone?" Edgar said. "She can't have moved away. Mum would've told me. Where did Vera move? Where's my mum?"

"No, not *moved*. Gone, *disparue*." Ratty waved at Edgar who stared blankly. "*Morte.*"

"Dead!" Corazon recognized that French word.

Edgar bellowed and dove into the lake. The plane pitched wildly, throwing Ratty against the passenger door. Edgar swam over to the clearing and stumbled onto the shale beach. He ran into the high grass of the clearing, shouting for his mum and Vera.

"Sorry, *désolé*," Ratty said. "I taut he knew."

Corazon's eyes narrowed. "Thought he knew what? What happened?"

"Big fire in March, five months ago. Winter, wood stove. Vera's cabin burn down. *Tout le kit*. She was inside."

"What about Edgar's mum? Did she burn up, too?"

Ratty spat into the lake. "I never saw her here. She lives down south with Edgar, *non*?"

Edgar had reappeared. He collapsed, sobbing inconsolably, on the beach.

"Vera get many visitors?" Corazon asked. Ratty shrugged. "Any of them Anglos? *Maudits anglais?* Anybody like that show up here five months ago?"

Ratty's expression lived up to his nickname. "Couple show up on skidoo. One was *anglais*, had a blue tattoo here." He traced a tear drop under his eye. "The other was Strine."

"What?"

"Strine, *australien*. You know kangaroo, jump, jump. White hair and beard. You know this guy?"

"You bet your ass I do," Corazon said.

Danny rushed up to the water trickling from the base of the granite outcropping. Close by, he found the plants he was looking for. He used Ricky's knife to cut several bunches of the shiny, dark green leaves, taking care that they stayed free of dirt.

He dove back into the woods. Ricky had pulled the thermal blanket from his vest while Danny was gone.

Danny kneeled down, shook out the shiny metal foil and tossed the plants on top of it.

"That better not be poison ivy," Ricky said.

"That's wintergreen. It's an antiseptic. My grandmother says you can use it to make aspirin, too." He worked quickly, crushing the leaves into two separate compresses. Using the knife, he cut two pieces from the shiny blanket and several strips of the medical tape. He pressed the first compress against Ricky's belly wound.

"Get that off me," Ricky said.

"Do you see a hospital here? Keep still." Danny folded the first piece of thermal blanket into a rectangle and secured it over the wintergreen bandage with white medical tape. "Now lean forward." He repeated the process with the far nastier exit wound. Finally finished, he gently pushed Ricky back against the pine and zipped up his combat vest to hold everything in place. The first aid kit contained three acetaminophen tablets. He handed them to Ricky, who gobbled them down dry.

"How are you doing?" Danny asked.

"Bad. Could use … Santa's nice weed …"

"I've got two 'shrooms left. Here, take them." He handed Ricky the last of his stash. "Come on, Macho Dude, time to haul ass. We need to get to that mine."

"Need water … take me back to the cliff …"

"There's no time. Can't you smell the smoke?"

"Yeah, I can smell it."

They stared at each other. Ricky wasn't going anywhere and both of them knew it.

"OK, have it your way," Danny said at last.

A sturdy sapling grew near Ricky's pine tree. Danny used the skinning knife to cut it down and whittle it into a pole. Ricky shoved his shoulders against the tree trunk and struggled to his feet, leaning on Danny and the stick for support.

They toiled back to the granite rise. When they reached the water, Ricky collapsed face down into it. Danny held his head so he could drink.

Finally finished, Ricky rolled clear and stared up into the darkening sky.

Danny retrieved the Aussie's pack from where he'd tossed it earlier. He settled it under Ricky's back to protect him from the ground and draped the remains of the thermal blanket over him.

"Time to go, Kid," Ricky said.

"I'm OK," Danny replied, not moving.

"Cut the crap. Give the bullet to McKenna. And this." He pulled out his ID and waited until Danny shoved it into his jeans pocket.

"Before I go …" Danny said. "I need to tell McKenna what happened out there. Did you … did you see Hendrix and Tear Drop do it?"

"Naw." Ricky shook his head. "Curtis … Hendrix's boy made me. Everyone drunk … found Morty's phone to radio McKenna. But phone … smashed to hell. Hit the woods."

"But you must have heard something."

"Nothing." Ricky coughed and gasped for air. "Heard plane … hid out. Surprise at dawn. Same as you." He groped in his vest and tossed out the LED flashlight. "Go on, take it." Danny bent down and picked it up.

"Why did Hendrix kill Curtis?" he asked. "Curtis was his bodyguard. He was paid to watch Hendrix's back. Did Hendrix think that Curtis ratted him out to the cops?"

"Nah, Curtis was loyal. He's ... Hendrix's brother ..."

"What!"

Ricky mumbled something inaudible. Pointed at the sky. In the distance the drone of Hendrix's plane, returning.

"He'll kill you," Danny leaned down to drag Ricky back under the trees. "He can't miss you out here."

"Wait ..." Ricky jabbed Danny's arm and mouthed: "Engine trouble."

The pitch of the motor did sound odd. Danny detected an erratic thumping under the normal engine noise. The roaring surged and faded, growing fainter and fainter as they listened.

"Gone home," Ricky breathed.

"If you say so."

Silence now. Danny bent down and drank as much of the muddy water as he could stomach. Finished, he offered the knife back to Ricky.

Ricky waved him off.

"Come on, man. What if the bears come back?" Danny said.

"Bear'll ... use it ... for a toothpick."

"OK." Danny searched for something to say. "Try to stay awake. You've got to, man, to signal the rescue copter. It's only for a few hours, hang on."

"Yeah, sure ... watch your back ... Kid."

His last image of Ricky was a pale hand waving him into the forest. As he pushed his way into the trees, he felt that he was embarking on an impossible, futile journey. Like The Traveler trying to recapture his lost horses.

30

They'd been coming for forty years, Logan knew, his sanctuary gone in the blink of an eye. In the rear-view mirror of the VW, he watched the camp people stream past Pasha's cage and charge up the stairs into the abandoned cafeteria.

Gotta get the hell out.

He crunched the engine into first gear and got the VW going, thumping and grinding over the potholes in the gravel parking lot. Screams and shouts behind him as he turned onto the overgrown driveway leading to Highway 11. He steered wildly over the uneven road, the branches of maples and chokecherries lashing the VW's dented sides, the windshield wipers breaking into mad motion when his knee rammed the lever under the steering wheel.

"I'm scared, Mr. Logan," Rachel said from the passenger seat.

Logan jammed off the windshield wipers, fighting the VW's transmission. Barry's people were chasing after the van, yelling at him to stop. As if their precious say-so would make him. Stupid, over-privileged yahoos, run all you want. You're no match for my internal combustion engine, he thought.

"Is Barry OK?" Rachel asked.

Logan sucked at his whiskers, thinking. "Kid, you're a good soldier. I won't disrespect you by telling you lies. He's gone. Fell off the damn cliff. Should've put up that fence thirty years ago."

"Santa pushed him!"

Makes sense, Logan thought.

Rachel started to cry with big, gulping sobs. "Santa wanted to kill me. Barry said he didn't want to, so Santa killed *him.*"

"Never mind, Santa can't hurt you now."

"We have to tell the police."

"Later, Kid." The VW burst out of the drive onto the gravel shoulder of the highway. Logan turned blindly onto the dark grey asphalt heedless of oncoming traffic.

"Santa told Barry to give him money. Because of the porno sites on his computers," Rachel went on, wiping her eyes.

"What?" Logan veered over the centre line, nearly smashing into an oncoming SUV. The driver blared his horn and flashed his lights. "Sorry, Kid." He pulled back into the northbound lane, breathing hard.

"I heard them," she said. "Barry said he didn't have the money. Santa got really mad."

"No kidding."

"Danny and I found the porno sites when we hacked into Barry's computer. Danny said Barry should go to jail. He wanted to tell the police only ..." She hesitated.

"Barry found out and fired him, I'll bet," Logan filled in. "That bastard. Barry doesn't deserve your tears." He found a crumpled serviette in the glove compartment. "Here, wipe your face."

Rachel took it and blew her nose obediently. He frowned, look-ing over his shoulder for any cars behind them. Nothing yet.

"Look, Kid, those camp people weren't chasing after us for nothing," he said. "I'm thinking Santa told them I pushed Barry over."

"But you didn't! If we tell Sergeant McKenna together, she'll have to believe us."

"It doesn't work that way, Kiddo."

"I know. She thinks I'm a liar, too."

Logan stared through the cracked windshield. Under the high overcast, the day had taken on a strange yellow light, like look-ing at the world through the celluloid lenses his foster parents, the Ericsons, used for their home movies. A dry wind whipped through the tangled weeds by the sides of the road and buffeted the sides of the van. Between the gusts, he could hear the faint whistle of the train. Tracking him.

Rachel turned her big yellow eyes on him and said: "What if … what if Santa comes after us?"

"I'll protect you, Flag. Don't you worry, I'll look after you."

He pushed on the accelerator, heading for Blue Sky Bookstore, the only refuge they had left.

Santa crouched in Barry's prissy beige *Prius* and cursed the dead camp director and his ancestors back to the primordial ooze. Couldn't get the wretched thing started because the bloody key wouldn't turn. He shoved and rattled the key in its slot, twisting it back and forth.

Have to stop, have to. He gasped for air, fighting for control. If he snapped the key, he was lost. He clutched his wounded thigh. Fresh blood had soaked through his red velour pants. No choice, had to get this useless trash-bucket moving. Couldn't foot it any longer. His chances of escape were growing smaller and smaller like Alice.

He burst into a frenzy, smacking every button, screen, and lever he could reach on the dash.

The *Prius* let out a sort of cough. The motor! It had turned over despite the bloody key. He'd conned it into working. He clutched the steering wheel and pressed down on the gas pedal.

The engine died instantly.

He screamed in frustration, couldn't help it. He hammered everything he could hit: the wheel, the armrest, the cupholder. The world was spinning. Couldn't see. Going to be sick …

He flung open the driver's door and vomited. Done it now. Shoved the old blood pressure over the top. Stroked out …

The grass under the open door was moving. Got to … got to get a grip. He hauled himself back up into the driver's seat. The wooden steps to Barry's office glided past the passenger window.

He stared numbly as the car meandered silently over the grass. Rolling downhill. He seized the steering wheel but the open driver's door slammed into Barry's prized Muskoka chair, knocking it over. He fumbled for the handbrake. Couldn't find it.

The *Prius* lurched forward up over a bank of weeds onto the gravel drive that led out of the camp. He wrenched the wheel hard to the left. The car continued down the road like a boat sailing over a smooth lake. How the hell ...

A video screen had popped to life on the dash, showing a circuit going round and round, one arm representing battery power, the other gas. So the stupid trash-bucket was running on battery power alone. No gas engine, *ergo* no noise.

You're going to save me, not the environment, you poncey car, he thought. Don't care if you steer like a bug in treacle. He leaned out, caught hold of the handle and slammed the driver's door shut.

Let's focus on the positive, as our dear departed Barry would say, he thought. He tore off his stained Santa hat and tossed it into the back seat. Spot of fun playing the full Shakespearean drama for those Camp Nirvana fools. He'd ranted and raved that Logan had gone bonkers and thrown Barry over the cliff. The twigs, dirt and blood on his torn suit backed up his story. He'd gone all noble that his wounds were nothing and that he'd race back to camp to call the police. And off the buggers went, tearing off to Logan's zoo like a pack of rabid dingos. Couldn't have hoped for better.

The car passed through Camp Nirvana's open gateway. He braked roughly at the drive's intersection with the highway. The *Prius* squatted in silence like a beige toad. Couldn't tell if the damn thing was stalled or idling.

Now what?

He looked south toward Santa's Fish Camp. Had to go back but that Corazon creature had probably raised the alarm. No choice but to wait for dark.

North lay nothing but trees.

Bloody dilemma. He pulled a loonie from his trouser pocket and flipped it. It landed bird-side up.

Tails. That meant north.

He pounded down on the gas pedal. The *Prius* surprised him by leaping onto the highway like a frenzied rabbit. He barely avoided a southbound pickup.

He steered into the right-hand lane. At long last, the gas power kicked in. About bloody time the *Prius* started behaving like a decent car. Calmer now, he retrieved the bottle rolling around on the passenger seat, unscrewed the cap with one hand, and took a long pull of Barry's rye whisky, the stuff for special guests only. Down with you and your precious, la-di-da camp, Barry, he thought. You deserved everything you got.

He stared at his thick hands on the steering wheel, saw them sinking into Barry's soft flesh ... Suddenly he felt icy cold. The shakes again. Always hit him after he did a dirty. He hadn't meant to throw Barry off the cliff, not really. Barry shouldn't have made him angry.

Risky that, getting angry. Always had to get angry to do the necessary. Not like Hendrix at all.

The glass bottle rattled against his teeth. Whisky spilled through his beard and soaked his tunic.

He'd screwed up royally last night at the Galaxy, smashing up Hendrix like that. Hendrix would be mad as a cut snake and out for blood, no point kidding himself otherwise. And when Hendrix got down to business ...

God, I'm too old to do another runner, he thought. Can't start over. No more gas in the tank.

He downed another slug of rye. Hendrix and Tear Drop would have trashed the cookhouse by now. Got rid of the product. Millions gone.

And he'd get nothing.

All that work – three years building up Santa's Fish Camp, nursing the grow-op, sucking up to the locals. It wasn't bloody fair.

A southbound car flashed its headlights at him.

He gasped and tromped on the brake pedal, shrieking to a stop inches behind a tractor trailer stopped at the end of a long line of cars. In the distance, a black and white OPP cruiser straddled the centre line, red light twirling.

So that's what the southbound driver was warning him about.

A copper was stopping each car, having words with the driver before he waved it past the barrier.

Bloody hell, Santa thought, shoving the whisky bottle under the driver's seat. No choice now: he had to take his chances and head south.

What a disaster, Corazon thought. Turned out that Ratty was indeed one of Sinclair's moonshiners and that bitter memories of Sinclair's sharp deal were carved deep into his black little heart. He'd refused to paddle out to fetch Edgar back to the plane. The smelly weasel only agreed after he took her last twenty-five bucks, even the dimes and nickels.

At least now they were back up in the air and the props drowned out the noise of Edgar's crying. He'd wrapped his soaking body in a stained grey blanket he'd pulled from the back of the plane. Where the hell had that old blanket come from? Maybe one of the hunters left it behind.

Normally she found flying meditative, but after taking off from Buggy Lake her rage and fear were leaking through her control. *Santa tried to kill me, he really meant to kill me.*

He won't stop, he'll try again, she thought. And I left Danny alone with those guys on the island. Oh, Danny, Sweetheart, forgive me.

"Oh God, why would Santa hurt my mum? She liked him so much," Edgar sobbed into his mike. "Where did he put her body?"

She could be anywhere, Corazon thought, looking down at the vast wilderness spooling out below them. "Maybe ... maybe it's time you went to the cops, Baby," she said.

"I-I can't go to the cops."

"Look, the cops scare me, too, but Santa's doing a helluva lot more than just growing weed on the side. He's killing people and getting away with it. Your mum was local, she was one of us. Do it for her."

"I can't! Santa and Mr. Hendrix, they'll kill me, too." Edgar rubbed his face. "They're not just growing weed, you see."

"Oh? Just exactly what are you guys doing at Santa's Fish Camp?"

"Nothing." He shook his head violently from side to side. "I'm upset. Forget I said anything."

Corazon adjusted their course, dragging her eyes away from the by-now-terrifying fuel gauge. "OK, let's talk about something else. How about canned bear hunts? I bet Santa got megabucks from those rich bastards to shoot poor Pasha."

"Geez, why can't you leave that alone?" Edgar wiped his eyes with his fingers. "Don't give me that look. It's not like I'm proud of it, OK?"

"How did Santa get Pasha away from Logan?"

"Oh, well, last spring Logan was getting drunk at the Galaxy 'cause Pasha was sick and he couldn't pay for a vet. So Santa spun him some bull about a hippy dude running a zoo for old animals down near Picton. He said he'd fix things so Pasha could stay at the Picton zoo for cheap till she got better. So Logan tranked Pasha and Santa, Tear Drop and me loaded her into the Hummer. Like Santa figured, Logan got real emotional saying goodbye, so Santa said I'd drive Pasha down to Picton and make sure she got settled all right."

"And Logan fell for that?"

"Well, he sort of knew Santa's story was bogus, but he really wanted to believe it. I mean, he's been giving Santa money for Pasha's food since April."

"Logan's on welfare."

"Yeah, I know."

"You scheming pair of bastards!"

"Hey, it wasn't my idea. Santa said Logan would freak out if we didn't keep collecting."

"No kidding." Corazon's hands gripped the controls so tightly they felt slippery. "Where did you keep Pasha?"

"Chained up in the woods at Santa's Fish Camp. Santa read on the Internet that some west coast dopers used a bunch of black bears to guard their weed plants. He thought he'd use her to guard the trailer. But Pasha just lay there. She wouldn't hurt anybody. I tried to take care of her but ..."

"Didn't anyone see her?"

"Nobody goes near the trailer. You want to keep your job at the Fish Camp, you stay away."

"So Santa decided he didn't want Pasha after all."

"Well, she just kept getting sicker and sicker. Santa got real mad at me. Then Mayor Fortin told Santa that Morty Gross knew this Norwegian guy who wanted to hunt Canadian black bear. Mayor Fortin said Morty had a big budget and orders to make this Anderson guy happy no matter what. Santa figured Pasha could earn him a hundred grand."

"*You sons of bitches!* How could you do that to Pasha? She was tame. She loved people."

"Don't you scream at me. You knew what was up when you flew out the hunters. You knew they were gunning for bear."

"Shut up!" Sometimes truth hurt so much it burned. She checked her GPS and steered back to her intended course.

Danny, oh, Baby, I'm never leaving you again.

Not now, not ever.

31

The blinds were still drawn over the windows at Blue Sky Bookstore. Logan rummaged for the spare key in the eavestrough above the front door. He found it, opened the store and shouted for Odile. By the cold silence inside, Rachel could tell she wasn't home.

They made their way to the kitchen at the back. Logan kept pacing back and forth along the counter by the kitchen sink. Clutching Odile's rifle, he paused every few minutes to check on the van through the back window. He'd parked it well out of sight in the woods.

"Maybe the cops sent the rescue helicopter out to find Danny," Rachel said, her eyes on the rifle. "Maybe Odile is still at the police station."

But Logan frowned and stayed quiet, the way Dad did when Mum went into the hospital for the last time.

"I'm going to tell you straight, Soldier," Logan said. "The cops won't go looking for Danny. They'll figure those foreign hunters knew the risks when they flew out into the wilderness. And even if the cops did rev up their fancy rescue helicopters and fly out there, they'll never find him. They'd need a flashlight to find their own butts."

"That's not true. Sergeant McKenna is smart."

"She doesn't know what she's dealing with."

Logan checked the window again. "You hungry?" he asked. She nodded. "Better eat something. Go help yourself from the fridge."

"I don't want to take Odile's food when she's not here," Rachel said.

"She'll understand. Wash your hands first."

Rachel sensed Logan wouldn't take no for an answer so she did as she was told, washing her hands at the kitchen sink using the dish detergent for soap. In the fridge she found a carton of milk, a loaf of bread and a jar of peanut butter. She set everything on the kitchen table and took the Blue Willow plates and the cutlery from the cupboards where she and Odile had put them away last night. She made sandwiches for herself and Logan and poured them each a glass of milk.

She nibbled at her sandwich while Logan chewed down his food by the window.

"You about done?" he asked her, a few minutes later.

She nodded. "I feel sick, Mr. Logan. I want to go lie down."

"OK, you go settle down in the van. I'll pack up our supplies."

"Where are we going?"

"North. Don't worry, Flag. Nobody's gonna hurt you. The train's coming but you're safe with me."

The prissy *Prius* had one bloody thing in its favour, Santa thought. At low speeds it ran dead quiet. He wheeled through a three-point turn behind the tractor trailer and headed south back to Red Dog Lake.

To keep out of sight of the coppers, he headed off in the wrong, oncoming lane. Hadn't driven on the left in years, not since Oz.

Lovely! He floored the accelerator.

For the next five miles, he had wonderful fun giving oncoming drivers a brain hemorrhage. He charged at their speeding cars, dodging back into the right-hand lane at the last possible moment. Eventually, though, he had to give it up. Barry's eco-car, brown and boring as marmite on toast, stood out like a blinking neon sign in Red Dog Lake where locals drove gas-guzzling pickups.

Must change wheels. He missed the Christmas Hummer – damn Edgar's eyes and blast his soul for making off with it – but now wasn't the time to be sentimental. The Hummer would never do for a runner. Tear Drop, on the other hand, drove a boiler-plate grey Hyundai on Hendrix's orders. Bit of challenge to snatch it if Tear Drop was still hanging about Santa's Fish Camp, but it'd do nicely.

Dark in a few hours. Nothing left to do but wait.

Ten miles north of Red Dog Lake, he spotted a familiar turn-off. He slowed down and, after making sure no traffic was in sight, he turned in. He steered the silent *Prius* down a long dirt track that gave onto a grassy slope. At the bottom of the hill, pressed up against a dark cedar hedge, languished a familiar, crumbling white trailer. The weeds surrounding it had grown waist-high, obscuring the vegetable garden and its rather unpleasant contents.

Often better that, simply let things sort themselves out. When Mother Nature had her way with Edgar's mum, simplest thing in the world to bury said evidence and keep collecting that lovely pension money. Easy to keep Edgar off the scent, at least at first. But you'd think Edgar's bloody aunt in Bugger Lake would have kissed his backside for his generous offer. One tiny lie and everyone stays happy. Was that so bloody hard? Brought the necessary down on herself, the old ratbag.

He opened the driver's door and shouted for Edgar just in case. The fat fool was supposed to be back at Fish Camp doing a last product run for Tear Drop, but you never knew. No sound except the sawing of crickets and buzz of mosquitoes. Nothing stirred under the heavy dun-coloured sky.

He settled back and took a long swallow of whisky, leaving the *Prius* to idle silently. He dared not turn the damn thing off because he'd never get it started again.

Edgar had been getting too teary about his mum lately. High time to do the necessary, long overdue in fact. Said elf had a gift for botanicals, but he'd failed high school chemistry – spectacularly and with passion – and Hendrix was most unhappy with the meth's quality. Maybe Tear Drop, for once, had taken operational issues seriously and saved him, Santa, the trouble of dispatching Edgar to the sweet hereafter.

"Here's to seeing your back end, Red Dog Lake," he said, raising the whisky bottle. "And that goes double for all your soiled inhabitants."

Next day he and the Hyundai would be over the American border, heading for Mexico. *Viva Zapata*, he thought. Tequila tastes better than rye whisky any day of the week.

Smoke from the forest fire had blotted out the sun. Danny had to use Ricky's LED flashlight to navigate the deep shadows under the pines.

Hard going now. The terrain was rocky, riddled with snaking tree roots. He sensed that he was moving downhill into a valley, where the bush promised to be even thicker. It might take him hours to struggle through a single mile. And the Archangel Mine lay several miles away.

Don't think about it.

He paused, eyes smarting from the drifting smoke. If Ricky was lucky, he'd bleed out before the forest fire hit him.

Or the bears came back.

Or Hendrix did another flyover.

Have to keep going. Have to get help.

I owe Ricky, he thought. So what if the locals call me a rat when I go to the cops. It's payback. Payback for Santa using me. Payback for hooking me into his scary illegal crap. And most of all, it's payback for Pasha.

He hadn't let on to Ricky; in fact, he'd tried to push the memory out of his own head, but he knew exactly where Santa had hidden his meth lab. Two weeks ago, he and Rachel had stumbled across it during one of Barry Tucker's excruciating field trips to Santa's Fish Camp.

And it was all because of Pasha.

A couple of locals claimed that Pasha was chained up in the woods at the Fish Camp. She was guarding Santa's weed plants, just like the black bears out in British Columbia, they said. Danny hadn't believed a word of it. Pasha was getting old, and even if Logan hadn't told him, he could tell she was sick. The last time he'd seen her was in April; one day she was sleeping like always in her old rusty cage, and the next day she was gone. He figured Logan had done something, something Danny really didn't want to know. The way Logan had been sinking all summer only deepened his conviction that Pasha was dead.

Still the stupid rumour had leaked into Camp Nirvana. He should have foreseen it: Rachel was obsessed about seeing Pasha, the dancing bear. During their field trip to Santa's Fish Camp, she'd asked to go to the washroom. He'd said, sure but be back at Santa's Fish Pond by noon. So she'd skip the rest of the tour past statues a three-year-old would find tacky, so what? He wished he could skip the tour himself. What harm could it do to let her go?

Plenty, as it turned out. Rachel didn't turn up at the fish pond and Barry went up like a volcano when he found out that Danny had let her wander off to the washroom on her own.

Worried sick, Danny chased after her. Barry had no choice but to let him: he and the other counsellors had their hands full over-seeing the other campers tear through the gift store. It took Danny an hour to track Rachel down. She'd ended up at the bottom of Mother Goose's Treasure Trail, as far from the central fish pond as the paths went.

She seemed unusually subdued. She hadn't managed to find Pasha, but she had tromped through rows and rows of suspicious, bushy green-leafed plants growing some distance from the trail.

"Tomato plants," Danny told her.

"No way," she replied. "Tomato leaves make perfume when you crush them, these don't. My dad works in public health. I know they're marijuana plants."

"Forget you saw them, Rach. I mean it."

By then they were fiendishly late for the bus back to Camp Nirvana. He tried to take a shortcut back through the woods. Bad move. In fact, scary bad move. Deep in the trees, they ran across a trailer surrounded by a litter of propane tanks and empty antifreeze bottles. Tear Drop, Santa's pilot, was smoking a joint while he lounged on the trailer's steps.

Never paid off to see what you weren't supposed to see, Danny knew. He'd hushed Rachel. To stay out of Tear Drop's sight, they'd stolen down the far side of the trailer, nearly choking on the sewage smell venting from it, until they could plunge back into the brush.

Rachel thought their narrow escape was a big, shiny adventure, but Danny made her swear not to tell anyone about what they'd seen. Thank God, she could keep a secret. For days afterward, he'd freaked out every time a car pulled into Camp Nirvana. When Santa had bought him that beer at the Galaxy, he'd nearly panicked.

I took the job even though I knew what Santa was. I'm so stupid I deserve to die, he thought.

Finally, the terrain began to look familiar. Corazon reached for the radio receiver. Time to call Morty.

"Hey, we're getting near Fire Island," Edgar broke off his snivelling. "Why're we flying way out here? I thought you said you didn't have enough gas to pick up the hunters."

"Shut up," Corazon said. She placed the call in to Morty. No response.

A grey mist of smoke was flowing through the trees below them, layering up into the atmosphere, cutting visibility.

Her radio stayed quiet.

"That's a storm, right?" Edgar gestured at the towering black cloud on the western horizon.

"No, that's not a thunderhead," Corazon managed to say. Under the black cloud, a raging rim of flame. Her hands shook on the controls.

"Oh man, that cop was right about the forest fire." He buried his face in his hands. "Oh man, oh man, oh man."

"Shut your noise! The hunters … Oh, my God, Danny … I gotta get closer." Fear was hollowing her out.

"Please turn around, Corazon. We got no gas left."

"*Sancta Maria*, I'm gonna go get him."

"Look, most like they left the island already. That's why Morty isn't answering. They're back in town. Santa prob'ly sent Tear Drop out in the Twin Beech right after he heard about the fire. He'd do that. Santa looks after people."

"Sure, the same way he looked after your mum."

"That's not fair!" Tears of anger stormed Edgar's eyes. "You take that back."

"Grow up! Check out your mum's Old Age Security payments. I bet Santa's been cashing her cheques since the day he killed her. Well, he's not gonna kill Danny, too."

"Turn around! Goddamn it, turn around!"

Edgar lunged for the controls.

The plane dropped like a stone. Through the windshield Corazon saw the earth rush toward them in a mad maelstrom of trees.

She shrieked in furious fear, fighting to wrench back the controls. She dug her nails into his meaty fists, but he hung on.

She scrabbled under her seat. Seized her shotgun and smashed it into Edgar's face with everything she had.

A loud, distant clap of thunder startled Danny. Even the forest floor seemed to shake.

He tried to spot the sky through the dense pine branches. Couldn't see anything. Where was the storm?

The thunder should be coming from the west, not the east. He shone the LED on the compass in the handle of Ricky's knife.

Still stuck. He sighed and stuffed the knife back into his belt.

A new rainstorm could slow down the forest fire, give him and Ricky a chance. It would give them water to drink. Even better, it would keep Hendrix out of the sky.

It was just what he and Ricky needed.

32

Logan finished loading the rest of the supplies in his VW and climbed in behind the steering wheel. Rachel had curled up on a pile of old blankets he kept in the back.

Poor kid, mixed up in all this, he thought. Didn't have the heart to tell her. He could think of several reasons why Odile wasn't home yet: none of them good.

He hammered the steering wheel in futile breathless pain. *Danny, you useless kid, sucking up to vermin for a few easy bucks. I'd kill you myself for what you've done to Odile, only the forest fire's probably beaten me to it.*

He started the engine and reversed the van out of its hiding place in the pines. A chevron of Canada geese passed overhead, the birds calling and trumpeting to each other. Heading south.

Winter's coming early this year, he thought.

He bumped out over the gravel parking lot, passing the old gas station clock on its rusty pole, and paused at the edge of the highway.

No traffic except for a black pickup heading south well over the speed limit. When it passed Blue Sky Bookstore, the driver astonished him by braking violently, slewing back and forth across the two-lane highway.

Logan reached for the rifle.

Somehow the driver got the pickup back under control. It stormed over the road and pulled into the lot.

Mayor Fortin climbed out, waving frantically. He rammed his white stetson over his bald head, hitched his gut over his tooled Western belt and jogged breathlessly over to the VW.

Logan rolled down the window on the driver's side, keeping his hand on the gun.

"*Tabernacle,* John. Boy am I glad to see you," the mayor panted as he reached the van. "Odile, is she back at home? Is she OK?"

"No, uh-uh, nobody here. Just pulled in myself. Place is locked up tight." Logan leaned out the window, blocking the mayor's view of the inside. "What's up?"

Fortin took off his hat and rubbed his bald scalp. "Bad news. That Sergeant McKenna, some guy ambush her cruiser five miles north of here. A bunch of guys from the Galaxy was going home after karaoke. They find McKenna's car smashed up on the highway. She got shot up."

"She dead?" Logan managed to say.

"No, she had on her safety vest, but it's not like TV, eh? The guys take her to hospital in Kirkland Lake. She got banged up pretty good."

"And the shooter?"

"Gone."

"McKenna had Odile with her."

"*I know,* I know. The OPP, they send one cop to close down the highway. Stupid, that shooter is long gone. The OPP they say they need all their other cops to fight that forest fire in Malartic. No one is looking for Odile. Me and a bunch of folks are searching up and down the highway. In case, you know, she is walking around hurt or something."

Or something. Logan shook his head. If he tried to speak, he'd scream. Not Odile, never Odile.

"When I saw your VW, I was hoping that she is safe back at home," Fortin went on. "You know how she sometimes walks in the forest by herself to do her shaman stuff. I was hoping she done that and she is home now." He looked Logan up and down. "You busy, John? We could use your help."

"Kirkland Lake. Doctor's appointment." Logan felt the lie slip out easily. "Back soon, I'll find you."

He rolled up the window, gunned the motor and pulled onto the highway before Fortin could ask more questions.

"Is Odile dead?" Rachel asked from the back.

Logan jumped. "How much did you hear?"

"The bad man, the windigo, he shot Sergeant McKenna, didn't he? Before she could get the rescue helicopter."

"Soldier, here in Red Dog Lake we look after our own. It's up to you and me to find Danny before Hendrix does."

"But there's no road in to Fire Lake."

"That's right, Flag, but I've got a fair idea how to find Danny, pretty fair."

Under the light of Ricky's LED, the ground flowed away in an unending, coppery plain dotted with twigs and rubble. Danny felt he was stumbling through a drowned world, the trunks of the pines the decaying pillars of a sunken wharf.

He stopped, coughed and rubbed his eyes. What if he was wandering around aimlessly like a fly on a screen?

He beamed the flashlight over the reptilian bark of the pines. Odile said that moss often grew on the north side of trees where sunlight was weakest, only it had to be the right kind of moss. Other kinds grew on the south side. And in the deep woods, where the forest floor lay in shadow, the moss grew all around the tree.

Like now.

Grandmother, I should have listened to you instead of bitching about getting back to my video games.

A rustling and a scrabbling. Something ran across his feet. He started and dropped the flashlight. In its last dying flash, he saw a chipmunk dive into the undergrowth.

He froze where he was, praying his night vision would kick in. He looked up. No stars overhead, no moon. He might as well as have fallen down the shaft of the Archangel Mine.

If I don't find the LED, I'm dead. Odile, Grandmother, I need your help.

Nothing happened.

What did he expect? That she'd appear in a mist of light, grab his hand and fly him out of the woods like Peter Pan? He could hear her berating him: "You are a man now, Danny Bluestone. You have been to college. You are a rational being. Think, take responsibility ..."

"OK, OK, I hear you," he said into the night.

All right, he *had* read on the Internet that dropped objects landed only eighteen inches away. He bent down carefully, running his hands over the dirt and stones in ever-widening circles.

There! His fingers struck the light's small smooth cylinder.

Talk about luck. He grabbed the LED and squeezed the on/off switch.

Nothing.

Broken. Now he was done for.

Another memory: Odile showing him her new flashlight, saying: "Modern flashlights are tough."

So maybe it wasn't broken: it had to be the damn batteries. He carefully unscrewed it, tucking the parts in his pockets, and extracted the batteries. Sure enough, they were gritty with corrosion. Thanks for looking after your stuff, Ricky, he thought.

He cleaned the ends of the batteries with his thumb, slipped the parts of the LED back together and tried again.

Light flared out, blinding him.

He scrambled up, heart thumping. No time to lose.

The bush had turned into a maze of vegetation. He wrestled with low-hanging branches, saplings and weeds. Often he had to stop and cut his way through with Ricky's knife.

This is taking way too long.

His throat burned, a harsh metallic taste invaded his mouth. Dehydration, already. Every muscle in his body screamed for rest.

If I sit down now, I won't get up.

"OK, I rest at tree number eleven," he said into the air. He fought past the tree trunks, counting one, two, three ...

"If you walk faster, I will tell you a story." Odile's voice echoed through his head again.

He thought back to the latest story he and Rachel had been working on, the one the Nirvana kids really liked at campfire.

"There once was a young brave who wandered far from his tribe into the lonely forest to hunt," he said aloud. "The days went by, but he caught no game. He saw no animals or birds, not a single living thing. He began to grow weak from hunger."

He paused for a moment. Getting hard to talk. No water around, the ground felt hard as cement.

"As the brave wandered deeper into the dark woods, he felt that someone was watching him. Someone evil."

He couldn't help looking over his shoulder.

"Just when he'd given up hope, he caught the scent of roasting meat. He crashed through the bush, following the smell until he came upon a clearing at the mouth of a cave. A tall man stood there cooking over a campfire.

"'Welcome,' said the stranger. 'I have been expecting you. You must be hungry. I have prepared us a feast.'"

Danny braced himself against a birch tree, thinking of Odile's blueberry pie and roast stuffed pickerel, hamburgers and fries at the Galaxy café …

Stop it!

He pushed off the tree and carried on. "The brave was frightened by the stranger's appearance. The man's skin was stretched tightly over his bones, and he gave off an odour like rotting flesh. But the brave knew he must eat or die, so he joined the stranger at the campfire.

"He fell on the food and ate the stew and roasted meat until he could eat no more. All the while the stranger watched him, licking his long, pointed teeth. 'You must be tired after your travels,' he said. 'Come into the cave, I have prepared a bed for you.'

"The young brave's instincts warned him not to enter the cave. 'I will stay by the fire,' he said. He lay down under the cold watchful eyes of the stranger and pretended to doze off.

"After a while, the stranger took a burning log from the fire and carried it into the cave. In the red light of the torch, the brave saw that the floor of the cave was littered with white bones: human bones. He knew then that the stranger was a windigo, a cannibal, and that he planned to make the brave his next victim."

Danny lurched forward, tripping over a rock. The LED was fading. He shook it, jostling it back to life.

"The windigo threw off his tattered filthy clothes and revealed his true form. His skin was the livid white of a corpse, his nails were yellow, curving claws and his fangs dripped with blood. A red star glowed on his forehead, the mark of evil.

"The brave leapt up and drew his bow, prepared to fight to the death.

"The windigo only laughed. 'Even if you kill me, you are doomed,' he said. 'I fed you human flesh. You will become what I am.'"

The flashlight was wavering like a fading ember. Danny shook it violently.

"The brave threw himself on the windigo. They fought brutally, tearing each other's flesh without mercy. The brave was gravely wounded but with his last strength, he threw the windigo into the fire. For a windigo has a heart of ice and only fire can destroy him."

The flashlight sputtered and died. The darkness was like water, suffocating him.

He felt his way over to the closest tree and slid to the ground.

"No happy ending," he said into the silence. "The young warrior could feel himself changing into a windigo. His heart was turning to ice.

"So to protect his people from evil and save his soul, he threw down his weapons. And climbed into the flames and died."

33

Through the windows of the van, Rachel could see it was night. In the distance, she heard the far-off rumble of thunder.

"You awake, Flag?" Logan asked from behind the wheel. "Storm coming."

She crawled over the ridged metal floor of the van, feeling the vibration of the road in her arms and legs. She climbed into the passenger seat, did up her seat belt and chewed her thumb – she couldn't help it.

She stared down at Odile's Winchester rattling on the floor between their seats. The camp counsellors would tell the police that Logan had killed Barry. Mayor Fortin would tell the police that Logan was driving north to Kirkland Lake.

Instinctively she looked over her shoulder out the back window at the empty highway vanishing behind them.

"Ease up," Logan said. "We're ahead of the cops. But we've gotta move fast to find Danny."

Rachel felt carsick. She tried taking deep breaths the way Dad had taught her, but it wasn't working. On early mornings when she went fishing with Dad, he'd tell her to think of a story or TV show, anything to take her mind off barfing.

"Tell me how you adopted Pasha," she said.

"Why did you have to go and bring that up?" He stared at her so long she got scared they were going to veer off the road.

"OK," he said at last. "Since it's you who's asking, Flag. Round about thirty-five years ago, I was driving past Sinclair's dump, the Galaxy now, and saw a bunch of locals hanging round a beat-up truck. Got curious so I pulled in for a look. Turned out it was a trapper with a load of live animals in cages. Two wolf cubs, a lynx and a black bear cub. Beautiful animals."

"And the bear cub was Pasha, the smartest and most beautiful of them all," Rachel filled in.

"Sure was. So I paid him fifty bucks for the lot of them and took 'em home."

That trapper was a son of a bitch, worse than any animal. He'd shot the mother bear for the hide and meat and Pasha was lying there pressed up against her dead body. He was figuring to drive south and sell the animals to a zoo he'd heard about in a drunken bar. Soon as he found out different, I knew he'd kill them for their pelts. So I gave him all the money I had on me, and when he tracked me down looking for more, well, let's just say I took care of business.

"So after you took them home, then what happened?" Rachel asked.

"I built my animals proper pens. Fed them leftover food from Sinclair's dumpy diner and whatever fish I could catch in Red Dog Lake. I named the wolf cubs Rusty and Brownie, and the lynx, Golden."

"And when they died, they got their own gravestones."

"That's right." Logan shot her a look. "Did I tell you this story before?"

"Some of it," she said quickly.

That seemed to satisfy him. "I gave Pasha a Russian name, like the trained circus bears I saw on TV when I lived with my foster parents. *The Ed Sullivan Show* – it was on TV long before your daddy was born. Anyhow, locals and tourists kept dropping by my camp for a look-see so I made 'em pay. That way my animals got enough to eat."

"And Pasha could do tricks so you could make the people pay more."

"You bet. Pasha was the most intelligent animal I've ever known."

"What was Pasha's best trick?"

"Well, my favourite was roll over and play dead. I'd give her a toy rifle. She'd be the sheriff and I was the bad guy. I'd run around and she'd chase after me on her hind legs. When she caught me, she'd shoot and I'd fall down and play dead. She'd roar, nudge me and lick my face all over. Then I'd leap up and say I was Sleeping Beauty brought back to life. That always made 'em laugh."

"Then she'd get her strawberry ice cream, right?"

Logan didn't reply. He slowed the van to a crawl, staring into the thick woods at the edge of the highway.

Abruptly he turned across the pavement onto a narrow gravel road. A short way in, he pulled up at a high chain-link fence.

"Kid, do me a favour. Get out and see if that gate is locked," he said.

Rachel threw open the passenger door and hopped out. The night air felt cold and bugs danced in the beams of the van's head-lights. She ran over to the metal gates and jiggled them before she saw they'd been secured with a chain. Hanging off the gate was a sign that looked like a black propeller on a yellow background. Radiation, bad radiation – that's what that sign meant. Dad had pointed out a sign like that at the hospital when they went to visit Mum.

She tried to warn Logan, but he was already out of the van, holding the rifle. He'd killed the engine, but left the headlights blazing.

"Mr. Logan?"

"Go round the back of the van. Crouch down behind the tire. Don't come out till I tell you," he said.

When he shot the lock, the boom was so loud, her ears hummed.

"You OK, Flag?" Logan had reappeared. He stood, looking down at her, the rifle resting on his shoulder. Rachel nodded. "See that?" He poked his index finger through a ragged hole in the side of the van. "That's a ricochet. Went right through. See why I made you hide outside?" She nodded again.

They climbed back into the van. Logan restarted the engine and drove through the gates down a dark corridor of pines and spruce.

"Why is there a radiation sign on the gate?" she asked.

"This here's the old Archangel Mine." He looked at her. "Uranium. They were tearing it out of the ground back in the Cold War when the Americans and the Russians wanted to nuke each other."

"But it's dangerous. Why would Danny come here?"

"Because it's the closest way to help, if he's coming through the bush from Fire Lake. The road from the Archangel Mine leads out to the highway: everybody in Red Dog Lake knows that."

Danny stared into the dark. Stones and roots dug into him no matter how much he shifted around.

Which would come first, the forest fire or the dawn?

He stared at a clearing in the trees just ahead. The ground was covered with a thin layer of sparkling snow. Odile stood there, wearing her faded blue house dress, her grey hair streaming over her shoulders. She held a sheaf of papers in her hands.

"*Mahikan*," she said. "Your writing is good." She flung open her arms. The pages of his and Rachel's graphic novel fluttered onto the snow like jewelled leaves. "Pay attention to what you have written."

She faded away and the snow melted into an opalescent lake. A black and white bird cut across it, one of the lost loons of Fire Lake. It let out a cry, and flew up out of the water with a great battering of wings, and landed in the pine tree beside him.

He came awake all at once, gasping for air. A loon landing in a tree was a terrible omen. Enough to frighten even a skeptic like himself.

The wind was picking up, soaring through the trees thirty feet above his head. Now and again, between the gusts, he heard a strange noise, a creaking and yawing like lumber breaking under a strain. Probably broken trees rubbing against each other, like the ones he'd found with his dad.

A brilliant flash of lightning arced across the sky.

He fumbled through the dark for the tree behind him and pulled himself up. Thunder exploded around him.

The next bolt of lightning threw tree trunks, weeds and stony ground into relief. He tried to memorize the layout of the ground and pushed forward blindly.

Rain came hammering down through trees. He threw open his mouth to catch the falling drops, grabbing branches and weeds as they hit him, for whatever water he could get.

Bolts of lightning tore up the sky continually. The thunder was deafening.

Rain drenched him as he pushed forward under the flickering light, but he felt like dancing. The thunderstorm would douse the forest fire. He'd find the mine and the highway, Ricky wouldn't burn …

A flash of silver. The ground was littered with twisted metal fragments. Glass crunched under his feet.

He froze. A massive bolt lit up the sky. A huge black cross was bearing down on him.

I'm going crazy, he thought. Then he smelled the pungent solvent smell.

"Avgas," he said even as he recognized the odour. "Oh, my God, it's a plane!"

A broken float plane was hanging in the pine trees above him, ready to go off like a bomb.

34

One spark hitting all that leaking fuel …

Danny knew he should run, but he couldn't. Lots of float planes look like Corazon's Piper Cherokee, he thought.

A flash of lightning. Rainwater streamed down the flanks of the broken plane. In the flat light, he couldn't make out its markings.

His dad had told him that when a bush plane got into trouble, the pilot would aim for the trees to cushion the impact. But both wings had to hit the trees at exactly the same instant. If the pilot couldn't pull that off, the plane would flip over, crash and burn.

Looked like this pilot had done the impossible.

The trees groaned as the plane shifted. Danny stumbled back, pushing wet hair out of his eyes.

More lightning. The passenger door was hanging open.

"Hey there! Are you OK?" he shouted into dark. "If you hear me, make a noise. Something, anything."

Flash – a dark bundle hanging out the passenger side.

Oh man, he thought.

He inched through the dark, feeling broken glass and pieces of metal crunch under his runners.

Flash – a body dangling by a strap, blue-white face distorted by gravity. A blue tear drop tattooed under the open left eye.

Danny cried out, he couldn't help it.

Breathing hard, he reached out into the dark and grabbed Tear Drop's leather jacket. He forced himself to check the cold limp neck for a pulse.

Pointless. Neck broken. Dead for hours.

The impact of the crash had tossed Tear Drop out of the cockpit. He must've hit the outside of the plane and died instantly.

Danny pulled out Ricky's LED. One last try, he thought. He shook it as though he was throttling Santa.

Miraculously it sparked back to life.

He beamed its light over the shattered plane. Rain ran in sparkling rivulets over the silver skin of the Twin Beech. The pilot's door stood open, the cockpit a dark hole.

He shivered in his wet clothes, listening to the storm and the cracking of the shattered pines holding up the carcass of the plane.

He moved the beam of the LED over the rubble field. Nothing resembling a body, thank God. Hendrix must be lying dead up there in the plane, but he wasn't about to climb up to make sure.

Must get out of here.

The storm was moving off, bringing on the most dangerous time for lightning strikes.

He stumbled away from the wreck and plunged back into the bush, the penetrating smell of avgas spurring him on.

"I don't like being outside in thunderstorms, Mr. Logan," Rachel said. Lightning crackled through the black sky. It felt as though they were huddling inside one of those wizard balls the comic book store had for sale back home.

"Safest place to be is inside the van," Logan replied. "But stay away from the sides. They're metal."

The van bumped off the end of the gravel road onto a pale, dusty pavement, pitted with deep holes. The headlights swept over a large looming building.

"That's the old mill." Logan gestured at the blank rusting walls. "That's where they'd crush up the ore, mix it with water and sulphuric acid and make yellowcake: eighty per cent pure uranium."

"That's poison."

"Uranium radiation ain't so bad. Less than an x-ray or at least that's what the Archangel's owners would have you believe."

He started driving past the building.

"Did you work here?" Rachel asked, wondering how he knew so much about the mine.

"No way. Archangel closed down a long time ago. I come up here sometimes to be alone. In a funny way, it reminds me of my childhood. My Pa kept me terrified the Russkies were gonna drop the big one on America. When I got away from him, I begged my foster parents to build us a bomb shelter."

A burst of lightning lit up a tall dark tower with a flat roof. To Rachel it looked like the sorcerer's castle in her video game.

"What's that tower?" She pointed at it as they passed by.

"That's the head frame," Logan said. "Sits on top of the mine shaft. It holds the cage, the elevator that hauled the men and the ore. Some miners call it the gallows frame."

"That's creepy."

"It's a good name for a place of death."

"Did many miners get killed here?"

Logan didn't reply. They'd reached the end of the pavement, a short distance from the mill building. The rain started up, battering the roof of the van. Their headlights shone down through the torrent over a vast dirt plain tufted with weeds.

"Can't see a damn thing," he muttered, trying to wipe the mist off the inside of the windshield.

Rachel leaned over to help clear her side of the window. "Where are we going?" she asked.

"Down to the tailings pond. If Danny made a straight line through the bush from Fire Lake, that's where he'd end up."

"What's the tailings pond?"

"Where they put the waste from the mill. They dumped it underwater to hold down the radiation. Why the face? You think a nasty old uranium mining company would lie and say that a bit of water can't protect you?"

He slammed the van into low gear and churned onto the bare dirt.

The rain will turn the dirt into mud, Rachel thought. We'll get stuck. Nobody's around to pull us out.

The van tilted and swayed so much, she had to brace her hands against the dash and the inside door even if it was metal.

He braked, pitching them both forward. The seat belt scraped Rachel's bare arm. Staring past the beating windshield wipers was like trying to see through a waterfall.

He sighed, turned off the headlights and killed the engine. Wind buffeted the thin metal sides of the van.

"How bad is the radiation in the tailings pond?" she asked as they stared into the night.

"Way worse than yellowcake. The waste rock is full of radium, which gives off much more radiation than uranium. And when radium decays, it gives off radon gas. That stuff really makes you glow in the dark."

"Does Danny know how dangerous the tailings pond is?"

"Hope so. Let's chow down some food while we wait for sunup. That's what a soldier does, Flag. He eats when he can."

She undid her seat belt and jumped into the cargo space where Logan had tossed the plastic bags with their food. She grabbed the bags, but couldn't help looking out the back window at the abandoned mine building.

"Hear the train?" Logan said from the front seat. "It's louder than the thunder now."

Lightning cracked open the sky above the towering outline of the gallows frame. In the square black opening near the top, the white outline of a man.

Rachel cried out. "There's a ghost. In the window."

"Oh, thank you, Blessed Virgin." Corazon slumped over the controls of the Piper Cherokee. "I will light you one hundred candles. Forgive me for doubting your grace. I will go to Mass, every week, I swear."

"You-you're amazing." Edgar clutched his nose, choking through a scarlet stream of blood. "Best pilot ever."

"Shut up!"

"I-I'm sorry." He tried to sop up the blood with a corner of his blanket. "Thinking about Santa killing my mum made me crazy."

"Then do something about it." She couldn't stop shaking. How she'd landed on Red Dog Lake in the dark with no gas and a storm coming on, she'd never know. It was a miracle, a damn miracle.

The Piper Cherokee coughed through the waves toward the dock. "Mess with me again, and I'll take my shotgun and blast you into space," she said. "I'll give you a flying lesson you'll never forget."

"I-I said I was sorry." He tried unsuccessfully to clear his nose. "Look, if we hadn't gone down low, we would never have seen that guy waving at us. Maybe, um, maybe that was Danny."

Oh, Holy Mother, make that guy be Danny.

Adrenalin coursed through her in great shuddering waves. Edgar had spotted the man on the cliff; she hadn't seen a damn thing. Too busy pulling the plane out of its deadly spin. Just the same, she'd broken her rule about cops and radioed in the sighting to the OPP. Now all she could do was hope for the best: that the cops would send out a rescue copter in time to save him.

The end of the dock was approaching. She glared at Edgar. "Give me the keys to the Hummer."

"What? What for?"

"You know what we gotta do. In Red Dog Lake we take care of our own. Are you in with me or not?"

"Yeah, yeah, I'm in." He swiped at the mess of tears, snot and blood on his face. "I loved my mum, I really loved her."

Must move, must go faster.

Thank God, Ricky's LED was still working, Danny thought. Branches tore through his clothes, scratched his bare skin bloody. He pounded over the rolling stones of a dry stream bed, tripped and fell heavily.

A strange buzzing sound. The back of his neck tingled. An eerie blue-white glow shot through the trees. St. Elmo's fire dancing on the silver skin of Santa's plane.

Lightning strike; he threw his arms over his head.

The explosion hit a heartbeat later. The pressure wave rocketed over him, wrenching the air from his lungs. Behind him, a furnace roar of flame as the avgas ignited.

35

The moment Logan turned to look for the ghost, a loud boom overrode the thunder. The ground, the van, everything was shaking.

"Wh-what's that?" Rachel asked. Through the misty windshield, she watched a scarlet sphere erupt in the forest.

Logan swore and swiped at the moisture on the glass. Rachel scrambled back to the front, leaving the bags of food where she'd dropped them.

Far away in the trees a fire was burning through the rain like a lighthouse.

"The lightning started a forest fire," she said.

"No, Soldier, that's artillery," he replied. "Coupla miles away, I'd say. I'm an old combat vet, remember? Heard a lot of those big guns in 'Nam."

A direct lightning strike on the plane.

Danny coughed and choked, desperate for oxygen. Slowly the air returned.

I can breathe. I'm still alive.

Metal and glass rained down through the branches. The burning plane bathed the forest in a red-tinged chiaroscuro.

Even though he was shielded by thick brush, the scorching heat of the flames was unbearable.

Must run. The brush will be an inferno.

He tottered to his feet, shaking a heavy litter of shredded bark and dirt off his back. Two arms, two legs, no gushing fountains of blood. A dull ringing in his ears. The thumping of his footsteps on the forest floor and the swish of branches and weeds sounded strangely muffled.

The explosion's knocked out my hearing.

He groped for the LED, but this time, he couldn't find it. And Ricky's knife, too, was gone.

"Why is the fire still burning?" Rachel asked. "Won't the thunderstorm put it out?"

As if in answer to her question, a rush of rain slapped against the van.

"Something's fuelling that fire," Logan said. "Too big to be rained out." He accepted the peanut butter sandwich she handed him. "I'm thinking we should get the hell out of here."

"But what about Danny?"

"OK." Logan took a thoughtful bite of his bread. "We gotta keep a close watch though. When the wind comes up from the west, that fire will blow over here in a heartbeat. We'll be trapped."

She felt cold stir in her stomach again. Fear, the wolf that circled round her even with Logan beside her.

She left the passenger seat and crawled over the heap of blankets to look out the back window again. Too dark to make out the gallows tower. If she reminded Logan about the ghost, he might decide to hunt it down. The thought of being left alone in the van in the blowing dark made her legs shake.

He leaned back in the driver's seat, chewing his food. "Sun-up's at 6:30. What does your watch say?" he asked.

She checked it. "Four o'clock."

"OK, I'll take first watch. A soldier grabs sleep when he can. You should, too, Flag."

Santa pounded the gas pedal, but the wretched *Prius* wouldn't stop hesitating and sputtering. The blinking fuel light on the narrow

display above the steering wheel now took on an ominous signifi-
cance. He ran his fingers through his sweat-drenched hair. He'd
been so focused on keeping the wretched battery alive that he'd
ignored the gas bit.

He stuck to the conventional right side of the road now, dimming the headlights as much as the *Prius*'s safety-Nazi design would
allow. In the wee small hours of the morning, he was unlikely to
encounter any OPP enemy sharks, but it never hurt to be cautious.

He passed the sign for Red Dog Lake.

He glided past Camp Nirvana's painfully outdated hippy peace
symbol. Gate closed and locked, mercifully no coppers. They must
have wrapped up their inquiries into dear departed Barry's most
unfortunate fall from grace. Still they'd be looking to interview him,
no point pretending otherwise.

A few miles later, he coaxed the *Prius* past the pink pile of the
Galaxy Motel. The stab wound in his thigh pulsed with pain. God
how he'd love to exact an exquisitely nasty revenge on that Corazon
bitch. No time now, he had business to take care of back at the Fish
Camp, but with luck he'd fit something in. Too bad he and Hendrix
were on the outs at the moment. Hendrix always had creative ideas.

The *Prius* – the Priapus more like – was chugging mightily, buck-
ing like a crazed goat. Finally, at long last, there stood his unholy
grail: the entrance to Santa's Fish Camp. About bloody time, too, he
thought and charged through the gate.

An almighty clang brought him up short. The *Prius* emitted a
last gasping shudder and stalled for good.

He tumbled out the driver's side to survey the damage. He'd
completely forgotten about the bollocking security chain across the
drive. It had never been an issue with the Christmas Hummer: he'd
popped through it dozens of times careening back from the bar.

He kicked the *Prius* with frenzied passion until blinding pain in
his wounded thigh prevailed.

His leg throbbing like a bastard, he scrambled over the remains
of the chain and plunged into the dark deserted grounds of Santa's
Fish Camp. The fibreglass statues along the forest trail glowed

moodily under the feeble light of the early dawn as he passed them by. Not a sound, not even the hum of an insect.

Behind Little Jack Horner and his plum pie stood a utility shed. He hobbled round to it and caved in the flimsy sheet metal doors with a kick from his undamaged leg. He pulled out a heavy metal spade and a black plastic garbage bag and headed back down the trail, making for Fish Camp Central, with its pond full of carp, Santa's Throne and Gift Shop.

As he limped down the trail, his pain and suffering were horribly augmented by some basic arithmetic. He'd only netted two thousand and ten dollars from Corazon, a laughable sum for effective decamping. Millions were locked up in the crystal meth, but the practicalities of seizing it from the trailer sent him into a panic. Hendrix and Tear Drop would snuff him out before he knew he was dead. Surprise, brute force and a reliably lethal weapon would be his minimum essential requirements, none of which, unfortunately, he had to hand.

Good thing he'd hidden away a tidy little insurance fund: the cash from the bear hunt.

Courage, Old Son, he told himself, catching sight of the dark waters of the fish pond. He hefted up the spade and limped over to the flimsy wooden dock. Here snotty little ankle-biters could pose with Santa for a twenty-five dollar photo. A fake fish on a string cost five dollars extra.

The carp had risen from the bottom of the pond in a writhing, wriggling mass, breaking through the murky surface of the water. Awful smell, like sewage and mud, with an undertone of ashes.

Well, he'd be well clear of the place in a minute. He hobbled the short distance over to Santa's Gift Shop. Lovely bit of irony to rest one's bum on the faux red velvet cushions of Santa's Throne, knowing that they held the salvation of said bum.

He aimed his spade to break through the glass door, when he noticed it was already standing open. *What the hell?*

He pushed his way inside.

Couldn't hear bugger all, but best not turn on any lights. No point in alerting that nasty sod Tear Drop who had an uncanny way of appearing round corners.

Visitors had to pass by Santa seated in all his glory before they reached the gift store proper. He fumbled over to the raised chipboard dais and grabbed the cushion on his gilded plastic throne.

He felt nothing but a heap of soft foam stuffing. Heart pounding, he plunged his hands through the ripped fabric, foraging desperately. His precious hundred thousand dollars had vanished.

Have to make sure, must make sure. He staggered over to the light switch and flicked it on. Santa's Throne was shredded as though that damn bear, Pasha, had used it to sharpen her claws.

He stumbled outside, dragging the spade behind him. The smell of smoke was undeniable now. A strange phosphorescence flickered over the fish pond.

Fire! A red light glowed through the trees, coming from the direction of Hendrix's trailer.

He started as a bulky dark shape separated from the shadows.

Danny was running blind through a funhouse of pitfalls and slapping blows from tree branches. He stumbled, legs numb, no longer conscious of walking. He only knew he'd fallen when he felt a stone pressing into his cheek and tasted blood in his mouth.

The rain from the thundershower would steam off the foliage like water off a stove. A freight train of fire would chase him down.

He tried to lever his body off the ground. Couldn't do it. He screamed at his muscles, swore at them, coaxed them.

Nothing, worn out.

Breathe in the smoke. Breathe deep, hold it in.

If I pass out, I won't feel the fire eating me …

Logan banged open the driver's door, letting in a rush of cold air. Rachel sat up and tossed off the old grey blanket. A watery light suffused the inside of the van.

She followed him outside, rubbing her eyes. No sun visible under the heavy overcast. The early dawn felt less like sun-up than a draining away of the night.

Logan was standing a short distance in front of the van. She ran up to him and together they looked down a long slope of dirt and gravel that ended at the tailings pond. To Rachel, the pond looked like a meteorite crater in the dark-green trees, a huge rust-rimmed pit filled with muddy water.

"It looks more like a lake than a pond," she said.

"Had to be big for what Archangel was doing," he replied.

A dark grey mist was curling through the trees.

"Is that the forest fire?" she asked.

"Yep, we're at risk, Solider." He shouldered his rifle. "Five minutes, down and up, that's all the time we've got."

"Danny!" Rachel shouted. She took off down the hill. Her runners sank in the cold damp earth. She struggled down the slope, trying to make her legs go faster.

The bottom of the hill ended at the edge of the tailings pond. She hesitated, not wanting to go near it. Under the water, the muddy bottom looked scaly and rusty.

She yelled Danny's name again, scanning the dark woods, searching for a human form, a campfire, a shelter, anything …

Nothing but silent dark trees.

She cupped her hands and screamed Danny's name. Logan stumbled down the slope to join her.

A flock of Canada geese flew over them and landed near the centre of the pond. Logan raised the rifle and fired into the air.

Danny was staring at white snow, lying in the forest clearing he'd seen in his dream.

I'm dying, he thought. Where is Odile?

Mahikan, you must get up. He heard her voice, clear and strong. *Get up. Save yourself and your little sister.*

He blinked. The white plain was a muddy lake. Around him, tree trunks took form. He saw pine needles, tall weeds and stones lodged in red-brown earth.

246 M. H. Callway

Someone was shouting. It sounded like a kid.

"Rachel?" he whispered. His mouth was parched, his voice a croak.

"DANNEEEEEE." She sounded desperate.

He swayed onto his hands and knees, started crawling …

His fists were sinking into mucky reddish earth. Before him stretched an expanse of shallow water. A flock of Canada geese swam leisurely at the centre.

A tiny figure stood on the opposite bank, shouting his name. At the top of a long dirt slope leading up from the water, he spotted an orange and white *Volkswagen* van, as tiny as a child's toy.

"Logan?" he muttered.

Rachel turned away, heading back up the hill.

"Ra – Rachel," he gasped.

The crack of a gunshot. The birds took off from the water in a thunderous flapping of wings. Rachel turned to watch them.

He lifted his arm, as heavy as lead. He reached up, tried to wave to her again.

"DANNEEEE!"

His arms gave way. He crumpled face first into the dirt.

In his dream he saw Rachel running toward him, skirting the edge of the water, and Logan's lanky form loping behind her, a rifle in his outstretched hand.

36

The shadow took shape.

"Edgar?" Santa couldn't conceal his surprise. "What the hell are you doing here?"

Edgar's overalls were darkly stained, his green elf hat sooty and torn. He was clutching a large red metal container with a long metal spout.

Santa smelled the sharp tang of gasoline. "Answer me, you sod."

Edgar tilted the can and poured a glittering stream of gas onto the pond's dock. He shuffled back, trailing fluid over the dirt to Santa's Gift Shop.

"For God's sake!" Santa said. "Bloody stop that, you mongrel. Did Hendrix put you up to this? Is that what this is about?"

Edgar's doleful cow's eyes swivelled his way. "No," he said, solemn as a bell.

The light through the trees was growing brighter. Now Santa could hear pops and bangs and shattering glass. "You set the meth lab on fire! You bloody fool, do you know what you've done? You've sent millions of dollars up in smoke."

"No, uh-uh." Edgar paused. "Mr. Hendrix and Tear Drop cleaned out the trailer this afternoon. They took your plane. Bye-bye Twin Beech."

"What?"

"Oh, yeah. But they didn't get far."

His heart made one slow thud. "You did something to my plane."

"Naw, Corazon took care of that."

"Are you saying ..." Santa blinked, throat dry. "Are you saying that Filo bitch buggered my plane? Did ... did Hendrix and Tear Drop go down?"

"Yep, big time." Edgar sloshed gasoline over the doors and windows of the Gift Shop.

All those millions and my plane, my soaring silver angel. Santa squeezed the spade handle as though he'd break it in two. "You barefaced liar! You couldn't possibly know if Hendrix crashed. Unless ..." he swallowed. "Were the police here?"

Edgar shrugged, shifted the can to his other hand while he foraged through the pockets of his overalls.

"Answer me, you cretinous bastard!"

Edgar rubbed his nose thoughtfully. "Corazon and I went up in her plane this afternoon. We saw the Twin Beech from the air. It hit the trees down by the old Archangel Mine."

"What?" Santa leaned on the spade for support, imagining a charred wreck. "Are they dead?"

"No kidding. The Twin Beech didn't burn but it broke up pretty good. Hard to see, though, on account of the smoke from the forest fire."

"Forest fire?" Santa echoed.

"Yeah, took out Fire Island, too. I spotted a guy on a bunch of rocks. He was waving at us. Corazon radioed the cops."

"Who ... who was it? Was it one of the hunters? Answer me, damn it!"

Edgar shrugged. "Don't know."

Morty and Anderson and Ricky Fountain: he'd put them out of his mind till now. They were all dead.

All except one.

He had to get out. No time left. "Where's my bear money, you thieving bastard?"

Edgar smiled for the first time. "Gave it to Corazon. All of it."

"What! Why, in God's name? Why?"

"Payback." Edgar pulled a plastic cigarette lighter from his overalls and held it aloft.

"Stop that."

"No."

"You utter turnip, what good will it do to burn down the Fish Camp? It provides the only jobs you and your mouth-breathing mates have in Red Moronic Lake."

"Shut up." Edgar flung a stream of gasoline Santa's way.

Santa leapt back, but not before fluid soaked into his tunic and trousers. "Are you mad?" he shouted. He felt a chill as the gas evaporated, the vapours searing his nose. "Come now, we've been working together a long time, Edgar. We're mates."

Edgar's fleshy face was as mournful as a medieval painting. "Corazon flew me up to Buggy Lake today."

"What!" *Check and mate.* "Vera had an accident." Santa's thoughts dashed about frantically. The words were scrambling out, catching on his tongue. "We didn't want to upset you, your mum and I. She's down in Toronto, I got her into a nice seniors apartment ..."

"Liar. You've been cashing her pension cheques, just like Corazon said."

"As a favour, to help her out."

"You killed her." Edgar flicked the lighter and tossed it at the pond.

The dock whooshed into flame. A string of fire raced across the dirt and burst into Santa's Gift Shop. The carp in the pond churned wildly as burning embers hit the water.

Immune to the heat of the fire, Edgar calmly picked up the gas can, the liquid sloshing inside. He advanced as slowly and deliberately as the monster in a science fiction movie.

Santa swung the spade. Full out, aiming for the fragile bone over Edgar's temple, trying to knock the ball out of the park.

The spade connected. Edgar hit the ground like a bull on the killing floor. The gas can slopped over his legs.

A floating ember ignited the gas in a burst of fire.

Santa backed away in terror. Then he remembered the gas-starved *Prius*.

The gas can had toppled on its side next to Edgar. He tore off his gas-soaked tunic and trousers. Nearly naked now, he reached through the fire and grabbed the can's metal handle.

He let out a shriek of pain. Blisters popped out on his palm.

Nothing for it, he needed that gas. Steeling himself, the flames singeing the hair on his bare arm, he snatched Edgar's elf hat from his bloodied head. He wrapped it round the handle of the gas can like a pot holder and dragged it clear of the fire.

"Oh God," he gasped. He collapsed a short distance from the fire. *Have to get away. Must run.*

He stood up and faced a vision of hell.

Edgar rose up out of the ring of fire. Wreathed in flames, he staggered across the charred dock and plunged into the fish pond. Water splashed over the banks in a heavy wave.

"Bloody hell," Santa choked.

Edgar floated quietly, face to the night sky. The pale bellies of the carp flashed as they thrashed around him.

A horrid metallic taste rose up Santa's throat. Helpless, he vomited into the dirt.

"EDGAR!" Corazon burst out of the trees, running like a mad Valkyrie, waving her shotgun. "Oh, my God, Edgar!"

Santa wheeled, searching frantically for the forest trail. He heaved up the gas canister and ran for his life.

"Get back here, you bastard!" she shouted.

The tree beside him exploded. The crazy bitch was shooting.

He ran into the dark of the forest, ignoring the screeching pain in his cut leg. He wove madly through the trees, hearing her fire again and again.

Thank God, her aim was every bit as bad as before.

He heard her slosh into the fish pond. "Edgar, oh my God, oh my God," she cried.

Thank God or whomever, she'd stopped shooting at him to save the fool. Charged with fear, he kept running, taking full advantage of her misplaced sentimentality …

"Edgar, *Sancta Maria!*"

Corazon felt her feet sink into the oozing muck of the pond bottom. The soft rubbery bodies of the carp squirmed around her. Thank God, the water only reached to her waist.

She tossed the shotgun onto the bank. She caught hold of Edgar's beefy shoulders and dragged him away from the fire to the far side of the pond.

"Get away from me. Get away, you mothers!" She pounded and thrashed at the carp to no avail. The rancid stench of the pond and the charring smoke were choking her.

"Help me, Blessed Virgin."

She struggled out onto the muddy bank. With her last bit of strength, she hauled Edgar's head and shoulders out of the water. She dared not look at his terrible injuries.

He let out a grinding moan.

Oh, my God, he's alive.

She fumbled through her sodden jacket for her cellphone. Miraculously it was still working.

She punched out a number, praying for him to pick up.

Hearing his familiar voice, she burst into hysterical sobs. "Oh, Joseph, thank God, you're home. It's Corazon. Edgar's hurt. I-I think he's dying. *Sancta Maria*, please God, we need your help."

37

"Water, give him water."

Danny saw Logan's bright blue eyes looking down at him.

Rachel leaned in, holding a large green plastic bottle with both hands. Danny felt cool fluid splash onto his face and run between his clenched teeth.

"Careful, Soldier. Pour that water into him a bit at a time," Logan said.

He felt Logan reach under his shoulders and lift him up. Water flowed into him, smooth and electric. His dry throat spasmed. He drank madly, his dirt-blackened hands clutching the plastic bottle, squeezing it flat.

"Ease up, Kid," Logan said. "Water won't help you if it comes back up again."

"I hear you," Danny whispered. He let Logan pry his fingers off the bottle and take it away.

"Rach, is it really you?" Her eyes were amber in the faint light. He reached for her hand. "You're really here."

"Danny!" Rachel threw her arms around him, burying her face in his neck, refusing to let go.

"You're cutting off his oxygen, Flag," Logan said.

"It's OK," Danny said. He curled his arm round her back and reached for the water bottle. Logan held it so he could drink. This time he was able to slow down on his own.

Logan tapped Rachel on the shoulder. She released her grip on Danny so he could sit up. He propped himself up on his elbows, head swimming.

"Can you get up?" Logan asked him.

"Give me a minute."

"Come on, we gotta move. That forest fire's getting too damn close," Logan stood up, tall as a tower.

"We saw it start!" Rachel jumped up to stand next to him. "The lightning came down and made a big red ball of fire. Did you see it? How close were you?"

"Too close. I need – I need something to eat. Anything you've got."

"Here, Danny." Rachel grabbed a plastic bag lying on the ground, pulled out a sandwich and handed it to him.

He sat up slowly and bit off a corner of the sandwich, chewing it carefully, mindful of Logan's warning to take it slow. The ordinary store-bought bread and peanut butter tasted better than anything he'd ever eaten.

"You done?" Logan asked. He was getting twitchy.

Danny shoved in a last bit of food and tried to stand up. The world was spinning again.

"I got you, Kid." Logan hauled him up and held him steady. "Breathe deep. Get your sea legs."

"Thanks," Danny said. The ground slowly levelled out.

"I'll help, too." Rachel threw her thin arm round his waist.

Leaning on Logan and Rachel, he stepped onto the rusty mud that ringed the tailings pond. Took one step, then another. Slow going. Thick smoke was rolling in over the water. A single bird swam in its centre, a smudged black spot.

The loon ... disaster.

Logan was right, they had to get out and quickly. "I'm OK now, John," Danny said after a few minutes. "Go on ahead, start the van. We're right behind you, as fast as I can make it."

Logan thought this over. "OK," he said at last. He plowed ahead of them up the long gravel incline, making for the VW.

Danny waited until Logan was halfway up the hill. "Rach, listen to me. We have to get the cops."

"No, we can't. Mr. Logan's in trouble."

"I know Logan hates cops, but there was a guy with me. He's hurt real bad. He needs the paramedics soon as we can get them out to him, if it isn't too late already."

"There aren't any rescue helicopters. All the cops are fighting a big forest fire in Malartic. Mr. Logan said we had to save you ourselves. That's why we drove out here to the mine."

"Logan's wrong. The cops will listen. This guy's one of their own."

"Danny, I ... I need to tell you something."

"Wait a minute." He rested a hand on her shoulder. "What's Logan doing?"

Logan had paused at the crest of the hill and seemed to be listening intently.

"He's listening for the train," Rachel said. "He's the only one who can hear it. And he keeps calling me 'Soldier' and 'Flag'. I don't know if I should feel scared or not."

Black smoke cloaked the tailings pond. The bird had vanished from sight.

"How did Logan know where to find me?" Danny asked.

"He said you'd end up at the tailings pond if you walked straight through the bush from Fire Lake."

"Grandmother told him I was on Fire Lake. She's amazing." He felt he could run the rest of the way up the hill to the van. "When I was out there in the bush, Grandmother came to me in my dream just like the old ones say. I used to think her mystic stuff was bogus. I figured I was dehydrated and hallucinating, but she was there, she was really there."

Rachel stared up at him, her lips trembling.

"What's wrong?" he asked.

"Odile, I-I ..." She burst into tears. "So many bad things are happening, Danny. Santa *killed* Barry Tucker. He pushed him over the cliff."

"What!"

"Santa wanted to kill me, too. I ran to Mr. Logan's. Now the police think Mr. Logan killed Barry. And Odile ..." Sobs choked her voice.

"Slow down, Kiddo."

Rachel tried to take a breath. "Sergeant McKenna was driving with Odile to the OPP station. She was going to get a rescue helicopter to look for you."

"Sergeant McKenna!" He grabbed her shoulders. "Are you sure? Ricky, the guy who's hurt – he's an undercover cop. He's working with McKenna. I have the proof with me."

"No! You don't understand. Mayor Fortin said ... he said Sergeant McKenna got shot. Before she got to the police station."

Cold spread through Danny like poison. "What ... what happened? Where's Grandmother?"

"She's gone. They can't find her."

She came to me as a spirit. She's dead because of me.

The world had stopped moving. He wanted to scream, but if he gave in to his feelings now ...

"Danny, I want to go to the police," Rachel said. "I want them to stop these bad things."

"We will, Little Sister, soon as we get out of here. Don't worry."

Logan had reached the van. Danny watched him throw open the driver's door and climb in.

A loud explosion. The tire on the passenger side vanished. Shreds of rubber burst through the air.

"Get down!" Danny grabbed Rachel and pulled her down with him onto the ground.

"What's going on?" Her voice sounded muffled against the dirt.

"Somebody's shooting at us. Stay down. Don't look up, promise me."

"OK."

Danny lifted his head to look up the hill. The VW had sagged heavily to one side. Logan's bearded form was hunched over the steering wheel.

John, get out of there.

Another shot. The VW's rear tire exploded. This time Danny saw a telltale puff of smoke from an opening near the top of the gallows tower.

"He's up there in the tower. Stay down, Rach."

A loud chain of noise. Bullets ripped through the thin metal sides of the VW. The driver's door flew open.

Logan tumbled out. He rolled into a combat stance and fired at the gallows frame.

"John, down here," Danny yelled.

Logan ran in a crouch and leapt down onto the hill. He slid and crashed down the gravel slope, landing just below them.

He crawled back up to them on his elbows, face streaked with mud and sweat. "Too old for this crap," he said. "You two OK?"

"Yes," Danny and Rachel answered together.

"Keep your heads down," Logan said. He squinted, aiming at the tower. "Can't get a fix on him. Got an old man's eyes, can't see a damn thing."

More bullets spattered into the dirt at the top of the hill.

"I don't think he can see us from up there," Danny said.

"Good thing," Logan said.

"Look, I've got an idea. If we go back down the hill a little way, we can get back into the forest. He won't see us there. We'll stay in the trees and work our way past the mine building. Then we can angle up through the trees and find the mine road."

"Won't work. Smoke's too bad in the woods."

"It's better than staying here waiting to get shot."

Logan looked down the hill. "OK, the fire hasn't hit the trees yet. You'd better get moving."

Rachel still had the plastic bag of provisions with her. Danny pulled out the plastic water bottle and a roll of paper towels. Quickly, he wadded up three clumps of paper towels and soaked them with water.

"Put this wet stuff over your mouth and nose," he told Rachel. "It'll cut the smoke. We're going to crawl back down the hill like snakes and get into the woods, OK?"

"OK." She threw him a grin, a flash of her old courage. She grabbed her share of the wet towels, turned around on her stomach to face down the hill and started down.

"Come on, John." He tried to hand Logan a sodden clump of towels.

Logan waved him off. "Keep them for Flag. Look after her. She's yours now." He broke open the rifle, checked it, and forced it back together. "You better find that road."

"Don't be crazy, come on!" When Logan didn't budge, he said: "Odile told me to look after my family. That means you, too."

"Do as I tell you or I'll put a hole in you like I should've before. The train's coming and I'm climbing aboard."

"I'm not kidding. I *saw* Odile out there."

"I know you did," Logan replied. "Now get the hell down into those trees or you'll lose Flag."

A bullet splattered into the earth three feet in front of them. Logan squeezed off a round in an ear-ringing burst of noise.

"Fine, I'll make sure Rachel's OK then I'm coming back for you."

Logan ignored him.

Danny started crawling down the slope. Rachel had moved swiftly. He watched the soles of her runners vanish into the smoke lapping up the hill.

He couldn't see her any more. No time to lose. He scrambled down after her, diving into the toxic fog bank of smoke. Immediately his eyes flooded. He couldn't breathe despite the wet paper towels over his mouth and nose.

"Rachel, where are you?" His voice was muffled. "Rachel ..." He was choking.

He heard a faint cough in front of him. He reached out and caught her arm. "Hold my hand ..." She grabbed it and held on.

They needed to travel across the hill about a hundred yards before they reached the trees. He couldn't see a damn thing, he could only guess at the right direction.

His hand tight round hers, he began dragging her over the choppy ground.

Bare-chested, dressed only in his striped boxer shorts and blood-soaked leg bandage, Santa leaned on the steering wheel of the *Prius*, breathing laboriously. He'd had an adventure forcing enough fuel into the wretched eco-car's gas tank. Barely got it going again using the usual slaps and gyrations on the dashboard.

Mustn't feel sorry about Edgar. Stupid sod asked for it.

He knew the shakes were waning when avarice eclipsed his frenzied thoughts of escape. He'd bloody earned those millions. Earned them a thousand times over.

Edgar said the Twin Beech was broken apart. It hadn't burned and the forest fire hadn't reached it yet. Hendrix and Tear Drop were dead and that lovely crystal meth was just sitting there in the wreck waiting to be had.

He'd find the crash site, how hard could it be? He knew the road in to the Archangel Mine. Knew it bloody well. He and Charmaine had driven out there in the Christmas Hummer often enough so he could sample her goods.

With luck, he'd salvage a wonderful retirement out of this dog's breakfast.

"Danny ..." Rachel coughed bitterly. "I can't ... breathe ..."

"Me either. We've got to ... go back up."

He turned back up the incline, clutching Rachel's hand. He stumbled blindly over the gravel, not stopping until they climbed out of the smoke into fresher air.

They collapsed on the ground, gasping.

"Stay down, Rach."

"I'm thirsty," she said.

He pulled the water bottle from the bag, opened it and gave it to her. She drank a couple of swallows and passed the bottle back to him. Hardly any left.

The forest beckoned, fifty yards away.

"OK, that's where we're going." He pointed to the trees, pushing away thoughts of an unseen bullet. "You have to run, like track and field at school."

"I can do it."

"If something happens to me, promise me, you'll keep going. Find the road. OK?"

"No, Danny, no ..."

High above them, he heard the rapid exchange of gunfire. "Now, Rach ..."

He grabbed her hand and shot out over the loose gravel. Heart pounding, he kept her close, shielding her from the tower with his body.

A bullet mashed into the soft gravel by his foot. He heard Logan return fire.

Don't think, run.

The soft earth and stones tripped them, made them clumsy and ungainly. He saw the trees ...

All at once they were caught in a dark maze of branches and weeds. He fought through them, dragging on her arm.

"Can we stop now?" Rachel asked.

"Yeah." He leaned on a birch tree and tried to catch his breath. "You OK?"

Her face was muddy and stray bits of leaf were tangled in her hair, but she was smiling. "You look like a crazy wild man," she said.

"No kidding. Come on, that jerk could fire into the trees any minute. This way."

He slogged through the bush, making sure Rachel stayed close behind him. "Once we hit the road, walking will be easy," he said. "Only ten clicks and we reach the highway."

"What about Mr. Logan?" she asked.

All he could hear was the numbing thud of their feet on the forest floor, the swish of tree branches and Rachel's tight breathing.

"That shooter won't get him, don't you worry about it." *I better not be lying.*

"I saw him in the tower last night. He looked like a ghost." Rachel rubbed at the insects that descended on them, moving or not. "I-I tried to tell Mr. Logan."

"Hendrix," Danny said.

So Hendrix had survived the crash of the Twin Beech. He'd climbed down from the shattered cockpit and walked out of the woods to the mine. When Logan and Rachel showed up in the VW, he took refuge in the gallows frame.

He left Logan and Rachel alone, but when he saw me he started shooting. I nearly got Rachel and Logan killed, he thought.

No witnesses: scorched earth.

"Sergeant McKenna said Hendrix is a real badass. He came to Blue Sky Bookstore," Rachel said.

"What!"

"Odile called him a demon, a windigo."

"Oh God … out there, that's what she tried to tell me."

"Danny …" Rachel stopped moving. "I don't hear Mr. Logan shooting anymore."

She was right. The world had fallen silent.

38

The mine road shone through the trees like a dusty river. They tumbled onto it, free of the smoky darkness of the forest.

"Rach, listen to me." Danny bent down and took her shoulders. "We're going to split up now. I want you to run out to the highway and get the cops. I'm going back for Logan."

"No! Hendrix will *kill* you." She clung to his torn shirt. "I'm coming with you."

"You can't." Gently he detached her hands. "It'll be easy. Just follow this road. The cops patrol up and down the highway all the time. Hide in the bush until you see an OPP cruiser. Then yell, wave, jump up and down, do anything to make them stop."

"What if they don't stop?"

"Wait for the next one. And promise me, swear that you'll hide until you see a cop car. A lot of weirdos drive along the highway."

"OK, OK, I'm not stupid." Her strange yellow eyes were wide. "I'll wait for you and Mr. Logan."

"NO! Get the cops." He stood back, silently urging her to run. "I'll be fine, Little Sister. Now go. Run!"

Face solemn, she turned away from him. She set off slowly down the road, each footstep an accusation.

"Sorry, Rach," he said softly.

Her footsteps became shorter and shorter until she was running. He waited until her small form merged with the distant trees.

The dirt road was humped like a hill in the middle and scattered all over with stones. How long would it take to run ten clicks? The longest cross-country race Rachel had done in school was only three clicks.

A funny pain in her right side under her ribs. A stitch, that's what Dad called it. He'd had one during his last triathlon and had to drop out.

She rested her hand on the pain, rubbing to make it go away. She slowed down to a walk, kicking the odd stone in the road, and tried not to think about Dad getting on the sag wagon during his race.

Why wouldn't her stupid side stop hurting? She stopped walking and took a deep breath to see if that would help. The forest was deathly silent now that she was alone. No animals, just stupid stinging bugs, and trees lining the road like the walls of a dark corridor.

A sudden cry like a baby in pain. She spun, looking behind her. A grey shape, soft as dust, skimmed over her head and landed on the top of a nearby spruce.

"An owl," she said aloud.

She rubbed her bare arms, feeling cold. Dr. Amdur, Dad's boss, got freaked out by owls. He said that back in England, where he grew up, seeing an owl meant bad luck.

She sensed the car before she saw it. It was gliding silently toward her.

Barry's beige *Prius*.

Santa!

Her brain told her to run into the woods, but her legs had gone rigid. She couldn't move. He's going to run me over, she thought. Still she couldn't move.

She watched the *Prius* creep over the dust of the road and stop ten feet away.

The driver's door opened and Santa got out. He wasn't wearing his dirty red suit any more. His hair was filthy and full of leaves and his bare torso was plastered with dirt. In those dorky striped undershorts, he looked like he was pretending to be a Maori warrior from New Zealand.

"Well, I'm damned," Santa said, leaning on the open driver's door and swinging a bottle in one hand. "If it isn't Logan's granddaughter. Aren't we the happy little Vegemite? Come over here. I want to talk to you."

"No!" Rachel forced out.

"Do as you're told. You've been a thorn in my backside ever since I clapped eyes on you."

"I'm not stupid, Fat-ass. You want to hurt me because I know you killed Barry."

"Such a heartbreaking loss to the youth of today, our dear departed Barry. He had you in his sights, you know, you social worker's nightmare. You should thank me proper for ridding the world of his useless existence."

They stared at each other.

Legs shaking, not daring to take her eyes off him, she leaned down and scooped up a fistful of gravel.

"Well, well, you vicious little monkey." He stepped round the door. "Bloody get over here."

"No way," she called back, forcing the vibration out of her voice. "Come and get me. I dare you."

"Move your skinny tail or I'll get back in the car, drive you down and flatten you proper."

Rachel lobbed a stone onto the hood of the *Prius*. Not a hard throw, but enough to make the metal ping. He reacted with irritation just as she'd hoped. She tossed a second rock, harder this time.

"Stop that," he shouted.

She winged a stone at the headlight, heard a most satisfying crack. Dad always said she'd make a great softball pitcher.

"Stop it, I said."

"Come and make me, Killer." A direct hit on the windshield, another to the window on the open driver's door, making him leap out of the way and drop the bottle on the ground. She threw freely now, dinging the car all over, watching his face grow scarlet.

Best for last. She leaned back like the pitchers in the American League and bopped him square in the middle of the forehead.

He roared in outrage and charged down the side of the car toward her.

She fled down the passenger side of the *Prius*, aiming for the trees, but he doubled back and caught her behind the trunk of the car. He seized her right arm, wrenching it so viciously the world glowed red.

She screamed the way Dad had taught her. *Use that microsecond of surprise to get away.* She twisted and let fly the gravel left in her free hand.

It struck him full in the face. He cried out, clutching his eyes.

"I am a ninja!"

She threw out her foot in a roundhouse kick, aiming her heel through the dirty grey bandage on his leg.

He bellowed like a shot moose. She jerked her arm free and ran past him to the open driver's door. She leapt behind the wheel, jamming the door closed an instant before he seized the handle.

She punched down the power lock button, sealing all the doors and windows.

He pummelled uselessly on the window. "Try and start it. Just try, you black-hearted little lizard," he shouted. "It's far beyond your weasel's brain. You're trapped. When I get my hands on you, you'll pray you'd never been born."

The key to the *Prius* was still lodged in the steering wheel. Awesome!

She flipped him her middle finger straight and tall. Grinning now, she rotated her finger and pressed the power button on the dash. Instantly the video screen woke up.

"What the hell?" He stared wildly.

"My dad's boss, Dr. Amdur, drives a *Prius*," she said through the glass.

Seeing Santa's expression was better than beating her best video game score.

"And Dad taught me how to drive." She shot the gearshift into reverse and backed up, watching the road through the back window, steering with one hand.

She couldn't see too well over the driver's seat, so she couldn't back up really fast the way Dad had taught her back at his old workplace, the body shop. Santa hobbled after her in a fury. His hands slid over the smooth hood of the car as he desperately tried to get a grip.

Abruptly she swung the wheel over in the first leg of a three point turn. He bellied over the hood, fumbling for the windshield wipers. She pressed down on the lever under the wheel and doused him with windshield washer fluid.

He roared, blue liquid streaming from his eyes and beard. She slammed the gear into drive, swung the wheel over into the second curve of the turn and tromped on the gas pedal.

Momentum rocked him off the car. He bounced and rolled like a dirty white barrel into the road.

"Yeehaw!" Rachel screamed and roared down the road.

He heaved onto all fours in a runner's stance. Battered though he was, he limped after her.

She pushed on the accelerator, knocking the *Prius* into gas-mode. He was running like a parody of a steam engine now, arms and legs pumping, face crimson as he wheezed for more oxygen. But no human had a hope of catching a car.

His frenetic form grew smaller and smaller. She plunged past the dark trees, howling with delight. In no time she was zooming through the Archangel's open metal gates.

No police cruisers on the highway.

She turned south, heading for Red Dog Lake and the first phone she could find.

39

Danny followed the mine road until the roof of the gallows frame appeared over the trees. Breathing deeply, he quit the road for the shelter of the woods, pushing through the brush until he reached the point where the vegetation gave way to the barren flats surrounding the mine.

He crouched down in the weeds, scanning the building and grounds for signs of movement.

Nothing.

Smoke from the forest fire loomed like a black thunderhead west of the tailings pond. A deadly grey mist flowed around the abandoned mill building, smudging out the sight of Logan's ruined VW.

He pushed back his tangled hair. He hadn't heard any gunfire for over half an hour. That could mean everything or nothing.

Doesn't matter what's happened. I'm coming to get you, John.

The only way to keep out of sight of the tower, and Hendrix, was through the derelict mill. He'd cut through the building, dodge past the old mill equipment, and get across to the side looking down over the tailings pond. From there he'd signal Logan, find him somehow.

He stared at the wasteland before him.

The dirt and broken pavement between him and the east end of the mill stretched the length of a football field. He'd have to run across it, exposed and vulnerable as a rabbit on a jet runway. He prayed that Hendrix was lying in the tower dead or injured, or at least that he was watching for Logan and not looking east, out in his, Danny's, direction.

Six years ago, back in high school, he and two of his Fortin cousins had tanked up on bootleg beer, driven up here and gone exploring. They'd all grown up hearing stories about members of The Community who'd died of leukemia or lung cancer after working at the Archangel Mine, but that hadn't stopped them. Beer, weed and stupidity had fuelled them. And had nearly gotten them all killed.

He hoped he remembered enough from their drunken adventures to find his way around the mill building.

He rubbed his burning eyes. The smoke was getting worse.

The end of the mill building held a shattered multi-paned window, big enough for a cathedral, but it was set fifteen feet above ground. He'd never manage to get into the mill that way. He'd have to edge down its long northern wall and find the cargo bay he and his cousins had used.

Tricky. The north side had no windows or door openings.

And the cargo bay lay just below the gallows tower.

The hell with it.

He burst out of the weeds onto the barren ground. He ran, leaping over gaping potholes, the pitted concrete banging through his runners. He saw nothing but the broken ground in front of him, rolling toward him in a blur.

Halfway across.

The darkening sky pressed down on him. His lungs were on fire. His leg muscles screamed with pain. He couldn't see, couldn't breathe.

A sharp clang of noise. Pain shot through his side. He hit the ground, wheezing.

Breathless, he lay on his back, ribs throbbing, staring into a white Arctic immensity. A strange flaky snow drifted down on him.

Am I dead?

Not dead, winded.

He heaved himself up and gazed at the white specks littering the rusty ground. Not snow, but paint. Flaking off the corroded steel wall of the mill building.

Idiot, he thought and dragged himself up to his feet. I was such a scared rabbit, I ran straight into the end of the mill building. Didn't even see it.

No time to waste. Move.

He limped along the eastern wall until he reached the northeast corner of the building. He began working his way down its northern side, pressing close to the blank, rust-stained metal that covered it.

He remembered his cousins joking that they might run across Logan at the mine. He probably had a big stash of rye whisky there, they'd said. If they found it, they'd have enough for ten parties. Everyone in Red Dog Lake wondered why Logan liked to hang around the Archangel Mine, but even as a disinterested teenager, Danny had sensed that the reasons for Logan's lonely vigils ran deep. And whatever those reasons were, he didn't want to know them.

He stopped halfway down the northern wall and wiped off his face. He didn't remember the distance being this far. The air was really smoky now, getting hard to breathe.

I'm exhausted. That little bit of food and water Logan and Rachel gave me won't wipe out two days of physical hell. I was running on adrenalin, now it's leaking away.

He forced himself to keep going. It took forever to get to the spot where the north wall bent round into the cargo bay. Gasping for air, he stopped to rest. And when he looked up, he saw the dark outline of the gallows tower, exactly as he remembered it.

He picked up a stray stone and tossed it round the corner into the loading area.

Nothing. No sounds, no movement.

With infinite caution, he peered round the corner. The loading area was filled with piles of jumbled cables and bags of pale, cement-like waste. Leaking oil barrels with black and yellow signs that warned of radioactivity were stacked like giant *Lego* pieces in front of the sealed cargo doors. And right beside them, he spotted a familiar window.

The way in.

Don't think. Go for it.

He slipped round the corner and picked his way through the toxic junk, mindful of anything that could tumble and make a noise.

So far, so good.

He ran up the crumbling concrete ramp that led to the window. The chipboard covering it had been so moist and decayed that he and his cousins had found it trivially easy to kick away a piece big enough to let themselves in. Now only a tiny piece of the board remained, clinging to a rusty nail, but the splinters along its edges looked fresh.

Hendrix!

Danny's heart beat faster. Hendrix had found the same way in. He'd gone through the mill building and found his way to the gallows tower.

What if he'd left the tower? What if he was hiding inside the mill?

Too late now. I have to risk it.

He eased himself onto the metal window frame, swung his legs over it and dropped down into the inky darkness of the mill.

He landed with a clang on a metal catwalk four feet below the window. Heart racing, he waited for his eyes to adjust to the dark, listening for any sounds.

Nothing but silence, thank God.

Light beams, murky with smoke, shone down through gaping holes in the roof. He watched the mill workings emerge: a strange, almost biological complex of pipes, ladders and tanks that stretched the entire length of the building. A yellow-brown dust coated everything. The smell of burning timber drowned out other odours he remembered: moisture and mildew, sewage and acid.

The catwalk he'd landed on ran along the northern side of the building twenty feet above the operations floor. Looking up, he could see another much higher catwalk close to the roof of the building: it seemed to run parallel to the one he was on.

Still can't hear anything; good thing.

A chaos of pipes and vats stood between him and the opposite side of the building, the southern side that looked out onto Logan's van.

He moved softly along the catwalk, following it past the mill workings, looking for a way down.

The catwalk ended in a flight of stairs that led down to the concrete operations floor behind a large leaching tank. He went down the steps, and hunkered down next to the tank. Beneath it, he spotted a heap of broken pipes. Much as he didn't want to touch anything in the dust-covered mill, he carefully removed a two-foot piece of pipe from the pile.

Not much help against a gun, but better than nothing.

He stayed close to the tank and tried to map out the layout of the building. Directly in front of him, on the other side of the operations floor, he could see the gigantic doors that once had given the ore trucks access to the mill. All sealed now.

He looked over his right shoulder and stared into the mouth of a dark tunnel-like corridor. He remembered it all too well. It was the passage that connected the mill to the gallows frame and the mine shaft.

He and his cousins had torn through it using their flashlights to light the way. His cousins claimed that Logan had hidden his liquor stash in the mine shaft. Even if that didn't make a lot of sense, they desperately wanted to find the shaft.

To look down it. And climb down it.

He remembered the beams of their flashlights criss-crossing through the vast darkness of the gallows tower. There was no way to get down the shaft. The cage, the elevator that lifted the miners up and down, had long since vanished. In the interests of safety, departing workers had fastened heavy wooden planks over the shaft opening.

His cousins couldn't pry off the boards so they jumped up and down on them, yelling like madmen, calling him a wuss for not joining them.

He'd let them get to him. He'd leapt up beside them.

The Archangel was called a shallow mine, because its shaft only reached down two hundred metres. Puny compared to the thousand-metre nickel mines in Sudbury, but an amply fatal depth, of course. Staring into that dark corridor now, he could still hear the crack of the wood plank giving way under him. Still feel his feet crashing through into the dark void.

He shuddered.

The hole in the wood hadn't been big enough for him to slip through. He got caught by the waist and hung there suspended, unable to free himself. The Fortins laughed their guts out while they snapped photos of him on their cellphones. Somehow he'd pulled himself out. He remembered going nuts, beating on them, though they were both into bodybuilding and much bigger than he was.

He'd lost the fight. Even now he wanted to kick their heads in.

Hendrix would've found his way to the tower through that corridor. Danny held his breath. He sensed no movement in the dark passageway. All he could hear was the faraway crackle of trees burning, like gunshots from a distant battle.

Forget about the mine shaft, he told himself. There's got to be a door or a window along the south side.

There! A human-sized door fifty feet down to his left. Tendrils of smoke were curling around its edges.

Leaving the shelter of the leaching tank, he crept down to the door over a litter of dirt, broken glass and metal. He flung it open and stared out at Logan's VW van.

The outside air was thick with ashes. He wiped his streaming eyes. The VW's rear door was hanging open. Had Logan climbed back inside the van?

A trail of black splotches on the ground, leading from the van back into the mill building.

Clutching the pipe, he noticed dark fluid smeared on the inside of the door. He reached out and touched it.

Too watery for oil. Blood!

It had to be Logan's blood. One of Hendrix's bullets had found him.

The sinister trail continued inside, fading into the dust and detritus of the operations floor.

He followed the deadly track, running, searching. It led from the door into the body of the mill, in the direction away from the gallows frame.

It ended at a rusty stairway halfway down the mill. Splashes of bright red blood filled the mesh treads of the stairs.

They led up to the former control room twenty feet above the operations floor. It resembled a railway car that had become entangled in the metallic entrails of the mill.

Something protruded through the control room's empty doorway: the sole of a cowboy boot, the heel scraped down so far, wear had bitten into the tooled leather.

Logan's boot.

"John," Danny cried out.

Logan's foot did not stir.

"John, for God's sake, answer me." Danny started up the stairs.

Something rustled in the darkness of the control room: a shimmering whiteness in the shadows.

Hendrix emerged through the doorway, his face dead white. Strands of his pale hair fell across a crimson gash in his forehead.

The star …

The windigo had emerged from his cave.

40

"Well, I'm damned," Hendrix said. "The rat has returned to the nest."

He pointed a grey rifle directly at Danny's heart. A twin of the one Anderson, the Norwegian, had emptied into Pasha's body, his pale eyes boring through his steel-rimmed spectacles.

Hendrix stepped over Logan's still form onto the platform at the top of the stairs. "Do us a favour, Mate. Set down that nasty bit of pipe."

Danny found his voice. "What for? You're going to shoot me anyway."

"Right you are."

Hendrix hobbled onto the first step. Danny flinched. Hendrix's flesh flashed crimson through dozens of tears in his black motor-cycle leathers. His right leg was a mess of blood and splintered bone held together with two flat bits of wood and a yellow bungee cord. How had he managed to climb up the tower? The pain must have been agony.

"You shot John." Danny's arms were shaking. He wanted to crash the pipe deep into Hendrix's skull.

"Self-defence. Wouldn't stop shooting at me." Hendrix was sweating, but he held the rifle steady despite his painful progress down the steps. "Hated to punch the ticket of an old soldier like him. Not many of us left."

"You lying, murdering bastard!"

"What?"

"I know you killed everyone on the island. You gutted Morty like a trout. You sliced off Anderson's arm, cut his throat and stuffed him under the lodge."

"No, Mate, wasn't me." Hendrix neared the bottom of the stairs. "No more talking, Rat. Time's short. Too tired to skin you alive. Consider yourself lucky." He pointed the rifle. "This is for Curtis."

"You killed Curtis. You murdered your own brother, you psycho."

Hendrix's eyes were a still, almost transparent grey. "Bollocks, you killed him."

"I never killed anybody!"

Hendrix eased off his ruined leg. "Well, not you precisely. More like it was that festering nark, Tom Rudd, the one masquerading as Ricky Fountain. Oh, yes, Curtis radioed me. Old Tom favours cowboy justice. Can't arrest 'em, kill 'em. Forest fire to erase evidence. Out in the wilderness where no one bothers. Tell us, did Tear Drop get him? Is he dead?"

"Yes," Danny lied, gripping the pipe. *Keep him talking.* "I'm not a nark. I'm a camp counsellor."

"Buying weed from Merry, all summer, weren't you, Rat? So you could shop him to Tom Rudd and that bitch McKenna. Tear Drop saw the obvious. Two natives thick with each other."

"Go to hell."

"What? Not politically correct enough for you?" Hendrix sneered. "If you're offended, I'm happy."

"Burn in hell, Windigo."

"What did you call me?" Hendrix rammed the end of the rifle barrel into Danny's chest. Danny felt the pipe slip out of his fist and heard it clang onto the concrete floor.

"I called you a demon," Danny said. "Because that's what you are."

Hendrix smiled. "That's what the old lady at the bookstore called me."

Odile, Grandmother.

"What did you do to her? What did you do to her, you son of a bitch?"

"The oldie? Nothing."

"Liar!" Danny caught the rifle barrel with both hands. Wrenched it up and away from his body.

Hendrix hung on, amazingly strong, struggling like a wounded tiger. Danny felt his hands sliding on the gun barrel. He was losing his grip, he couldn't hold it …

A loud guttural cough behind them.

"Charlie?" a familiar voice said. "My God, you're alive."

Santa!

Hendrix twitched in surprise. Danny let go the rifle. He snatched the pipe from the ground.

And smashed it into Hendrix's shattered leg with everything he had.

Hendrix screamed in agony. He staggered against the stair railing.

Danny scrambled into the jungle of pipes, ladders, and cables under the control room. Breathing hard, he weaved his way through the maze.

Get to the other side. Find the catwalk. Get to the window.

An ear-shattering explosion. Dust spurted from a pipe by his head. Metal fragments stung his cheek. Hendrix had fired and missed.

Danny ran, ducking and weaving through the workings. A ladder appeared in front of him.

He climbed the rusty rungs one after the other. He reached a metal landing and bellied onto it, gasping for air.

Shouts and bangs below him. He rolled over, pressing back into the shadows by the crumbling wall. He saw that he'd landed on the highest catwalk, the one that ran along the roof of the mill. From here, he had a full view of the plant.

He looked down through the rusting metal mesh of the platform and watched Hendrix and Santa as they searched for him. They emerged from under the control room.

Santa was naked except for a filthy pair of boxer shorts. His hair was a wild tangle, his limbs and torso caked with blood and dirt. In one fist, he held a bottle of coppery liquid that looked like rye whisky.

Hendrix could barely walk, but he swung his rifle, looking, hunting.

"Leave him, Charlie," Santa said. "He's a wanker. Here, have a drink."

Hendrix spun with astonishing swiftness and crashed the rifle down on Santa's head. Santa screamed and fell on his knees, clutching his ear.

"For God's sake!" Santa cried.

Hendrix stood over him with the gun. "That's for starters. You didn't just turn up here."

"Edgar saw the Twin Beech. He saw the crash from the air. I was worried sick. I had to find out if you and Tear Drop were all right."

"Tear Drop's dead. Broke his neck in the crash."

"I-I'm sorry."

"Bollocks, you're after the product."

"Oh." Santa wiped his nose with his fingers. "All right, fine. So what if I am? You stole the whole bloody lot. You crashed my plane. You've ruined me. I didn't deserve that, Charlie."

Hendrix hit him again. "You lying, murderous bastard, Tear Drop said you buggered the engine. You made the Twin Beech go down. And us with it."

"No, never." Santa cowered, hands over his head. "You know me, Charlie, I've got no mechanics. Wouldn't know where to start messing about with the engine even if I wanted to. And I wouldn't want to. I'd never do that to a mate."

"You self-serving rat. My brother's dead and it's your bloody fault."

"I didn't know there'd be a forest fire. Please God, be reasonable. How could I possibly know?"

"You ratted me and Curtis out. You planted those two narks on the island. I know you, Merry. You'd cut your own Ma's throat for a dollar." Hendrix braced the end of the rifle barrel on Santa's glistening forehead. Danny couldn't breathe.

"All right, all right, I'll tell you," Santa shrilled. "Edgar was the rat. Edgar ratted us out."

"That lamb brain? That's a pathetic lie, even for you, Merry."

"I had no idea until last night, I swear. Told me to my face, the sod. Boasted about it. He's a monster. He killed his own ma for her pension money."

"Bollocks. Fleecing old women, that's one of your habits."

"No, no, for God's sake, hear me out. Edgar buggered the Twin Beech. He told me. Think about it, Charlie. Other than Tear Drop, Edgar was the only one who knew how to fly the bloody thing."

"Knew? That's past tense, Mate."

Santa let out a huge sob. "I've made an awful mess, Charlie. Shouldn't have trusted Edgar, but you get close to a man when you work with him for three years. I got sentimental. It's a weakness of mine. B-but I did the necessary. Not pretty, but I got it done. The coppers are after me. I've got to get out. Please, Mate, we're losing time here arguing."

Hendrix lowered the rifle. "All right, go on, get up."

Santa wiped his face, teetered to his feet and took a long gulp from his bottle.

"The crystal's in my pack," Hendrix said. "Left it in the tower. Too heavy. Go on, fetch your car."

"Car?" Santa echoed.

"You don't travel farther than six inches without driving, Fat Gut. It's twenty miles to Red Dog Lake. Where'd you leave it?"

"I-I don't have the car," Santa said. "The kid took it."

Rachel! Danny crawled to the edge of the catwalk, straining to hear.

"What kid? You mean the little girl with the old soldier?" Hendrix said.

"She's not a child, she's a hyena," Santa said. "I stopped to water the roses. She got in the car and drove off. Stole it when my back was turned."

Rachel! Danny bit his hand trying not to scream.

"You lying snake," Hendrix said. "The kid ran off into the woods with that native. Saw them from the tower. You hit her with the car, didn't you? Didn't see her running down the road, did you? You ditched the car after, didn't you, you bloody coward?"

Danny lunged for the catwalk railing. "What did you do to Rachel?" he shouted.

Hendrix turned and fired.

His shot went wild.

Danny raced away down the catwalk, hugging the decayed inside wall. Behind him, a ringing bang of metal. They'd found the ladder.

"Can't do it ... You go up," he heard Hendrix say.

"There's no time. The forest fire, we've got to get out," Santa said. "My leg's bad."

"Get up there or I'll blow your guts out."

"All right, all right." Santa began grunting up the ladder.

Danny ran on. He looked down through the iron mesh and saw Hendrix on the operations floor, tracking him through the rifle scope to get a clear shot.

A whoosh of noise. Santa had flopped off the ladder onto the upper catwalk. Danny passed the top of the leaching tank.

"He's over by that tank," Hendrix shouted. "Get him."

There has to be a way down. There has to be.

The catwalk was too high up; he couldn't jump. Frantic now, Danny looked for a set of stairs, a ladder, anything.

The catwalk ended. Ended in a ladder, thank God.

He leapt onto it. Went down, the rungs trembling under him. Suddenly he felt air. The ladder was broken.

How far up was he above the floor? Couldn't see, too dark.

Using only his arms, he eased his body down rung by rung, his feet dangling in the air.

He reached the last rung.

"I've got him," Santa shouted above his head. "He's here, Charlie."

Danny let go the ladder.

The ground rose up and whacked him in a teeth-jarring blow. A bolt of fire shot up his right leg. The pain was incredible. He rolled onto his back, clutching his knee.

"Charlie, get over here," Santa shouted.

Danny struggled onto all fours, his hands sinking into soft yellow dust. He stared into the darkness of the passageway into the tower.

He hobbled onto his feet. Each step on his right leg was excruciating.

He tottered into the vastness of the gallows frame.

It was filled with a faint opalescent light. Smoke was flowing in through cracks in its wooden walls. A large black backpack rested on the ground next to the timbered platform over the abandoned shaft: Hendrix's precious product.

A shattered stairway spidered up the inside wall of the tower, leading to the roof. He started crossing the room to reach it.

"Now I've got you," Hendrix said. "Dead to rights."

41

Danny threw himself at the pack. Only two planks covered the mine shaft opening now: silver wood beams forming a cross over complete darkness.

Arms straining, he heaved the pack onto the plank closest to him. He crouched behind it, using it like a shield.

He watched Hendrix trudge into the dim light of the gallows frame. His pale face seemed to glow.

"That pack won't stop a bullet. Hiding behind it won't do you a bit of good," Hendrix said.

Danny had seen what Anderson's gun could do. Hendrix's bullets would pass through the pack, through him, through the wall of the tower and out into the woods.

He stood up and tilted the pack over the black void of the shaft, holding it by the straps.

"Fine, shoot me and watch your meth go down the shaft," he said. "Six hundred feet straight down and no ladder to bring it back up."

"I'll risk it." Hendrix took aim.

"Stop for God's sake!" Santa staggered up to Hendrix, bottle in hand. "Listen to me, Charlie. Don't chance it. We'll never haul it back up in time. The fire's on top of us. We've got to get out of here."

"Don't interfere," Hendrix said.

"The crystal is worth millions. Throwing it away won't bring Curtis back," Santa said. "Millions! Do you hear that, Danny? Millions. Come on, be a sport. We'll split it three ways."

"No way," Danny said.

"The little rat wants it for himself," Hendrix said, still aiming.

Danny leaned the pack so far over the opening of the shaft that his arms shook from the weight. "Get out of here, both of you, or I let go."

"For heaven's sake, Danny, now you're being a complete bloody idiot," Santa said. "You're holding a fortune. It's more money than you and your entire monkey town will see in three lifetimes. Don't be insane, Mate."

"Hey, I'm just a banjo-playing native from Red Dog Lake. What do I know?" Danny retorted.

"You know you don't have a choice," Hendrix said.

Danny stared at him. "Yeah, Demon, I do."

He let go the straps.

"NO!" Santa screamed in furious disbelief.

The pack crashed down the mine shaft. Echoing, banging. Faded out of the range of hearing.

Danny felt calm now. He felt ready.

He faced Hendrix. Stared into the small dark hole at the end of the gun.

Maybe I'll see Odile again. Maybe Rachel, too.

A huge noise exploded through the tower.

The red star on Hendrix's forehead burst open. A fountain of blood poured over his white face. For a moment he seemed to be wavering in indecision.

Then he slowly toppled into the dust.

Santa made a strange mewling sound. "Oh God. Oh my God, what's happened? My God, my God ..."

A tall figure staggered in from the corridor. A tall figure wearing a battered cowboy hat.

"Logan!" Danny screamed.

Blood soaked Logan's denim shirt. He was deathly pale, barely able to stand. He lowered his smoking rifle. "You OK, Kid?" he breathed.

"Yes, yeah." Danny felt his chest with numb hands. *I'm alive, I'm still alive.*

"What have you done?" Santa collapsed on his hands and knees next to Hendrix. "You killed him. You killed Charlie."

"Damn right." Logan reached down and jerked the rye bottle out of Santa's fist. He wiped the neck on his shirt and took a deep swallow.

"Logan!" Danny stumbled away from the shaft. "I thought you were dead, man. I thought Hendrix killed you." He limped over and threw his arms around Logan's thin frame in a fierce hug.

"He tried. One side, Kid." Logan pushed Danny away, shoved the bottle into his hands and aimed the Winchester at Santa.

Santa was on his knees. "No, please, don't kill me."

"You hurt Flag," Logan said. "I heard you. You hurt her and you're going to die."

"No, no, I swear I didn't touch her," Santa shrieked. "She started screaming she was a ninja. She kicked me in the leg. The little wretch knows how to drive a *Prius*. She got away from me."

Danny seized Logan's arm. "John, wait, I think he's telling the truth for once. Rachel … Flag … knows how to drive. She told me her dad taught her when he worked at the body shop."

"I am telling the truth," Santa pleaded. "Danny, please, make him understand."

"You murdered my bear. Pasha was worth ten of you," Logan said. His rifle didn't waver.

"You're right. You're absolutely right. I needed Pasha to guard the operation. But the money. I'm weak, I'm the first person to admit it. Please, for heaven's sake …"

In the distance, the faint whine of a police siren.

"John, hear that?" Danny said above the noise of Santa's sobs. "I think it's the cops."

He strained to hear the siren again.

"Listen to me, John. Santa wasn't lying. Rachel got through to the highway. She's bringing the cops. John, please, leave Santa for the cops. Flag is all right. She's safe."

Logan stared at him.

"Flag is all right," Danny repeated. "We have to get you to a hospital."

"Forget it. He's the rot at the heart of this mess," Logan said. "Pasha's dead. I have to kill him."

"John, don't do it," Danny said. "He's a crook and liar. He's not worth going to jail for. Too many people have died. Don't throw your life away." He heard a trickling sound. A rank odour of urine overpowered the woodsmoke.

"Oh, hell, I've wet myself," Santa cried.

Slowly Logan lowered the rifle.

"Oh, thank you," Santa sobbed. "Bless you, Danny. Thank you, thank you, thank you."

"Oh, shut it," Danny said. He seized Logan's arm. "Come on, leave him. We have to get out of here."

"Gotta deal with something first." Logan handed his rifle to Danny who took it and set the rye bottle down on the ground. Kicking Hendrix's rifle aside, Logan grabbed the dead man by the arms and dragged his body over to the mine shaft.

"What are you doing?" Danny said. "We're running out of time. Leave Hendrix. He's dead."

Logan rolled Hendrix's body over. Hendrix's limbs spasmed. His eyes rolled sightlessly.

"He's alive," Santa whimpered. "Charlie's still alive."

"Not for long." Logan heaved Hendrix's torso over the lip of the shaft.

"John, no!" Danny hobbled toward Logan, but his throbbing knee crippled him.

Logan seized Hendrix's legs and shovelled him headfirst into the shaft. The thumps of his fall echoed endlessly.

"Murderer!" Santa shrieked.

He crawled like a deranged crab toward Hendrix's fallen gun, but Danny was faster. As Santa scrabbled to get hold of it, Danny crunched his undamaged foot down on the older man's wrist.

Santa yelled in outrage.

Danny wrenched Hendrix's gun away from him. One gun in each fist, he kicked Santa's bandaged thigh to make sure he'd stay down.

A helicopter rotor thumped loudly overhead. Danny heard it pass over the mine building and head west over the tailings pond. He prayed it was the rescue copter dispatched to look for Ricky.

"Come on, John, it's the cavalry," Danny said. "We've gotta get out so the cops can see us."

"OK," Logan grunted in reply. He limped back, picked up the rye and snatched the Winchester from Danny.

Danny threw Logan's arm over his shoulder, holding him upright. Together they stumbled down the passageway back into the mill.

"Where are you going?" Santa demanded. "What the hell! You're leaving me. You're leaving me to burn. Come back here. I need help."

"Shut up. Find your own way out," Danny called back.

Together he and Logan groped their way down to the door Danny had found earlier, the one that looked south onto the van.

A wall of furnace heat struck them when they stepped outside. Flames circled the tailings pond. Trees bent like charred matchsticks in a scarlet gale. The smoke was a thick black fog. Embers were landing on the old mill building. It would go up in a matter of minutes.

Where the hell was that police car?

"Gotta ... gotta sit down," Logan gasped. "Can't ... breathe."

"The heat ... get behind the van," Danny coughed back.

They struggled over to the VW, but it barely shielded them from the intense heat. Danny tossed Hendrix's gun into the van through the open cargo door and eased Logan down onto the ground on the side away from the fire.

Leaning back against the rear tire, Logan took a long swallow from the rye bottle. A flock of birds passed over them, crying out in panic.

"Hear that? The animals are leaving," he said. "Won't be long now."

"We'll make it. The cops'll be coming down the mine road any minute," Danny said to convince himself as much as Logan.

Logan took another deep swallow. "Tell me how she died, Kid."

"Rachel's fine." *She has to be.*

"Not Flag. She's too smart to let that sorry rat get her. You know who I'm talking about."

"John, I ..." He had to face this, he had no choice. "I swear on Odile's heart and spirit. I didn't know the bear was going to be Pasha."

Logan stared down at the bottle.

"I'm not asking you to forgive me. I don't deserve that."

Logan bent his head. "Answer my question, Son."

"Like a hero. Pasha died like a hero."

"The truth now." His brilliant blue eyes bored into Danny's. "Did she suffer?"

"The hunt ... it was over real fast. The hunters ... all they cared about was getting back to drinking. Pasha didn't feel a thing."

They both knew he was lying.

Logan took another drink. He stood up and gazed down at the cauldron of smoke covering the tailings pond. "See that? Pasha's come to get me," he said.

"That's not Pasha, John."

"Yes, it is. I'm leaving now. The train's arrived at the station and I'm getting on board." Logan started walking away from him, the Winchester in one hand, the rye bottle in the other. "Don't try to stop me."

Danny grabbed his arm. "I won't let you walk into the fire, John. That's insane. You're family, you're one of us. The cops won't do anything to you. Hendrix shot you, he was going to kill me. It was self-defence."

"I enjoy killing sometimes." Logan smiled at the flames. "Violence burns inside me. I grew up nourished on hate and hell-fire. Pounded into me from the day I was born. Good people tried to help me, and all I did was cause them a world of pain and ruin their lives. I'm dangerous. I should have stayed in the military. I'm a bad man, Danny."

"That's not true."

"Sorry, Kid, it's not in your nature to understand a man like me."

Danny felt hollow; the smoke burned his eyes. "You killed them, didn't you? You killed the hunters on the island."

"Yes," Logan said. "Took you long enough to figure that out."

"You knew you'd find me here at the Archangel Mine. You came looking for me because you knew I was still alive. Why didn't you kill me, too, on Fire Island?"

"Because of Odile. She's a saint and she loves you, God help her. I'd never hurt Odile. And Flag liked you."

It all made horrible sense, Danny thought. Hendrix had called Logan an old soldier: he'd been a commando in Vietnam; he had the training to kill Morty, Anderson and Curtis quickly and quietly. That's why Ricky hadn't heard anything out in the forest. And Logan had been too smart and careful to hunt for him in the dark. It spoke of a terrible premeditation.

"Who told you we were on Fire Island?" Danny asked.

"Charmaine did. Santa likes to talk big in bed."

"Did you fly out in Santa's Twin Beech?"

"No, I borrowed Corazon's Piper Cherokee: that way they wouldn't suspect me when they saw me land. Knew Corazon flew them in. Heard that Morty character talking on his cellphone outside the Galaxy." Logan rubbed his face. "I'm going now."

"John, look, we'll explain to the cops. I'll get you help."

"You can't help me. Nobody can."

Logan pushed him away. He left the van and started trudging down the hill that led to the tailings pond. Danny limped after him. The heat blistered his skin and tore at his lungs.

"I won't stand by and watch you kill yourself," he cried.

Logan shook his head. "Don't try to stop me. If you do, I'll kill you." Danny stepped back, knowing he meant it. "I told you I was evil. Give me the freedom to do this my way. That's the way you can help me."

He forged down the hill, not feeling the fire, though Danny could feel it singeing every cell of his body. The siren sounded close now. He turned and caught the red flash of a police cruiser at the point where the mine road gave onto the mud flats surrounding the mill.

Logan was already halfway down the slope.

"John, come back up. The cops are here," Danny shouted.

Logan paused for a moment. "There's a letter. In the glove compartment of the VW," he said. "I've left the zoo and the land to Odile and Flag. It's worth maybe two bucks but it's all I got and I want them to have it. If they're gone, well, who gives a damn what happens to it."

The siren cut off. Danny saw the police cruiser shoot out of the trees, bumping across the barren ground toward him. It skidded to a halt close to the smouldering mine building.

The cruiser's doors flew open. Sergeant McKenna got out. She was wearing her navy OPP uniform and black bulletproof vest. Rachel jumped out the passenger side. She tried to race toward Danny, but McKenna nabbed her and held her back against the heat of the fire.

Danny felt relief crash through him. Rachel *was* safe.

"Danny, get over here," McKenna cried. "The whole mine is going up any minute."

"Logan!" he called down. "Rachel … Flag is OK. She's here. She's with McKenna in the cop car."

"Danny," Rachel yelled out to him. "Odile's OK. She's back at Blue Sky. Sergeant McKenna found her."

"Logan, did you hear Flag? Odile is OK."

Logan stopped and smiled, the smoke curling around him. "Yeah, I heard," he said. "That's good. Do me a favour, Kid."

"Anything. Just come back up."

"Don't tell Flag. Promise me whatever happens you won't tell Flag."

"I promise. Now come home."

"No." Logan shook his head. "I am going home now."

He turned and vanished into the smoke.

42

"HEY, SPORTS FANS! IT'S KARAOKE STRIP BENEFIT NIGHT!" the lead singer of *Black Thunder* screamed into the mike. "Here's George Thorogood. Come on, you buggers, *Get A Haircut.*"

"And get a real job," the audience roared back.

The band began pounding out the classic Thorogood favourite. Danny had never seen the Galaxy Tavern so jammed. Seemed like the entire population of Red Dog Lake had turned up to raise money for Edgar's bail. Didn't matter that nearly everyone was back on pogey, now that the cops had closed down Santa's Fish Camp and Camp Nirvana.

Danny, too, was collecting.

"Hey, Danny boy." Ricky – Special Agent Thomas Rudd – punched his arm. "Come on, wake up and drink up or you're gonna be playing catch-up with me all night." With his shaved head and black muscle shirt, he blended right in with the Red Dog Lake crowd.

Danny sighed and finished off his bottle of *Brador* beer. Corazon had reserved a prime table for him and Ricky. They sat squashed up against the stage, close enough to count the sequins on the costumes of the amateur strippers. No doubt this tantalizing proximity was fuelling Ricky's excellent spirits. The free beer and bourbon Corazon had sent over from the bar certainly helped too.

Despite the heavy silver medical bracelet that clanked against the *Rolex* on his wrist, Ricky looked well for a man who'd been airlifted half-dead out of the bush just four weeks before. McKenna had fought hard to free up a rescue copter from the Malartic disaster after getting Corazon's radio report, but it took the crew nearly eighteen hours to find Ricky. Luckily the thunderstorms held back the forest fire; Ricky's tough physique had done the rest.

Ricky leaned across the table to make himself heard over the noise. "Weird to be sitting here raising bail for Santa's dirty little helper. Ironic, a college type like you would say." He cracked open a can of *Budweiser*. "Hey, what can I say? Corazon talked me into it. She is one fine lady."

"She is that," Danny said.

"I owe her, man. If she hadn't being flying low, looking for us after the island went up in smoke, well, let's just say I wouldn't be sitting here sucking back these cold ones." He looked sober for a moment. "Should have said this before, Dan the man, but I really owe you. You saved my life."

Danny shrugged. "Hey, you pulled me out of the lake. I figure we saved each other."

"Well, I'm ordering you to haul your butt down to Kentucky. We'll listen to some real music and do some real drinking." Ricky drained his beer. "Though you Red Dog Lakers sure can knock it back."

"We try."

"I meant that about you coming down. Gonna have time on my hands from now on."

Danny sat up. "What's wrong? Did the doctors say something this morning?"

"Nah, not the docs, the Bureau." Ricky rolled his empty beer can between two meaty fists. "My op blew up. Too much collateral damage."

"But a bent cop tipped off Hendrix. That Constable Michael who used to patrol round here. By the time McKenna dimed him, we were already on the island."

Ricky grimaced. "The Bureau doesn't see it that way. Someone has to carry the can and it looks like it's gonna be me. A lot of people died because Hendrix went crazy and killed everybody."

"But Hendrix, Curtis and Tear Drop are dead. The meth lab is gone. That should count for something."

"Yeah, but Morty and Anderson don't count as collateral damage. They had friends in high places, if you know what I'm saying."

"Yeah, I guess I do."

Ricky reached for another beer. "Didn't help either that your buddy, Santa, gave McKenna the slip."

After the forest fire had burnt itself out, the OPP had combed through the charred remains of the Archangel Mine building. No trace of Santa.

"The forest fire was on top of us," Danny said. "It felt like a blast furnace. McKenna couldn't chase after him. We barely made it out of there ourselves."

"I know. Like I said, I wish my superiors, and McKenna's boss, saw it the same way." Ricky popped the top of a fresh *Budweiser.*

"Dude, there's no way Santa made it out of there even if he got into the woods. He was beat up and down to his boxer shorts. He's dead, he has to be."

"Don't kid yourself, Easter's a resourceful bastard." Ricky seized the gleaming bottle of *Jack Daniel's* resting on their table. "Come on, grab your glass. I want to ask you something."

"Sure, ask away." Danny watched him fill their shot glasses to overflow.

"What did Logan say to you before he walked into the fire?"

Danny stared down at the dark brown bourbon, hoping Ricky couldn't read him in the dim light. "John wasn't thinking straight. He'd lost a lot of blood." He fiddled with his shot glass. "He ... he mumbled something weird about getting on a train. Meaningless stuff."

"What did he say about the bones in the mine shaft?"

"Nothing. Nobody knew about them till McKenna and the OPP found them. Ask around. Everybody here will tell you the same thing."

"Guess they would." Ricky gave him a long, hard stare: a cop's stare. Then he relaxed and downed his shot. "Fire's a helluva way to off yourself. Why do you think Logan did it?"

"I don't know. I can't stop thinking about it." Danny swallowed his bourbon, feeling it burn all the way down.

The band broke into Corazon's signature disco tune, *Hot Stuff.* Thank God, Danny thought.

Corazon strutted onstage wearing a blazing gold-sequined tunic. "You bet I'm hot stuff, baby tonight," she shouted into the mike. "WELCOME, ALL YOU MOTHERS!"

The audience shrieked and howled, banging the tables.

Corazon covered her mouth in mock horror. "Oops, I gotta watch my language 'cause there's so many kids and seniors here. But hey, you gotta excuse me 'cause we're stripping for a great cause tonight, right, people? We're gonna show all we got to keep our Red Dog Grizzly out of jail."

"How's he doing?" someone shouted.

"Glad you asked, Baby," Corazon said. "The docs are kicking him out of the burn unit tomorrow. He's waving you all a big hello with that trouser cobra of his, all the way from Toronto, the Big Smoke. So drink up and get hot and horny 'cause it's time to get down and dirty!"

She pranced past Danny's table and threw Ricky a broad, lascivious wink. Ricky grinned back and raised his shot glass in salute.

So that's it, I get it, Danny thought. Well, the two of them are both in their forties. Why not?

Corazon had stopped inviting him to stay over for breakfast. He couldn't blame her: he'd avoided her, and everyone else, since the events on Fire Island. Just the same, he felt hurt. Even if it was high time for both of them to move on.

First up onstage was Charmaine, Santa's old girlfriend or Edgar's new girlfriend, whichever way people chose to look at it. Ricky gazed in rapture as Charmaine jiggled her way through a popular Shakira tune. The noise, the flashing lights, the cigarette smoke … the show was just getting started and already Danny had had enough.

He stood up and said: "I'm stepping out for a minute. My grandmother ..."

Ricky choked on his shot. "Your *grandmother's* here?"

"Yeah, she's at the back with some of the elders from The Community."

"Sure, sure, man." Ricky grinned. "And roll one for me while you're at it. I'll smoke it later."

"No problem." Danny grinned back. He pushed his way through the crowd and escaped outside into the fresh air.

The night was soft, dark, and full of stars. Warm weather for September. Sergeant McKenna had parked her cruiser in the middle of the parking lot and sat alone in a bubble of blue-white light. No doubt she'd heard that if she ventured into the Galaxy, Corazon would make her strip.

Danny slumped down on the wooden bench beside the tavern door and felt for the spliff in his shirt pocket. Had to rely on local bush weed now that Santa's Fish Camp was out of business. He pulled out the spliff and wet it. McKenna was looking straight at him, but he doubted she'd interfere. Judging by the fragrant fog bank of smoke around him, she'd have to arrest half the town.

He lit up, wishing he'd stayed at Blue Sky tonight. There stillness and contentment flowed like water between the bookshelves. He'd moved back home with Odile after the doctors and the cops were through with him. To keep busy, he'd offered to run the bookstore for her.

She'd simply inclined her head and said: "The bookstore is yours now, *Mahikan.*"

He'd insisted, too, on doing his fair share of the cooking. Dinner tonight had been Rachel's favourite: pan-fried fresh trout and Odile's blackberry pie. True happiness, Danny thought, releasing a lungful of smoke.

Rachel was back at school down south, but they spoke on Skype and connected on Facebook thanks to the satellite Internet Corazon had installed at Blue Sky Bookstore in an unusual burst of generosity. For a time, he'd feared that he'd never see his little sister again. Rachel's dad had checked himself out of rehab after

McKenna called him and he'd driven through the night to bring Rachel home. Luckily he'd calmed down once he met Odile. He'd even agreed to let Rachel spend Thanksgiving at Blue Sky next month: Grandmother had that effect on people.

Now that the tourists were gone, the bookstore remained quiet. Danny had had plenty of time to work on the graphic novel. After long reflection, he'd decided to finish the windigo story. To his relief, Rachel's illustrations of the demon resembled Hendrix, not Logan, but the young brave looked disturbingly like himself.

He started as the wooden bench creaked. Odile sat down beside him. She had an uncanny sense of knowing exactly when he lit up a spliff. He sighed, put it out and stowed it back in his shirt pocket.

"It is time for me to leave," Odile said. "Mayor Fortin has decided to strip. He will have much to tell our priest at confession tomorrow."

"Right." Danny cleared his throat. "I heard Corazon kicked in ten thousand bucks for Edgar on behalf of the Galaxy."

"Yes, Madame is a remarkable woman." Odile folded her hands in her lap. "She told Joseph she wishes to thank him and The Community for saving Edgar's life. She has set up a fund: bicycle economics, she calls it. Giving back to Canada's First People."

"Anybody ask her where she got the money?"

"Not really." Odile smiled. "Our Community is most grateful for her help."

Danny watched McKenna adjust her radio, head bent as she listened to the OPP dispatcher in Kirkland Lake.

"Raven stopped by the diner this afternoon," Odile said. "I have asked her to dinner tomorrow."

"What for? McKenna's a cop. She can talk to me any time she wants. We don't have to give her dinner," Danny said.

"Raven is investigating a cold case that troubles her very much."

"I see." Danny shifted on the bench. "She's coming on shaman business."

"Yes, she is asking for our help. Unofficially."

"Our help? No, Grandmother, *your* help."

"You are being too hard on yourself, *Mahikan*." Odile paused. "Your vision is there if you wish to use it."

"No." Danny shook his head. "Vision goes to the women in our family."

"Your mother's vision was very strong. And you are forgetting your grandfather, Albin. His gifts were remarkable."

They sat quietly together, gazing at McKenna's cruiser and the empty highway.

"Grandmother," he said at last, "what happened after Hendrix shot at you and McKenna? Where did you go?"

"Raven told me to run so I did. I hid in the forest by the side of the road until the young men found her and the windigo left on his motorbike. Then I went walking."

"Everyone was looking for you."

"They should not have worried. I have known how to survive in the woods since I was a child. Besides … you needed me."

Danny hesitated a moment then said: "Out in the bush, I had, well, these vivid dreams. I was dehydrated, and pretty traumatized so that probably explains it, only … were you really there?"

"If you believe I was there, then I was there." She rested her hand on his. "I know you are troubled, Danny. You are thinking of Logan."

"Yes," he admitted.

When the cops hauled up Hendrix's body and the meth from the Archangel Mine shaft, they'd made a grisly discovery: skeletal remains, dating back decades. McKenna had pressured Danny for answers – just as Ricky had tonight.

Don't tell Flag. Promise me you won't tell Flag.

"Logan saved our lives," he said. "Mine and Rachel's. I tried to stop him walking into the fire, but I couldn't."

"Maybe you were not meant to." Odile looked thoughtful. "John lived too close to evil for much of his life. He feared – perhaps he knew – that his heart had turned to ice."

Danny felt his eyes burning. "Do you know … do you under-stand what he did on the island?"

"Yes, you have just told me, *Mahikan.*"

"Rachel must never know. I promised John …"

"We will keep his secret."

Danny wiped his eyes. "I can't stop thinking about the horrible way he died."

"We must try to forgive him. He is at peace. His spirit is with Pasha's now." Odile squeezed his hand. "Come with me tomorrow. We will light a candle for him at Mass."

Acknowledgements

First of all I want to thank my publisher, Maureen Whyte for believing in *Windigo Fire* and for making my book part of the Seraphim Editions family. I feel blessed to work with my editor, George Down, who reviewed my prose with respect, care and unfailingly sharp insight.

Behind every developing writer stands an army of friends, teachers and supporters. My teachers, Rosemary Aubert, Maureen Jennings and Peter Robinson, were more than generous in their encouragement and in sharing their knowledge and remarkable skills. Authors and close friends, Gail Hamilton, D. J. McIntosh and Roz Place, read the manuscript of *Windigo Fire* and offered valuable suggestions and warm support when I needed it most.

I owe enormous thanks to my two literary critique groups, collectively known as the Mesdames of Mayhem. They are sixteen wonderful women authors whose thoughtful feedback and long-standing friendship continue to be more than important to me. The Mesdames are: Catherine Astolfo, Rosemary Aubert, Donna Carrick, Melodie Campbell, Vicki Delany, Lisa De Nikolits, Catherine Dunphy, Cheryl Freedman, Sylvia Maultash-Warsh, D.J. McIntosh, Rosemary McCracken, Lynne Murphy, Joan O'Callaghan, Jane Peterson-Burfield and Caro Soles.

Mitch Kowalski, founder of the Toronto Writers Centre, provided a safe haven that allowed me to create and research *Windigo Fire*.

Last, but not least, thank you forever to my family: my husband, Ed Callway, my daughter, Claire Callway and my son-in-law, Mitch Risman for their unfailing love and belief in my ability as a writer.